DOVE

Paisley Hope is an avid lover of romance, a mother, a wife and a writer. Growing up in Canada, she wrote and dreamed of one day being able to create a place, a world where readers could immerse themselves, a place they wished was real, a place they saw themselves when they envisioned it. She loves her family time, gardening, baking, yoga and a good cab sav.

 @authorpaisleyhope

Readers can't get enough of the *Soldiers of Bedlam* series:

'One of the best books I have ever read!'

'I could not read this book fast enough'

'Perfect'

'Ten stars!!'

'Read within a day and couldn't put it down'

'I devoured this in one sitting'

'Another masterpiece from Paisley Hope'

DOVE

PAISLEY HOPE

PENGUIN BOOKS

PENGUIN BOOKS

UK | USA | Canada | Ireland | Australia
India | New Zealand | South Africa

Penguin Books is part of the Penguin Random House group of companies
whose addresses can be found at global.penguinrandomhouse.com

Penguin Random House UK,
One Embassy Gardens, 8 Viaduct Gardens, London sw11 7bw

penguin.co.uk
global.penguinrandomhouse.com

Published in Penguin Books 2026

001

Typeset in 10.86/14.03pt Fanwood by Six Red Marbles UK, Thetford, Norfolk
Printed and bound in Great Britain by Clays Ltd, Elcograf S.p.A.

The authorised representative in the EEA is Penguin Random House Ireland,
Morrison Chambers, 32 Nassau Street, Dublin d02 yh68

A CIP catalogue record for this book is available from the British Library

isbn: 978–1–911–74622–5

Your soulmate doesn't have to be a knight in shining armor. Instead, he can be covered in ink, clad in black leather, and love you from the first moment he pins you up against a wall with his hand around your throat.

Glossary of Club Lingo

MC: *Motorcycle Club*

Club business: *Illegal /non-illegal activity that benefits the club*

Cut: *Leather vest or jacket bearing the club insignia*

Sweetbutt: *A girl who hangs around the club, often offered for sex or help, hoping to become a member's ol' lady*

Ol' lady: *Wife or serious girlfriend of a club member*

Rockers: *Patches fixed to the back of a motorcycle, cut with the club's insignia*

Patch over: *When one MC takes over another*

Sprite: *Good girl, fairy, princess*

Squid: *A poser rider the club looks down on, someone who lacks biker common sense*

Code: *The rules club members live by*

Chapel: *The room in which the club conducts their daily/ weekly meetings*

Service: *The meeting to discuss club business*

President or Prez: *The highest level of power, the boss, the conductor of business*

VP: *Vice president*

Enforcer: *Upholds club laws, protects patch holders, defends the club's reputation, assists in conflict resolution.*

Sgt. at Arms: *Sergeant at Arms, protector of the president, his number one*

Prospect: *A club apprentice—usually wears the prospect patch for one year to prove his loyalty through service, trust, and a series of really shitty tasks no one else wants to do*

Rally: *A gathering of bikers, normally for fun but club business is generally conducted as well*

DOVE PLAYLIST

1. *Way Down We Go*—KALEO
2. *Fortunate Son*—Creedence Clearwater Revival
3. *Kashmir*—Led Zeppelin
4. *Dreams*—Fleetwood Mac
5. *Pour Some Sugar On Me*—Def Leppard
6. *Back Door*—KALEO
7. *Barracuda*—Heart
8. *Deuces Are Wild*—Aerosmith
9. *More Than a Feeling*—Boston
10. *Take Me To Church*—Hozier
11. *Feeling Whitney*—Post Malone
12. *Where Did You Sleep Last Night*—Nirvana
13. *Howlin' For You*—The Black Keys
14. *Hunger Strike*—Temple of the Dog

CONTENT WARNINGS

This book is an interconnected MC romance that houses darker elements. It is intended for people 18+. Please read these trigger warnings before you continue your journey:

Violence, as expected with the life of an outlaw motorcycle club, including but not limited to: mild torture, gun violence, murder, discussion of sexual assault of a sixteen-year-old (nothing descriptive—on-page talk of past occurrence). Mild alcohol and drug use. Discussions of life in the military; traumatic combat flashbacks.

Sexual triggers are not fully listed to conceal plot points and pivotal moments but are of a darker nature. They include but are not limited to: blood, breath and knife play, anal sex, sex that feels ritualistic, consensual non-consent, degradation.

PROLOGUE

Sean

The Altered Compass

"Today you take the first step to becoming a man, Sean." My father grips the back of my neck, giving me a pat with his bloody hand, his chest heaving. I look at the man on the floor and swallow down my own rage, because that man tried to steal from us and he hurt my mother. She's being taken away now by my aunt Theresa, a bloodstained rag to her face. Switch and Ray, my dad's VP and president, stand behind us. I shouldn't be in here, I'm only fifteen years old, but I needed to make sure my mom was okay when I heard her crying out for my dad.

"I won't be here forever. One day you'll inherit this family, and you *will* need to protect yourself and your mother. So, it's time, son." I look up at him, unsure and afraid, but I can never admit that to him.

"For what?" My voice cracks and I swallow down my fear. There's no sense in being afraid, it doesn't change the outcome.

"It's time to alter your compass." He pats me on the chest and walks me closer to the body on the floor with his arm around my shoulders. The man lying in front of me is barely breathing.

"See, son, morality only exists in a man's mind."

"W-what do you mean?" I ask as my heart thuds in my ears.

"I mean that only you can decide what is truly moral and what isn't. If you decide the world is a better place without your enemy, then I believe you were put in his path for a reason. It's up to you to decide, no one else. In this case"—he nods to the man on the floor—"I would say it's up to you to finish him off. For your mother, for the club. But the choice is yours."

A rush of fear and excitement that I can't explain vibrates through me with his words. I know my father—when he tells me to do something there is no arguing, so I don't try to think of a way to get out of this. Instead, I sharpen my focus, trying to evaluate the most effective way to complete my task. I can't use the floor to crack this fucker's skull, and I can't break his neck. My father won't respect that. He has to die by my fists. It will show my strength.

"You use your fists," he orders, like he's reading my mind.

I take a breath and focus on the man's face, remembering the way my uncles have taught me to fight. Pressure points, where to hit him, what will kill him the fastest. I swallow my fate and drop to my knees, pushing down every ounce of fear I feel, and I go to my thinking place. The part of my brain that solves my problems. The part that makes sense to me when I have to analyze something.

I quickly calculate my body weight and the force needed for a punch directly to his temple. In his deteriorated state, I should be able to do the job in five punches or less. *If* I hit him with everything I've got.

"Go ahead, Sean," my father encourages from behind me. I roll my sleeves up to my elbows, twice evenly on each side, and take a deep breath. I picture my mother after he bounced her face off the concrete wall. I can't let my father down. I close my eyes, still mentally calculating, and I swing. I think I cry out but I still keep swinging. Again, and again. I swing through nine punches, until my knuckles are busted up and bloody.

Then rage mixed with a need I can't push down suddenly bubbles up and I keep striking him. I don't know for how long, but I know I don't stop until my father pulls me off him. I fight back against my father's hold, thrashing. I *need* to make sure I've done my job and my task is completed.

"He's dead, son," my dad says, pulling me from my haze. I relax and blink back tears so he doesn't see me cry as he lets me go. What kind of a pussy cries? I'm fifteen, for fuck's sake.

When I look down at my bloody hands then back to the man's face, I know my dad is right. I check the imaginary box in my head and breathe a little deeper when he says, "Atta boy," and wraps his strong arm around me. "Your moral compass will be different now. It's still intact, but altered."

"How?" I sniff, resisting the urge to look back at the man I just killed.

"Well, it'll still help you navigate, but it'll never point true north again. From now on your path will be different from that of a man who hasn't handed out death. This will be your truth, and that's okay as long as you know why you took his life. As long as you know it was justified, and it *was*."

I nod, feeling proud of myself, stronger. Feeling like *him*. My father squeezes my shoulder and kisses me on the top of my head.

"You did good. The kill doesn't have to be perfect your first time, son. There's room to improve . . . Now, let's get you cleaned up . . ."

The altered compass is a piece of my father I've remembered every single day, in the desert and in the streets.

The things I've seen and done would horrify most men, but there isn't a single thing I regret. I don't think about my choices after I've made them, or look back, because time can't be changed, and it never stops. At the end of my time on this earth, the only man who has to live my truth is me. A truth that runs through my head repeatedly because I never, ever stop thinking.

I was dubbed a prodigy, a genius, at a young age. I suppose I could have been an epidemiologist, or I could have gone to MIT and become an astrophysicist, developing technology NASA hasn't even dreamed up yet. But that was never my future for two reasons: One, I don't follow the rules of any other man well. And two, by my twenty-fifth birthday I'd killed so many men that I knew I would never fit inside the box that is the norm of society. And I carry on my back the memory of every single man I've killed. I remember the way each man's pupils grew as they filled with fear while the last glimmer of life drained from them.

Those memories and a compiled stack of double standards are one part of my truth, because when in combat, death is justified by fighting for my country. For those deaths, society tells me I should be proud and they call me a hero. They give me medals for those deaths, for Chrissake.

But the lives I take on the streets, in a different kind of war—those earn me a different title.

Outlaw. Criminal. Monster.

The double standard is that death is only allowed when you're granted permission from a rich man behind a desk who can't wait to measure his dick against those of his enemies.

Death because some scumbag thought he could hurt the woman who would surely be my wife? Illegal. Unfortunately for the scumbag, death for my country and death in the streets is all the same to me, and I'm not ashamed to admit that.

Killing this man will just be adding another body to the pile and another clip to the never-ending reel in my head. One I won't lose a minute of sleep over.

As I ride as fast as possible through the streets between my clubhouse and her home, I imagine all the ways I'll torture him to make him pay for thinking he could go anywhere near her. I think of the way her voice sounded when I answered the call . . . muffled, distant and afraid. I didn't know what was going on until I heard a man's voice and then that was *all* I needed to know.

I get from my bike to her door in seconds, then enter the house on silent feet. I can hear him before I see him, and my blood boils as I pull my gun from my hip and take aim at the unknown, ready for anything and laser-focused.

"You have her eyes . . ." he bites out, his voice shaky and low. "It's like seeing a fucking ghost . . ."

I hear her whimper softly and plead for all of one second—"Why? How did you find me?"—before I figure out where they are in her century-old house.

The stealth training ingrained in me doesn't allow him to hear me coming. Even if he could, the adrenaline rushing through my veins at the sight of her pinned against the living room wall gives me the strength of ten men. The man holding her is a waste of breath, and he's wearing a cut I can't wait to burn. "Please, just listen to me . . ." His tall, lanky body is pressed to hers, which makes me want to rip him to shreds. He's already taken so much from her.

I think I hear him muttering something like, "You're looking for answers and I'm gonna fucking give them to you . . ."

Then the familiar haze lines my vision and the monster in me takes over.

I replace my gun at my hip and yank his head back while allowing my fist to come down on his face with a deafening crack, breaking his nose instantly. My arms wrap around his thick neck in a sleeper hold before he gets another word out or has the chance to lay a finger on her pretty head. I drag him out the back door, not wanting one drop of blood to spill on her floor.

The sun is starting to sink behind the trees surrounding her property. It's private and quiet out here, and I toss him to the ground behind a bush while garbled words do their best to spill from his blood-filled mouth.

"Motherfuck—"

I commit fully, straddling him as my fist comes down again. The sound of his jaw cracking is like music to my fucking ears. The thrill of the capture is subsiding, but the satisfaction of his demise is on the horizon. And judging by the fear-soaked smell and this fucker bleeding all over his shitty, good-for-nothing cut, he knows it. I keep hitting him as blood leaks from my busted knuckles. Time passes, I don't know how long, but it's in this moment, with blood covering me, that I feel clearer than in any other.

At peace.

This is the other part to my truth.

I simply don't give a fuck. Feeling this way isn't barbaric, it's cathartic.

It's not just an eye for an eye. It's a loose end that I *need* to tie up. A mental itch that must be scratched at all costs.

"Sean . . ." Her voice is shaky and soft, calling my name from somewhere behind me. Even after such a short time, it's the only voice that can stop my raised fist from crashing down on him again. I blink, coming out of my haze and looking down. Her attacker is out cold, but for now, he's still breathing.

I let go of his blood-soaked shirt and turn to face her.

"That's enough," she commands softly. I take one look at her and grimace as I stand and make my way across her yard. Relief that she's unharmed and pure admiration for her ability to make it until I got here washes over me for the first time, and I feel like I no longer have my legs beneath me. I take her into my arms and crush myself to her, muttering her name as she grips me tight. I have no idea how long we stay like that before I finally move to the side of the house to turn on the spigot connected to a coiled hose. I give my hands a rinse before ripping off a small length of fabric from the bottom of my t-shirt and running it under the water, then return to wipe her tear-stained face, removing his splattered blood from her soft neck and shoulders. I can't bear the thought of this worthless piece of shit's blood anywhere near her.

"H-he says he has answers . . . could he?" she stammers, as I run my hands over her bare arms, warming her.

"I'm gonna figure that out." I swipe her soft, fiery hair from her forehead and gently kiss her there before pulling her close. She takes a deep breath, and I feel her body start to relax.

"That's better," I whisper, inhaling her sweet scent. Another detail I can't forget. Even now, everything about her calls to me. When I should be focusing on how to get this cocksucker back to my clubhouse, all I can think about is the taste of her skin. I pull my phone out and send a message to Kai and Jake, my club's enforcer and vice president, knowing they'll be here inside of ten minutes.

"What do we do now?" Her voice is muffled by my chest.

"I do what I do, and you decide how deep into my world you wanna be."

Her sultry brown eyes look up at me expectantly.

"I was hunting him. I wasn't planning to kill him, but now . . ." I flex my aching fist. The one that just pummeled that motherfucker's face into the ground. "You know exactly who I am . . ." I stroke her cheek with my thumb.

"Yes," she answers, reaching her warm hand up, placing it over mine.

"But knowing that reality and *seeing* it are two totally different things, understand?"

She swallows down the fear I know she's feeling and nods, side-eyeing him. "Of course," she whispers softly.

I move into her sightline to bring her eyes back to mine.

"Don't look at him. He's lying there like that because he took from you, and I will never tolerate that. No one will ever harm a single hair on your head, or anyone you love, ever again."

"I don't have many of those . . . people that I love. But . . . do you think he does?" Her pretty face knots in confusion as she comes to terms with the fact that this man will likely die simply because he hurt her.

This is a "right from wrong" she's never had to contemplate. I tilt her chin up to me. "Don't do that. Look at me. He isn't worth an ounce of regret. He made his choices in life . . . the wrong ones. This is his fate."

I remind myself as I watch her struggle with this new reality that my brain works differently than hers—that she won't find it easy to separate emotion from business when it comes to ending a human life, even one that took from her so viciously.

For me, this is *only* business. I don't worry about this man's family, or anyone who might care when he doesn't come home tonight.

I only worry about two things. My club, and now . . . *her*.

I wait with bated breath as her fingers slide over mine, removing my hands from her face. She straightens her shoulders and smooths her thick copper hair but doesn't speak as she tucks the bottom of her shirt back into her cutoff jean shorts. As if putting herself back together on the outside will hold her emotions together on the inside too.

I let her push past me and move to stand over her attacker's unconscious body. Her chest rises and falls evenly. She doesn't look afraid now. She looks bold and in control. She looks powerful. Her long hair blows loose and wild in the late evening's summer breeze as she focuses.

I wait for questions that never come, for a more prominent fear or shock that never rises. Instead, she shocks *me* by simply embracing the calamity.

"I'm stronger than you think, Sean," she whispers before dropping to her knees. Her small fist comes up and slams down onto his face as she cries out, and I watch in sheer fascination as she picks up a heavy, jagged rock from her garden, and her fist rises again.

CHAPTER ONE
Layla

Days Earlier . . .

"It's so nice to see you dear. It's been a long time. You're looking . . . different."

I nod and force a smile onto my face as I place menus down in front of the elders from my parents' church, Judy Pryor and her husband Roy. I ready my mini tablet to take their order and resist the urge to tell her to take her judgmental eyes elsewhere and go fuck herself.

"It has been a long time," I respond, ignoring her comment about my looks as she eyes the floral and vine tattoos that run down the length of my bare arm. "You're doing well?" I ask politely. My voice is sickly sweet, and from another life.

"I am. Always so busy with the church, you remember how that is?"

"Of course," I answer quickly. What she really means is: *You know, when you used to come to church?* Her eyes continue their judgment as I rattle off the specials. When I'm done, she looks up at me with mock care.

"Are you okay, Layla? You haven't been around since . . . well, you know . . ." Her voice trails off as she takes in my much longer, now more auburn hair. It used to be a very dull shade of brown in my younger years—a lifetime ago, when I checked all of her boxes.

She didn't know me then any more than she does now, but she didn't need to. I was *there*. I could've been murdering squirrels in my spare time, but if I was in that building on Sunday, I was "a little dear" and "a real sweetheart."

"I'm perfectly well, thank you for your concern." I fight the sarcasm in my tone. Giving her nothing but saying everything all at once. *Fuck right off, Judy.*

I take their order and click "submit" on the tablet to send it to the kitchen.

"It's good to see you both," I say politely. Before I can turn away Judy reaches out and touches my arm, invading my personal space.

"I have to ask, do you have a new church family? A fellowship group to pray over you?"

I remind myself that I desperately need the tip from their bill and gently pull my arm away. "It's been a long while since I've had time for a fellowship family," I answer. It's true, and it's also the understatement of the year. Not that she could know, but being in school, in a fast-track program for massage therapy, takes up most of my free time. Not to mention I work thirty hours a week just to keep myself fed and housed. Plus, I'm still grieving the death of my best friend in the whole world, so making the church a priority isn't really on my radar right now.

"Well, if you ever feel called to come back to the church, we're all here for you. And we're all praying."

"Thank you, Mrs. Pryor," I say through my fake smile. "That's very kind of you. Your drinks will be out soon."

I turn and blow out a breath. Simmering anger courses through me. Not one of them was actually "there for me" when my mother was stolen from me. None of them knows she died on the very night that she was finally going to set herself free. No one but me knew she was leaving, because on the outside, my parents' marriage was a thing to be admired. But on the inside my father was controlling, misogynistic and abusive. Sometimes, when he drank too much, he would hit my mother, and then spend the next week apologizing and gaslighting her into believing she'd deserved it. All the while he was having affairs and gambling their life savings away. But all that mattered was that they were there front and center every Sunday morning, so they were a real blessing to the community.

They portrayed that false image better than anyone could have imagined. But none of that matters, because they're gone now—and one thing my mother's death has taught me is that a public image is complete bullshit.

I can't go back, but I can promise myself I will never end up like my mother, in a loveless marriage taking shit from a man in the name of his church.

I will be myself and be happy, however that looks.

I haven't lost my faith, and I don't need to draw closer to God. God and I have an understanding. We're good. I most definitely don't need people like Roy and Judy to tell *me* how to live in order to please God when they're holding onto countless sins of their own.

For example, Judy is a shit disturber who loves to gossip about anyone and anything at the church. I bet she goes to her women's meeting this week and tells everyone there how she saw poor Layla Monroe . . . *"And she's got so many tattoos now and she's colored her hair. She's lost her faith. Everyone pray for her."* Then she'll talk about how I'm working as a server when I was supposed to be a teacher.

I see through her sad existence though. Her false goodness. Because if her faith was truly her cornerstone, it wouldn't matter to her where I work, how many tattoos I have or that I've drifted away from the church. It would only matter that I was a good person, which I am, and she would truly care about me, which she doesn't.

And it's not like where I work is a dive bar. The Palm Club is the most upscale boutique restaurant in Harmony, Georgia. It's the place people come to eat on a first date, or an anniversary. Its cozy atmosphere boasts warm brick interior walls, wrought iron tables with live edge wood tops, and accent lighting. Greenery and twinkle lights cover the ceiling, and the whole place bleeds hip and rustic local hangout.

They also don't know that teaching was my mother's dream for me, and that when she died, I figured at that point there was no reason to follow her dreams and instead began to follow my own. Even if that means exhausting myself just to afford this semester's tuition, and putting up with the judgy glares from people like Judy and the roaming, hungry eyes of her husband.

I bring them their drinks and force another fake smile as the restaurant becomes busier and the sky outside darkens with clouds. It's a typical evening for Harmony in July. Our town is close to Savannah and the water, which means we don't go many days without a thunderstorm to cut the humidity in the summer. Today is certainly no exception. It's a scorching 103 degrees outside, so I barely even flinch when the loud crack of thunder rocks the large pane-glass windows just after six.

"You need to take that break," my friend and coworker Chantel reminds me. Her full pouty red lips turn up in a grin. She's got this job down pat after two years here. She's teaching me all about choosing clothes that are just revealing enough, yet still classy. Chantel calls the look "classy fuckable." And she's a master at it, with her long blonde tresses hanging down her back in waves, her black pencil skirt, and the white sleeveless blouse that shows just the right amount of cleavage.

It's a style I've tried to emulate tonight, in my black leather skirt and off-the-shoulder white bodysuit with a more open and revealing back. My thick, wavy hair is a soft shade of copper. It's piled into a high ponytail with face-framing bangs and some wisps left out to accentuate my brown eyes, which everyone always tells me are my prettiest feature. My lips are the perfect shade of crimson and my nails are manicured to match, painted by my own hand to save money I just don't have. A fleeting memory of paying upward of a hundred dollars to get my nails done flashes through my mind, but those days are gone. Now I thrift my looks, and thankfully, Chantel has an incredible collection of heels she lets me borrow to make my legs seem longer than my five-foot-four frame allows.

"I'll take my break soon. It's a packed one tonight. I'm alright for now," I tell her as my drinks order comes up and I grab them with ease.

"Uh-huh," she mumbles. "You never learn," she says with a laugh. I've only been here since March, when I left the retail job that was making me half the amount in a week as I earn in two shifts here.

"Well, babe, if you aren't taking yours yet, I'm taking mine. Cover me for a few?" she asks.

I nod, and am just getting ready to deliver table two's Long Island iced teas when the glass double doors bearing The Palm Club's logo fly open. The humidity from outside rushes in—warm air and the smell of rain—but a shiver runs through me as three very wet, very ominous-looking bikers take up the entire entrance.

They're completely out of place among all the after-work businesspeople and the town's upper crust, and they wear the colors anyone living in Harmony would recognize: the Hounds of Hell Motorcycle Club. Anyone here will see dangerous outlaws, but the moment I glimpse their leather and the ink on their skin, all I can think of is my mother's face the last time I saw her—and the police sketch that's lived in my head for almost two years.

CHAPTER TWO

Layla

Chatter slows around me and the music playing through the sound system becomes more prominent. A chill ripples down my spine as I watch the man who is front and center stalking toward me, wearing a black t-shirt under his cut, black jeans and black motorcycle boots. His face is partially covered by a black bandana. The look of him sends my pulse into an unexplainable rush. I swallow, trying to calm it down and ask myself *why?* All I should feel when I look at him is anger and trauma.

He keeps coming my way and I do nothing but shift from one foot to the other, frozen by his dark and rugged beauty. His head is shaved close, and his vibrant green eyes are fixed ahead—the windows to a demon's soul—as he walks with an air of authority and his men follow behind. I watch carefully as he pulls his bandana down and the rest of his features come into view. His beard is a deep brown, covering his wide jaw, and his features are straight and masculine. His furrowed brow makes him appear almost angry and stern. I can't explain the way my knees weaken as he quickly closes the space between us. Those emerald orbs snap unexpectedly to mine, I have no time to look away, and my stomach drops with their violent, deep hold. He reminds me of a fierce gladiator as his jaw flexes and his thick neck pulses. I look away from his stare to take a breath and let my eyes trail over the rest of him. There are dog tags hanging around his neck and, of course, there's the telltale sign of the life he belongs to.

That fucking cut.

The Hounds of Hell, the biker gang that my small town has been wary of my whole life. We all know their ways, and I remember my mother telling me not to look at them when we heard the deafening sound of their Harleys as they rolled in a solidified group down Main. I was warned not to look at them in town, not to get in their way. We know of the bodies that have turned up outside town that belong to rival clubs. We know how our law enforcement sweeps every illegal thing they do under the proverbial rug. "It's not in the township's interest to pursue" is often the statement. We know what that means: they work for the club too.

The Hounds of Hell are the dark underside of Harmony, so I should be afraid of this gladiator and what he's capable of. His scent washes over me as he gets closer, pulling me from my memories, but instead of the fear or anger I expect, an unstoppable want rocks me to my core. He smells of cedarwood, leather and smoke, and it speaks to my senses, drawing me in . . . I'm completely entranced.

The biker pauses and looks down at me intentionally, like I warrant his scrutiny simply because I'm standing in his way. I swear I stop breathing as his surprisingly beautiful eyes linger on mine and then trail the planes of my face. My lips, my neck. My heartbeat thunders, and it feels like time pauses before he finally looks away, uninterested. I blink, trying to clear my senses, and eye the patch over his heart: *Sergeant at Arms*.

The three of them don't wait to be seated, heading right into Chantel's section. The one I'm covering while she's on break.

Snapping out of my stupor, I move quickly to table two, placing their drinks down, telling them their meal won't be long, and I think about the gladiator's patch, trying to remember what the rank means. The other two wear *Enforcer* and *Treasurer* patches. I have no idea what those mean either, but it's obvious the Sergeant is the leader of the three just by the way he walked in front of them. I give my head a shake and ask myself why the hell I'm even still thinking about him as I take another table's drink order and pray for Chantel to hurry the hell up so she can take the biker table. The storm outside rages on.

I head toward the bar to wait on my next round of drinks. Another hour and I'll be behind it for the rest of my shift, when the drinking crowd pours in and the restaurant transforms into more of a pub. The music gets louder, the row of pool tables in the back gets busier, and the bar becomes packed. I don't mind working the bar though—in fact, I prefer it. The later it gets, the more cash I make.

I look up when I've finished delivering the drinks, knowing the club members are my next table, but Chantel is still not back yet. I give in and glance over at them. The Sergeant is leaning back in the padded leather booth, deep in conversation. His legs are relaxed, his inked forearm rests on the table, and his sculpted hand is covered with more ink and rings. He uses his thumb to spin the ring on his first finger methodically as he looks over. It's almost as if he can sense my eyes on him, and then he beckons me with his first two fingers and an upward nod of his chin.

As I grab their menus and silverware, I feel the heat creep up my throat. His bold demeanor and the way he slowly looks me over from my cherry red heels to the hair on my head unnerves me. It's not subtle, but it's not degrading either. I can't put my finger on the way it makes me feel. Somehow it has me wanting to cover up, and at the same time tear every shred of clothing from my body so his gaze can make a permanent home on my naked flesh. Then his eyes leave me to go back to the men sitting across from him.

I lift my chin in fake confidence as I approach, and something in me takes over. I don't know if it was my encounter with the elders from my church—or the way this man just looked me up and down as if it was his right, and then dismissed me just as quickly with his eyes.

The need to let someone, *anyone*, know I'm not who they think I am overwhelms me as I set down the three menus on their table.

"Next time, you need to wait until someone seats you," I say as confidently as I can. "Will you all be eating tonight?" I ask, looking from one to the other.

The handsome blond one, the enforcer, laughs and scrubs his scruffy jaw with his hand; his smile is megawatt. He looks sort of like Heath Ledger and I wonder how he didn't win at life just on his looks alone.

"Depends on what you're serving up, beautiful." That all-American smile widens with his words.

I narrow my eyes at him. "Drinks and food," I enunciate in a *don't fuck with me* tone as I set down their silverware tucked into napkins.

"We don't take this one out much," the man beside him says in a low voice, hiking his thumb over his shoulder. I look at him pointedly for the first time. The treasurer. He's all sharp edges with messy brown hair and piercing blue eyes that house the look of past torture.

The two men chuckle, and it only serves to make me more pissed and uncomfortable.

"Forgive these fuckin' idiots." The deep, smoky voice of the sergeant stops their laughter immediately. It's smooth like thick honey, as if he has all the time in the world to speak because no one would dare interrupt him.

I let my eyes move to him, willing myself to stand strong and not appear fazed by the grace he carries himself with. He leans forward, straightening out his knife and fork on the napkin with perfect precision, before folding his hands together as he props his elbows on the table.

He's muscular in a way that says he's strong as hell, like he works out seven days a week. His corded forearms flex with rigid veins and I notice that even his knuckles have symbols and words on them. I'm a sucker for tattoos on a man, but I haven't known any personally who have this many, so I shamelessly take them in. My eyes settle on his right hand and what I can catalog quickly. A cross made from detailed-looking daggers covers his finger. It's on the end of an ornate chain that winds down his hand, connecting to a cracked compass, on top of which sits a peaceful dove. It's not unlike the one I have inked on my own shoulder that I put there in memory of my mother, only mine is in flight. I like to think that when she passed, she escaped her cage. I wonder briefly why he would choose a cross, and the dove. Then I blink and scold myself for even noticing. He clears his throat, taking in my stare. I bring my eyes back to the depth of those dark, emerald pools, and I swear I see a hint of amusement in them as he cocks his head and speaks to me again.

"We'll take three bourbons—Hellbender. And . . ." He pauses for a moment. "Yeah, we'll all be eating tonight." His voice is strong and poignant, sending another current up my spine with the flash of an unexpected vision, one where his face is buried deep between my thighs.

I suck in a breath, needing to get out of his sight. I don't know what the hell has gotten into me, but instead of feeling the disgust I should toward him, he sends my blood racing as I try to push the image from my head.

"I'll give you a few minutes," I say, heading for the bar.

My back is turned while I put their drinks order in, but I can feel the heavy weight of his stare on me. I'm certain he's watching me. The feeling is eerie and exhilarating all at once.

"Thanks babe," Chantel says as she breezes up to me, looking around.

"Perfect timing." I exhale a long breath.

"You okay? You're shaking." Chantel's face is lined with concern.

"Yeah, just . . ." I nod at the table of men I just left and Chantel's eyes flit toward them.

"Oooh shit, some bad-boy Hounds of Hell members? Mama likey," she says, eyeing them all up. I shake my head with a scoff, keeping my eyes away from that deep gaze.

"They're all yours," I tell her, heading to pick up table four's appetizers. I should be glad I'm free of the sergeant's stare, but moments later, I can't help myself. I decide to glance up at his table, feeling the pull of his gaze—and when I do, I find those dark eyes still unapologetically fixed on me like he can't look away any more than I can.

CHAPTER THREE

Layla

The rush of the bar never stops as the dinner crowd transforms into the drinking crowd. Our dance floor opens up at eight and fills right away under the soft glow of the string lights.

I head to work behind the bar as two more servers come in to take over the late shift. I get on with Tyson, who's the manager and weekend bartender. He's funny and kind. He sort of reminds me of my older brother Dell, and we've gotten into a flow. He takes care of his end, I take care of mine, and sometimes we meet in the middle. We manage the hectic bar with ease most weekends.

People come and go as the night continues, but the one nagging constant is the three Hounds of Hell members sitting in the corner. Aside from their periodic laughter and the consumption of an absolute feast, you'd never know they were there. Unless you were me and could physically feel the eyes of their leader on you.

I duck down and grab a Corona from the cooler beside the overstock. I crack it open and pass it over the bar to a regular and take another order from a man beside him.

"You have beautiful eyes," he yells over the music. "Name's Ryan," he adds, not that I asked.

I nod and smile at him. "Thanks, what can I get you?"

"A drink for me and a drink for you?"

Ryan, if that's his real name, is a business type, wearing dress pants and a button-down. He looks like he's lost his jacket and tie at some point since he arrived—as well as his wedding ring, but the tan line is still present on the ring finger of his left hand.

"I don't drink while I work," I say, taking the order of the woman beside him while he takes his time with his drink choice. I pass her a glass of house white and glance back at Ryan.

"Have you decided?" I ask.

"I've decided I don't want to stop looking at you, so if it takes me longer to decide . . ." He offers me a cheesy little grin, and I must be out of sorts tonight because I'm losing patience. Fast. I try my best not to roll my eyes, and instead glance over his shoulder at the sergeant and his crew still sitting there in the corner. My stomach drops as I notice *those* eyes on me, glancing up over the rim of his glass. Then the sergeant turns to face me fully and holds me with his gaze for a beat before he stands up. Probably ready to leave. I will myself to look away and offer Ryan a very fake smile, ignoring his attempt to hit on me.

"We have some excellent local craft beer—"

"I've also decided that I'd like to know what makes you smile. I saw you smile earlier." He cuts me off, flashing me another grin and thick-lashed blue eyes. I sigh deeply, bracing myself to shut this man down as politely as possible. Then Ryan reaches down and grabs my wrist as I set a napkin on the bar. My body physically rejects his touch and I tug my arm back.

"It feels like . . . well, it almost feels like the heavens start to open every time—"

"Van Morrison?" a deep voice asks, sounding almost annoyed. "That shit works for you?"

I flinch and turn to face the sergeant, realizing he stood just to come over here.

"You don't pick up a woman like that, squid, especially when she's just trying to do her job, yeah?" The sergeant turns his furrowed gaze intently to me, leaning into the bar and, in turn, pushing Ryan aside. One large hand reaches out to circle my wrist. I look down and notice that the tattoo of a chain on his right hand almost looks like a bracelet of sorts. His thumb grazes the soft skin of my inner arm. This touch doesn't repel me; this touch makes me weak. I break out in goosebumps, and he immediately pins my eyes with an intense stare.

"Me and the boys are gonna stay a little later and rack some, *babe*. We'll need another round of Hellbender."

My mouth pops open and so does Ryan's. Even I will admit this outlaw is devastatingly gorgeous in the most unconventional way, and for some reason, it seems he's pretending we're a *couple*?

I tip my head to the side and narrow my eyes at the way he speaks. His tone is almost affluent, unexpected, and I can't make sense of it as I look from Ryan back to the man's eyes, which are making me feel very unsteady. I pull my arm away.

"And whatever your new friend here is about to have, add that to my tab too," he says, flashing a gorgeous straight smile—one that doesn't quite reach his vibrant eyes. It somehow only serves to make him even more threatening.

"T-thanks man," Ryan stutters with a cautious smile. "I'll take a whiskey sour. Sorry . . . I didn't know she was taken—"

"I'm not taken," I interject. That anger I was looking for when he came up to the bar has finally arrived. *Who the hell does he think he is?*

The sergeant shoots a warning glance at me.

"I promise I won't hurt him. Now that he's apologized . . ." he says pointedly, but his words are more of a threat than an

24

assurance with the wicked smirk he wears just for me. I feel almost hot with the way he's publicly claiming me—the shameless way he seems to think he has the right to pretend I'm *his* as I make Ryan's drink.

I set the whiskey sour on the bar and Ryan makes a move to grab it, but the Sergeant is faster. "Oh . . . just one thing," he says to Ryan as he passes the drink over to him. "You're going to fuck off now, and be sure never to look in this direction again, unless you'd like to know what it feels like to have your eyes plucked from their sockets. Understand?"

He clamps his large hand on Ryan's shoulder and Ryan almost buckles as his eyes widen. I instantly know as well as Ryan does that this man wouldn't hesitate to do *exactly* what he threatens. Then he lets go with a clap to Ryan's shoulder and it somehow makes *me* feel bold, despite our workplace mantra that "the customer is always right." This customer doesn't have the right to hit on me.

"Actually, two things . . ." I turn to Ryan, a hand on my hip. "Put your wedding ring back on, you look like a jackass."

Ryan looks between us for all of one second before he disappears without a backward glance, faster than I've ever seen a man scurry away from a bar in my life. I can't help but feel the rush of just speaking my mind for once. That felt damn good. I let a small smile slip onto my face when I meet the Sergeant's eyes, and he smirks back.

"You're welcome. But I really do want those Hellbenders," he commands with a gleam in his eyes and a knock on the bar top. He turns to leave but I stop him. I spread my arms out wide on the bar, leaning in so he can hear me, feeling almost high as his eyes narrow and he comes closer.

"I'm not available for you either, and I'm not thanking you for acting like a Neanderthal. I'm a grown woman, and I've worked here for months." I look up at him pointedly. "I can handle myself."

The sergeant spreads his own arms outward, matching my stance and leans in so his face is inches from mine as he looks me up and down—slowly, hotly, as his incredible scent washes over me.

"Can you now?"

"Absolutely," I bite out in response. He's overwhelming, to put it mildly, but I can't let this man know he ruffles my feathers even one bit. Something tells me he wouldn't respect me if I faltered, but as his eyes trail over me, something also tells me that I'd be shockingly down to be *disrespected* by him.

This man actually smirks. "Those Hellbenders, yeah?" he says, swallowing me with his eyes.

I toss my ponytail over my shoulder and turn to reach on my tiptoes to grab the Hellbender off the second-highest shelf. When I turn back and pull four glasses out from under the bar, tingles erupt all over my skin, because my sergeant's gaze has changed from the playful one he had before. This gaze is ruinous and almost hungry.

My sergeant? What the hell, Layla?

I ignore it as best I can and pour his four shots, then slide them across the bar. When the last shot reaches him, our fingers brush, sending a trail of goosebumps up my forearm, just as his friend, the blond, slides in beside him.

"Ax, fuck, what's taking so long? It's your shot . . ." he says, looking at me, his words trailing into a grin. *Ax?* I'm not surprised his name is Ax. Isn't that what all these bikers' names are like? Ax? Razor? Tank?

"Oh . . . got it." His gaze bounces between us. "Still hungry." He chuckles. Ax backhands the blond man in the chest as he takes three of the shots in his own hands and leaves Ax's with him.

"Your name is Ax?" I ask without thinking, as I wipe down the bar.

"That's what my men call me," he answers, his eyes never wavering as he takes his drink.

"Like a lumberjack? That's the most original offering your men could come up with?" I blurt out. Ax looks at me for a split second like he almost doesn't know what to say. Then that same amusement I saw earlier lines his eyes. He brings his shot up to his plush lips and knocks it back in one go, never breaking eye contact. I watch him as he licks his lips after and uses one ring finger to swipe along the bottom one. I swallow as he sets the glass down on the bar and waits, spreading his hands wide, his muscled arms flexing.

I raise an eyebrow. The *audacity*.

"Would you like that filled, Your Majesty?" I ask.

He nods once with the hint of a smirk. I lift the bottle up and pause.

"I don't enjoy being told what to do with just a look," I say hotly. I should probably tread carefully with him; I have no idea who he is, but I also get the strange sense that he wouldn't hurt me, and right now he's just pissing me off, wasting my time, costing me both customers and tips.

A line is forming behind and beside him, but he doesn't seem to notice or care because he just walks around everywhere like he owns the fucking place.

"Filled. *Please*." His emerald eyes burn as he assesses my expression while I pour the bourbon.

"That wasn't so hard, was it?" I ask him as though he's a small child to whom I'm teaching a lesson.

"You're not afraid of me," he notes with a curious fascination as I finish pouring the amber liquid. I let out a small laugh.

"Ax?" I ask. His name on my lips feels as dangerous as the weapon it symbolizes, and I slide his drink to him. "I've been through more than you can guess, and it takes *a lot* to scare me." I look him up and down. "But if scaring me is your thing, by all means, do your best, *babe*." I offer him the same nickname he called me and my lips pop on the B, making my words sound sort of like an invitation. Instead of walking it back I continue, my body tingling. "Oh, and if you happen to cost me any more tips tonight, then it's *you* who should be afraid," I add before looking away, straightening the glasses under the bar. I know nothing about this man, but I know I can't just stand still in front of him or he'll notice the trembling in my hands.

Ax smiles wide and tips his head back, a deep rumble of laughter vibrating through his chest, and as I swipe a ten-dollar bill left on the bar from earlier his hand comes down over mine. His palm is warm and his fingers are thick and wide enough to make my hand disappear under his. It's dominant and . . . settling. I try not to let him see me shudder as I feel the power behind it. The *warning*.

He's close enough for me to smell his delicious scent again and it's clouding my senses along with those eyes. Heaven mixed with the beckoning call of the devil himself.

"You use your pretty mouth as a weapon," he muses. "But that won't deter me. In fact, it only serves to tempt me, so be careful what you wish for." His voice is low, stunning me. The way he looks at me almost makes me feel like I'm someone else entirely. I don't quite know who she is, but the feeling spurs me on.

"You have *no* idea what I do or do not wish for, Ax," I rasp, almost breathless.

"Mmm," he hums. "I think I do, little dove."

He gives my hand a light squeeze before backing away and disappearing into the heavy crowd with his freshly filled glass. I blink and blow out a breath, quickly working to serve the line that formed around him, trying to keep my head straight the whole time.

What the hell was that? *Little dove?* I'm still trembling as I look in his direction. *Shit, did that just turn me on?*

A few minutes later, when the line is finally tamed, I motion to Tyler at the other end of the bar that I'm sneaking out back for a few minutes.

"Can you bring some limes up when you come back?" he calls out.

"Sure thing," I answer, just trying to get out of there as the storm rages outside. It has nothing on the one that raged in Ax's eyes when I challenged him. Just the thought sends my heart racing.

Damn. I definitely need that break now.

Chapter Four

Sean

Sweat and dust sting my eyes as I lie waiting, focusing on the bird not hindered by space or time. It can fly away any time it chooses, unlike me, and I'm jealous. It should fly away. It should get the fuck out of this fucking desert, but it doesn't. Instead the music plays. Over and over it plays while the dove looks down on me as if it's guarding me, and I use it to keep my focus for as long as I can, willing myself to stay awake as the sound of the chopper gets closer.

"Why don't we come here more often? Fuck." Kai cuts into my flashback as I arrive at our pool table from the bar with my drink in hand. My back is tight after riding so far and I know the whiskey will soften the tension there for me, even if it's only temporary. I watch as Kai takes his shot and sinks the yellow ball in the side pocket, glancing back over his shoulder at two brunettes in the corner.

"All this uppity pussy just does something to me, bro." He shakes his head with his bottom lip between his teeth and smiles wide. "Mmmm-mmmm-mmmm," he hums as he takes in the woman and her friend. Both of them look to be in their mid-thirties, older than he is. I scrub my face with my hand. Fucking whore.

Mason chuckles and stands to line up his shot. "I think maybe I hooked up with that one once. I swear I've seen her at the club." He nods to the blonde leaning over the bar. She's smiling at the woman who stole my attention and hasn't let it go since the moment I walked through the door. Something was leading me to her, telling me to seek her out. It wasn't just her beauty; it was something more. I never doubt my instincts, and the second she turned to reach for my bourbon, and those long copper tresses trailed off her shoulder, I *saw* why. Call it an epiphany of sorts, but I knew I wasn't done with her yet.

So I watch her work now, planning my next move. The curvy hips that lead up to her small waist and full tits that would fill my hands so fucking perfectly. The long copper waves, high cheekbones, big brown doe eyes and a heart-shaped face with full pouty red lips. Her soft skin is tanned and silky-looking. She's got a highbrow way about her, like she was raised on the upper-class side of town, but she's full of a sass and feistiness I didn't expect when I first saw her. I can't tell whether it's real or if it's just the armor she wears. But real or fake, watching her in the dim bar lights I find myself imagining all the ungodly things I could do with those full hips, namely gripping them tight while she rides my fat cock.

Her beauty is undeniable, but when she turns and holds my eyes, still speaking to her friend, I feel it again. Something deeper that is pulling me in. But while I'm cataloging her details, I can't yet form the root or solution of her—and that leads me to *need* more, because usually women don't entice me, they don't perplex me or call to me, yet she does.

I sip my drink thinking of how she looked at me with such

disregard yet her nipples hardened under her thin white shirt as I approached her. How she shuddered under my touch but her eyes went wide when they met mine, screaming *please worship me* and *defile me* all at the same time.

I look out toward the rain and see it isn't letting up yet, then back to *her*.

"You gonna take your shot, motherfucker, or keep making eyes at that stunner behind the bar?" Kai jokes. "Christ I may have to—"

I push past him, hard enough that he steps back a bit. "Don't even think about fucking looking at her," I mutter.

Kai and Mason both guffaw at my words.

"She's fucking tasty. I'll give you that, so if we're gonna have to wait while you rail her in the bathroom, let us know and we'll rack another game without you." Kai's eyes drift toward the bar and I move to stand in his way, flexing my fist and pissed off at myself more than him. I have no idea why I'm instantly so protective of her, because it isn't my fucking style.

"I said, *don't* fucking look at her."

Kai pats me on the shoulder. "You got it, boss, but you better make your move quick. Looks like she's heading out, and we should too, as soon as that rain lets up. Shel and Prez will have our fucking heads for being late."

I glance toward the bar again and find her eyes across the room; she involuntarily licks her lips. Fascinating. It's clear that she has no idea the look she's wearing is one of pure unfiltered lust. Her cheeks pinken as we lock eyes, but she doesn't look away how I would expect her to and I let myself imagine all the other ways I could make her blush like that for me. Then she turns, her eyes fluttering as she casts another glance at me over her shoulder before disappearing behind the doorway to the back, her hand sliding down the frame as I hear her words in my head.

Do your best, babe.

I flex my fists as I contemplate her words. An invitation she didn't even understand herself. With just the memory of those words, I feel the same sort of itch that spreads under my skin when I'm about to hunt a man down. It's this hyperawareness of not letting go, of making sure I follow through, cleanly and precisely. Only, I don't want to kill her. On the contrary. I want to make her feel alive—and then, if I discover she is like every other woman I've ever touched, I can just move on with my fucking day.

Mason hits the pool table when he sinks an impossible shot and I give my head a shake, though my mind is already made up as I set my cue in its holder and turn it so it lines up perfectly to match the rest. "I'm not finished here yet. Text Prez and tell him we're gonna be late."

"Christ," Kai breathes out. "Just don't get us arrested. This face wouldn't last a day in jail."

I hear him chuckle as I leave them behind and begin my hunt.

I've learned over time that if I move with enough confidence, no one will ever question me. Even when I walk right into the back of a restaurant where I clearly don't belong.

The servers scurry like roaches under a Maglite as I stride to the back in a steady, even pace, breathing in the sweet scent she left behind. All of the employees pretend they don't notice me because no one wants to be the one to tell me I'm not authorized to cross the threshold of the bar. They're best to stay out of my way anyway. I'm full of unbridled need, and I don't know what I might be capable of if someone gets in my way, because in all of my thirty-two years, I've never chased down a *woman* like this before.

The more I think about her, the more the anticipation and need to find her consumes me. The sweetest hint of vanilla and peach fills my senses, and as I walk I grin with the satisfaction of knowing she's close and that my chance to unravel her, to find out if I'm right, is coming.

CHAPTER FIVE
Layla

I swallow the burn of a shot of whiskey in the break room. We aren't really supposed to drink during our shifts, but I think I need it to get through tonight. I've just closed the magazine I've been staring at for the last ten minutes without reading a word.

"Holy shit, it's a busy night out there!" Amber, one of the night servers, says as she breezes into the break room and reaches for the cigarettes in her bag. She's pretty and kind. Her family is from Thailand and her parents split their time between here and there still, but she rarely goes back with them when they travel, choosing to stay alone in their upscale home when they're gone. She was the first one to befriend me when I started here, and she smiles at me now. Her dark hair is cut into long layers with wispy bangs, and she's always styled to perfection.

"It's the rain," I tell her as I stand and straighten my skirt. "It brings everyone in, because what else are they gonna do in a hundred-degree heat and a thunderstorm?"

"Yeah, and it's still pouring. I heard it's supposed to last all night."

Great.

"Makes you wonder how long the bikers will stay. Don't see them around here, ever." Amber pulls the thought from my head as she fiddles with tucking her shirt into her tight black dress pants.

I look at my reflection in the mirror, seeing the eyes of my mother staring back at me. Grief washes over me and I swallow down the lump in my throat. There are moments I almost see her. Almost feel her hand over mine, or see her eyes crinkle in the corners as she smiles.

I've had this vision since she died and it clouds my mind— the woman behind the bars, clinging to them. The woman isn't either of us per se, more a mix, but she looks like us and she's begging to be freed. It isn't unusual to see me in her, but after the encounter with Ax at the bar just now and the way I spoke my mind, she looks different—a little bolder now, as if there is a glimmer of hope. As if her freedom might be a possibility.

"Three bikers in our club is like mainstream news," I comment, keeping my eyes on my reflection.

"They aren't difficult to look at, if you know what I mean," Amber snickers as she applies her own lipstick and pushes her tits up. "God, the biggest one is *hot*. Like, I'd scale him like a tree if I wasn't afraid he'd do some weird shit like tie me up and spank me red."

The idea of the sergeant's hands on me flashes into my mind again. I push it away and fix my necklace in the mirror.

"Well, spankings aside, hopefully for Chantel's sake they were good tippers," I laugh, turning to check out my ass in my skirt. It registers with me that we don't really have a time limit for customers, so as long as they keep ordering, they could stay here until close.

I lean into the mirror and fluff my ponytail, then carefully touch up my lipstick, rubbing my lips together with a slight pop. I'm trying not to romanticize someone who is probably just a cocky, womanizing criminal, because he's the exact opposite of what I've always thought I want in a man. My mind drifts to the lines of his sculpted hands and I remind myself that those hands have probably done terrible things in the name of his club. What those hypnotic green eyes have witnessed would probably give me nightmares. And then I ask myself again why the hell I'm so transfixed by him. *Why the hell do I care?*

But try as I might, while Amber rambles on about another server she doesn't like, the vision of Ax stalking toward me with his face partially covered by that black bandana floods my mind and I let myself take it a step further. I imagine his body over mine, pressing up against me and whispering into my ear in that gruff, deep voice. Those rough, experienced hands drifting down my sides—

"Are you behind the bar for the rest of the night?" Amber asks, cutting into my headspace as she spritzes hairspray. I blink and force myself to take a deep breath.

"Yep," I say, keeping my eyes on the mirror as I release the breath. "But I still have some time left on my break."

"Alright, I'm going for my smoke. See you out there," she calls. I smile, knowing Amber is heading out to our covered patio. She only allows herself one or two cigarettes a day. She calls it "stress balance."

"Sure thing." I snap my eyes to her in the mirror as she leaves the room.

I give my ponytail one final tighten, and I swear the shadow of something catches my eye behind me. I turn, suddenly feeling like I'm not alone. My breath quickens as my eyes move back and forth, waiting, but I hear nothing.

"You're losing it," I mutter under my breath, then decide I might as well get back out there early. Sitting in the break room thinking about how the big bad biker's hands would feel sliding up my naked thighs isn't helping anyone. Namely my thin cotton panties that already feel a little more damp with just the thought.

All the storage is partway down a long narrow hallway of warm brick, flanked with black sconces every so often for the same ambience as the restaurant itself. Right in the middle sits the giant dry goods walk-in pantry, and across from it is a massive walk-in cooler that houses all the cold goods and frozen items. The door to it looks like a bank vault and the lights turn on automatically when we open the door and walk inside.

I pull the heavy door open and make my way in so I can grab limes for the bar, only the light doesn't turn on. I pause and step backward over the threshold, then back into the cooler, hoping to trigger the motion sensors and waiting for the light. But there's nothing. I lean outside the door to reach for the manual switch, wondering why the automatic sensor is off, when two strong arms wrap around me from behind and pull me in. His scent washes over me and I instantly know exactly who is in this cooler with me. I open my mouth to scream, my blood thickening with fear, but I can't call out because a heavy hand is clamped down over my mouth as my chest is pushed up against the frigid cooler wall. His deep, gruff timbre fills my ears as my vision from earlier comes to life.

"Let's see if fear is what you wish for, little dove . . ."

CHAPTER SIX
Layla

"Let me go!" I bite at his hand, but my words are muffled and I lodge my elbow into his ribs. Ax grunts with my bite then chuckles darkly as he glides his hand down my arm, grasping my wrist in front of me and holding me tight.

The truth is I *should* be afraid, but instead something else is happening as I struggle uselessly against Ax's strong hold. His cedar and leather scent washes over me and sends my body into a frenzy I've never felt before. His breath is even and calm as he holds me tight and kicks the door closed with his foot. With one hand he drops the safety latch to lock us in the freezing space, while dipping his head down to my neck and taking a deep breath in, running his nose along the column of my throat.

"*Fuck . . .*" he groans, as his nose brushes the shell of my ear and he inhales. Just the way he says it has my skin erupting with goosebumps, and every cell in my body tingles with the rush of danger and a kind of deviant desire I've never felt before. I lean my head back on his chest, realizing this is an untapped fantasy, buried deep within the darkest corners of my mind. To be taken, to be forced. But even still, I fight to be released from his hold, because that's what I *should* do. I shouldn't want him to sneak in here and put his hands on me the way he is.

"You can't just come in here and touch me like this," I whimper as my cheek is pressed into the freezing cooler wall. Right and wrong bleed together like a shockingly vibrant kaleidoscope of desire and need. It clouds my head when he tightens his hold.

"Your body is *screaming* a different story." He reaches down and grips one of my hips tight and I realize I'm rolling them back, rocking against him instead of away. "My ego is big enough to handle you pretending you don't want me. In fact, I fucking love this little game."

His lips drop to my neck again, and the moment they do I'm filled with two things: anger and *need*. The two feelings colliding is like a sonic boom—and it's something entirely new. I feel rage toward him because he's mysterious and frightening and beautiful. And yet there's stability, because I've never felt empowered in any man's arms the way I do right now in his. This connection to someone I've just met is completely foreign, and although it's a hard truth I'll only admit to myself, I *want* him to touch me.

"Maybe you're just not as scary as you think you are," I taunt, my voice sounding much raspier and in turn sexier than I intended.

I begin to fight again, against both him and my own desires, grabbing at him anywhere I can as he spins me around. I gasp when my bare back is pressed into the cold cinderblock wall. Ax's hand comes up to my throat and he circles it with ease as his lips hover over mine.

"You have no idea how scary I can be, but I can already tell." He pauses to watch my lips. "You want that fear, and you want to be forced to feel it."

I whimper in response, unable to deny his words.

"I bet the idea of you not having a choice makes this tight little cunt weep for me." He slides his free hand down and squeezes under the curve of my ass as my blood races. His other hand stays at my throat, his thumb grazing back and forth over the center. I imagine that the chain inked on his skin now looks like a necklace around my throat, and it's eerily settling.

"You're only afraid because you know you want me . . . the same way I want you, and you can't explain why," he notes in a gruff whisper.

"If you scare me, it's only because I know what you're capable of, but I don't . . . know *you*," I breathe out as my core throbs with his words and the admission that he feels the same unexplainable connection I do.

"You think you know." He rests his forehead on mine. "And that's *exactly* why you like it. But babe . . ." He pauses to bring his hand from my ass to my chin, bringing my gaze up to meet his. "You *will* know me."

My mind races as I look into those haunting eyes, comparing this to what I've had with any man before this moment. The boring dates I've had to force myself not to yawn through. One serious boyfriend for a year in college who seemed sweet when we met but couldn't even make me come without my help. What I'm being offered at this moment isn't any of those things.

This is sheer magnetism. Passionate and raw. This asks nothing of me. This is only right now. But I can't *want* him . . . can I? I've only just laid eyes on him. In one last desperate attempt to stop this, I force myself to remember that a man just like him is the reason my life went from hopeful to complete shit in a single day.

Despite the logical part of my brain that's doing its best to take over, I cling to my monster in the dark. And not only do I cling, I pull him closer, fisting his t-shirt. My nails scratch through it and rake down his hard, warm chest. He hisses and tightens his grip on my throat. My pussy throbs as I let a moan escape.

"That's it . . . that's the sound I want, little dove."

We breathe in unison, our chests heaving in the dark, frigid space. I can barely make out the profile of the strong angles of his jaw and cheekbones in the glow of the emergency light. Every muscle in my body is on fire, despite the chill, waiting for him to move, to do something. To make the decision for me so I don't have to admit he's right.

"Your mind tells you no, but your body begs for something more, doesn't it? A little bit of fear, and maybe a little bit of pain? Your body begs just the way I knew it would the second I laid eyes on you." He brings his arm down and wraps it around my waist to pull me tight to his body, and that's when I feel him. Big and hard, pressing into my abdomen. Fighting him turns him on as much as it does me.

"You can't . . . know that about me . . . just from looking at me," I breathe out, desperate for some form of control that I simply no longer have as his chest presses to mine and the leather from his cut grazes my nipples, making them harden and ache for his hot lips.

"I don't even need to look at you." He pinches one of my nipples, hard. "I can fucking *smell* you." He slides his hand down my side. "And I know you're fucking soaked under this tight little skirt." His fingers just barely slide under the hem.

"Fuck you!" I bite out, my teeth chattering from the cold and the rush of adrenaline. But I give in and fuel him further, reaching up to hit him in the chest. It lands, but Ax doesn't flinch. Instead, he smiles a satisfied grin and pushes his hardened cock against me again. My body shivers as the desire surges.

I succumb to the reality that he's right. I *want* to fight him. I want to *test* him. I want him to take every last shred of innocence I possess. I want this stranger to take my free will from me.

"It's obvious that you're not from my kind of world. You

know I can offer you more than any man who's ever touched you before."

A soft moan slips from my lips as he releases my throat and sinks his fingers into the hair beneath my ponytail, then grabs it and pulls it tight, tipping my head back so my lips pop open.

"You're a caged little rebel," he whispers. "Searching for a man who can satisfy every depraved desire you've ever had." His tongue lightly skates across my bottom lip as I pant, desperate to kiss him, desperate to squeeze my thighs together—but I can't, because he's holding me in place. When he lets go of my ponytail I don't move, I don't fight. I wait with bated breath as his eyes trail my face, my neck.

His words are true.

I've dreamed of a man who can take control of me sexually. Even when I thought it was wrong, I dreamed about it. One who will claim me and handle me and teach me what it means to be desired. As wrong as this is, I *want* Ax to want me. My soaking wet panties and my aching core are the proof.

I give in, pressing my pussy against his thigh and moan, and he pushes back.

Just this once can I indulge? Can I let him set me free?

Ax spreads my legs wider, as much as my leather skirt allows. It inches up my thighs as he tightens the hold he now has around my waist.

"If you want to be ruined by a man you fear, then *I'm* the man who ruins you," he says, bringing his thumb from one side of my bottom lip to the other, smearing my freshly applied lipstick. Another groan leaves him as he breathes me in once more, and the sound ignites me. "You've fucking bewitched me, little dove. I don't ever want *any* woman. But I fucking want *you*."

With his words, something in me breaks. I let my want take over as I grip his cut tight with one hand and let my free hand move up, my first two fingers ghosting my nipple. I whimper with desire as I look into his eyes.

"Maybe . . . this was my plan all along?" I lick my lips as I trace the outline of my nipple with my fingers again, and a low growl leaves his chest as his lips descend to my neck, hurried and crazed, biting then sucking in deep pulls. His mint-and-bourbon-laced breath is hot on my skin as I mewl into him while he tortures me in the best way, plucking a nipple through my cotton bodysuit.

"*Ax* . . ." I moan the only name I have for him, sliding my hand from his cut to his waist, then under his t-shirt, exploring his abs and the wide expanse of his hard muscles and warm back. My fingers trail over what feels like a long jagged scar. Everything is cloudy and hazy as he pushes my skirt up enough to slide his hand between my legs, cupping my soaking pussy through my panties. The heel of his palm gives me just what I need as he circles it there with perfect pressure. It suddenly hits me that he's going to make me come and he's barely even touched me.

"Poor little rebel. No one has ever given you what you need, have they?" he asks as he pushes harder against my needy clit.

His words mixed with the freezing space cause shivers of pleasure to race through me, and I shudder in his arms.

"So fucking desperate . . . let your body take what you want now," he coaxes, his voice gruff.

"Please . . ." I whimper, without even knowing what I'm pleading for as I press harder against his hand.

"That's it," he praises as he slides his thumb under my panties, through my soaking slit and up over my aching clit. A greedy growl leaves him as he confirms my secret need for him.

"Mmmm . . . I fucking love being right. Look at this fucking mess you've made. All for the man you don't want." I feel his smirk against my lips as he sweeps his thumb over me, but I'm too far gone to care about his gloating as he pulls the top of my bodysuit down, allowing my breasts to bounce free. He doesn't waste a second, sucking a nipple into his mouth. My mind floods with nothing but unfiltered desire and thoughts of him. I move against his fingers as his tongue flicks, sending tiny sparks through me.

My hips rock into him, and I grip his leather as I ride his hand, both of us still fully clothed. I've never experienced anything so erotic. He pinches my clit before pushing his first finger into me, then a second. They're thick and stretching me as my core spasms. Waves of pleasure pulse through me as my orgasm begins to take hold.

"They'll hear me . . ." I whimper breathlessly, the sounds of my pussy being fucked by his thick fingers filling the space. He slides my arousal up and toys with my clit again, and my eyes roll back.

"Let them," he growls. My legs shake as I shamelessly grind against him.

"I-I'm going to come . . . Ax."

"*Sean*," he says, commanding. "My name is Sean."

My eyes flutter open and connect with his in the dim light. I can see how much he wants his name on my lips, but I'm not ready to give him that.

Instead, I simply cry out as pleasure washes over me.

"*Fuck! Please* . . ." I beg for him as I come, looking into his eyes with his name on the tip of my tongue. Sean's jaw sets as he watches me, as if he's fighting both anger and lust.

He groans. "Look at you, dripping down my hand. You won't say my name, but I promise you *will* remember who made you come for the rest of the night," he murmurs as static lines my vision, my breathing shallow. I moan into his chest, biting into my bottom lip, and he holds me up as I let the rush of him race through my blood—the rush of this . . . freedom. My whimpers are the only sound in the cold, dark room.

I'm still so sensitive when Sean pushes my panties fully aside and firmly slides his first two fingers through my soaking slit, and my head falls back as he brings my arousal to his lips. He sucks his fingers clean, pulling them slowly from his mouth, and I watch with fascination as his eyes close while he savors the taste of me. He licks his lips, and when his eyes open, I can see even in the dark that they're hooded and stormy.

"*Fuck me*," he murmurs.

I try to catch my breath as I watch him. I've never seen a man be so brazen, so unashamed before.

"Give me your name," he commands.

"L-Layla," I whisper, my body shivering now that the adrenaline is wearing off. It's only thirty-five degrees in this fucking cooler.

An odd look I just can't place takes over his face as his jaw falls slack before he whispers, "Layla." Then his eyes close as he draws me close and breathes me in deeply before opening them. "Such a pretty mess you made for me. So fucking sweet," he rasps before dropping his lips to mine. He doesn't fully kiss me, but I taste myself mixed with him as he pulls my bottom lip into his mouth, sucking until I feel blood rush to the surface. Even though I shouldn't want this stranger, the moment he backs away, my body begs as I drop my hands—and I fight the loss of him.

I try to force some semblance of control into this situation. I squirm away from him, then grip his arms and push him with all my strength into the cooler wall I was just pinned against. He lets me, a shocked look taking over his face, and I bring my lips up to his in frustration.

"You've made me late, *Ax*," I whisper accusingly, desperately trying not to kiss him. It isn't without effort, and that just pisses me off all over again, yet still I grip his cut tight. "Are you about done? I need the ladies' room before I head back to my

46

job," I mutter. *Because I'm sure my lipstick is all over my fucking face.*

His eyes meet mine and shock gives way to a glorious yet hauntingly beautiful smile that takes over his whole face, before he tugs me closer one more time.

"*Layla . . .*" He draws my name out again as he bends down, and just the sound of it on his lips settles something deep in the marrow of my bones. I use all my inner strength to push back from him, giving him one more look before grabbing the limes and opening the heavy cooler door, leaving him behind. I hear that deep chuckle as I walk away and wonder if that actually just happened or if I've just hallucinated from hypothermia.

CHAPTER SEVEN
Sean

Well this just got really fucking interesting.

I'm rarely shaken or intrigued. I may not be a good man, but one thing I am is an honest man. So I'll admit that hearing my little dove's name was Layla, coupled with her pushing me into the cooler wall after she came all over me, shook me to my very core and definitely intrigued the fuck out of me. She has no idea how close I was to hiking up her skirt and claiming her like a fucking animal right then and there. Her fire is an invitation that I won't ignore, only my resolve managed to stop me. I *will* fuck her. But the first time I sink into that tight, needy cunt I want her to be able to unleash the wild side that I'm now positive is living within her, and she can't do that in the back of a restaurant full of people.

Layla.

The name on loop that pulled me through my worst moments. The lyrics I hear every single time I remember lying in the dust, looking up at the lone laughing dove on top of our mutilated Humvee. My fucking saving grace. I don't question why her existence lines up with my past. I don't believe in fate,

destiny or whatever you want to call it, because fate isn't quanti-
fiable. But I do believe in the chemical and physical connection
between two souls and mine is most certainly connected to hers.

Of that, I'm positive.

I watch her now as the bar begins to empty out a little. My
men left but I've stayed the extra hour until close, slowly sipping
my bourbon right at the end of her bar.

When I came back from the cooler five minutes after her,
she glanced up at me, perfectly put together and dismissive. Perfectly poised, aside from the flush of her cheeks and the glassy
look in her eyes that gave away that she had just come all over my
fingers with that heated look in her eyes and those moans on her
pouty lips. Something about this woman hating that she wants
me just fucking makes my dick hard.

The combination feels like my undoing, but I want more of
it. I want all of *her*. I don't know where she comes from, who
her family is, what she likes, what she hates, what drives her or
what turns her on, aside from fear because that's already apparent. But I *will* find out. I have no choice but to now. She's a knot
I need to untie, a mystery I feel the need to solve. Covered in
ink with a penchant for danger. Cocky and standoffish, yet trembling with want. A caged little rebel without her cause, because
she simply hasn't discovered what her cause is yet.

I breathe deep with satisfaction as this challenge presents
itself. I never doubt my gut, and in this case I already know I'm
right. My little dove is about to find out that *I* am her cause.

CHAPTER EIGHT
Layla

What was I thinking? What came over me? How did one touch turn me into a begging slut for the big bad biker? I work on autopilot for the last hour of the night, trying to wrap my head around why Sean is still here, sitting at the other end of the bar watching me. He isn't drinking quickly; he's been sipping one bourbon and a water. But he's making me feel completely on edge in a million different ways.

"Avoiding me isn't going to help you forget about me," he offers, as I stand from crouching down to empty the bowl of peels into the compost bin. I fight the urge to wipe the cocky expression off this man's face.

As the bar empties, Sean stands and moves toward me, swallowing the last of his bourbon finally and fishing for his wallet inside his cut. I notice it's simple black leather as he pulls enough bills out to pay my rent for at least three months. Chantel told me their food bill cost a fortune and that they gave her a forty percent tip.

Because he's a criminal and is paying with blood money. And I just let him finger-fuck me until I came all over him.

Not your finest moment, Layla.

Sean pulls two hundred-dollar bills from the stack and drops them on the bar top. I look at the cash and then back up at him, and his jaw flexes. Our silence is charged with unspoken electricity.

"What the *hell* is that for?" I ask in an angry whisper, already thinking the worst.

Sean understands me immediately and leans in on his forearms.

"I don't pay for women, Layla." The sound of my name hits me square in the chest, even though it isn't the first time I've heard him say it. "This is to cover my drinks from the night, and a tip for you since I held your line up earlier."

I fold my arms over my chest. The strange thing is that, even though I know he must be a bad man, he seems . . . oddly trustworthy. I have no idea how, but I can feel it.

"If you're uncomfortable you can ask your friend. We tipped her the same percentage," he adds, that hint of amusement back in his vivid eyes.

I sigh, taking the money, and sign his receipt with my name, like we are told to do with every bill, then hand it to him along with his change. *All* of his change. It's too much of a tip and I don't want any signals crossed here. Although I desperately need it, I also need to show him that I'm not someone who can be bought and that I'm still somewhat in control. At least, I'm trying very, very hard to be.

Chantel returns to the bar and Amber follows behind her, both of them carrying spray bottles and rags from cleaning tables. The last patrons fix to leave as I eye the door behind Sean then look back at him.

"So . . . then, see you never?" I tell him, not knowing what else to say. Chantel and Amber take one look at us staring each other down and freeze in their tracks.

"You'll see me tomorrow." He smirks. It's a stated fact, not a question, and it unnerves me that he's enjoying this so much.

"No," I say instantly, shaking my head.

"No?" Sean asks with one eyebrow raised.

"That's right." I point between us. "We aren't happening."

I can see the girls back away in my periphery as Sean's grin grows, and he pulls a stool back out, carefully taking a seat as he watches me. He spreads his arms wide and drums his fingers against the bar top in thought. I can already tell that time isn't something he concerns himself with as he sits here like the bar *isn't* closed and it *isn't* time for him to go.

"I'm serious," I say, looking around. "This was a one-off."

He shakes his head and stares at me for a beat.

"Nah," he says simply.

"*Nah?*" I ask incredulously.

"That's right. I find it rude that you've already made up your mind about me and you don't even know me." His gaze trails down my body then back up. "Especially after you had no problem using me."

I laugh. "Well, I'm sorry to tell you this . . ." I cock my hip and place my hand on it. "Actually, maybe I'm the first one to *ever* tell you this, but the world doesn't revolve around you and I didn't exactly have time to think about making a choice in that cooler."

Sean folds his thick arms over his chest and strokes the underside of his bearded chin with his tattooed knuckles, studying me with those knowing eyes. I'm full of shit and he can tell.

"Yet you had time to push that needy little pussy into my hand *instead* of pushing me away."

I suck in a breath, glancing around to make sure no one heard him. He analyzes my response as he leans in closer, folding his hands carefully in front of him on the bar top.

"Using me to come is fine, you can do that any time you like, but I'm not gonna be your dirty secret, little dove." He says the last words just loud enough for Chantel to gasp audibly from the back corner, where she and Amber are finding busywork. I shoot daggers at them quickly then turn back to Sean's menacing emerald eyes.

"This is my reputation. My job. I *need* this job to pay my bills and get through school. I need every single cent." Something in me breaks with the admission of my vulnerable financial state to a stranger, and my voice cracks with my last words. "And we would never work. *This was a one-off*," I repeat.

He watches me as I compose myself, leaning away from him and straightening out my skirt. He stands and pushes in his stool, taking a moment to make sure it's in line with the rest, then looks me directly in the eye.

"You've got a dove inked into your skin. How much do you really know about them?" he asks.

I blink and look up at him, not understanding why we're talking about this when I just told him to leave. He rests his hand on the bar, the one with his own, larger dove.

"When they find each other, they don't just bond for the night, so *nah*," he says before turning to leave without another word. I follow him, walking briskly.

"How long do they bond for?" I ask behind him.

He just turns and smirks at me over his shoulder, like he knows something I don't.

"I mean it," I call after him, trying to sound as tough as I can while he pushes through the glass doors into the now cloudless night. The moment he's out of the door I lock it much more violently than warranted and let out a frustrated huff. The click of the deadbolt echoes through the glass foyer.

I mutter obscenities under my breath as I move back toward the bar to finish up, turning when I get there and leaning back on it, blowing out a breath. I'm not there for more than a second before Chantel and Amber are at my side.

"*Whaaaaat* was that?" Chantel asks, pulling out a bottle and pouring us all a shot.

I put my head in my hands and groan. "*That* was a mistake. Five minutes of thinking with my pussy and now he says he'll 'see me tomorrow.' I don't know what to do."

Chantel hands me a shot glass. "I do," she snorts.

I look at her expectantly. She looks from me to Amber as she hands Amber hers. "Give whatever that mountain of a man wants a try, and enjoy every single second." Chantel laughs. "It's not the end of the world."

They both laugh harder and knock back their shots.

"I've been to a party or two at the Hounds of Hell clubhouse. They get up to some pretty crazy shit, and to be honest I think I may have hooked up with one of them a couple years ago. I was pretty drunk but I just remember it was *hot*." Chantel nudges me. "You could have some fun with him. It's a distraction from your constant routine of work and school, and it's not like you're a prude. You'd like it, I'm sure."

I look toward the door, shaking my head. Remembering where he comes from, who he most likely is at his core. The police sketch released of my parents' killer fills my mind. I remember the tattoos, the distinctive leather vest. Sure, it wasn't unequivocally a Hounds of Hell vest on the killer, but it was someone just like him, wasn't it?

"Earth to Lay?" Chantel says, snapping her fingers. "Oh my God, this is why you were late coming back from break!" She whistles.

Oh God.

This night just needs to be done. I want to go home, have a hot shower and then fall into bed because I have a 10 a.m. class tomorrow on campus and then I have another full shift here after that. I also have to ride the bus both ways, since my mom's old Lincoln died on me a couple weeks ago. The very last thing I need is a persistent outlaw showing up here tomorrow night and distracting me like this again.

I run through what happened tonight and calm myself down as we continue to close up, feeling like I might be gaining some clarity now that I'm away from his gaze.

This *must* just be his game. I want nothing to do with his world and I'll make that clear over and over if I have to. Yes, he played right into fantasies I hadn't even fully admitted to myself yet. But men do this sort of thing every day, so why can't I? It's no big deal. I don't owe him anything. I'll just stay clear if I ever see him again, which I probably won't.

"Stop worrying about it," Chantel calls with a laugh from the other side of the bar, surely taking in the way my brow is knotted as I work. She knows me pretty well after only a few months. I look up at her and she shrugs. "He probably moved on the moment he left. Men like that don't have a long attention span."

"Yeah." I nod. She's right. He's just fucking with me because he can. He'll forget all about me.

By the time I head out and climb into Chantel's car for the ride home she offered me, I *almost* have myself convinced.

Chapter Nine

Sean

"At least she's getting out of the house again. Before you know it, she'll be back at school, one day at a time." I grip Mason's shoulder beside me in our club meeting—our service.

We're seated in the chapel room at the clubhouse. It's a large space that houses a heavy walnut table, big enough to seat twenty-five. An intricate metal replica of our cut hangs on the wall, an homage to where we came from. Wolfe's grandad Ira designed the insignia with his own hand. The deadly wolf skull with a snake slithering through. A reminder: *Keep your friends close but your enemies closer.*

The room is sparsely furnished, just the table with ashtrays on it and in the far corner a fully stocked liquor cabinet. This is our safe space, the place we can speak freely about anything and everything. Business or personal.

"She'll get past this. We'll find and fucking gut whoever did this to her, but in the meantime, she's got the family, and her therapy right?" I ask.

Mason nods. "Yeah, seems like it's helping."

The entire table offers similar support after my words. It

wasn't much more than three months ago that his youngest, now seventeen-year-old, sister was assaulted by a man who had lured her through a social media app. She thought he was a college student, one she had developed feelings for. He covered his face, drugged her, raped her and recorded it, stating on the video that she'd consented, that she'd *begged* for it. She hadn't. Fucking disgusting. The videos were released online with the man fucking her, his middle finger raised to the camera. It was taken down, but the whole thing has come close to ruining her life. And the police keep saying she's just another statistic. They haven't been able to figure out who did it. But *we* know it's a personal retaliation targeted at our club. We know it was a Disciples of Sin member because of a tattoo on the guy's wrist in the video.

Spare none. That's the motto of our rival club. We don't know for sure who exactly did it, but we have a damn good idea, and we'll leave no stone unturned until we find out for sure and bring him and whoever else was involved to club justice.

It's our most sacred rule. You never, *ever* fuck with women, children or our families. If you do, we'll make you wish the devil himself got a hold of you before we did.

Our conversation turns to business, and we listen to our club president, Gabriel Wolfe—my brother for all intents and purposes—talk about next week's drug shipment being brought in from Canada for our clinics.

Wolfe has been club president for a few years now, and he's done a hell of a job upholding not only our business but our reputation in both Savannah and Atlanta. His father was in the club before him, although he was a total fuckup and waste of space. Wolfe redeemed his family name and learned how to be a true leader from his uncle Ray, the prez before him who passed him the torch. He's also found a way to use the club and anything illegal that we sell to give back not only to the community but to our fellow Veterans. He was an officer in my unit during all three tours in the desert; we've been through it all together and then some.

I've always found it odd that Wolfe's uncle asked him instead of his own son, Jake, to carry on his legacy. But Jake doesn't seem to mind and is now our VP. He's kind of a flake anyway, and I'd never say this to another living soul, but I've never liked the guy. He's usually looking for a quick fuck or a quick high. He isn't calculating, and he never thinks before he acts. A recipe for disaster in our world, and his haywire actions alone can drive a man like me to the brink of insanity. You can never count on him.

"Alright, so get through this week, and Kai, keep looking for our culprit," Wolfe says. But even though we're finished with the conversation, Mason is still seething.

"I fucking know it was someone from the Disciples. The things I'm gonna do to that motherfucker Marco," he says through gritted teeth, mentioning the Disciples of Sin president, Marco Foxx.

"We all *think* it was them. But we can't do shit until we *know*," Wolfe says, leaning back in his chair. His voice is commanding. "We have to do this with clear heads," he adds.

"I'm getting closer," Kai pipes up from the other side of the table. He's smart as fuck with anything tech. At first, I thought he was just some pretty boy when he prospected. I didn't think he'd last a week. I figured he just wanted to get his dick wet and prove to the world he was a badass, but after eight months of prospecting and now two years with his rockers, he's proven *me* wrong. He has a deeply dark and twisted side just like the rest of us, but his seems to be fueled by some sort of revenge almost. His backstory isn't mine to tell, but parts of it are grim enough to bring this peaceful sort of smile to his face when he's peeling back someone's fingernails.

"I'll find out where the video came from. I fuckin' promise

you that," Kai adds. Mason grits his back molars. The day he gets his hands on the man who violated his baby sister will be a reckoning that I'll not only welcome, I'll happily assist with. That man will wish he was never born.

My eyes snap to Wolfe's for direction as I spin my ring on my first finger. He sits at the head of the table, tipping the gavel on its head against the wooden plate. The room is lit with spotlights and the walls are paneled with wood. I always sit at Wolfe's left and Jake sits across from me. My job is to protect Wolfe first, at all costs, and the club second. After serving with him overseas I'm already used to that, so this has seemed like the natural progression of things for me, and it isn't a job I take lightly. I'd take a bullet or a life for him in a heartbeat, and even though it's not his job to do so, I know he'd do the same for me.

"Alright, enough of that. Off the record, what took you fuckers so long last night?" Wolfe asks me, Mason and Kai.

I shift in my seat, trying to loosen my tight back, feeling my brow furrow.

"You good?" Wolfe asks, always concerned about our well-being. I nod.

"Fucking rain yesterday," I retort. He knows it always aggravates my back and the chronic pain that lives there.

"The rain, and running down two K-6ers," Kai chuckles, mentioning a low-level street gang. We scared them off when they were dealing in front of one of our clinics last week and gave them a good beatdown—so yeah, that didn't help either.

"Well? What happened last night?" Wolfe coaxes an answer out of us. "You were supposed to be here at nine to help Shelly move tables around for the party, and she isn't gonna let you get away with that shit. She was bitching all night about how hard it is to find good help around here." He mentions my mother by name. She's a fireball, and she's been the den mother around here since my dad died. She didn't have to stay, but I was deep in it by then and it was the only life she knew. She gets a little crazy when it comes to hosting and we're having a party next weekend for one of our members. It's Flip's fiftieth birthday.

"Sorry Prez, we got caught in the rain and we were fucking starving. We stopped at The Palm for a steak," Kai says, speaking for me.

"The Palm? That would've been a sight. Did you clear the place out?" Jake asks with a chuckle.

Mason shrugs. "No one tried to take our pool table."

The room laughs around us.

"We would've been in and out but this prick went and fell in love with some bartender chick and he wouldn't let us leave," Kai says, pulling out a smoke with his teeth from the pack in his inside pocket and lighting it with the flick of a silver lighter. "Fucking stalker," he adds on his inhale. The table chuckles as he blows out a steady plume of smoke. "So if you're gonna blame anyone, blame him for tripping over his own dick."

Wolfe looks at me for a long moment, stroking the scruff along his jaw and leaning back in his seat.

"It couldn't be helped," I grit out. "Fucking woman bewitched me."

Wolfe is a beast of a man and serious as all hell most of the time, so when he smirks, even in the slightest, you just know he's gonna fuck with you.

"You expect me to believe a woman put a spell on you?" he asks.

"Magic tits?" Robby J jokes from his end of the table.

"Christ . . . her tits, ass, ohhh that fucking ass," Kai says, mimicking taking a big bite of her ass with a sort of growl that would have me cock-punching him if I was sitting next to him. My fist hits the table.

"Shut the fuck up," I say to Kai, instantly shutting him up.

I'm the only one at the table not laughing over his actions.

The moment they all realize I'm actually serious, the laughter stops.

I shake my head. "Talk about Layla like that ever again, and your ass-eating days will be over. You'll be eating through a fucking tube."

Kai takes another drag on his smoke. "Fuck man, I was only joking. Are you *actually* gonna see this chick again?"

"Holy fuck, now *I* want to know what she looks like," Flip says from the end of the table. Another chorus of laughter.

I turn to face him. "You might be old, but I'll still fucking beat the shit outta you," I warn him, and I'm only half joking. The idea of anyone looking at Layla besides me is causing my blood to boil, and Christ, I may not understand the chokehold this woman has me in, but I will figure it out—and until then, they *won't* talk about her like that again.

I need more time to solve this.

"When I bring her around here," I add. "All of you will fucking behave." I look around the table.

"*We'll* all behave, but will Shell?" Wolfe asks, and he's right. My mom is definitely going to go overboard when I bring a woman around. I knot my brow in thought. I'm going to have to talk to her about this.

"I'll deal with my mother," I say to the table.

"Better you than us," Jake pipes up, which causes more laughter.

"Does *Layla* know she'll be here soon?" Mason asks with a smirk.

"Not yet, but she will," I toss back.

"Alright, unless anyone has anything else, we're done. Everyone get out. I've got shit to do," Wolfe says, snapping the gavel down. We all stand as Kai stubs out his smoke.

I clap him on the shoulder. "Don't go anywhere. I need your help for a minute."

He nods. "Sure thing, Loverboy," he says with his sinister grin.

Cocksucker.

I'm nothing if not a creature of habit. Most days are the same. Chapel in the morning if necessary, then my daily training regimen, which has been the same for over ten years, finishing with an ice-cold shower.

I step out of that shower now, giving my back a good stretch to loosen the tension that lives there as I wrap a towel around my waist, letting myself mostly air-dry. My muscles are extra sore after I went hard this morning, but it's par for the course. I don't like feeling out of control, and right now I'm fighting that feeling hard as I scroll through the texts on my phone from the guys and my mother.

> **BOSS WOMAN**
>
> You're bringing a woman here? Who is this sweetbutt?

Fucking pricks. More than likely Kai told her, because he's my mother's little bitch.

> She isn't a sweetbutt. She's new to this world and I'll be the one to introduce her.

> **BOSS WOMAN**
>
> Well, Christ on a fucking cracker. I didn't believe them when they told me.

> This is exciting. What does she like to eat?

For fuck's sake. I pull up my chat with Kai and message him.

> You need to get off my mother's tit.

KAI

> She's the only mama I've got.

> Should've seen her face light up though. Classic.

> Fucking shit disturber.

KAI

> Check your email. I sent you what you wanted.

Fucking Kai. A pain in the ass, but it looks like he came through for me today, so I'll let it slide. I tell my mom I'll talk to her later and put on a pair of black jeans and a flannel button-down. Then I open the file from Kai. I quickly scroll through, reading quickly what I can.

Layla June Monroe, age twenty-four. Christ, she's eight years younger than me. Dropped out of a Georgia State program leading to a teaching degree after her parents' deaths nearly two years ago. Now in a fast-track program with just over one semester left to becoming a registered massage therapist. I read through the rest of the info, the schedule of her classes, including some this summer, and I check out the clinic she has her placement at. I note her acceptance into a kinesiology program but that she hasn't accepted the offer yet.

I wonder why.

She's an honors student and seems to spend all her time at school and at her job at The Palm Club. Just as I suspected, she's a good girl dying to be bad. One boyfriend a few years back, looks like he was part of her parents' church. Some photos of her at a dedication on the church's social media page. Her and another girl in their teens. Layla's hair was more of a chestnut color then, and the other girl's hair is black. They're hugging and holding tambourines. I read through her parents' file too, not making it past their tragic deaths. Kai has included the police file and I see it's still an open case. I spend the next thirty minutes reading every single thing I can about her. I don't need to make notes, I'll remember it all. That's just how my brain works; it's like a sickness sometimes, but it's helpful for things like this.

I read on, realizing I was right about her social status. Her father was a government accountant and her mother a home-maker who volunteered with their church quite frequently and taught Sunday school.

Kai is a master at finding everything there is to know about people, and Layla has been easy enough to figure out with just a few clicks of a mouse. It seems like she leads a charmed life, and there aren't any skeletons in her closet.

I reopen her class schedule and memorize it, then I move to my home office.

My house sits at the end of a quiet street in a century-old neighborhood of Harmony. We all spend time at the clubhouse, but we all have homes. Some guys have families, and most have real jobs like I do.

I switch on my computer and my three monitors light up. My house is a Craftsman, modernized for the latest security features, and my office sits behind locked glass doors and is secure. I'm a retired active-duty Marine, but I still work for a branch of Veterans Affairs. For the most part, I don't agree with any government policy, but I do have a deep respect and love for my country and every single person who serves it.

Pretty much the moment I was discharged, I learned that

you can't change anything for these soldiers and Vets unless you do it from the inside. So that's what I spend my time doing, and the bonus is I get paid very well to do it. Not to mention my schedule works around me. I can check in at will and rarely have to put in more than a couple days of work a week.

I pride myself on being a Vet's best advocate, and I help them in any way I can, and if that means pushing the government to give them more assistance, so be it. If it means fighting to give them better care, so be it. If it means keeping only a small portion of what I earn so I can financially assist with better programs for the soldiers I personally know, so be it. There's no limit to what I would give to my brothers and sisters who fought alongside me, and those I don't even know. We're all family.

After printing the documents from my phone and deleting the digital files, I place the hard copies into a folder marked *Layla* in the drawer of my mahogany desk, pushing away the image in my head of her defiant face as she came last night. Refusing to call out my name. My cock twitches with just the thought of the complex puzzle she presents, but I force myself to pull out my notes for my video meeting with the deputy assistant director of Veterans Affairs. I get through almost my entire meeting before my mind is racing again with all the things I've just learned about Layla and how much more I *plan* to learn. A plan that will start the moment I get off this call.

Chapter Ten
Layla

I rub my temples and will the headache forming behind my eyes to go away. I've had a full day of Pathology, which has been an info dump for our midterm next week, and I've barely slept because every time I close my eyes all I can see are the intense green eyes of the man who looked at me like I belonged to him.

I tossed and turned all night wondering if he will in fact show up at work tonight, and I've already planned out some possibilities of what I'll say to hopefully get him to move on.

I don't date.

I'm focusing on school.

I have a husband and four kids.

You scare the shit out of me.

My phone buzzes on my desk as my professor finishes up his lecture.

CHANTEL

Amber's gonna be late. Can you come in at six?

Fuck. I check the time. It's three now. All I want to do is go home for an hour and take a hot bath before I have to put heels on for the night. I'm not scheduled until seven. I breathe out a tired sigh.

Sure.

Only a few more nights of work until I actually get a day off. A day I will spend on my sofa in my PJs, eating ice cream while I work on my assignment.

"I'll see you next week. If you have any questions, you can email Gloria," my prof says, motioning to the TA in the front row.

I make it outside and immediately feel like I've been slapped in the face by the sun. It's a damn scorcher again. Humid as hell, and the idea of getting on the sweltering bus makes me want to call an Uber, but I know that's a luxury I can't afford.

I pull my sunglasses out of my crossbody bag and pop them on, glancing in the direction of the bus stop. But I stop dead in my tracks, because that's when I see him, and I swear my soul almost leaves my body.

Parked directly across the street, leaning back on a monstrous matte black and deep bronze Harley, once again dressed in all black, wearing aviators and his club cut, is none other than Sean.

He pulls his sunglasses off and looks at me in the same devastating way he did last night. Like he can't look away. His thick arms are ripped and folded over his chest and his brow is furrowed in that mysterious scowl, like a million thoughts are running through his head.

You are stronger than how good he looks, I repeat to myself as I sort through all the questions running through my brain.

Should I pretend I haven't seen him?

How the hell does he know where I go to school?

What does he really want?

Why do I want to know?

All of them fly right out of my head as he stands and begins to walk directly toward me in an even stride with his long lean legs. Sean's moves are calculated, like even the cars coming down the street would stop and wait until he's safely across. As he places his sunglasses inside his cut I watch him carefully; he just has this powerful confidence about him that I don't think anyone questions.

Well, I know one thing, he better be ready, because I'm about to fucking question him. I *should* run in the other direction, but instead I head straight for him, my annoyance at him digging into my life, however he was able to do it, taking over.

It takes us a moment to meet in the middle of the busy sidewalk, but then I grip his arm and pull him toward the shade of a tree, away from the campus pathway, ignoring how his skin feels against mine. Summer classes means the campus isn't as busy as it would be throughout the school year, but I still don't need anyone from my classes watching me argue with this gorilla of a man.

"What the *hell* are you doing at my school?" I glance over his shoulder toward where I know the bus that's due in five minutes will be coming from, and then look back up at his searing green eyes, which are now brighter with the sun.

"Did you follow me? Because, if so, you're fucking unhinged," I tell him louder than I should. We've garnered some attention; he's clearly out of place here, and a few passersby have turned to look over their shoulders at him. He pays them no mind and ignores my shock. Instead, Sean moves his hands up and loops the first two fingers of each hand into the front pockets of my light, ripped jeans, and pulls me forward until I bump into his chest.

"You have no idea." He looks down at me with a dark chuckle.

"Is that supposed to make me feel safer?" I hate how much my body likes touching his.

"It's irrelevant if you *feel* safe, but just so we're clear, you *are* safe with me."

"I somehow doubt that," I lie.

Sean narrows his eyes at me, and I realize I haven't pulled away from his hold. In fact, I'm leaning into him, gripping his shirt. I let go suddenly and push away.

"The biggest problem you have is that you try very hard not to want me when you actually very clearly do," he says, assessing me like he can read my thoughts. "That takes way more energy than just giving in."

"I don't even *know* you!" I whisper-yell. "*That* is my biggest problem. I met you less than twenty-four hours ago. In that time, you've invited yourself into my work cooler"—I use air quotes around *invited*—"you've followed me to my school, and you've obviously dug into my personal business or you've just been stalking me all day!" I bite out between clenched teeth, a new thought occurring to me. "I hate to break it to your gigantic ego, but when a girl says that what happened with you was a one-off, it is *not* an invitation to keep trying."

Sean chuckles. "I didn't hear you complaining about the lack of invitation when you were coming all over my hand."

He nods toward his bike. I shift nervously from one foot to the other.

Good. He's leaving, and just in time as I see my bus round the corner—

"Let's go," he bites out.

My eyes widen and I look from his bike back to him.

"I'm *not* going with you," I tell him, putting my hand on my hip. He sighs, lifting his eyes upward before looking back at me. I can see his wide jaw tic from a foot away and I just know I'm pissing him off.

"Yes, you are. One, because we both know the last thing you want to do is get on that bus in this heat."

His eyes trace the lines of my face as I watch the bus approach.

"Two, you *want* to ride with me."

His voice reaches a lower octave, one that hits me in all the right places. I want to follow him, but because I refuse to give into him so easily, I move to push past him, heading toward the bus stop. I don't even get two steps before a deep growl sounds behind me and I'm being picked up and hoisted over Sean's shoulder.

"And three, because I *fucking* said so, woman," he growls.

My breath catches in my throat and I hit his upper back. "Put me down!"

Sean carries me the rest of the way, and everyone in the vicinity is watching us as he sets me down beside his bike. My chest heaves as I push my hair back off my face and look up at him.

"*Now*," he commands, passing me a helmet and climbing onto his bike. I wait all of five seconds before I take it from him, like an absolute fucking lunatic who clearly needs her head checked. Then I huff out a breath and clip it onto my head, because I *do* want to get on the back of his bike instead of on that bus . . . I just don't want to admit it.

"You don't even know where I live," I fire at him, but then I hear the deep rumble of his chuckle again as he ignores my comment.

Right. Of course he knows where I live.

CHAPTER ELEVEN
Layla

Being on the back of Sean's custom Harley is a sensation I simply wasn't prepared for. He tells me where to put my feet and what not to touch because it's hot. When I take my place behind him, his heavy hands squeeze the outsides of my knees and he tugs me closer in one fluid movement. I let out a little yelp with the action, and when he's satisfied with my position, he pats one hand on my leg and then moves it up to his grip. Another caveman-like action that doesn't fail to make my heart rate sputter. There's just something so unabashedly masculine about him. So sure and confident. When he starts his bike, my arms wrapped around his firm waist, the heavy, methodic rumble is almost comforting. But the way it feels when I lean my head against him and breathe in his sinful scent is intoxicating, and for this one moment, I give in. It actually feels good to have someone to lean on. My breasts press into his back, and the warm leather of his cut brushes my cheek. I'm holding on tight but not tight enough that it could ever hurt a man of his size, so I find it confusing when I feel him tense under my arms. I know enough about the human body from my studies to know he's harboring some kind of pain in his lower back. I remember the scar I felt under my fingers and wonder what happened to him.

Sean reaches back and slides his open palm from the top of my thigh all the way down to my knee, giving it a light squeeze before he lets go, and I shudder from the steadying gesture.

"I've got you. Let's fly, little dove." He gives me one slow smirk over his shoulder, and the completely fucked-up thing is, I know he *does* have me.

The wind whips my hair around my shoulders as I watch city workers water the hanging baskets of flowers on the lampposts outside the quaint little shops that make Harmony a summer destination. I must admit that this is worlds better than taking the bus. But I know I've thoroughly lost my mind getting on his bike when Sean passes the turnoff for my street. I panic for a moment when I realize I don't know where he's taking me, but a few blocks later he backs his bike into an open spot in front of The Henhouse, a charming lunch bistro off Main, and pops his kickstand.

"What are we doing?" I ask, working at the clip on my helmet as I get off the bike. Sean follows suit and stops my fingers from fumbling. He undoes the clip gently and pulls the helmet from my head, letting it hang from his grip.

"We're eating."

"I was going to go home and have leftovers and a bath," I tell him.

"No leftovers." His eyes simmer behind his words. "I'm buying you lunch."

I look up at his face—the look he's wearing isn't stern, but his eyes are, and I am starving. All I had a chance to eat this morning before I left was Greek yogurt. He probably somehow knows that too.

Sean leads me with a hand on the small of my back to a booth. This isn't the type of place where you wait to be seated.

Thankfully he's behind me, so he can't see that the moment his hand connected with my back my nipples hardened to points. As if my body is addicted to his touch exactly the way he thinks it is. I clear my throat and try to get it together, sliding into the booth across from him.

"People don't just meet and do things like this, you know. It's unstable behavior," I tell him, picking up the menu from the table and beginning to flip through it.

He doesn't pick his up, he just leans back and watches me. I run my eyes over the choices and try not to feel the heat from his gaze. It's an impossible feat.

"Says who?" he asks.

"Pardon?" I ask.

"Who says it's unstable to know what I want?"

"Everyone."

"*Everyone* doesn't have to live my life, or yours, so fuck them," he tosses back.

I don't really know what to say in response, but I'm saved by the server as she approaches the table. She's maybe my age, with long dark hair and ocean-colored eyes. She sort of looks like my high school best friend, Brinley, who lives in Atlanta, only not quite as soft and innocent-looking.

"The usual, Ax?" she says as she eyes me up, then turns her pretty eyes back to him. He doesn't even look up at her.

"Yep," he says. "Two of them, and one San Pell and one coconut water," he adds.

Now I know he's a stalker if he knows I used to drink San Pellegrino when I could afford it.

He takes the menu from me and hands both his and mine to the server.

She scurries off with a look of disappointment on her face, and I take a minute to look at him through her eyes. His veiny, corded forearms rest on the table, and the spread of ink there interests me. The intricate designs and numbers, mixed with phrases in cursive. My eyes move to the cross on his finger, and I again wonder who the hell this man is at his core, because I truly couldn't figure him out if I tried.

"How do you know I'll like what you ordered?" I quiz him, giving into the moment, resting my chin on my palm.

"Because it's the best burger in town, and they hand-cut their own fries."

My stomach growls in response.

Sean grins. "See?"

"You don't even know me, yet you know *way* too much about me. How is that?" I question, folding my arms over my chest.

"I don't know it all yet, but I will," he hedges as I watch him shift in his seat a little as a knot forms between his brows.

"What hurts?" I ask, my curiosity getting the better of me as the server comes back and places two glasses on the table. She sets my San Pellegrino down and an organic coconut water for Sean.

I watch with curiosity as he moves my glass in line with his, then picks up the bottle of San Pellegrino and pours it into my glass. When he sets the bottle down, he turns it so the label faces me, then pours his coconut water into his own glass, doing the same with his bottle, facing the label toward him.

"The chivalrous biker who drinks organic coconut water? Interesting," I muse.

"It rehydrates me after a workout," he says without looking up, and I admit to myself this is not what I expected when I saw him walk through The Palm Club's doors last night.

Chapter Twelve
Layla

"How can you tell something hurts?" he asks, setting his glass down after taking a long drink.

I shrug as I take a sip. God that's good, after being out in that heat. I must take too big a mouthful because a tiny bit spills from my glass and lands on my chest. One lone droplet of water trickles its way into my white tank top between my breasts. I use my middle finger to scoop it up before it falls any further and move to wipe it on the napkin, but Sean is faster. He reaches out and swipes my hand up to his lips, bringing my middle finger into his mouth. His hot tongue pulses against the underside, and I clench my thighs together as my breathing increases with his simple yet barbaric action.

"We're in the middle of a restaurant, for God's sake," I whisper, checking to see if anyone is looking. He just smirks at me, before pulling my finger from his mouth with a slight pop. It's insanely erotic. Absolutely overbearing. Yet I have to physically hold in a moan—and the worst part is, I didn't even try to stop him. When he places my hand back down on the table, I blink rapidly, trying to regain my composure, wondering if I'm hallucinating again. He isn't even shaken. Alarm bells fire off in my head. *This is not normal.*

"Well?" he says.

"Well?" I ask, totally out of it.

"How do you know something hurts?" he asks. I blink again.

"Oh, um . . . I could tell by the way you tensed up on your bike, and the face you made just now when you changed positions." I lower my eyes. "I'm assuming from the scar on your back that's where the pain is?" I add, still feeling a little self-conscious about what happened last night.

Sean takes a sip of his own drink. "Yeah, my back bothers me sometimes."

I look at him expectantly.

"I was an active-duty Marine," he starts.

I nod, having gathered something like that from the dog tags.

"I was injured during my last tour, and I suffered from a slipped disc among other things. The scar isn't from that though. When our Humvee went end over end, glass broke and it cut me. It cut me here too." He holds his t-shirt up and shows me another large scar across his abs.

My mouth falls slack for a full second because *holy shit, those abs.* I close it and look back up to meet his eyes, momentarily stunned stupid by his body.

"Oh . . ." I mutter, forcing myself into professional mode. "What kind of treatment have you had?"

The server comes back with our meals and places them in front of us.

"Can I get you anything else?" she asks Sean.

"No, we're all good," he says, sending her on her way, again without taking his eyes off me.

He takes a big bite of the delicious-looking burger and I follow suit. *Damn. So good.*

"Months of physio after I got home," he says around chewing. "I fucked up my arm pretty good too. Broke it in two places and cut it to shit, so I was sort of limited on what I could do. It's fine now but my back still bothers me from time to time, and I tweaked it last week."

"What'd you do to it last week?" I ask, popping a fry into my mouth.

He just takes another bite, his eyes housing an evil sort of glint.

"We don't know each other that well yet," he says simply.

A chill runs down the length of my spine, and I'm reminded of my Google search in class this morning—*What is the job of a Sergeant at Arms?*—which told me that Sean has to be willing to do anything to protect his club, but especially his president, so I know this man in front of me is very much capable of violence. Yet in this setting, he seems more calm and controlled than any man I think I've ever met.

"Did they offer you meds?" I ask, dodging the visions of him as that violent persona.

He shakes his head. "I don't take that sorta shit, not even Tylenol."

I nod again. *Noted, no drugs.*

"Have you ever tried a deep tissue massage?" I ask, dipping another one of my thick-cut fries into the really good house-made sauce.

Sean looks up. "I don't like people's hands on me, so no," he mutters, taking another bite. I watch him closely, thinking of the times he's let *me* touch him.

"There are stretches, daily yoga practices, even foods and natural things you can take that promote healing."

He looks at me in silence while he chews, and I realize that when he focuses like this and watches my expression, it makes my palms sweat.

"It can really help. It's what I study, but something tells me you already know that," I offer nervously.

He leans back. "Mmm-hmm," he answers noncommittally. "Why haven't you accepted your offer yet for Kinesiology?"

"I swear . . ." I mutter, shaking my head. "How do you—?"

Sean leans a little closer. "To be clear right now so there's no guessing involved . . . I know everything about you."

I hate the rush that courses through my veins with those words and how much I like the idea that he *wants* to know everything about me.

"How?" I ask.

"We have someone who gathers information for us," he says simply as he eats.

"Most vague answer ever," I comment, with a half-smirk. Sean shrugs.

"Before I decided I wanted to . . . spend more time with you, I had to know about you, and now I know," he states, as if it's the most natural thing in the world.

"I can't afford it," I blurt, returning his honesty. "Kinesiology, I can't afford it."

I expect to see the same look of pity my parents' church friends offer me, but instead Sean's face contorts in confusion.

"You live in the nicest part of town, your father earned a strong six-figure salary. So, poor? That just doesn't add up," he retorts. It's not a judgment, it's simply an assessment.

I push down years of bottled-up anger at the image my parents portrayed.

"Your investigator didn't find out everything then, did they?" I fold my arms over my chest as he looks at me questioningly.

He just takes another bite, waiting for me to continue.

"My parents' life was a lie. They died and I inherited nothing but my father's financial problems and the grief of losing my mother, who was my best friend. I can barely cover my tuition for my last semester so I can graduate, and I'm working as many hours as I can," I bite out with a sigh. "All because a man wearing a cut, most likely from a club just like yours, robbed me of my parents and left me with my father's sham of a life." I force myself to soften my tone, trying not to sound so hostile. If nothing else, I'm fairly certain Sean wasn't my parents' killer. "According to the police, it was all for a measly four hundred and eighty-three dollars," I add. "They died for nothing."

Sean takes me by surprise and leans in, placing his heavy, warm hand over mine, I inadvertently take a deeper, more settled breath. "I didn't dig into their finances, but I saw the address of your home. There are no poor families in that part of town."

He's just assuming what everyone else does and I can't fault him for that, but suddenly I'm no longer hungry. I don't talk about my mother or how much I miss her every single day with anyone, and yet here I am, talking about my parents to a total stranger.

"You were close." He says it like a statement, and I feel the sting of tears in my eyes, because I can't actually remember the last time someone spoke about them. My brother Dell rarely does.

A tear spills over my cheek, and I pull my hand free to swipe it away.

"To my mother, yes. She was my best friend, but she . . . wasn't strong enough to leave until it was too late," I tell him, struggling to hold back the tears that so desperately want to come.

"I can assure you that it wasn't a member of our club who took the lives of your parents."

We sit in an oddly comfortable silence for a beat. "We don't rob public places, and we don't kill innocents. It's not our MO."

I look away from his direct gaze, but for some reason I believe him.

A few more moments of silence pass. Sean leans back again, and as I eat a few more fries, I can feel his eyes on me. Like the wheels in his head are turning.

"You're going to work for me." It's not a question; he states it like a command. "You need help with your tuition and this works perfectly."

My eyes flick to his. "I will *not* be working for your club." A million thoughts flood my mind, but Sean just calmly shakes his head.

"I said you're going to work for *me*. Not my club. You need the money, and I would just give it to you, but in my experience, people feel better about taking money if they feel they've earned it."

"I would never take it anyway," I say defiantly. "There's no such thing as free money."

He nods. "Smart girl. But this will be a job, and if it helps with the cost of your schooling, then it's a win-win."

"What could *I* possibly do for you?" I say. I am the slightest bit curious, and as much as I want to fight it, the idea of seeing him again is too appealing to turn down.

"I need help healing my back, as you pointed out."

"I thought you didn't like hands on you," I retort.

Sean watches me carefully. "I'd allow your hands on me, little dove."

I eye him up. "Is this just your way of getting me to spend time with you?" I ask, glad to be free of the heavier conversation about my parents. "Because, I'll be honest, all I have time for is work and school. I don't even have time to do my laundry or clean my house."

"I can work around your schedule." He pops the last bit of his burger into his mouth.

"And what about your schedule? Do you work?" I bite my lip. "Aside from what you do with your club?"

He nods. "I do, but it's very . . . flexible."

I can't for the life of me guess what he would do for a living. *Bodyguard?*

Contract killer?

"I do want to spend time with you, and you'll learn very quickly, Layla . . . I always get what I want."

I shrink a little with his words because they're so commanding.

"There's no point in pretending otherwise," he says easily. "I want to help you and you're the perfect person to help me heal my back." He takes a drink of his coconut water. "The sooner you admit you're curious and that you want to get to know me, the easier this will be. And just so we're clear, this life . . ." He pats the patch over his heart. "It isn't black and white, and we are not all alike."

He's so fucking sure of himself it's contagious. But he isn't wrong. I'm curious about working for him—and also who he is . . .

"And just how long would I work for you?"

"How long will it take to see a difference if I do exactly what you say when it comes to a rehab plan?" he tosses back.

I take a sip of my drink before I answer. "Maybe you'll notice a difference within a month if you're dedicated, but it is a long-term process."

"Well, then it's a good thing I have lots of time, and there isn't a worry about me being dedicated," he says. I think of his abs and don't doubt him. "So it's settled. You work with me, and in turn I'll pay the balance of your tuition for the year."

I just about choke on the sip I'm taking before folding my arms over my chest, looking out at the busy restaurant. "That's twenty-four hundred dollars."

Sean doesn't even flinch at the number. "Done. Seems worth it to me."

My mouth falls open. Now I'm *really* curious about where and how he gets his money. "I'm not a whore," I blurt out.

Sean leans back and watches me for a beat, using his napkin to dab at his mouth and then folding it perfectly in half before setting it down. The silence between us after that statement is deafening.

"If you were, you wouldn't be sitting here." His voice is deep and even. Just the sound alone makes the little hairs on the back of my neck stand up. "And if *anyone* ever suggested you were a whore, I'd rip their tongue out with my bare hands."

His jaw tics so aggressively I fear he may tear a tendon. He taps his first two fingers on the table for a beat, then a moment later he's breathing deeper, calmer.

"An excellent personal trainer, a massage therapist, and physiotherapy would all separately cost me more than your fee, so in my opinion having one person handle everything is worth it. And if that means you have to spend time with me, then all the better."

I say nothing as I register that he's probably right about the cost of all those things, but still, I weigh up my options.

"I don't fuck around. I don't like to beat around the bush." His voice is gravel as those green eyes pull me in again. "You're more than welcome to pretend that you won't want me to touch you, that this will remain purely professional. But you'd be lying to yourself." He smirks. "Lucky for you I'm extremely patient, and I'll wait until you're begging me to touch you again if that makes you more comfortable. Because you *will*."

I laugh and avert my eyes from his. He's so damn cocky.

"Again, I'd like to point out this is not normal behavior for two people who just met," I reiterate. Everything between us feels so charged, so intense. It can't be real.

"And again, I'd like to remind you that I don't give a fuck what anyone but me and you think," Sean says gruffly.

"What makes you so sure I'll be begging for it?" I ask, unable to stop myself.

"Because, Layla, I may not be the man you *think* you want, but I am the man you *need*. And soon, you'll see what I already know."

Fuck. Well that just hit me some kind of way,

He eyes me up, shock flickering in those depths at my unwillingness to instantly agree to whatever the sergeant wants. "Fuck it, I don't even need the month, I'll do it in half that time."

"You can't heal in two weeks. My clinic is fully booked, I wouldn't be able to get you in for at least a week."

"No, you misunderstand me. If I'm right, which I normally am, I'll show you this connection between us is real and there's no reason to fight it. And when you realize that to be true, I can promise you, you'll be begging to be *mine* . . ." His eyes smolder. "*Before* those two weeks are up."

Hearing him say those words sends a flush to my cheeks that I can't control. The thought of being *his*.

"You're even crazier than I thought." I force a laugh, incredulous. "You can't convince someone they're your soulmate in two weeks, Sean," I tell him, liking the way his name sounds and feels rolling off my tongue.

"The fuck I can't." He takes a big drink of his coconut water.

"You expect me to believe all I have to do is help you heal your back, and you'll pay me twenty-four hundred dollars?"

"I don't like to repeat myself," he says. "But yes. I think this is the best idea I've ever had actually." His face is smug and satisfied as he pulls his buzzing phone out to check a text.

I blow out a raspberry and pick up a fry, my appetite coming back while he responds to the message. I swallow slowly, just thinking, his cockiness fueling me.

"So, you agree then?" he asks, sliding his phone into his pocket.

I narrow my eyes and take my lower lip between my teeth for a beat, balancing on the point of a knife.

Sean leans forward and pulls my hand toward him. "So we're clear, I can't for the life of me figure out why the fuck I'm so drawn to you either, which is why I'm committed to finding out."

"So I'm a puzzle that needs solving?" I raise an eyebrow.

"You've perplexed me," he answers. *So yes.*

I slip my hand out from under his and extend it for shaking.

"I agree to take the job," I say evenly, trying to keep this as professional as possible.

He accepts my hand, his eyes never leaving mine. The feel of my small hand in his large one, the way we fit together, it's a comfort I feel familiar with already. And I can't deny our touch makes me feel like there's a live current rushing back and forth between us.

"Let's get my number in your phone then, yeah? I like to have my trainer on speed dial." He smirks.

I pick my phone up and unlock it. "Just one thing." I set my phone in his hand. "I'm used to looking after myself. And so we're clear," I say, throwing his words back at him, "I don't ever beg anyone for anything."

That hauntingly beautiful smile takes over his face as he enters his number into my phone and then hands it back, stroking his wide jaw.

"We'll see, little dove. We'll see."

I shake my head and smile. The way he's so convinced there's something deep, something otherworldly, between us almost makes me believe him, but I remind myself I have no idea what kind of darkness lurks in his world, or the things he's seen and done. I decide maybe I owe it to myself to at least find out, though, because damn, the way he's looking right now sitting across from me is almost enough to make me give in. *He could change his mind tomorrow,* says the little voice in my head, and I know it's right. Men like Sean always like the chase. And if that's what I am, at the very least I'll help him work on his chronic pain and earn some extra cash. If he loses interest after that, so be it. I'll just remain prepared and professional. I can do that; I can fight whatever this is I'm feeling.

"Looks like we just made a deal. For now, you belong to me," Sean says, low and even, holding his hand out. I take it and question my logic and my sanity, because the prospect of belonging to him doesn't scare me as much as it should, and nor does the feel of my hand in his.

A strange memory I haven't thought of in a very long time comes to mind as we get ready to leave the restaurant. My mother, just days before she died, out of nowhere said to me, "The devil never comes dressed as your worst nightmare, he comes dressed as everything you never knew you wanted."

Sean looks at me with that satisfied smirk, as if he already *knows* I'm his, and I can't help but feel like maybe I did just sell my soul to the devil himself.

CHAPTER THIRTEEN
Sean

It's always fucking Eric Clapton. After a hundred and thirteen days out here, you'd think this motherfucker would listen to something else, anything else. But he never does, and I'm at the point where I'd rather listen to the incessant grunts of my newest bunkmate fucking his hand beside me at night than listen to my Staff Sergeant's continuous Clapton tracks. As we drive through the desert on the outskirts of Kandahar, I glance at Private First Class "Buck" Buckman, beside me.

Fucker's gone to the dark side, tapping his first two fingers on his knee and humming along to the opening strings of "Cocaine" as my Staff Sergeant, Keenan, sings the words out loud and off key from the front passenger seat. He spits some chew out the window so he can really get the lyrics out.

Telling my Staff Sergeant to shut the fuck up wouldn't lead to a very good start to my day, so instead of doing that I just keep my mouth shut and look out at the same beige landscape I've been looking at for months. A mirage in the never-ending stretch of sand happens every four seconds at this speed. I count them as we drive. The closest we've gotten to anything green was when we *were stationed outside Herat for a few weeks, but it's June now and that was April.*

I glance ahead, seeing the city in the distance through the glimmer of another mirage. The sun reflects off every building and you can almost see the steam rising from them, like we're about to enter hell itself.

It was a short ride in from our base to carry out this non-combat evac operation. We're 11th Marine Expeditionary, Special Ops. We're capable of handling anything, but today it's our job to meet six embassy staff brought in from another city and offer them an escort to a deemed safe site. Standard procedure.

Standard Tuesday in the hottest fucking place on earth. Like I said—hell.

"Deep dish Chicago," Buck calls over the music and the road. I cuff him upside the back of the head as my stomach growls just thinking about real food.

"Pussy," Wolfe, my lifelong brother, says from the driver's seat.

We all chuckle. On the list of things we miss, eating pussy is probably number one.

"Oh yeah, what I wouldn't give for a big old plate of pussy right now," Buck says, turning to face Wolfe.

"With a side of soft skin and cherry red lips," Keenan says from the front seat. "Fuck, I love a woman with red lips."

I stay in a sort of trance . . . one, two, three, four . . . listening to their chatter for the next few minutes. There's no sense in chiming in.

Wanting something out here is both pointless and useless. Because out here we have nothing, we are nothing, and longing for the luxuries of home doesn't help the days go any faster. Dust spews from our heavy tires to make a near constant cloud around us as the opening strings to the next song begins. "Layla." For the millionth time this tour. We don't even make it to the first verse before a deafening, vicious blast rocks our Humvee. It takes me a second to realize we've been hit, and by the time the realization settles in my head, we're already airborne.

"Is this what you need me to tow?" A heavy voice cuts into my flashback the next afternoon. The past feels even more prominent now, and I blink to get my bearings then glance toward Layla's open garage. Sometimes the memory is so vivid, so present, that I can almost feel the pain, smell the desert and the diesel fuel.

"Yeah." I point to the Lincoln SUV waiting in her garage for a tow. "Thanks for taking it right in, Mikey. I'm pretty sure her alternator is shot, and the battery."

He nods. "We'll take a good look at it."

I gesture to my bike. "I'll follow you over."

"I need you to have a look at the body for me," I say, turning to Wolfe. He owns the custom body shop next door to our mechanic Mike, and now that it's been towed, Layla's SUV is sitting in the lot between Wolfe's garage and Mike's. I tell him all the places I noticed rust, remembering them all from when I first looked it over in her garage.

Wolfe eyes up the Lincoln. Simply repainting isn't really his forte. He designs and creates really kickass customs for some pretty high-end clients. He's an artist when it comes to this shit.

"Yeah, I can slide it in." Wolfe scrubs his jaw and examines the rust along the bottom of the SUV, then clears his throat, pulling his gloves off and stuffing them into his overalls. "It won't take much to fix, and we'll clay-bar the underside when we're done to give her a couple more years."

"Thanks, brother." I pat his chest, offering him no explanation to the question I know he's got running through his head.

But he scoffs. He isn't letting it go. "Alright, I fuckin' give in. The fuck is really going on with you? With this woman?" Wolfe stares at me. "I've known you a long fucking time. Are you having some sort of breakdown? You need anything?"

There's no rational explanation yet as to what I'm doing here. My need to look after Layla when she's stubborn as fuck and doesn't want to accept help easily is unexplainable, and the need to be near her is part of an equation I just can't solve yet. There *has* to be a logical answer, but right now I don't have it.

I shake my head. "I think it's the exact opposite of a breakdown," I tell him, thinking of the way her eyes darken to a rich chocolate whenever I look deeply into them.

"Fuck off," Wolfe says. "After a few days?"

I look him dead in the eye. "This woman—fuck, within the first few seconds."

As I looked around her place this morning after she'd left for class, I realized two things: her back door is way too easy to get into, and there's more to the story of her losing her parents than I initially dug up. She doesn't know who killed them, and the look of pain in her eyes when she talked about them triggered something in my brain. Now finding their killer is like a dripping faucet in the back of my head I can't ignore. I *need* to know who did it. I need to know *why* and make it right for her. With one phone call, I already have the hunt started.

I continued through her house alone, spending way too much time doing things I probably shouldn't. Cleaning, organizing, reorganizing. My obsession grew as I breathed in her perfume and looked at photos of her on the walls. Her smile never truly reached her eyes in any of them. While I worked, I tried to find any rational explanation as to why I can't stop thinking about her, and the only conclusion I've come to is that a rational reason doesn't exist. The feeling of peace that spread over me when Layla wrapped her arms around my waist on the back of my bike yesterday is a kind of calm I've only felt once before—when I was deep in the desert—and all I know is I need *more*.

Wolfe folds his heavy arms over his chest. He knows me better than anyone, so I get why he'd be skeptical. I've never seen Wolfe with a woman for any longer than it takes to fuck her and move on. I'll admit that was my way before too, but now . . .

"I don't get it." He fixes me with a questioning stare.

"I dunno, man," I offer, running my hand over my head. "All I know is this woman sets something off in me. It's like I'm just acting on something before I even know what the fuck I'm doing." I shrug. "I can't explain it, *yet*. I'm working on it."

"You vetted her good?" Wolfe looks me up and down, switching to club business. He's good at not pressing any kind of emotion for too long. The club sits above all else, and he'll want to be sure we know every little detail about her before I decide to make her mine.

"Of course," I retort.

"So you're gonna make her your ol' lady? Be a one-woman man? For real?" he muses, his face breaking into a rare smile. "You sure you didn't eat some of those shrooms Robby brought in?"

I shake my head. "Never been more sober," is all I offer as I walk towards my bike.

"Chapel at eight tonight," he reminds me. "Stop at Belgrave first—and fuck, keep your head in the game *before* the pussy," he adds, mentioning the clinic where I'll need to grab our weekly cut of profits on my way to the club.

"On it," I call back. I straddle my bike and move to put my helmet on, suddenly remembering the way it felt to have Layla's warm thighs pressed against me. My mouth waters, just recalling the way she tasted. If she was anyone else, I would've fucked her already and moved on, but the part of this puzzle that consumes me is that I *need* her to admit the truth to herself. That she wants me in the same unexplainable way I want her. I *want* her to beg for me.

I don't just want part of her body—I want *every* part, and I already know I won't fucking stop until I get it. I clip my helmet and pull my bandana up, but before I fire up my bike I feel my phone vibrate in my pocket.

When I pull it out I see that it's Frankie Steadman, our town's deputy sheriff and friend of the club. I tug my bandana down.

"Been waitin' for you," I answer. "You better have some good news for me."

CHAPTER FOURTEEN
Layla

DELL

We're having the lemonade auction next weekend if you want to come. Mandy is baking, you could see some of the congregation.

They always ask about you.

My brother's text popping up stalls the video I'm silently watching at my desk in class: "The Power of Tai Chi for a Slipped Disc."

I have to work.

Dell is six years older than me, and I mostly hear from him when there's something to discuss about the house or when he's inviting me to something at church, because when it comes to everything else, we just don't really align. We just . . . see things differently. He's a successful architect for a homebuilder downtown. He has a steady girlfriend, Mandy, who he's probably going to marry, even though I don't think he loves her, and he has no problem living in complete denial about our parents.

I wait for the message about making time for my faith. If I know Dell, he isn't done trying to convince me. The last thing I want to do is spend time at the church and get side-eyed by everyone there and have advice that I didn't ask for handed out to me. I already get enough of that surface-level care from him. The reality of it is, he doesn't really *want* the truth. Whenever I tried to talk to him about the way our dad treated our mom, he straight up said he didn't want to know. He actually thought living in an abusive, unhappy marriage was what was best for Mom. For better or worse, he said, and he told me that every marriage has its problems.

Just those words alone told me he'd rather live with them in their lie than face the truth, and I knew then that I was completely and utterly alone.

As if on schedule, my phone buzzes again.

DELL

> Well, if you change your mind, you know where I am and I'll be around on Saturday to cut the lawn.

I respond to his message with a thumbs up but don't offer him anything else, then I get back to focusing on my healing plan for my new boss.

I spent the first half of class today calculating how much it's going to help me financially to work for Sean over the next month. The idea of my tuition being covered was almost enough to bring me to tears. I might even have enough to fix my mom's SUV so I can get it out of the garage again. But I'm going to do this right. Take it seriously and treat him like any other client.

I've spent the rest of class coming up with a plan for him and dreading the bus ride home.

But as class ends and I head through the doors into the Georgia sun, it's apparent Sean is a creature of habit because he's here waiting to pick me up again. In the very same spot he was yesterday, with a spare helmet hanging from his finger. He looks pissed off and relaxed all at the same time. A force to be reckoned with.

A biker god.

There's no argument from me today about accepting his ride home. One, because I'd rather not be thrown over his shoulder again. And two, I have a shift at the wellness clinic to get through before I'm finally done for the day—and I'll admit it, I'm dog fucking tired. Getting a ride home and actually having time to change and eat is an idea that is really working for *me* right now, and not because he says so.

"So, is this a regular thing now?" I ask, moving toward him, feeling a sense of ease that I still can't quite understand.

"No arguments today?" he questions, one eyebrow raised. "You ready to admit you like this kind of power between your thighs?" He pats the seat. He's all big biker dick energy right now as I stop in front of him and look up. He comes even closer and brushes my hair off my shoulder, then puts the helmet on my head and checks that it's fastened, just like he did yesterday, and I hate that it draws me in. His finger tips up my chin to pull my eyes up to his as he stares down at me, then slowly he slides both his hands down my bare arms, giving them a light squeeze.

I look over at the bike and shrug. "Meh . . . feels pretty much the same as riding the bus."

He looks at me with disbelief and amusement in his eyes.

"Nah, I know your secret." His deep voice mixed with the feel of his calloused fingers lacing through mine makes me break out in goosebumps.

"Which is?" I query.

He leans in and his green eyes turn molten. "You feel free as fuck on my bike, but it's cute as hell when you lie to yourself."

"I'm not lying," I retort with a little more fire, fighting this attraction with everything in me. The hint of a smirk still plays on his lips as he lets go of my hands and climbs onto his bike, then fires it up. The sound vibrates through me but he doesn't look back. He just uses two fingers in a come-hither motion over his shoulder.

I roll my eyes at the command, but the moment I wrap my arms around his waist and his hands slide over my thighs again, tugging me closer, an easy familiarity I haven't felt maybe ever before washes over me. I know he's right.

I smile wide. I do feel free as fuck.

CHAPTER FIFTEEN

Layla

"You're gonna need this now." Sean drops a shiny silver key into my hand as we walk up the path to my back door fifteen minutes later. I look down at it, then back up to his eyes. From this angle with the sun on him, there's an almost grayish hue to the green.

"For . . . ?"

"Your back door. What you had before wasn't a lock. This one will actually keep your house secure. That little click-button lock wasn't keeping anyone out."

Holy shit. "You changed my *lock*?"

"Yeah." Again, the epitome of cool, as if this all just makes sense. "Like I said, you weren't keeping anyone out with the old one. I'm surprised you haven't been robbed yet."

"Obviously I'm not keeping anyone out." I look him up and down, then turn to unlock my door. The shiny new deadbolt sounds. I push the door open, ready to ask him if he's ever heard of boundaries, but the words die on my lips when I step inside.

"*What the* . . . how long were you here?" I ask, entering my now very, *very* clean house.

I set my bag down and look around. Sean picks it up and puts it on a hook by the door, making sure it's hanging straight.

The whole place smells like cinnamon and orange. My back door opens into the kitchen, and I can see the living room from where I'm standing. The blinds are slightly parted, giving me a view straight onto the tree-lined road in front of the house. The air is cool and everything is organized. My mail is even in a little basket on my counter, and there's a bowl full of fresh apples in the middle of the butcher block island.

I turn to face him.

"Did you use my homemade *cleaner*?" I ask him in disbelief as my voice rises an octave. Panic mixes with this warm feeling that overcomes me, knowing he was here cleaning. It doesn't even bother me that he was here without me. I realize it's because he wanted to take care of me, and no one else has done that since my mom.

"I did." Sean nods and takes off his cut as he follows me in, hanging it over the back of a kitchen chair as I kick off my sandals. The thick, shag area rug in my living room even has straight, uniform vacuum marks across it. I'm not a messy person, but I just don't have the time to deep-clean my house, so this is just . . . on another level.

"You said the other day you don't have time to clean, but I do." And apparently, he doesn't know when to stop, because this place is absolutely spotless.

"I don't know what to say," I reply, stunned.

"Say thank you," he answers simply.

I close my mouth and blink, still in shock. "Thank you." I look back at him, realizing he must be getting to me if I feel like I owe him a thank you for this very unhinged, stalker-like, yet somehow sweet gesture.

I turn and run my hand along the shining counter. Everything is folded neat and straight. *Perfect.*

Sean nods toward the fridge. I follow his gaze because, as astonished as I am, I know I have to eat in order to get to the clinic on time. I narrow my eyes. More shock follows as I open my fridge, finding it's also been cleaned and restocked.

"You made food?" I ask as I pull out the glass container that's resting on the top shelf. That same sense of panic washes over me, but I do my best to push it away as I head to the cupboard for a plate. I pause, because my plates are no longer there. The cupboard is filled with drinking glasses and coffee mugs. I turn to face him, a hand on my hip.

He doesn't look even the slightest bit apologetic for rearranging my kitchen.

"It made no sense to keep your plates there. Plates should be on the other side; glasses should be closest to the sink."

I pull a glass down and fill it with water from the tap.

"This all goes way beyond boss–employee relations you know," I comment before I take a sip.

"Every boss–employee relationship is different, Layla." He leans on the counter, his brow furrowed.

I just shake my head and open the container. It's so pretty I don't even want to dump it out onto a plate. It's deep green leaves of romaine with tiny tomatoes, evenly sliced avocado and bocconcini cheese. The chicken is grilled and sliced perfectly, lying neat and evenly spaced across the top.

I look up at him and wonder if he knows the depths of the compulsive tendencies that I'm beginning to notice in him. I recognize them in so many ways because my mother had them. A product of always trying to control her environment. As if everything being perfect would prevent my father from blowing up or nagging at her. I imagine that, after serving overseas and the things he's seen during his life, Sean has these tendencies for very similar reasons.

"I'm supposed to be planning your diet, not the other way around, you know. You have a problem giving up control?"

He stands to his full height. As he comes closer, it seems obvious that it's impossible for him to be still for long. My stomach turns queasy with the feeling of someone taking care of me. I'm just not used to it, and it scares me more than anything else. If I ever got used to it and then it was gone . . .

"No, little dove, I have no problem letting you take control, but you have a problem letting people help you." His slow, easy tone strikes a chord deep within me. It settles me, calms me.

"Are my forks still in the same place?" I ask with an eyebrow raised, moving toward the usual drawer.

"Yes," he says evenly. "Because where they were made sense."

"I'm glad you approve." I can't help it. I smile at him, pull a fork out and take a bite of the salad. It's really fucking good. Of course.

"Did you make this dressing?" It's honey mustard and it's delicious.

"Yes," he answers quickly. "The shit you buy from the store is garbage."

I lean back against the counter and watch him as he retreats to take a seat at my kitchen table. He's relaxed here, one arm leaning on the table and his legs spread, the other arm resting on his thigh. His black t-shirt clings to all the right places on his upper body, yet it's obvious he never tries to be hot; he just *is*. Every look he gives me with those intense green eyes exudes raw temptation and certainty. He looks entirely too large for this space, and after doing these unexpected, crazy things for me— things I'd never have expected him to be capable of when I first laid eyes on him—he looks way too enticing.

"You're staring," he notes, watching me take a bite and chew carefully. His eyes show an authentic interest. "What're you thinking?"

"I'm wondering who you are," I say truthfully. "You don't behave the way I'd expect."

Sean ponders my question for a moment. "Then the problem is with your expectations, not how I behave."

"So this is how it'll be now? Like it's normal for you to come into my house when I'm not home? For you to pick me up every day?"

Sean grins and strokes his chin. "What is normal?"

"It's normal for me to at least know more about you. You seem to know everything about me."

Sean stands and takes my now-empty dish from me. He sets it down and fills the sink with hot soapy water.

"You can ask me anything you want." His face doesn't show any hint of emotion and I can tell he doesn't share information about himself easily as he starts to scrub the dish.

I ask the simplest thing I can think of: "What's your last name?"

"Hunter," he answers instantly.

"Fitting." I smirk. "And . . . why do they call you Ax?"

"My middle name is Axel. There were three men named Sean in our unit. Ax was more identifiable. It stuck."

"And you still have ties to that life? Marine friends?" I lean against the counter and fold my arms over my chest, watching as he works carefully to dry the dish, making sure to rid every drop of water from it, as if it's his sole task.

"My club prez was a Corporal in my unit, and I've known him all my life. He's as close to a brother as I can get." Sean's thoughts are somewhere else as he looks out my kitchen window and wrings out the dishcloth, folding it neatly before he brings his eyes to mine.

"How did you end up with the Hounds of Hell?"

I watch the muscles in Sean's jaw tic. I've already noticed this happens when he's in thinking mode. I wait as he moves back to the kitchen table and picks up his cut, putting it on before coming back toward me. I set my glass of water down, not sure what he'll do next. I'm quickly realizing that the moment he comes too close or takes over my space in any way—hell, even the moment he looks at me a little too hard—my pulse goes into overdrive and my brain stops working properly.

Sean stands in front of me, only inches away, and he studies my face for a moment before answering. Meanwhile I'm frozen, watching his features in return, trying to understand him. Straightforward and tough on the outside, but I can already tell he's a deep well of things the outside world doesn't get to see.

My eyes involuntarily drift to his neck, where there's an inked phoenix, wings spread wide over the column of his tanned throat. I breathe him in, imagining the way his skin tastes—

"Another time." He smirks, and his voice makes me flinch. "Now go get ready. You don't want to be late for your appointment." Those knowing green eyes drink in my momentary desire and fill with satisfaction.

I clear my throat and push him back. His warm, hard chest tempts me to keep my hands on it rather than drop them to my sides.

"That . . ." I remark, pointing up at him. "You knowing my schedule better than I do—that is *not* normal." I move past him, listening to his chuckle as I head down the hall, trying to catch my breath. I'm already in way over my head with Sean Hunter on day two of this arrangement—and even I know that *that* is not normal.

CHAPTER SIXTEEN

Layla

I'm making my way down the hall from the staff room at the clinic, pulling my hair up into a high ponytail as I get ready for my appointment. Reception has told me this client is new, so I have a sixty-minute slot booked for an assessment and the first treatment.

I put my phone in my cubby at the front desk. I don't take it into sessions, and I find myself wondering what will be waiting for me when I finish. I'll admit, life has been a hell of a lot more interesting since I met Sean. He doesn't care what anyone thinks, or about fitting into anyone else's version of normal. In turn, that makes me care less and less about fitting into anyone else's mold.

I actually found it funny when a horrified Mrs. Fielding, my elderly neighbor who also happens to attend my old church, glared at me as Sean and I started off down my driveway to come to the clinic. I've seen her out there the last couple of days, milling about, probably wondering whose Harley is parked at my house.

Waving at her like I didn't give a fuck felt like I was shedding one more layer of my old life. The old me would have cared what she thought. But the version of me when I'm with Sean just can't be bothered. He is unapologetically genuine, and that gives me a kind of confidence I've never had before. I actually laughed at the look of pure horror on her face when the sound of Sean's bike almost shook all the houses on our quiet street. But I'll need to brace myself for the questions that will come, because I can almost guarantee that when Dell next sees her at church, he will hear all about the big bad biker who was at my house.

I pick up my client's file and knock on the door, then freeze as the name on the intake form practically jumps off the page. I push the door open to a familiar scent as the harrowing green eyes I can't get out of my head meet my gaze.

I close the door behind me and drop the file onto my desk with a little extra force, never breaking our stare. The only sound in the room is the spa music that plays quietly on a loop.

"Anyone ever tell you you're relentless?" I ask rhetorically.

"I just seized an opportunity," Sean answers. "You said I couldn't get in until next week, but it seems there was a cancellation."

"Mmm-hmm." I sit down across from him at my small desk and look down at his file, not even wanting to know how he managed to pull this off. I read the answers he provided on his questionnaire like I would with any other client, and do my best to focus, but under my outward professionalism I can't stop thinking about what he looks like under those clothes, both dreading and anticipating that I'm going to have to put my hands on him.

We spend the next few minutes talking seriously about his treatment. Or rather, it's me talking—stalling. I explain what I expect from him, how we'll start adding yoga and deep stretching into his routine. He answers truthfully about when he feels the most pain and describes it as I take notes. When I can no longer stall, I take a deep breath. "Alright, let's see where you're tight and what we can improve," I tell him as I stand and make my way to the cabinet beside my massage table to set up.

When I turn back around, he's already behind me.

"Where do you want me?" he asks in a low voice, from only a few inches away. My entire body heats with thunderous desire as I look up into those eyes.

Fuck. *On top of me?*

He pulls his cut off and hangs it over the back of the chair.

I swallow before I answer, questioning my sanity. "The massage table is fine." I have to figure out how to separate and compartmentalize working with him and wanting him, because I'm a total goner for this man the moment he comes anywhere near me.

"Perfect," he says, then—using one hand to reach behind his neck—he pulls his t-shirt off and folds it, setting it on the same chair his cut is draped over. I think he begins to speak but I have no idea what he's saying, because under that shirt is the kind of body I've seen only in my dreams.

Sean's so defined that I can see every ripple of his tight abs and the deep V that disappears into his black jeans. His chest is thick and solid. Ink lines his arms and shoulders. My God, *his shoulders.* His arms make me want to curl up with them around me and make a home there. There isn't much of him that isn't covered in ink, but what I can see is smooth and tanned. The dog tags remain around his neck and remind me of his sacrifice, his bravery and his strength, somehow making his allure even stronger, as if that were even possible. Goddamn.

Sean Hunter is all man and fucking incredible-looking.

"Jeans too?" he asks, grasping for his buckle, snapping me from my living daydream as I focus on his eyes, which are watching me intently and filled with that cocky amusement. It hits me then that *I'm* the one who's going to suffer the most through this massage.

Okay . . . maybe I didn't think this through very well.

CHAPTER SEVENTEEN
Sean

All the restraint I've used to stop myself from tearing every single piece of clothing from Layla's body since the first moment I saw her is worth it when I see the way she's looking at me right now. Striving for optimum physical health has its perks, but I'd never once cared what a woman thought about my body until Layla's warm, whiskey-colored eyes turned dark and lustful the moment I pulled my shirt off. Just knowing she wants me the way I want her is electrifying, and proves she's one step closer to admitting she wants to be mine.

"Wait!" She stops me, holding a hand up as I work at the buckle on my jeans. "I have to leave so you can get undressed." She straightens out the sheet on the table with a blush creeping up her throat. "And a reminder? I'm not *that* kind of masseuse. I'm a *massage therapist*."

"Thanks for clearing that up." I grin, removing my holstered gun and my knife, both of which I carry everywhere with me, before setting them on her desk. "I'm not self-conscious. You can stay." I shrug, just wanting to fuck with her.

I begin to toe my boots off as she moves toward me and

presses a warmed towel to my bare chest. I take it from her, brushing my fingers over hers.

"As much as you *think* I'd like to see you naked, there are rules here. This is a respectable place and I have to leave the room while you prepare for your treatment." She looks down to the sheet in my hand and her eyes trail over my chest one more time. "And we're not working on your glutes, so leave your boxers on. I'll be back in a few minutes."

I chuckle to myself at the way she fights the inevitable. It all serves to twist even further into the most complex puzzle I've ever tried to unravel. "For such a small person, you're really fucking bossy," I tell her as she opens the door.

She shrugs, brushing me off. "Maybe it's just you who brings out the worst in me?" she fires over her shoulder as the door closes behind her and I'm left standing in the middle of her massage room with my boots off and my pants undone.

I try to remember the last time a woman said no to me. Every time I think I've moved closer to understanding Layla, she throws me off my game. I know she does it to prove her strength, but all it makes me want to do is fuck the fight right out of her, repeatedly. I shake my head and pull my jeans off, folding them over the side of the chair where the rest of my clothes are, then I look down at my rock-hard cock and ask myself what the fuck I'm supposed to do with that now.

CHAPTER EIGHTEEN
Layla

Taking a deep breath, I stare at myself in the mirror outside the treatment room. Looking at my mother's eyes inside of my own, I wonder how she lived a life with no temptation, how she made it through each day giving to everyone else but never herself and still always having a smile on her face. To leave Sean standing there looking like every fantasy I've ever had was difficult to say the least, but I remind myself that I did leave and maybe that's a small victory in itself. I'm pretty sure he expected that he'd show me his beautiful body and I'd just be putty in his hands. And although I almost was, I refuse to be like every other woman he's rustled his belt for and had them drop to their knees. In Chantel's words, *I have the pussy. I have the power.* There's something incredibly strengthening about knowing that, even though I'm at Sean's mercy, he's moving at *my* pace, not the other way around. I don't think he does that a lot.

When I knock and push the door open a few minutes later, he's face down on the table, arms under his chin. I close the door as I always do.

"You can put your face in here," I say, patting the donut at the end of the table. He glances up at me and my stomach drops.

All his dark, delicious beauty is focused on me as he lets out a sigh while I try to ignore how perfectly the height of his face lines up with my core.

"Tuck your arms here, if you can," I tell him, running my hand along the very limited space on either side of his thick body. That fucking body, goddamn.

Any. Other. Client.

"That was longer than a few minutes," he comments, as I check something on his paperwork about his back.

"I was checking in with reception."

And trying to find the guts to come back in here and forget about how big and hard you were under your jeans.

I decide the only way I'm going to get through this massage is to talk. And by talk, I mean explain all the technical things I'm doing to him as I go. To keep some semblance of the professional barrier between us. Every step of the way, I'm hoping it serves as a reminder for both him and me that this is *my job*, and whatever I'm feeling for him, however intense, shouldn't happen here.

As much as I feel the urge to run my tongue over the expanse of his wide back and the defined muscles of his shoulders, I focus intently on the ink in his skin as I grab my oil from the counter beside the massage table.

"This is coconut oil," I advise him as I gently shake the bottle. "Your chart didn't mention any allergies."

Sean's three biggest scars on his back, including the one I've already felt, run in jagged disarray over his skin.

"No allergies," he says, as I notice how the scars weave through the letters tattooed on his lower back, but they seem older than the ink, as if the ink surrounds them. *HOUNDS OF HELL.* All capital letters, the same as his cut, and a glaring reminder of the world this man comes from.

"I'm just going to adjust your sheet," I tell him as professionally as possible.

I pull the soft cotton down with a shaky breath and fold it neatly, tucking it just under the band of his boxers, below the two dimples above Sean's really, *really* incredible ass. An ass you just know comes from years of intense physical training. The ass of a fit-as-fuck soldier.

The entire right side of his upper back is free of ink, but the left houses a very detailed piece that takes up most of the space. Bodies, many of them cloaked and faceless, all shaded in black and gray, lie haphazardly in a pile, bloodied. Above them, coiled in a tight spiral, is a snake. Maybe a cobra? A mean-looking one, jaws open, fangs out and ready to draw blood. I fight the urge to trace the lines and ask him what they mean, and force myself to move to the head of the table instead.

More writing on his shoulder in a thin, cursive font is where I choose to drop the small amount of oil that I need to begin his massage.

Liberation of the human mind from the dominion of religion.
Liberation of the human body from the dominion of property.
Liberation from the shackles and restraint of government.

And right below that:

The pact of three:
Soldiers. Brothers. Blood.

I contemplate what it all means—why he has these bodies and these words inked into his skin. I shudder with the obvious thought of them being people he's maimed himself, because there are so many. Somewhere deep inside me I know there are things about him I might not be able to comprehend or want to know, yet I think I *like* that somehow. The unexplainable heat and want that rushes through me at the danger he represents threatens to obliterate the professional line between us. With him, I struggle to keep it in place.

I massage people every time I'm in the clinic. It always feels medical, closed off and therapeutic, and there are clear boundaries. Which is one of the reasons I was happy to get a placement here. I've never had to worry about my clients ever getting inappropriate. But there is absolutely nothing professional about the way I feel the second my fingers connect with Sean's warm skin. I stand above him and take a deep breath in as silently as I can, grateful for the spa music that I turned up much louder than normal in the hope that it would break the tension between us. Sean stiffens, but otherwise doesn't give any indication I'm affecting him one way or another as I slide my shaky hands from the base of his neck downward, beginning to massage, beginning to warm him up. And almost causing me to overheat in return.

"I'm going to begin by connecting and clearing the deep muscle tissue and fibers in your upper back," I tell him.

He doesn't answer, so naturally I ramble on.

"The reason is b-because of the nature of human tissue." I silently curse myself and the way my nerves are making me stutter as I slide my hands down his spine, the pads of my fingers pressing into his sacrum. He's so big and solid, he makes me feel small, like he could swallow me whole, and I've never wanted to lose myself to someone like this.

"It's tight," Sean grunts as I work my magic on the knots under his shoulders.

Stress knots.

I wonder again about the probable horrors of his daily life, and what he saw as a soldier.

"It is," I confirm. "But I'm going to do my best to help with that."

These aren't sexual words, so why am I sweating? When my hands press deeply, sliding over his sacrum, he *groans*. It's a deep, sensual sound and my knees feel weak. I fight with everything in me not to keep going and slide my hands lower, squeezing his perfect ass in my hands. *Fuck*, I'm like a cat in heat just from touching him.

I blink and try to swallow, going back to my professional plan, making sure to keep my eyes on the space I'm massaging.

"In order to improve things, we need to do this twice a week at least. Muscle tissues want to go back to doing what they've always done, but connective tissues we can structurally align by doing this sort of work regularly."

"And that's what you're doing now?" he asks, acting like he's actually curious.

"No, not yet," I tell him as I work his QL muscle. "First you have to warm up the muscles. You don't want to . . ." I swallow. "Go in too deep, too fast."

"Mmm-hmm," he hums.

Oh God. I've never been more glad that I don't have to look someone in the eye than I am right now.

"Why?" he asks, and I note the hint of amusement in his tone. Right away I know he's trying to make me uncomfortable, but the joke's on him. I'm already at my breaking point with him being practically naked, laid out before me, while I stand here knowing what it feels like to have his hands on my body. The air is thick between us and I'm hanging on by a damn thread while I answer his question as honestly as I can.

"Because if you go in too deep, too fast, the body just isn't ready. It'll fight you. You want these muscles nice and warm," I say, pressing into his mid-back. "Ready to . . . take it harder, before you really get to work." My voice is almost breathless.

I add a little more oil and run my hands down his sides, pressing harder now, knowing he can take it. I spend the next few minutes working the area where I know his disc was damaged, loosening him up and ridding him of various knots in places that I can feel need the most work. I don't know how I manage to do it and keep myself together. Through it all, Sean breathes deeply and evenly, and by the end, I'm a hot, disheveled mess.

When I'm almost satisfied with my work for this first session and thoroughly turned on, I ask him to flip over so I can finish working the trap muscles that connect his neck to his lower back. I hold the sheet up so he can roll over easily, but when I let it drop back down it does nothing to conceal the heady bulge of his swollen cock in his boxers. He reaches up and folds his arms behind his head with a smug look that says he isn't even remotely embarrassed that he's turned on. It's almost admirable.

"Arms at your sides," I correct him quickly. He keeps watching me but does what I say as I force myself to finish the massage. Sliding my fingers carefully over the sides of his neck, I start massaging. His eyes are open now as I work, watching me, studying me, which only makes me more nervous as I move to his right side. I favor the area below his rib cage, the muscles there connecting to the place in his back where he was injured. I lean over him, working the other side for good measure, my fingers gliding firmly over the muscles along his abs. It's under the sheet at the base of his hips that I press my fingertips into his flesh harder, almost panting, both of us knowing the pace of our breathing has nothing to do with this massage. I could so easily push this thin cotton sheet out of the way, rid him of those boxers and lower my face down.

His eyes fall closed and he groans again, and it fuels me. His right hand moves from his side to the back of my thigh as I stand beside him, letting my hands move over the ink that runs along the length of his ribs. His eyes flutter open and we watch each other for a beat before he gives in and moves first, sliding his heavy palm upward with perfect pressure to the threshold of my ass and resting it just below the curve. All I can do is breathe in a shallow gasp. I need to tell him to stop but I don't. *I can't.*

I say nothing as he grips my upper thigh and it fills his hand. He squeezes, hard, and I whimper, biting my lip as my eyes flutter closed. I turn away, trying to focus on finishing the job even though all I want is his hands on me.

The alarm on the counter quietly goes off, causing me to jump, signaling the end of his time with me. I finish the area I'm working on and slowly stand back, just looking at him.

"Ax," is all I whisper. He wastes no time sitting up, swinging his legs over the side and pulling me in to settle between them.

"Sean," he corrects. His abs flex as he leans closer and breathes me in, my face only inches from his.

"This is where I work, I have to be . . . professional," I tell him, barely breathing as his hands come up and grip my ass tighter.

He looks me over, slowly. "There's nothing fucking professional about us, Layla."

I stay still for a beat, just breathing the sweet air between us.

"I have *no* idea what you mean," I whisper defiantly. Sean chuckles darkly, pinning my eyes with his as his thumb comes up to trace my jaw, and I shudder.

"You make *me* weak, Layla, and that's something I've never been before." He moves his lips closer. The alarm continues its relentless chiming on my desk.

"I need *you* to be strong. I need *you* to push me away, little dove, because I'm not strong enough to make you, and if I kiss you right now, I won't stop. I'll become something I never am." With his hard warm body pressed against me, I'm frozen in place.

"And what is that?" I ask.

His breath is even. Outwardly he seems calm and collected, though I can see a struggle in his eyes.

"*Really* fucking out of control."

Something in me snaps with his honest words and I realize that maybe I can be that honest too. I can be *both* the weakest and strongest versions of myself with him. I reach my arms up around his neck and move even closer.

"I think . . . I want you out of control," I whisper as I lean in and take what my body wants. I press my lips to his and the world around me ignites. He stiffens at first, sucking in a breath as if he didn't expect this from me, so I move slowly, teasing. My kiss is soft, my lips pressed against his plush mouth cautiously as his hold suddenly tightens around my waist, and then he groans, deeply. It hums against my lips and sears every part of me as Sean takes over with a hunger I could have never prepared for. My lips part and every thought of winning or losing, of being weak or strong, leaves my head. All I can feel is him as I let him in.

"*Fuck*," he growls as his tongue sinks into my mouth, and I grip him tight as we kiss with an intensity like we were made to be one. The more we kiss the faster we move, and the deeper and more desperate the kiss grows. He's hard and pressing into my abdomen. I'm slipping, losing control as every delicious swipe of his tongue searches my mouth with perfect pressure. He tastes me as if he's memorizing the way we move together.

I moan into him and his name is right there, but I kiss him deeper to silence myself. I know the moment I say it like this I'll be his, and I can't promise him that yet. He kisses me back without hesitation, but a low growl rumbles in his chest with frustration as footsteps sound outside the door and remind us that anyone could hear. Something about it makes my core throb even more and it takes every single shred of self-control that I possess to pull my lips from his and remove his hands from my body, backing away.

"I . . . have a staff meeting in ten minutes," I tell him in a breathless whisper as the alarm continues to sound. Sean watches me, and I see the effort it's taking for him to hold back; his own chest heaves and his eyes are crazed with lust. A second passes between us and I realize that he isn't going to let me out of this room. He may actually try to fuck me right here during my workday, and I don't want him to think this is that kind of place.

My heart begins to pump even faster. I've pushed him too far. He told me not to kiss him. He told me to walk away. I start to back up slowly, but Sean stands, stalking closer in nothing but his black boxers, tight around the outline of his solid cock. There's a dark glint in his eyes as he shakes his head slightly and taps the alarm so it stops beeping. I turn to bolt for the door, and I almost make it. My hand grips the handle, but Sean is faster and more calculated. One heavy hand covers mine, turning the knob back, and the other rises above us to keep the door firmly shut, making sure my escape route is taken from me swiftly and quietly before he locks the door from the inside.

Our breath is heavy as I spin around and stare up at him in shock, caged in his arms, waiting for my fate as his lips come down to hover over mine.

"Stay."

Chapter Nineteen
Layla

Sean is someone else entirely right now. One strong arm wraps around my waist, lifting me up and depositing me on the massage table.

My legs are pushed apart, and he settles between them, his arms caging me in on either side as his lips once again hover over mine, my body begging for his as he watches my quickened breathing with fascination. He *is* actually going to fuck me right here in the massage room at my clinic with my boss just down the hall.

"I warned you," he murmurs.

I can't cry out, or risk attracting attention to what's going on in here. I can't move at all as he brings his mouth even closer.

"I wasn't done," he growls as his lips press to mine. This kiss is different from the first; it's instantly all-consuming as his big hands move over my body in a way that makes me feel as though he's been holding and kissing me forever. I reach my hands around to his upper back and rake my nails downward in a silent plea for him to stop before someone knocks on the door, but my body doesn't want what my head does and, before I even understand what's happening, I'm tugging him even closer as I kiss him back. I'm half clinging to him, half clinging to my self-control, my sanity.

Sean slides his hands up and over my ribs to find my nipples hard and begging for his touch. He toys with one through my shirt and I whimper.

"I'm at work . . . I can't . . . please," I whisper, but it's a pathetic attempt and he knows it.

A deep groan rolls through his chest as his lips move to my neck, my collarbone, then the shell of my ear.

"Then you better come fast and quiet, little dove. Your tight, needy pussy on my tongue is the consequence of making me lose control."

Sean kisses me once more and I don't care where we are, I just want him.

"And now, I'm not leaving here until I'm done eating."

A shiver ripples through my whole body as he pinches my nipple, and his lips on mine grow urgent. Sean moves his tongue with mine in a steady pace that could make me come all on its own.

"My boss . . . my staff meeting," I mutter, trying to get my words out, but I want him so badly . . . I grip him tighter in spite of myself.

The deviant glint returns to his eyes as he pushes against me, hard and ready. I moan and wrap my legs around him.

"*I'm* your boss," he rasps. "And I'll make you come in under a minute. You won't be late." His voice is lust-filled and I desperately want what he's offering. Just to feel settled, just to take the edge off of whatever this is so I can think clearly again.

"One minute?" I ask breathlessly, trying to make sense of this in my mind. I angle my hips into him, searching for any sort of friction, and he wastes no time. Sean drops to his knees before me and pulls my pants off, tossing them to the floor before pushing my cotton thong aside and pulling me closer to the edge of the table.

"Feel free to count if you like," he offers with the cocky tone that normally pisses me off. Right now it's only serving to make me grip his shoulders tighter, my head tipping back. There's no stopping him now, as he presses his nose against my pussy and breathes me in, then makes a *tsk*-ing sound.

"Imagine trying to run away when you're this fucking soaked for me," Sean muses as he runs one finger slowly through my wet slit and I brace my hands against the table for support. "You're not fooling anyone by trying to escape, Layla. You're just a desperate little slut for me, aren't you?"

I look down at him, this steady bear of a man between my legs, looking up at me. He uses his free hand to spread me apart and he runs his tongue firmly through my slit, groaning into me, his eyes closing as he tastes me properly for the first time. I bite my lip to keep from crying out. I'm panting so hard I feel dizzy as my body quakes for him, and desire rolls through me with just this sight. I moan as he sucks my clit into his mouth and those eyes open, vibrant and light as he burrows his face deeper, watching me.

"Mmmm. Start counting in that pretty head." He reaches up and clamps a hand over my mouth as he feasts on me in a way no one before him has. I do what he says and count. *Ten, eleven, twelve . . .*

I can't breathe. I can't think. I exist only for the pleasure his perfect mouth offers me. Even after just a few days I know him well enough to know that he won't stop until he's satisfied with himself. He can't. *Oh God . . . twenty-six . . . twenty-seven . . .*

Sean is too good at this. I can't keep up as he trades between licking, sucking and nipping at me. My legs shake, and in mere seconds I feel the orgasm ready to crash over me. His hand over my mouth grips tighter and angles my face downward. My eyes meet his and he groans as his tongue laps against my clit. *Forty-two . . .*

"I want those eyes on me as you grind your desperate little cunt down on my tongue. Come now, Layla. Come for me, little slut," is all he says, and something about those degrading words mixed with his worshipping gaze sends me over the edge.

My nails scratch at him, and his hand covering my mouth makes it hard to breathe as he sucks hard on my clit, his arm flexing as I rock my hips into him, riding his face. *Fifty-three . . . fifty-four . . .*

His tongue flicks over me, then he sucks my clit in again and I'm instantly done for. I cry out into his hand as I come, hard. My eyes flutter shut as waves of pleasure roll through me. I try to breathe as I scratch his shoulders so deeply it's possible he's bleeding.

When I open my eyes he's still fixated on me, running his tongue through my sensitive center, smug and tasting everything I offer him.

"Such a good girl, doing just what you're told."

I squeeze my thighs tighter in retaliation.

"Fuck you," I whisper, breathless. I've never seen anything so fucking frustrating or beautiful as him in this moment. He looks like an animal desperate for me, and I know *I* did this. I also know I want more.

I try to get my breath back as Sean stands. He kisses me deeply, and the taste of myself mixed with him keeps the fire burning between my thighs.

"Layla," he whispers. "That's *exactly* what I intend to do." He pulls me close, his pupils blown wide, full of want. "Neither one of us is strong enough to resist this." He kisses me once more. "Don't be late."

I scramble to pull my pants back on and stand, slowly backing away as he watches me, smug and satisfied with himself. He wanted me to be weak for him; he wanted me to prove I couldn't resist the temptation between us. Somehow, he knew I couldn't.

I unlock and open the door, still feeling lightheaded with desire as I close it behind me and lean back against it for a moment, trying to compose myself. My breath has just returned to normal when my boss rounds the corner. I straighten up.

"All set, Layla?"

I nod, frustrated with myself. I let whatever this is between Sean and me bleed into my place of work. This isn't a game. I can't lose this placement. Sean tells me neither one of us is strong enough to resist this and he's not wrong. Right now, for him, I'm fucking weak.

Chapter Twenty

Sean

That fucking kiss.

Another twisted piece of the puzzle I keep trying to solve but never really get ahead of. It wasn't even Layla's perfect dripping cunt on my tongue that did me in. It was that fucking kiss.

I sit at the bar across from Layla's clinic, sipping a double bourbon while waiting for her to finish work. It's a drink I fucking *need* after the last hour. I'm aching and hard beneath my clothes just thinking about her and about how fucked up timing is, how unpredictable. I palm my cock through my jeans, willing it to stand down. It has crossed my mind that this woman is a sheer test of my will. I'm fucking desperate for her in a way I've never been desperate for anyone or anything, after only days. Every single time I think I have her figured out, or have the upper hand, she completely flips the script on me.

But when she took control and leaned in to actually take what she wanted from me? Kissing me like that when I distinctly gave her the choice to walk away?

Fuck. Those pouty lips on mine and that sweet, tight pussy on my tongue caused my entire fucking soul to shift.

I swirl the bourbon in my glass as the seedy bar bustles around me with an early after-work crowd.

That kiss sealed my fate, and her withholding my name when I knew it was on the tip of her tongue sealed hers.

I want everything from her, yet something in her refuses to give herself to me completely, and that forces me to uncover exactly what it is that's holding her back.

I need to break the code of her psyche. She's turned me from a man crazed to a man *obsessed*. I'm deeply obsessed with Layla Monroe, and it's an obsession I already know I'll never come back from. I could almost hear the dirty thoughts running through her head as she whimpered into my hand, and even without her uttering my name that kiss gave me everything I needed.

That kiss was her permission.

CHAPTER TWENTY-ONE
Layla

I'm still hot and bothered but I try to keep composed, taking notes as my boss talks the staff through the new infrared therapy clinic we're opening in our building in a month. I wonder if it's obvious that I was just my client's main course down at the other end of the hall not even five minutes ago. Being around Sean is like coexisting with a whirlwind. A big, rugged, sometimes scary whirlwind. It's easy to imagine belonging to him fully though, and I've never really belonged to anyone. Not where I feel like I can be *exactly* who I am without shame.

DELL

> Mrs. Fielding said you were on the back of some man's motorcycle. Is everything okay?

I glance down at my phone as my boss continues our staff meeting.

> What did she do, call you?

I figured I had at least a few days before she snitched on me.

DELL

We had a Bible study meeting this afternoon. She was worried.

I hold in a scoff. Worried is the last thing she was. Excited she had something to gossip about? That's more likely.

I'm fine, he's a friend.

I never saw it quite as much before, but I can't believe how truly judgmental the people I've grown up with are. They don't know anything about Sean, but because he has tattoos and a motorcycle I need to stay away from him altogether?

DELL

She also said he had a Hounds of Hell leather jacket.

It's called a cut.

DELL

Are you okay, Lay?

I roll my eyes.

I'm fine. Tell Mrs. Fielding that next time I'll be sure to bring Sean by for tea.

DELL

That isn't funny, are you in some kind of trouble?

I silence my phone and flip it over, focusing on finishing the rest of my meeting. When we're through, I check the appointments for my next scheduled shift.

When I exit through the front door of the clinic a half hour later, Sean is waiting for me, leaning against his bike, and the vision of him between my thighs flashes through my mind, sucking all the air from my lungs.

"So this is just how it is? Every day you'll be here?" I say, to taunt him and break the intense heat still lingering between us after this afternoon.

"You're never taking the bus again," he says gruffly, tugging me close and dropping his lips to mine right in the parking lot. "Mmmm, can you still taste your sweet pussy on my lips?"

I back away, feeling the eyes of my coworker on us as she heads to her car.

"You can't be a caveman. This is where I work. Don't make me actually get on that bus." I nod to where the bus is in fact approaching.

Sean pulls me closer still and kisses me again with a growl.

"Keep fighting, little dove, but you're coming with me," he says in a low voice, sending my stomach into a frenzy.

"Where are we going?"

He traces my lips with those haunting eyes. "I have club business. You can come with me and meet my mother."

Wait, what?

"Your *mother*?"

"Yeah, my mother."

My mind races. "I don't even know what this is with us, how can I meet your mother?" I ask him, honestly.

I watch as a serious look fills Sean's eyes and he brings his thumb up to lightly trace my cheekbone, holding me tight around my waist with his other arm. "She already knows about you, she wants to meet you, and what my mother wants my mother gets. She's a bulldozer."

I blink up at him, not understanding.

"There are no secrets in my club. Especially not when fucking Kai knows them."

I watch his face and secretly wonder about this woman he so obviously holds up high on a pedestal.

"You don't care what anyone thinks, but you really care about her opinion, don't you?" I ask him. His jaw sets and I can tell this isn't something he talks about. I can feel how difficult it is for him to open up at all.

"My mother and I . . . we've been through some shit. We've been through it *all*, and all she's ever wanted is to see me with someone."

"How do I know that someone is me?" I'm secretly afraid of the scene I'm about to walk into, picturing this woman judging my every move and whether I'm the one for her son.

"I already know enough for both of us, but if you aren't ready to admit it yet, you can pretend. Either way, we're going."

He grins a real smile that reaches his eyes, and it's so beautiful it stuns me.

"She's harmless, just don't piss her off, especially if she's standing near the gun cabinet."

I can't tell if he's kidding or not as he secures my helmet. I know he can't help himself; it's his way of making sure I have it on and it's secure. As he climbs onto his bike before me, I try to think of *any* reason not to go meet his mother. I can't even imagine what kind of woman it takes to raise a man like this. Thoughts of a TV show I watched as a kid, *Xena: Warrior Princess*, fill my mind. A strong woman, a commanding one who could take charge and be fierce when needed.

"You're at least taking me home first so I can change. I'm already nervous enough, I don't need to be in my work uniform."

Sean glances back at me over his shoulder.

"I've got a change of clothes for you."

Of course he fucking does.

"Come on, she *hates* when people are late."

Oh fuck.

I climb on the bike and wrap my arms tight around him, and just as I expect, he pulls me closer. I try desperately to settle despite the nervous energy coursing through me. *Gun cabinet?*

Well, this should be fun.

CHAPTER TWENTY-TWO
Layla

My heart pounds in my ears and my palms sweat as the Hounds of Hell clubhouse comes into view at the end of a gravel side road off the main highway. The driveway seems to go on forever, with a wide creek running beside it. The closer we get to the clubhouse, which is really a huge barn with a black metal roof, the easier it is to see the line of Harleys parked at the edge of the drive. There are more out behind the building as well, along with a few trucks and a van. The Hounds of Hell insignia looms front and center on the building and the fierce wolf head is intricately cut from black sheet metal. It's impressive and fierce. At the side of the clubhouse there's a large, covered patio with an outdoor kitchen. There are a few people milling around smoking weed and talking as we park Sean's bike in between a matte black Harley and a vintage chrome one with high, chopper-style handlebars. That heady smell of pot mixed with cigarettes hangs in the air.

Sean takes my helmet off, and tilts my face up toward his.

"Chin up, little dove. You're with me, yeah?" he says as he takes my hand. I nod, focusing on the clubhouse as we walk.

When we approach the side of the building, I can hear Pink Floyd playing through a Bluetooth speaker sitting in the middle of the outdoor table. There are two women sitting there, both of them in barely there clothing. Little black skirts, tank tops and over-the-knee boots. It's obvious they're doing everything they can to keep the men's attention. I suddenly feel a little more confident in the light jean shorts and white tank top that I changed into when Sean stopped at the gas station to get fuel. I hold my head up, toss my loose, wavy hair over my shoulders, and follow close behind him.

Six pairs of eyes turn to face us—namely me—as Sean says hello to them. One man stands up with a big smile, like he hasn't seen Sean in a while.

"Ax, brother, looking a lot cleaner than the last time I saw you."

Sean smiles wide at him and leans in to give him that sort of manly clasp of hands mixed with a half-hug. They both pat each other on the back.

"Yeah, a little less dirt on my boots," Sean answers.

"And a little less blood on your hands," the man adds. It hits me again that I have no idea what goes on in Sean's club life.

The group laughs—particularly one woman who's just joined them, She can't be any older than I am, with a short blonde bob and blunt bangs. Her lips are cherry red and she wears cutoff black jean shorts and a red tank top.

She eyes me up, then looks at Sean, like she's trying to make sense of who I am and why he was holding my hand.

"This is Layla," he says to the group. "This here is Ron and his buddies from up north." Sean introduces me to the man and his crew.

All the other men are surprisingly friendly and extend hands for me to shake. The women just give me fake smiles.

"You must be made of magic, Layla," Ron states as he shakes

129

my hand then pats Sean's shoulder. "Winning this one over, either you're magic or he's just gettin' old."

"Fuck off, old man," Sean grunts, then grabs my hand. "Anything shiny and new, they just can't help themselves," he says to me.

"Lucky me?" I retort, which makes the group laugh again.

Sean leans down and kisses my forehead as sparks run the length of my spine with his lips on me. I make eye contact with the blonde woman again as we start to head in. She looks at Sean in a knowing way and then glares at me as she takes a joint from the man next to her, watching me while she takes a deep hit.

"Come on, let's meet my ma," Sean says. "Catch up with me for a drink later, yeah?" he says to Ron. Ron holds up his beer in salute and Sean and I disappear through the side door to the building.

The scene unfolding inside is somehow both exactly what I pictured for an outlaw clubhouse and also not even close. The ceilings are high and wood-beamed, the lights are low, and people are scattered throughout at round tables.

A few people are playing pool at one of two tables in the wide-open space, and there's an area where couches are set up facing each other and people are drinking and talking. Behind them on the wall are framed cuts in glass cases that I assume belonged to people that have since passed. There are people dancing to Aerosmith on a makeshift dance floor. The music blares through a sound system that seems to be state-of-the-art. One whole wall is basically a bar area—full service from what I can tell, and not unlike the one at The Palm Club. It's fully stocked, and a Hounds of Hell wooden sign hangs in the center. There's an older woman behind the bar acting as bartender, but patrons aren't paying as she passes beer and shots of whiskey to them. The vibe in here isn't one of danger, it's one of family. Comfort and safety. Would I want to mess with anyone in this room? Not a chance. But do they seem like they would keep me safe? Absolutely.

Sean stops at the bar and knocks on it twice, and the woman makes her way over. Now that she's close, I'd say she's in her late forties.

"Can we get two Hellbenders?" he asks her before turning to me.

"This is Remi, she's Robby J's ol' lady. She helps us with the bar."

"Hey, darlin'," she says, passing me a shot of whiskey with a friendly smile. I take it gratefully, hoping to calm my nerves, letting the burning liquid slide down my throat as I wait for Sean's mom, aka the woman I picture as Xena, to emerge at any moment and club me.

"There she is." Sean nods to the back, grabbing my hand, surrounding me with his warmth again as he pulls me to a corner where an older woman with hair so platinum it looks white sits at a table with a glass of what looks like sweet tea and lemon. Her lips are red, and she has deep lines around them, as if she's been a smoker all her life. The bridge of her nose has a noticeable scar, but it's faded and she's done a good job of covering it with makeup. She looks to be in her mid-sixties.

When we get close, I realize she's doing a large puzzle and there's a bag of crochet yarn and a hook sitting on top of the table. She's puzzling and crocheting in the MC clubhouse?

I'm in the upside down, I'm pretty sure.

"This is my mom, Shelly," Sean says, as the woman looks up from her puzzle. She has the same green eyes as Sean's. On her first finger, in the same place as Sean's, I notice the same intricate dagger-cross that he has, only hers isn't anchored by a chain or compass.

They have matching tattoos? Shit, that's really cute.

I look down at her work, expecting a field or lake, and just about laugh out loud when I realize her puzzle is in fact a picture of a completely naked man, his body muscled, Michelangelo-style, with flowers covering his cock. She smiles up at me, and out of nowhere I really miss my own mother. Her smile used to light up any room, just like Sean's mom's does. This woman hasn't even spoken to me yet and I instantly love her. I can already tell that here, in this place, the last thing I'll be is judged.

Shelly stands and gently pats Sean on the face.

"I was just taking a break. I can only clean up after these assholes for so long before my back starts to bug me." Her voice is raspy but sweet as she turns and offers me another warm smile, one that puts me completely at ease. She throws her arms around me in a hug.

"You're Layla, then, I take it," she asserts confidently, backing up to look at me like a long-lost aunt.

I hug her back when she comes in again.

"You're so beautiful," she says.

"Thank you," I answer, totally charmed, as I tuck my hair behind my ear. "So are you," I add. She really is.

Shelly smells like Chanel with a hint of smoke, but somehow it's comforting. Another pang of missing my own mother punches me in the gut. I look up at Sean over her shoulder, in complete disbelief because she's not like Xena, she's more like Tinkerbell. I think she's even smaller than me *and* she has heels on. Her button-up cheetah sweater is soft and her jeans hug her slim hips perfectly.

"I am, aren't I?" she quips, sliding her hand down to hold mine and pull me toward the table. "Pull her chair out, boy," she commands.

"Christ, give me a chance to," Sean replies, doing just what she orders, sliding a chair out for me and then one for her. I don't miss that they're pulled out exactly the same distance from the table.

"I forgot to tell you how fuckin' bossy she is," he tells me as

Shelly hugs him. She's a third of his size and it makes me wonder how on earth she birthed this man.

"I'm not bossy, I'm assertive. There's a difference," she corrects. "And his dad was a big man," Shelly says to me. My mouth falls open and I look at her quizzically.

"You just look like you were wondering where he got his size from."

"I was," I admit with a laugh.

Shelly leans in and cups Sean's face with her hand. "Don't worry, he was only an eight pounder when he was born, thank Christ."

I laugh in spite of myself. "Thank Christ," I echo.

"Has he had his manners about him?" She narrows her eyes at Sean.

"Fuck, Ma," he gripes, running a hand over his head. I stifle a giggle. It makes Sean seem so much more human and shows me the level of respect he has for his mother as he pushes her chair in when she sits. This big, bad outlaw biker at the mercy of this tiny, spunky woman?

"Just say the word, honey, and I'll give him a smack," Shelly says as I take a seat across from her. He pushes my chair in for me too and I laugh. I don't doubt her for a second.

I look up at him. "Sometimes he remembers his manners," I say with a grin.

Sean's jaw falls slack and then his green eyes darken as he bends down and whispers the words "You're fucking done for" into my neck.

"Boy, I tell you—" Shelly starts.

"He's actually been quite a gentleman when it counts," I tell her, stopping her just short of standing to smack him. There's something just so real about this moment, as Shelly asks me to start finding the edge pieces for her puzzle. I oblige, as someone in a Hounds of Hell cut pulls Sean away to the table next to us.

"Who's the new girl?" A middle-aged blonde woman drops into a chair at our table a few moments later as I find Shelly a few pieces she was missing and add them to the puzzle.

"Layla," I answer, smiling at her.

"Maria," she introduces herself as she pulls a cigarette out of a red case and lights it.

"Layla came with *Sean*." Shelly waggles her eyebrows at me. I smile at her; she's clearly enamored with her son.

Maria eyes me up, but in a way that says she's genuinely curious about me, not like she's judging. "I'm like his aunt. Known him since he was ten and I was twenty-two."

"Since long before his dad died," Shelly adds. I nod, absorbing all the info about his dad and cataloguing it.

"Was his dad in the club too?" I ask, trying to appear nonchalant.

Shelly looks at me for a beat, almost like she's wondering if she can trust me.

"He hasn't said anything, I was just curious," I add. "He's kind of a closed book."

Shelly and Maria lock eyes and I worry I've overstepped until they both start to laugh.

Maria takes a drag from her cigarette. "Go easy on him. You're the first woman he's ever brought around here, honey."

Now it's time for my mouth to fall open, because *what the hell?* The first?

CHAPTER TWENTY-THREE
Layla

"Ever?!" I ask.

"Ever." Shelly smiles then gets back to her puzzle. "And yes, his dad was in the club. His name was Kurt."

She takes her phone out and pulls up a photo. It's a younger Sean in a Marine uniform standing next to a man who looks strikingly like him. Neither is smiling. Their eyes are menacing.

"May I?" I ask her. She nods and hands me the phone.

His dad had longer hair and I notice as his arm is draped over Sean's shoulder that he also has the dagger cross tattooed on his finger, only his is an exact replica of Sean's, chain and all.

"That was taken before Sean's second tour overseas," Shelly tells me. "Kurt died the way all of them hope to." She doesn't look up as she speaks, and I gently set her phone down as she places another puzzle piece in its home. "On the back of his bike."

"How old was Sean when Kurt died?" I ask without thinking.

"It was ten years ago, he was twenty-two. He was in Iraq when it happened. He doesn't talk about it much, but his dad was his best friend, aside from me of course." She winks.

My heart drops. I look over at Sean. We were the same age when we lost a parent we loved, and he wasn't even here when it happened, so he didn't get to say a proper goodbye.

"I'm sorry you lost him," I offer Shelly, feeling like I already know her. This is not what I expected to walk into when I got off Sean's bike. I feel at ease, not out of place at all, and I have to keep reminding myself that this is only my first time being here.

She smiles at me. "I have Sean. I've always had Sean. He's my protector. He has been since he was a boy." She looks pointedly at me. "You'll never find anyone more loyal."

"I second that," Maria adds. I turn to her.

"What about you? Are you someone's . . . ol' lady?" It sounds weird, but it seems natural to them.

Maria laughs. "I'm no one's *old* anything sweetheart, but I'm with Chad," she says. "Sometimes." She winks, pointing to the man Sean is talking to. He looks to be about forty-five. He's much shorter than Sean and has a big burly blond beard.

"He isn't from this charter, but he rides in a few times a month. He's here for a few days," Maria adds.

"And thank God, because this one gets cranky when she doesn't get laid," Shelly comments, hiking her thumb at Maria.

I laugh as Maria swats at Shelly, then gives in with a smirk. "It's true, I do."

"What do you mean 'charter'? How many of these clubs are—?" I'm cut off by the sound of chairs scraping against the concrete floor. The men at the table next to us where Sean is sitting all stand simultaneously.

I look over my shoulder toward the door to see the reason they've stood, and quiver a little bit in my sandals.

The man who approaches their table is just as big as Sean; his hair is long, dark and unkempt, and he's inked everywhere, just like Sean. He's built like a tank with violent gray eyes and a wide jaw. He's got that gladiator look too, and he wears the same kind of dog tags around his neck. And on his cut is the one word that confirms what I already know: *President*. This is Wolfe.

"Stand, honey," Shelly whispers. I do what she says.

"Prez," Sean says in greeting, hugging him. They clap each other hard on the back and the president hugs Chad too. The mysterious Wolfe and Sean are almost the same size and I can tell they share a deep bond. Sean is intimidating on his own—I've only just started to get used to his size and the presence he has—but these two men together?

Terrifying. No wonder no one messes with this club.

"This is Layla," Sean says, turning to face me, introducing me to Wolfe.

"Wolfe," he says in a deep voice with a smooth-as-silk timbre, extending his large, tattooed hand to me with a nod.

"Are you all just gigantic?" I blurt out, then gasp and clear my throat. "Shit, um . . . sorry, nice to meet you," I offer.

Wolfe chuckles darkly and nods in return.

"Same to you. Ax's been talking about you." He smirks and side-eyes Sean.

"Chapel, real quick." Wolfe nods at Sean. "We have some stuff to go over. It can't wait."

Sean pats him on the shoulder, as Wolfe turns to look back at me with his deep gray eyes.

"Make yourself at home here, Layla. Whatever we have is yours. Shel will take care of you and we're gonna get some barbecue going soon, so stick around, meet the other guys, yeah? Just don't let this one show you the ropes or you'll be dancing barefoot and topless before midnight." Wolfe points to Maria, who scoffs. "Bite your tongue, kid." Then she winks at me. "And it would be before eleven, just for the record."

I laugh as Sean squeezes my hand.

"Fuck, you smell so fuckin' good," he rasps in my ear, sending goosebumps down my neck before he backs up. "Stay. I'll be back soon. We can eat if you want before I take you home." The moment he utters the word *stay*, another round of nerves fizzles up my spine. I've already hit my limit today; I don't know if I can take much more of him. I'm running out of reasons not to just give in to him entirely.

It dawns on me that maybe that was his plan all along.

You'll be begging me.

"Don't be too long, she's already got a crowd watching her," Maria comments.

"My ma will fuck up anyone if they even think about touching her," Sean says over his shoulder.

"Damn straight," Shelly agrees as we sit back down and continue working on the puzzle together, as all the men in the room with cuts disappear behind a large wooden door. I watch as they all drop their cell phones into a basket sitting on a table outside the room. The music keeps rolling as Remi brings us another round of drinks, and then another after that. We let the whiskey sink into our blood and chat like old friends while we work our way through this puzzle like it's the most natural thing in the world.

I'm still pretty sure I'm in the upside down, but the more of this whiskey I drink, the less I care.

CHAPTER TWENTY-FOUR
Sean

"We'll start watching every member of the Disciples. Their higher-ups are in New Mexico this week at a rally, but technically speaking we have no issues with them right now, so a trip to Lush or Lavish might be in order?" Kai mentions the strip clubs in Lakeside and Perrytown owned by the Disciples. We try not to go to them unless we absolutely have to.

I run through the faces of every ranked member in their club, remembering them all by name.

"A few of the girls that hang around here work over there. We'll see where we get," Kai tells the table. He's been laying out all the information he's found on one of the Disciples of Sin members, Bryan Freeland, a piece of shit they call Gator. It's no secret that their club and ours aren't friends. There have been times of peace, but also times of all-out war between us. Right now, a war is brewing on the basis of Gator being involved in Mason's sister's rape.

"And we're sure Donny knows it was him?" Wolfe asks, mentioning the K6 member who leaked the info to us. He leans forward, folding his hands in front of him.

"He said he'd put money on it. Kinda hard to miss a guy with a blunt-smoking alligator inked on his hand, and the Disciples crest on his neck."

Jake chuckles and fires up a smoke. "What kind of a fucking twat buys GHB with a tat like that and doesn't cover his hand?"

"The kind with half a fuckin' brain," Wolfe answers, then looks at Mason. "But it's good for us. The K6s are the only ones who sell it around here and the timing is bang on. It's enough to find out for sure if it was him, and who gave the order."

I shake my head and turn to Mason, who's almost vibrating beside me.

"We're gonna get what we need," I tell him, patting his shoulder.

"The thought of that fucking piece of shit anywhere near Nicola is enough to make me burn their entire fucking club-house to the ground with every fucking one of them in it."

"Nicola is our family too," Robby says from his end of the table. He's right. We've known her since she was twelve, and now at seventeen she's gonna need years of therapy and recovery to get past this. Even Mason's other sister, Emilia, had to take a semester off school to help Nicola through the worst of it. It's affected them all.

"What do we know about the last time he was seen?" Robby pipes up, stubbing out his smoke.

"Apparently, he could be in hiding. But it's all lining up. Donny said he's got a perc problem. If he's buying, we'll find him," I offer.

"It's retaliation," Wolfe tells us. "It's too close to us shutting down Seventh and Lark, and too close to us cutting a deal with the building on Fourth Street. It's prime Disciples territory." Wolfe swirls his bourbon in his glass, mentioning the Disciples of Sin's most notorious place in Atlanta to unload fent—that is, until we moved one of our clinics in and cleaned up the block, essentially putting them out of business on their most profitable corner. It would've set them back big-time until they could get themselves set up elsewhere.

"No man, it's my fault. It's because of what me and Jake did at Lavish," Mason bites out. "Never should've went there to meet Jared. Should've picked somewhere else," he adds, mentioning the prez of our sister club, the Titans.

I nod. It could be. Lavish is known as a place where anything goes, and the Disciples's prez, Marco, didn't like the way one of his girls was hitting on Mason. Apparently, he wanted the girl for himself, but she was new and was trying to lure Mason into the back. Mason of course went with her, and fucked her in the bathroom. Then Marco found out. He's an irrational cokehead, so he pulled a gun on them and told them to get the fuck out. Naturally, Mason broke a beer bottle over his head and cut him up real good. Fucker almost bled out on the floor before their club doctor came, but by then Mason and Jake were long gone. We heard that girl's now Marco's ol' lady.

"Marco told Donny they were gonna hit us where it really fucking hurt, for Bridget," Mason bites out. "He has some kind of obsession with her. He told Donny it was personal."

I lean back in my chair. "The moment we can get our hands on this motherfucker it's gonna be game over for him. Until then, we have to bide our time." I look at Mason as the sound of Stevie Nicks suddenly blares through the wall of our chapel.

Jake and Kai turn to glance over their shoulders. They can't see anything because the blinds to the main space of the clubhouse are drawn.

"The fuck is going on out there?" Kai grins. "Got your lady here, yeah?" he says to me. "She stirring up some shit with Maria and Shel?"

I look at the clock on the wall. It's getting late and this place will be filling up with hang-arounds and people looking for a release. Friends of the club are always welcome here.

"Fuck only knows what'll happen to your girl if you leave her with Maria too long," Jake chuckles. "She'll be corrupted for sure."

I shake my head. "No one's corrupting her but me," I tell him with a grin.

"Alright, let's fuckin' eat then, we're done here." Wolfe looks around the table to make sure none of us has anything to add. "Let's organize a tail on Gator's crew." He looks at me and Kai. "Hit up Lush in the next couple days, not Lavish. Aiden runs Lush, we know some girls there," he says. Lush is the club that Marco's stepbrother and VP, Aiden Foxx, handles. It's notoriously cleaner—much more of a high-class gentlemen's club than the sister club, Lavish—and I already know what Wolfe's thinking. If the girls there aren't fucking for money, they may need it and be more likely to hand us intel discreetly. "Ask around about Gator. We'll see where it leads." Then he snaps the gavel down to end our meeting.

I pull Kai aside quickly before he leaves the room. "That other thing we talked about this morning. Are you on it?"

Kai nods, lighting a smoke. "Yep, we'll find out who it was."

"Good man," I tell him, giving him a light pat on the back, ready to get back to Layla. I'd like to say my mind wasn't on her the whole time I was in service, but I'd be lying.

The crowd is thick already when I exit the chapel and pick my phone out of the basket. I look around for a minute but don't see her where I left her with my mother and Maria. Someone has the grill going and the smell of steak wafts in from outside when the door is opened.

"She's fitting right in," my mom says, posting up beside me.

"I told her to stay with you." I look down at her. "She

alright?" I strain, trying to see over the crowd, but I still can't see her through the group of dancing sweetbutts and hang-arounds.

My mom laughs and pats me on the hand. "She's more than alright, baby. She's a little sweet and a little sour. A keeper." She backhand-cuffs my chest. "You really like her, don't you."

"Christ, we're not having this talk," I breathe out.

My mom laughs, linking her small arm through mine. "She made herself right at home and it ain't even dinnertime yet." She nods toward the back of the room. "I'm heading out, baby, busy day tomorrow." She works as an accountant for Wolfe three days a week.

She squeezes my arm and grabs her purse as she readies to leave the club. I follow her glance to where Layla and Maria are, with two of the regular girls Maria drinks with on any given night. They're dancing to "Dreams" by Fleetwood Mac in a dark corner, but Layla still commands all the attention in the room. Her hips sway to the music and her back shimmers with a thin veil of sweat. My mouth waters just thinking about tasting her again.

I make it to her in under ten seconds, watching as she sways her hips to the music. She's definitely been drinking and she's losing all her inhibitions as she throws her arms up over her head.

"Oh look, it's my boss," she mutters with a sass-filled fuck-me look on her face.

"Hell, she's dancing us under the table," Maria says, patting me. "She's all yours." She heads off for the bar with the other girls and leaves me and Layla alone.

Layla's eyes flutter closed when I don't waste any time gripping her tight around her waist. As my fingers slide under the hem of her shirt, she fucking moans, pressing into me.

"It's not normal to dance with your employee like this, you know, unless you want to fuck her," she says, challenging me. This fucking woman.

"You're done with alcohol tonight, Layla." I say her name evenly, sliding my hand under the waistband of her shorts. Her breathing increases with the feel of my callused fingers moving over her silky waist.

"You're not telling me what to do, *Ax*."

I let my fingers graze the side of her satin thong and grip it tight, twisting my fingers around the soft fabric of her underwear. She sucks in a breath. I know I'm pushing her, because I'm fucking pushing myself.

"Shit . . ." she whispers into my lips. "Did I hit a nerve?"

"Did *I*?" I smirk, tugging at her thong. She moans as the fabric pulls tight and nestles right up over her swollen clit. I kiss her lightly once, then twice, remembering what it feels like to have the full force of her lips on mine. Just the thought of kissing her makes me hard. It's a foreign feeling, something I haven't craved in as long as I can remember.

"No," she lies, fighting me with everything in her, but I don't miss the way she presses up against my cock a little harder. Her beautiful lips turn up into a smile and the tipsy glow of her cheeks flushes even more as her inhibitions fall completely away and she reaches between us, pressing her palm to my rock-hard cock in the dark corner we've drifted to.

"There's a lot of people watching us." She looks around and grips me a little tighter. "But if this is what you want, two can play that game, Ax."

"Sean," I correct. "And by the look in your eyes right now, something tells me you like that all these people are here. You like being watched."

I suck in a breath as she squeezes my dick again, harder this time, letting her free hand reach up to rest on my shoulder.

"I like it when *you* watch me," she moans in a breathy whisper. I give in, letting go of her panties and pressing my hips into her, kissing her with a groan.

"Fuck, woman, what are you doing to me?" Flames lick up my spine as she lets out another throaty moan, then pushes me back. She starts to laugh. An evil little laughing dove.

"It must be so *hard* for you not to get exactly what you want right when you want it." She squeezes my cock again. "That I don't just bend to your will, Mr. Always-In-Control," she whispers. "*So hard* to hover just before your breaking point all the time." Another squeeze of my cock.

Christ, I'm about to fucking blow in my pants.

"I'm not hovering," I growl, gripping her so tight her breath hitches. "To be very fucking clear, you *are* my fucking breaking point." I reach between us and grip her throat tight—just enough to take back some semblance of control.

"So why aren't you taking what you want? You don't seem like the kind of man who waits."

"I'm *not*," I admit. "But you will work for my cock. You will beg me for it, Layla, just like I told you you would." I trail my finger down her cheek and over her lips, then down the valley between her full tits, before gliding even lower, pressing my palm against her clit. My cock throbs behind my zipper with the feel of her wet heat as her palm still grips my cock, only now she's moving it slowly over me.

"You'll beg for me to make this pussy mine." I kiss her. "You're almost there, baby, so close to begging. This soaking cunt proves everything I need to know."

Her plush pink lips pop open as she whimpers. She smells like peaches and bourbon as we both pant. All the sounds of the room are lost; there's only us.

"Mmmm . . . yes." She trails off with a moan. "And I think you're about to come for *me*. And that proves everything that *I* want to know." Another squeeze to my dick, so hard it almost hurts. The corner we're in is just dark enough to shield us from sight as Layla starts to undo my buckle and slips her hand inside my boxers. Her warm palm presses to my cock and she squeezes again.

"Shit." She looks down then back up to my eyes. "No wonder you're so fucking confident."

Fucking hell.

"Look how hard you get when I fight you, *baby*," she purrs with another tight squeeze, and then she's softly gliding her hand over me. She has no fucking clue what she's doing when she's this drunk, but fuck . . .

"Show me I'm right and come for me, *Sean*."

"Holy fuck, Layla." My body shudders with the sound of my name on her lips and I stiffen even more. *"Fucking Christ,"* I breathe out, and then I'm kissing her, and as her tongue enters my mouth, meeting mine in a searing kiss, she whispers again: *"Sean."*

I unload against her palm, sliding my hand from her throat into her thick hair and tugging tight at the roots. She bites into my bottom lip with the pain while I come.

I claim her mouth while she moves her hand with ease, now covered in me. I breathe deep when I'm through, shell-shocked and half crazed.

Layla looks down at her slippery fingers after pulling her hand out, then her gaze flicks back to mine and I pull her to me.

"Clean up your mess," I growl, half pissed off that she just made me come in my fucking jeans but also more turned on than I've ever been. Her eyes grow wide with my words and I bring her hand to her lips, soaked with my come.

"Suck it off, every last drop."

A wide, smug smile breaks out over her lips as she pulls her fingers into her mouth one by one.

"Can I do anything else for you, *boss*? Or is that enough?" She looks down again, my buckle still undone, my cock obviously still hard in my boxers.

"Fuck." I tip my forehead to hers, still breathless. She hums with satisfaction, and I kiss her again. "I've never come just from kissing a woman before, but that gets you off, doesn't it? Knowing that you're the first?"

"Not as much as it gets you off," she whispers, licking at my lips devilishly. She tastes like the two of us together.

I'm just about to tell her what a sassy little brat she is, when she flinches in my arms as the music cuts off abruptly and Robby uses the loudspeaker to call out, "Food is ready, you bunch of miscreants!"

Then Layla reaches up on her tiptoes, just to torture me a little further, and kisses me on the cheek with her soft lips.

"Time to eat," she whispers with a smirk, then pats my jaw. My own come soaks through my boxers as I pull her close just before she's about to back away.

"The funny thing about pretending, little dove . . . if you pretend long enough, you might forget why you're pretending in the first place," I say as I drop one more kiss to her lips.

She just backs away without a word and turns to link arms with Maria like she's right at home, as I stand there fucking dumbfounded. I came out onto this dance floor to tease *her* and instead I wind up coming in my fucking pants like a teenager?

Fuck me. I'm in love.

Layla is sexy as hell, and she's been dancing for the last half hour with Maria while I keep a close watch with my boys. After I made my way down to my room at the back of the clubhouse and cleaned myself up before we ate, of course. I've never been happier in my fuckin' life to have fresh clothes here. And now, here I sit. Sipping bourbon while every man in this room looks her way. I've contemplated breaking at least five jaws in the last few minutes alone while she dances to "More Than a Feeling" by Boston.

"You could just piss on her, really stake your claim. That might be easier than looking like you're ready to kill someone," Wolfe chuckles beside me.

"Left her with Maria, what'd you expect?" Boyd, one of our older prospects, adds. "She's nice. She was asking me how long I'd prospected for." He snorts back laughter and I look out at her as she smiles and bumps hips with Maria. Fuck, she's cute.

"And here she comes," Jake pipes up, grinning. I turn to face him as he looks her up and down and licks his fucking lips.

Make that six jaws. I punch him hard in the shoulder. He flinches and I shake my head no. He shrugs.

"Sorry, I'm not used to this whole, 'Ax doesn't share' thing."

Layla looks around the full table and doesn't hesitate. She slides in right beside me. I pull her onto my lap, making sure no one can see up her shorts.

The heat from her sweat-slick body is almost too much for me to bear with her ass in my lap. She leans in and whispers in my ear, her sweet scent washing over me.

"Take me home, Ax," she whines. "*Fuck me.*"

I stroke her thigh and the feel of her skin under my fingers almost sets me on fire.

"Please," she adds, placing a soft kiss on my neck, her hand pressed to my chest. I hear Jake chuckle. I count in my head how many seconds it would take for me to stand up and smack his head off the table.

I set my jaw and squeeze her thigh.

"I'm gonna take her in your truck," I call over to Jake, not trusting her to hold on to me on the back of my bike right now.

He tosses me his keys.

"I'll bring it back in an hour," I tell him as I stand, helping her up.

"Take your time." Jake snickers, knocking back a shot. "I would."

This time I don't have to hit him. Wolfe does it for me, cuffing the backside of his head. I nod to Wolfe and follow my drunken little dove out the door.

CHAPTER TWENTY-FIVE

Sean

It only takes fifteen minutes to get to Layla's from the club. The roads are empty this time of night.

"You scare me, you know?" Layla says as I unlock the back door of her house and usher her in.

"Do I?" I ask, tossing her keys into the basket on a side table.

She laughs and looks up at me with a teasing look on her face. "And not in the way you think," she whispers, moving away from me. I watch as she kicks her sandals off and moans. The sound alone makes my cock twitch as I pull my cut off and hang it on the back of a chair before locking the back door. Layla stumbles into the living room, swaying slightly from side to side.

I follow her in and take a seat on the sofa, nodding to the seat beside me.

"Sit."

She listens and joins me, but instead of sitting down beside me she climbs right into my lap, straddling my legs and pressing her hot pussy against me. I'm quickly learning that, regardless of the circumstances, when she's near me, I'm instantly hard.

Drunk Layla is more open and obedient. There's nothing

holding her back and she's really fucking difficult to resist. She rests her forearms on my shoulders and tips her forehead to mine, her copper waves falling over her shoulders.

"I'm afraid because I've felt alone my whole life. I don't trust people easily." It's a tiny whisper as I slide my hands up her back. "I'm afraid because I trust *you* and that doesn't make sense to me," she adds, letting her lips graze mine. "And . . . mostly I'm afraid because I never want to end up with the wrong person, like my mother did." Her last words are the quietest whisper. "I want to live. She never did."

I'm desperate for her, but I'm sober and clear-headed as I stiffen under her.

"Your truth is nothing like hers. There's a reason you won't ever end up like that."

She laughs. "Oh yeah? And what's that?"

"Because you're strong, little dove, and bold. You don't take shit from anyone, even me." I stroke her face and hope she remembers some of this. "Strength commands worship. That's all you'll ever know with me. I will worship you, Layla, every single day, and no one will hurt you. Ever."

She whimpers and touches her lips to mine. Want floods my cells as I breathe her in and she presses into me further.

"Um . . . I'm drunk and you probably have some rule about not fucking drunk women, right?"

I flex my fists then let my hands trail over her hips, pulling my own strength from somewhere deep. Layla's plump ass fills my palms and I rock her close to me. She moans and it almost breaks me.

Almost.

"I don't give a fuck that you're drunk," I bite out. "I know you want me just as much as I want you. Drunk, sober, it doesn't matter. But when I take this pussy for the first time, you're going to be stone-cold sober, little dove, because I want you to remember every fucking second of me filling you. Understand?"

Layla leans back and crosses her arms in front of her. Gripping the hem of her tank top, she pulls it off over her head. Her full tits spill over the top of her lacy bra and her long red hair tumbles down. I take a second just to look at her.

She is fucking stunning.

"You sure about that?" she whispers in a challenge.

I reach up and pluck at her nipple through the lace of her bra.

"Oh, how the tables have turned." I grin as her head falls back and she whimpers.

I pluck again and she rocks her hot pussy into me and bites her bottom lip. "Please . . ." she moans, already knowing what it does to me when she begs.

Fucking Christ.

It takes every single stitch of restraint I possess to stop myself from fucking her. But I meant what I said. I want her to remember everything. I want to look into her eyes while I claim her and she screams my name for the first time, and I can't do that when she's drunk like this.

"You want me, Layla?" I ask her. "You want me to take this tight pussy for my own right now?"

"Yes," she whispers, grinding into me. "God, yes."

I still her hips with my hands.

"Then you can fucking tell me that when you're sober."

She blinks. "What?" she asks breathlessly as I lift her off me. My petty side loves this payback for her making me come in my pants in the middle of the clubhouse dance floor.

She climbs right back into my lap. *Persistent little brat.* Her face is knotted in confusion as she grips mine in her hands.

"You said when I begged you, and I'm begging. *Fuck me*," she orders.

I bring her lips down to mine. I bite her plush bottom one. She winces.

"Go to fucking bed, Layla," I say gruffly, lifting her off me one more time. I hand her shirt back to her, looking her dead in her pretty whiskey eyes. She just stands in front of me, her chest rising and falling rapidly, shocked I'm not giving her what she wants.

Then she lets out a little huff and takes her tank from my waiting hand. She's all piss and vinegar because I turned her down, and even that makes me smile.

Another discovery. She's fucking adorable when she's angry.

She turns on her heel and heads down the hall to her bedroom.

"I wasn't going to fuck you anyway, Sean Hunter," she calls out. I scrub my face with my hand as I chuckle into it. I look down at my rock-hard dick and shake my head.

The sound of Layla opening and closing drawers in her bedroom tells me she's trying to get ready for bed as I pick up her purse and hang it on the hook on the wall in her kitchen. I wash my hands and can't help but make sure everything is clean and shut off. I think about how fucked it is that I'm here with her, *not* fucking her, because I care about her being clear-headed in that moment.

I analyze why, and the only thing I can come up with is that I want her to remember it more than I care about fucking her.

I hang the dish towel up, folded neatly in half, and look around. Everything is in order and it's quiet now at the end of the hall.

I pour her a glass of water and walk down the hall, and when I reach her bedroom I pause in the doorway for a moment, just watching. She's already in bed, face down, wearing a fresh tank top but she still has on her shorts. She's passed out cold. I scrub my face with my hand, and set the water down on her bedside table. I can't just leave her like this.

I make my way to the bathroom and run a facecloth under warm water, then return to her room. I sit down on the edge of her bed and pause, watching her sleep, pushing a lock of hair out of her face as she stirs slightly and hums the sweetest sound.

"I don't want . . . to be alone," she mumbles.

"Just be a good girl, Layla, and get some sleep." I take the opportunity to roll her onto her side and I start to wash her face. She sighs as I gently wipe, pushing her long hair off her shoulder and washing there too. It was hot as fuck in that clubhouse tonight and she'll want to feel clean when she wakes up. When I'm done cleaning her up, I undo her shorts and pull them from her body. All her silky skin comes into view and I'm instantly hard again, but she's snoring softly and doesn't even flinch when I tuck her into bed. The thought of any other man doing this for her sends my blood racing. I push that thought away because it's never going to happen.

Pulling her robe down from the hook on the back of her door, I drape it over the end of the bed and push her slippers to the side so they'll be there when she wakes up.

I look down at her, sleeping soundly. I'm rock hard and out of my mind for her.

This woman is gonna be the fucking death of me.

CHAPTER TWENTY-SIX
Layla

"What happened?" I set my purse and keys down on our kitchen table. I rushed straight home from the meeting with my high school guidance counselor when I heard my mother was at the hospital. She stands and hugs me, moving her arm in its cast carefully.

"It's nothing, baby, I tripped. You know how clumsy I am." She tucks a lock of her dark hair behind her ear. My mom is still very pretty and youthful in her forties, which comes from walking every single day and never sitting still. She's always involved with something at church or in the community.

A heavy sigh leaves me as I watch her face, because my mom isn't clumsy at all.

"Tell me how it happened." My eyes narrow as I wait for her response, because I know somehow it was him. She had a different injury like this the last time my dad came home from the track after having too much to drink, when he was angry at her for donating to the church roast beef dinner without asking him. A fucking double standard, since he throws money away at the track without ever discussing it with her. "Tell me Dad wasn't there and you weren't fighting when you 'tripped.'" I put air quotes *around the last word and she just looks up at me. Her brown eyes are filled with a deep sort of longing. A longing to tell someone the truth that we both know but never say.*

"We were . . . arguing, but it was my fault. He was right, and I should've been more communicative with him. It's my duty as his wife to make sure I run his home the way he needs me to."

I grit my teeth. My mom was a teacher when she was younger, but now she only works for him. She could work; there are many women at our church who have day jobs. Something to fulfill them outside of their marriages. But my dad likes her home. I'm sure it's to keep her vulnerable at all times.

"That's bullshit!"

"Layla June Monroe!"

"It is, Mom. You don't deserve to live in fear of cooking the wrong dinner."

"It wasn't his fault." Her eyes plead. "Yes, he was there, but I stumbled backward myself. He had nothing to do with it."

She would sound sincere to someone who didn't know better. But I don't believe her. I know. I know it's him. It has been for years.

I groan as I look in the bathroom mirror after splashing warm water on my face, reliving the dream I just woke from. Those dreams come less often now, but when they do they're vivid and heart-wrenching, because every time I think maybe it will end differently. Staring at myself now I can see her eyes staring back at me more clearly than ever. It's the same vision as always. The woman behind bars, clinging to them and begging to be free.

I sigh and gently pat my face dry before setting the hand towel down. The smell of bacon and coffee and the feeling of my pounding head wash over me. I have a full morning at the clinic before a shift at the club tonight. I think it was sometime after one when we got back here and I know I drank way too much.

I'm not prepared for what greets me when I reach my kitchen.

The man who happens to be my last appointment in the clinic this afternoon, after another spot miraculously opened up, is standing at the stove cooking us breakfast. *Sean*. I grip the wall and watch, as a new wave of grief smacks me square in the chest from the dream.

I close my eyes and lean against the wall. He's the first person to stand there, at the same stove my mother used to cook at. We'd have our girls' brunches almost every weekend, and she'd make us pancakes with fruit and we'd talk about school, boys, our faith. Everything and anything. The kitchen has seemed so empty, and now . . . it's not.

I think of her smile. Tears fill my eyes and I try to remember the way her laugh sounded. It doesn't come to me, and grief washes over me again, making me nauseous. I open my eyes and take a breath. The realization she's never coming back hits me once more.

Sean's phone buzzes as he cooks, and he answers it.

"Yeah?"

I wait. Maybe I shouldn't be eavesdropping but I'm curious to know what he does when I'm not with him. I duck back into the hall so he can't see me.

"It's a start. I don't wanna leave any stone unturned. It won't be the Disciples."

What won't be the Disciples?

"Could be, but I can't see that either. It doesn't make sense for them to kill for no reason."

I wish I could hear the other side of this conversation.

"If you get him, no one touches him. His broken bones are mine, got it?" There's a pause. "Yep, and keep me posted. We can use the cabin if we need to. If he doesn't want to talk, we'll make him."

Equal shots of fear and desire run through me. Sean is speaking so casually about hurting someone, and the first thing that happens when I hear it is that I *want* him? There's no hope for me—

"You're not as stealthy as you think, little dove. You can come out now."

CHAPTER TWENTY-SEVEN
Layla

Fuck. I look up at the ceiling. When I peek around the corner, Sean looks freshly showered, his hair is buzzed even closer than yesterday, and he's wearing his standard black t-shirt with his dog tags tucked in, black jeans and he's got AirPods in. He looks like he's in his cooking element. There's fresh fruit, orange juice and coffee set out on the counter, and he's scrambling eggs in a skillet on the stove. I've never seen anything so beautiful so early in the morning. He turns to look at me and pulls the AirPods out while I take a seat at the island.

He says nothing to me about me listening in on his phone call as he slides a glass of orange juice and a freshly poured coffee toward me, turning the handle of the mug to face me, and then follows it up with a bottle of Tylenol.

"Thanks. I think I need that this morning," I groan, twisting open the Tylenol.

"You have to pace yourself when you come to the club," he says as I pop the pills in my mouth and use the orange juice to swallow them down. "But I don't hate the sound of you begging me to fuck you." His voice is full of teasing.

I pause mid-sip, broken memories flashing behind my eyes. Me, pulling my shirt off in front of him when we got back here. Climbing into his lap on my sofa, telling him how badly I wanted him.

I threw myself at him. And he turned me down. Visions of him pushing me back flash into my mind and I cringe. *"When I take this pussy for the first time, you're going to be stone-cold sober, little dove."*

Another of him tucking me into bed. *"Be a good girl, Layla, and get some sleep."*

Another of me asking him to stay. *"I don't want to be alone."*

Oh God. I begged him, alright. Begged him to stay with me.

"All coming back to you?" He smirks as he plates my breakfast, passes it to me and sets a fork and knife above it.

"Did you leave?" I ask on account of his new clothes.

"No. I had Boyd bring my bike and some clothes from my room at the club."

"Where did you sleep?" I ask.

"Next to you," he says, like it's the most natural thing in the world. "You snore." He smirks. *Oh my God.*

"Only when I've been drinking," I retort.

"It was cute as fuck," he adds, which settles me. It's an odd sensation not to have to worry about being what he wants—that who I am *is* what he wants.

"Do you all have rooms at the club?" I change the subject from my alcohol-induced sleep habits, ignoring the fact that I was drunk enough to be completely unaware of this beast of a man in my bed.

He looks up. "Just myself, Wolfe and Jake have private rooms there, but I rarely stay. Only if there's an emergency."

"What kind of emergency?" I ask, taking a bite of bacon. It's maple bacon. *God that's good.*

Sean looks at me as he sits down on a stool with his own

plate. "In case of a lockdown, or if someone is hurt and we have to stay with them, things like that."

"Lockdown?"

Sean takes a big sip of coffee. "Sometimes if we have problems with other clubs, things can get dangerous, and so it makes sense for us to stay at the club. But if that happens, the club is the safest place you can be," he says reassuringly.

We sit and eat in silence for a beat.

"My mother used to cook us breakfast like this," I tell him, changing the subject, taking another bite. "It's weird having someone else cook for me."

"What do you miss most about her?" he asks, and I look up in surprise at the question. I just didn't expect it. The bridge of my nose stings with just the thought of her. "She was my person. The one person I had who loved me for *me*. But she kept secrets, and she protected my father. She was just about to break free from him when she died." I've offered way more than he asked for, but it feels good to talk about her without judgment.

"Your dad was a prick, yeah?" Sean asks. "I looked into him a little more. Lots of debt. Gambling is deadly."

"It wasn't just that. He had a temper."

I watch Sean's fist flex and his jaw harden instantly. "Did he hurt you?" he growls.

I shake my head. "No, but sometimes he'd hurt my mom, and then he'd apologize. She stayed with him, she supported him. She even went to meetings for spouses of gambling addicts so she could support him *better*. She stayed because she was worried what the church would think." I smile softly as I break a piece of bacon apart. "We had a plan though."

Sean doesn't say anything, just lets me talk, eating his breakfast and watching me.

"The night she died, she went to a last-minute dinner with my dad. She wasn't supposed to go, and I was here. We spent months planning, I had a place off-campus I was staying at in Atlanta. I don't know what changed—maybe she'd just had enough—but we got her a bank account and she funneled her own savings into it. Enough to start her off. She had a teaching degree, and a decent résumé. She just hadn't worked since Dell and I were young. She was going to freshen it up and had finally gotten everything sorted out."

I shake my head, my eyes filling with tears.

"All she had to do was make it through that dinner with his work colleagues, then when he got home and went to bed early like he always did, we were going to leave together. She already had the divorce papers drawn up, and she had all her favorite things packed." I lean back in my chair and look at him. "She was excited to start fresh. She had a new sort of gleam in her eye that I hadn't seen before. But that night I just waited and waited. They never came home. The police said . . . the man was wearing a cut, but the witness couldn't see which club, they just saw him taking off on a bike and it was dark. I wouldn't be surprised if my dad did something to bring this to them."

"With the gambling?" Sean asks.

I shrug. "I don't know, maybe."

"He'd have to owe a lot for them to kill him."

"Three hundred grand?"

"That could do it." Sean moves his chair closer to me and wipes the tears from my cheek, then places his hand on my face. "Some clubs demand loyalty to earn their rockers, to patch in. Killing innocents is one way."

I nod. "It makes the most sense. My parents were just in the wrong place at the wrong time, I'm sure."

"Our club would never do that," Sean says firmly. Strangely, I believe him.

"They still have no idea who did it. Just a police sketch. I just wish I knew why." I swipe my tears away and steel myself, looking down at my half-empty plate. The Tylenol has kicked in and my headache is thankfully subsiding.

I glance at the clock and then back at Sean. I have to be at the clinic in an hour.

"This must be worlds away from your life. Your mom said you've always been a part of the club, even as a boy," I say sincerely.

"My father was the previous president's enforcer for a while, and then his Sergeant at Arms. My grandfather was an enforcer." Sean folds his napkin perfectly in half and leans back in his chair. "My mother stayed even after my dad died. He was hit by some drunk college kid. She kept the club as her purpose because that's what he would've wanted."

I breathe out a sigh. "Shit. I'm sorry."

Sean shrugs. "It was ten years ago. I still miss him and his guidance, but he died the way all of us hope to. On his bike. It was his time."

"Was he in the military too?" I ask as I sip my juice.

Sean nods. "Both my father and my grandfather served. My grandfather in Vietnam and my father in Desert Storm. I knew it was my future but I didn't do it the way they did. I didn't start out as a boot. I joined as a Second Lieutenant."

"How?"

"I earned a degree." He takes a sip of his coffee. "From Duke."

My mouth falls open. *Damn*. I did not expect that. "*Duke?*"

He looks up at me. "With honors."

I shake my head and blow out a breath.

"What?" he asks, setting his mug down.

"I just, I mean, I didn't . . ." I feel the blush of my assumption creeping into my cheeks. "You surprise me, is all."

"Life is all about making smart decisions. Calculated choices. I knew they wanted me, I knew it would be a free ride." He shrugs. "I remember things."

"I suppose I shouldn't be surprised. I know you're smart, and sometimes it seems like you never stop thinking." It's something you notice about him almost right away.

"It's not about being smart. It's my memory. I've been told it's photographic. I remember faces, names, text, formulas. School just came easy to me." He says it like it hasn't always been a blessing.

"That must have been hard when you came home from overseas?"

I watch his face as he looks down to his plate, and I can tell he doesn't talk much about that time.

"It's why I always wanted the next tour. I sought it out, because being there, in the fucking carnage, never having time to think or remember, seemed easier than being here with nothing to distract me. Understand?"

I nod. "Were you worried every time you went that you might not come back? Were you afraid of dying out there?" I ask.

Sean leans back in his chair and folds his thick arms over his chest.

"My bunkmate, Buck, he used to read poetry. Old-world Spanish poetry, and one in particular always stuck with me. *Contented, the righteous nest searches for the ominous blackbird to fill it / The darkest of beasts rest soundly in the most hidden dens, / The dead in their shallow grave, and the sad in their oblivion, / Only through this peace will my soul become sand in its desert.*"

"That's beautiful," I say softly. The look in Sean's eyes tells me Buck is no longer alive, and I don't want to pry.

"For me it means that, even at death's door, from flat on my back in that fucking desert, I knew I couldn't let the beast win. The darkest parts in me needed to stay hidden in the beast's den. The good I had left in me? I had to choose to let that overcome the bad. I had to *choose* which part of me got to take flight. I chose to use my demons to help others learn how to do the same."

I watch him as I take my last bite of toast.

"The government I had ruined myself for mentally was nowhere to be found when I was done with my active service. I didn't turn to drugs like many of my brothers. I joined the club and I started a career where I knew I could help. Is what we do illegal? Yeah, but we do it to help fund the things that matter. Sometimes you have to do a little bad to do a lot of good. I made the choice to be involved, to make a difference for anyone else returning home who was feeling lost and ruined, because I knew our government wasn't going to be there for them either. I can't help every soldier, but I can help some."

Sean sits up straighter and his brow knots for just a fraction of a second.

"Your back?" I ask him quietly.

"Yep. It's always a little tight in the morning."

We sit in silence for a moment before I say, "We'll work it out with the next massage. It's a process."

Sean watches me, then nods toward the end of the hall.

"Go get ready, I'll clean up and get you something packed for lunch," he says, setting his fork down. He leans closer and kisses me. "And you'll be my good girl and eat it, yeah?"

Another wave of emotion hits me square in the chest, but this time it isn't grief. It's the feeling of him looking after me, yet again. He does it like it's second nature to him, whether I need him to or not. I've just spent so much time looking after myself that I don't really know how to respond other than nod and head down the hall like the good girl Sean Hunter wants me to be. The truth is, even with him living a life outside of what anyone I've ever known would deem to be honest or right, even with him having threatening conversations about breaking someone's bones while he cooks me breakfast, I'm feeling more and more like *his* good girl every single day.

CHAPTER TWENTY-EIGHT
Sean

"Make sure he tells us where it all is." I push the K6er's head down and more blood drips from both the gash on his brow and his mouth as he groans. He's already looking rough, but before we're done he *will* tell us where our product is.

Kai comes back into the room we're holding them all in, ready to make their nightmares become reality. We're in an abandoned house in the shittiest part of town. The fucking windows are boarded up, for Chrissakes, and it smells like piss. There are two women, if you can even call them that—they look more like high schoolers—sleeping on sofas in the living room. They're high as fuck and still dressed to pick up. Meth bowls, cotton, a few spoons and lighters, and used needles are strewn all over the table. One of the girls still has her arm banded up from her last hit. I've seen at least one of these women on the street outside our Bleaker Road clinic. She barely fucking looks eighteen.

The moment Kai pulled up our security footage and we saw who was behind the break-in at the clinic late last night, we were on the hunt. It didn't hurt that Kai thought they might be able to help me with my search for the man who killed Layla's parents.

Now that she's talked about it with me and I've seen the pain behind her eyes, it isn't just a want for me to find him, or them, and get her the answers. It's a *need*.

We found them in the alley behind this shithole, handing off one of their girls to some guy in a van. She looked scared, and it was obvious she didn't want to go. An all-out fight followed, and one of them punched her in the kidney. He'd never hit her in the face because he wouldn't want to damage his moneymaker. They're dealers of drugs and pussy, but most of them are avid meth users themselves. And one thing about junkies like that, they get freakishly strong when they're high and they don't feel any pain. We beat the shit out of them and dragged them back, but we all took a couple good knocks before we were able to overpower the five of them and drag them back into this place. One of them hit me with a piece of wood that was lying in the alley and split my cheekbone open, but we got them inside and tied them up and then we got to work.

I look at the old clock on the wall. I'm supposed to be at my clinic appointment with Layla in five minutes, but it's not like I can call her while Kai and Jake are slicing these fucks open and breaking their fingers, so I pick up my phone and call our prospect Boyd instead.

Thirty minutes and five more broken fingers later, one of them finally breaks and tells Kai where a week's supply of our methadone and a massive stash of clean needles is. That's the problem with what we do—junkies want needles, and we have them. They also steal our methadone mistaking it for something that can get them high.

"He also told me a rumor he heard about a couple getting shot at an Atlanta gas station a couple years back, and a certain Wretched Souls member," Kai tells me before speaking to Jake. "In the bathroom, under the sink, lift the bottom of the cabinet out, you'll find it all there." He turns back to the junkie that spilled all and grips his face hard. "Unless you're fucking lying to me. Then I start taking teeth."

I shake my head. Fucking Kai. He loves this shit way too much.

Kai kicks him hard and the prick cries. He's already tweaking for his next fix.

"Shouldn't have caved so early, I was looking forward to breaking the rest of those fingers," Kai says to him, genuinely disappointed.

I make my way through the dark house, doing my best not to step on a rat as I open the kitchen window to take a breath that doesn't taste like the inside of a sewer while I pull my glove off to call Boyd. There's shit everywhere—garbage and booze bottles.

Fucking pigs.

"Hey," Boyd answers.

"You pick up my package?"

"Yeah, your package didn't want to be picked up," he responds with a chuckle.

"Not surprising," I answer as Jake comes back inside from our van with a small tan duffel bag. I follow him back to what I guess you could call the living room in this shithole, where we have the K6ers tied up, and watch as Kai pulls a suppressed Glock 44 out of the bag Jake just brought in.

"I'll deal with it. I'm pretty much wrapped up here," I tell Boyd. "I'll be twenty minutes, just don't let her out of your sight."

"Okay, but boss? She said she didn't need a babysitter and, uh, she seems kinda pissed at you."

I chuckle. "Yeah, the feeling is mutual," I mutter as I hang up.

I've just sent her a text when Kai takes aim at our resident tweakers without an ounce of hesitation and the biggest fuckin' smile on his face. He quickly takes the first one out, then the second, both clean double taps to the head. The sound of their brain matter and blood hitting the wall behind them makes more of a sound than the gun. The other three are so badly beaten they hardly even notice that Kai just killed their buddies as they hover in and out of consciousness. Even though we're in the shittiest part of town, we still wouldn't shoot them without a suppressor. Cops are everywhere around here, and gunshots are the fastest way to bring them to the door. There's no reason to draw heat to us if we don't have to, but we have no choice but to kill them. I won't leave any loose ends untied.

I watch as Jake takes aim at the next one. It's part of our code; we all participate. All for one. I think about Layla giving Boyd a hard time about babysitting her as Jake takes his shot. I can almost see the defiant look in her bratty eyes.

"You're up." Jake hands me the gun. I take it from him and move closer, needing the junkie's eyes, needing to see the soul of the man whose life I'm taking. I kick him and he looks up at me, fucked up and glazy. He has no idea what's even happening. I don't waste a second, I just aim and fire, hitting him twice right where I want to—between his eyes. It's at this moment the last one comes around.

"Hey . . . what? . . . Don't fucking . . . shoot me . . . please," he begs, noticing the guy beside him is now leaking from a massive hole in his forehead. I move in front of him and focus on his eyes. Even high, they're pleading, but I'm going to finish what we came here to do. We've been looking for two of these men for a while. But these fuckers have stolen from us for the last time. The one I just shot is the low-life pimp that's been known to take in girls from the street—some underage, some just desperate to belong to someone—and he feeds them drugs, using their bodies for money until they have nothing left. Until they're just machines that work for him. He beats them when they get out of line or even try to complain, and he takes almost every cent from them. A waste of lungs using up fresh air that someone better could be breathing in. Guys like him are the bottom of the barrel.

"Rock paper scissors?" Kai asks hopefully, but I'm done fucking around. I'm sick of the smell in here and my back has had enough. I look at the last junkie, raise the gun and pull the trigger, ending him. He slumps forward.

Five less K6 dealers make Harmony a better, safer place.

"Ax, fuck, that was rude," Kai says, cuffing my shoulder, annoyed I didn't give him the chance to take out the last one.

"Let's just get the fuck outta here," I tell them all. I've got other shit on my mind.

Layla might not be willing to admit she's mine yet, but when it comes to her safety, I simply don't give a fuck what she wants. She's about to learn that I won't tell her what to do very often, but when I do, she's gonna fucking listen.

CHAPTER TWENTY-NINE
Layla

My head is a total clusterfuck during my shift at the clinic.

It's filled with the way Sean looks at me, the life he lives, the life I don't have anymore, and the admission that I'm still grieving that life I could've had with my mom free of my father. I've been grieving my mother more than I've let anyone know.

Having Sean in my space has shown me that. He's a force that's both pulling the air from my lungs and breathing life back into me in a way I didn't know I needed. I make it through most of the day without hearing from Sean at all, which is odd.

The thing about working in a profession where talking is limited, it gives you way too much time to live inside your own head. By the time Sean's appointment rolls around at three, I'm splashing cold water on my face while I wait for him to arrive. Just the thought of his skin under my hands sends a rush through me I can't ignore. A rush I don't want to ignore.

But by three thirty he still hasn't shown, and I'm thinking I was right to be so hesitant about him. I'm annoyed with myself for giving into him so quickly as I exit through the doors of the clinic at the end of the day, but I stop in my tracks when I see

Boyd, one of the prospects I met at the club, in the same truck that Sean drove me home in last night. He's clearly waiting for me. When he looks up and sees me, I get a polite, tight-lipped smile and a nod as he starts walking in my direction.

"You have to come with me, ma'am . . . umm, Layla," he says as we meet in the middle of the sidewalk and I shoot him a glare. Boyd is a shorter guy with jet black hair that's cut close. He's only a few inches taller than me, but he's built like a brick shithouse, as if his height fueled him to work out five hours a day—and unlike the other guys, I don't see one visible bit of ink on his skin.

"Where is he?" I ask sharply, wondering if I should take the ride home or wait for my bus just to prove a point. "I don't need a babysitter," I tell him as I start walking toward the bus stop. "If Sean wanted me to go home with someone from the MC, he should've come to get me himself."

"He . . . can't."

That stops me. I turn and face Boyd. "Why?"

Boyd looks up at the sky, then back down to me. "I can't tell you that. But you have to come with me. He wants you at the club when he gets back."

I put my hand on my hip, my suspicion growing. "Why didn't he tell me he wasn't coming?"

"Listen, Layla, I get you're pissed, but can we talk in the truck? I don't want to get my ass kicked for not getting you back to the clubhouse. It's for your safety."

"For my *safety*?" I ask, my voice hitting a higher note. Boyd's eyes are pleading. He seems like a nice guy, polite and well-mannered, and the way the patched members seem to give him shit constantly almost makes me feel sorry for him, but how do I know Sean really sent him?

"I think I'll wait right here."

"Fucking Christ." Boyd rubs his forehead and pulls his

phone out. I watch for my bus as he texts, and not thirty seconds later a message comes through on my phone.

> **YOUR BOSS**
> Get in the truck, Layla.

> You're late.

> **YOUR BOSS**
> Something came up, this isn't a game. I won't tell you twice.

A chill runs through me. I know there's no playing with him right now. I look up at Boyd, who's still waiting expectantly just as my bus rounds the corner.

"We good?" Boyd asks.

Fuck. "Yes." I scowl at him and head for the truck. "You have to stop at my place so I can at least change." I look down at my scrubs.

"As long as you're quick. Ax said to take you right to the club."

"I'll be quick," I say as he climbs in and starts the engine. I look out the window as he backs out of the parking space. It's not his fault Ax is a caveman who sent someone to fetch me like I was his property. I'll take that up with him though, the first chance I get.

"What do you mean? I thought you had to take me to the club?" I ask Boyd as I stand freshly showered and dressed in comfortable jeans, a white t-shirt and my favorite Chucks. My feet are too sore to put heels on tonight.

"He changed his mind. He wants us to stay here, said he was on his way. Like I said, I'm not trying to get my ass kicked and I don't question when he tells me what to do."

"A lesson you should take to heart, little dove." Sean's voice speaking directly to me makes me jump. I didn't even hear him come in. I spin around to face him, already pissed that I was picked up by his guy like some package, but the moment I see him, my anger dies and turns to fear. I've seen him serious, I've seen him commanding, but I've not seen him angry and right now he looks really fucking angry. As he turns to face Boyd, I gasp. His cheekbone is split open and a bruise is blooming there. Dried blood is caked to his skin and a few smears of fresh blood line his cheek below the gash. He's also filthy, with what looks like dirt and sweat covering his neck and shirt. My eyes move to his knuckles as he approaches the kitchen sink. They're busted open and bloody.

"Wait outside on the porch," Sean says to Boyd. "Keep watch until we leave." That's when I notice something else in his eyes, something I haven't seen before. Like he's holding the horrors of the day there. "You need to call into work. You're not going," he says to me.

I don't even argue, I just nod, because there's no arguing with the look in Sean's eyes right now.

Boyd doesn't waste time arguing either; he just nods at me and leaves as Sean begins to scrub his hands clean. My breathing increases as I begin to understand why he didn't show. He obviously couldn't, and was involved with something for the club that I probably don't want to know about.

Sean keeps his eyes trained on mine as he walks by me and heads down the hall to my bathroom. "We'll talk after," is all he says.

I wait a few seconds while a silent war wages in my head. The second I saw Sean come through my door battered and filthy, my heart dropped, and the last thing I care about now is him missing his appointment. The last thing I want to do is fight what is happening. All I want to do is go to him, crawl into his strong arms and make sure he's okay, the same way he made sure I was okay last night.

I move quickly toward the bathroom door. It isn't fully closed and there's a sliver of light peeking through. When I push open the door, Sean is standing at the sink. I can tell he's tense, because the muscles in his back are rigid. The water is running as he checks out his injuries. He looks at me over his shoulder in the mirror. After I grab a fresh cloth from the linen closet, my eyes can't roam his skin fast enough. Sean's naked body is on full display, and he's a force to be reckoned with. He's taut and flexed, covered in sweat, with blood dripping down his face, and he isn't self-conscious in the slightest as he stares at me with those haunted eyes. He's incredible. My gladiator.

I'm desperate to reach out and touch him.

CHAPTER THIRTY
Layla

I move closer, handing the cloth to him, and he takes it, running it under hot water before shutting the tap off then beginning to wash his face. He hisses when he hits the wound and it starts to bleed even more profusely than it already was.

"It looks deep," I say.

"It's fine," he grunts as he runs the cloth under the water again and wrings it out.

"It needs stitches."

"Nah, don't worry about that right now." His voice is low and firm.

I can no longer help myself—I rest my hand on the middle of his back and my entire being comes alive with the feel of his skin under mine.

"What are these bodies?" I ask, letting my fingers trace the inked designs.

Sean looks at me in the mirror again. "They're the bodies of my past."

He stiffens under my touch as blood trickles slowly down

his cheek and then over his neck. I move to stand in front of him and he backs up to make room for me as I slide my hand down his arm. In the soft glow of the bathroom lights, I can see his cock is solid and ready for me, and my mouth waters at both his size and how perfect he is.

"And today, did you add more bodies to that pile?" My question is a whisper.

"If I say yes, how would that make you feel?" His emerald eyes search mine as he waits for my answer, as if he's afraid I won't speak the truth.

My heart drops but its pace escalates at the same time. "I would want to know why," I answer boldly.

Sean leans down and kisses me. "Because they were a waste of human existence, and they needed to die." His voice is thick and smooth. Certain.

"How do you justify that?"

He lifts my hands up and holds them tight as he speaks. "You watch a group of men abuse a girl, give her drugs to keep her just high enough that she'll fuck any dick they put in front of her, and then steal from our clinics where we try to help people just like her. Then they keep all the money she earns selling her body and her soul. You watch that happen and then tell me that those men should live while she suffers."

I look up at him. "I . . . can't."

"In war, we wouldn't hesitate for one second to kill a man like that, but on the street, the law says we can't."

I swallow, trying to determine whether or not I can live with that.

"You shouldn't hesitate." It surprises me that I don't feel any differently about him now that I know without a doubt he's taken someone's life—and not only that, I understand. I look down at him again. His cock is so ready for me as I slide my hand down to skim my finger along his shaft, unable to help myself. He shudders against me and adrenaline fills my blood. I look up into his dark eyes.

"Those girls were admitted to one of our recovery clinics today. Maybe there's a chance for them to get cleaned up, or maybe not, but we have to at least try."

I don't say anything. I just reach up on my tiptoes and kiss him. Hearing his side of things makes what he does sound almost reasonable, and I can't make sense of the various shades of gray right now. I just need to feel him close to me. My fight not to give into him dies a little more with every small detail I learn about him. I can hear myself panting and I feel like I'm having an out-of-body experience.

"You drive me out of my fucking mind, Layla June." My knees go weak just imagining him inside me. He traces my cheek with his knuckle. "You take a man who's never wanted and *make* him want." His voice is a whisper. "You take a man who doesn't care, and you *make* him care."

Heat and wetness pool against the cotton of my panties with his words.

"But you *will* listen to me when I tell you to do something that's for your own safety, Layla." His tone is one I wouldn't argue with. But the danger he presents turns me on even more, and I know there is no going back for me now. I'm positively fucked. I want his danger and I want him. There's no line that divides the two.

"I was mad when you didn't show up," I say softly.

Sean looks down at me, still serious. "You've had a lifetime of people telling you what to do. I won't do that unless it's necessary, but when I do give you an order, you *will* follow it."

I *have* had a lifetime of people telling me what to do. I've only felt at home with one person before him, and now she's gone. The fear of losing him now almost crushes me. I battle with the thoughts I'm *supposed* to have versus the ones I *actually* have.

"You talk like I belong to you, but it's only been a few days," I whisper, still not believing this can be real.

Sean's eyes are ominous, his pupils blown wide, and the heat from his body along with his gaze makes me lightheaded as he brushes my hair off my face and I notice again how busted up his hand is.

His knuckles are swollen, red and angry. I'm still looking at them when he uses his hand to tilt my chin up so I'm looking at him, leaning down as if he's about to kiss me—but I stop him, bringing his wounded hand to my lips instead. I kiss the cuts there, one by one as he breathes evenly, never taking his eyes off me. Then I look up at him when I'm done, my eyes searching his.

"I don't care about your past, I want you just as you are," I tell him, reaching up to kiss his cheek, the blood from the fresh wound there lining my lips before I pull away and place my hand against his jaw.

Sean's eyes turn urgent and hungry as he realizes this is me accepting every part of the man he is, and he uses his thumb to slide his blood across my lip. Slowly he brings his hand up and swipes his first two fingers through the fresh blood still dripping down his face. I stand frozen as he paints it over each of my cheeks, then gathers more and paints it down my nose, then even more along my bottom lip. My heart beats so quickly and my breaths are so shallow that I feel like I might faint. He's marking me with his blood, and a flush creeps up my neck at this animalistic ritual.

He's intent as he leans in, analyzing his work. When he's satisfied, he turns me around to face the mirror and stands behind me.

"Look at this woman, marked by the blood of the man she belongs to." His deep voice is quiet as I stare at my reflection.

"Look at how strong she is." I look at the blood painted across my skin and realize he's claiming me.

The woman behind bars flashes through my mind again, only this time she's smiling as *he* begs to set her free from the cage she's in. Empowering her to be free. Empowering *me* to be the woman I am becoming *with* him.

Sean moves the hair that's escaped my clip off my shoulder and bends down to kiss the skin at the base of my neck.

"Time means nothing to me. Our next second could be our last. You *are* mine, Layla. I've never been so sure of anything," he whispers, spinning me to face him and pulling me so close that I gasp when he presses against me. I dart my tongue out over my bottom lip, and when I taste his blood, the sadistic part of my brain rejoices and my pussy throbs.

"You think I'm strong, but I'm not strong, Sean . . . I'm weak." I'm silently begging for his lips on mine but he doesn't give me them. Instead, he backs up and turns the water on in the shower, but then he's in front of me in seconds, trailing his finger over my cheek.

"We might be weak for each other, but together we're strong," he growls, as I close my eyes and tug him closer, shedding the remaining pieces of my former self. "We're unstoppable." He kisses my cheek. "Unshakable." He kisses the other. "Infinite."

The last word is barely out of his mouth before his lips come crashing down onto mine. My heart pounds in my chest as his kiss consumes me. Sean holds me so tight that it's almost hard to breathe. He groans as his lips part mine and he forces his tongue into my mouth, pulsing and frenzied. Sean Hunter kisses exactly how he *is*. Wild, yet so calculated. My arms wrap around his neck and I push into him, moaning into his lips. Everything feels so surreal as his hands knead every part of me they can reach, and he kisses me in that demanding way. Licking, sucking, nipping at me, sending little sparks through my blood and driving me to the brink of insanity with every soft, deliberate pulse of his tongue meeting mine.

Sean leans deeper into my lips as I eagerly kiss him back. He unclips my hair and lets it fall down around my shoulders. The kiss is only broken for a fraction of a second, just long enough for him to pull my shirt up over my head and toss it to the floor, then he's unclasping my bra with one hand and adding it to the pile as steam begins to fill the bathroom.

He backs up slightly and his gaze ravages my topless body like he can't get enough. I can't help myself—my eyes move down and I cautiously run my fingers along the side of his solid cock, then look back up at him. Sean reaches down and takes my hand in his own, wrapping it tighter around his cock as precome leaks from the tip.

"*Fuuuuck,*" he breathes out, and then his lips are back on mine and my naked chest is pressed against his as his hands move over me the way mine move over him. I rock my hips into him, removing my hand from his cock to allow us to meld together, searching for the sweet friction I so desperately need. Anything to soothe the savage ache between my thighs, the need for him that I haven't been able to shake since the moment I first saw him. Both his hands come up to frame my face, and he anchors me with the lust and fire in his emerald eyes.

"You're so fucking beautiful." Sean's voice is deep and gruff as he backs up to look at me, and his eyes are feral. I lean in, nipping at his full bottom lip, biting hard enough to hurt him.

"Stay . . . I . . . wasn't done kissing you yet," I whisper to him playfully, which pulls a deep growl from him that feels very much like a reward to me.

The release of being completely myself is freeing. Sean gives me what I want. He lets me kiss him for so long I don't even know what time is anymore.

Still kissing me, he unbuttons my jeans with one hand and

pulls them from my body along with my panties. Our naked flesh pressed together is as close to ecstasy as I've ever felt. When he finally breaks the kiss, I'm breathless and boneless, and then his hands slide down my ass and I'm being lifted, my legs wrapping around his waist as he walks us into the shower. His strength is evident as he pins me against the shower wall, the hot water rushing over us. "Layla," he chants as he kisses me, sliding his finger down to sweep over my clit. "I can't wait to taste this soaking cunt."

I tip my head back and moan, then focus on his eyes again, knowing exactly how to get what I want. To command him just a little bit stops the thinking side of his brain from taking over, the side that always has to be in control, and *that* is where he seems to find his release.

"No, Sean," I draw his name out in a whisper. "It's *my* turn."

CHAPTER THIRTY-ONE
Sean

Layla removes herself from my grasp, clearly with her own agenda as she slides her hands down my chest and drops to sit on the shower seat behind her, looking up at me with those big siren eyes and my blood on her face.

Just the feel of her hand wrapping around my cock as she takes control makes my eyes roll back, for fuck's sake. Everything about this woman drives me crazy. I skate my thumb over her bottom lip as I look down at her, wanting everything she's willing to give me. I commit this to memory—her pretty face stained red with me. I'll fucking remember it for the rest of my days.

"Open up for me then, little dove. Show me where you want my cock."

She taps her lips. "Here," she breathes out, leaning in to swirl her tongue over the crown of my dick. Her long copper hair is a wild tangle around her shoulders and her pretty pink nipples are on display. All I want to do is bury myself so deep in that sweet fucking pussy I can't stop thinking about. But first I need to stuff my cock down her throat to take the edge off or I won't last five minutes in her tight wet cunt. It's been too long, and she's tortured me too much.

Water hits her lashes as she looks up at me, a wicked gleam in her eyes.

I fucking love being right. I knew this woman was made for me. I graze my hand over her wet hair as she tastes me, slowly at first. Then her eyes turn from curious to desperate as fuck in a heartbeat as I stroke her cheek with my thumb, washing my blood from her face. I'm aching against her lips. I finish washing away the red from her skin and move my thumb down to her bottom lip, popping her mouth open before reaching to the back of her head and collecting her hair in my fist, pushing her toward my cock. I watch in awe as she takes me fully into her mouth, and I slide into her throat with ease, pressed against her tongue, and groan.

Motherfucking perfect.

She gags when I hit the back of her throat, and I slowly pull out while I look down at her.

"Suck," I order, and she smiles with sass and fucking nips at me.

I hiss and shake my head no, reaching down to pinch her nipple hard in response. She whimpers as if the pain fuels her, then she takes over, wrapping her fingers around the base of my cock. Covering me with her lips again, Layla takes me deep a second time and moans around me. I watch as she clenches her thighs together on the seat.

"*Fuck*," I breathe out. "You like tormenting me? It makes you wet to show me how well you can take my fat cock?" I love the feel of her tongue against me, sliding along the underside of my shaft. The sass in her eyes holds my attention as I tangle my hand in her hair again, holding her exactly where I want.

"You look so pretty like this, Layla . . . fucking beautiful," I murmur.

184

She shivers at my praise.

"Yeah, you love being my filthy fucking girl, don't you?" She nods with her big doe eyes looking up at me and my cock in her mouth and my knees weaken at the sight. I set the pace for her and cover her hand with mine at the base of my cock. "That's it . . ." I'm lost in the feel of her.

She moans around my length again as I push deeper. She has no idea how good she feels. *Un-fucking-real.*

She trades between swallowing me down and teasing me with small licks and whimpers that tell me she's as desperate to come as I am.

I slide out of her mouth almost all the way, and Layla's tongue glides over me before she takes me as deep as she can. Her eyes are full of fire, water glistening on her long lashes, mascara running down her cheeks. She's fucking perfect.

"Fuck, I wish you could see what I see right now, how well this pretty mouth takes my thick cock."

But I need more, it's not enough. I've never wanted more with any woman, but with her, I just can't get close enough. I need to taste her, to come with her, and I don't have the room to do that in this shower. I kill the water, lift her from her seat, and her legs wrap around my waist as I step out of the shower. A cool rush of air surrounds us and she gasps. Water drips everywhere while we move the short distance to her room, and I kiss her deeply all the way. I sit on the bed with her on top of me, and groan as my cock slides through her slit. She moans and lets her head fall back.

"Come here," I whisper. I don't know what the fuck is wrong with me, but I don't want to fuck her yet; I want to savor every single second of this first time with her.

She looks at me questioningly as I grip her hips and guide her movements so I can devour her while she swallows my cock.

"No, here." I tap my lips. "Come sit on my face, Layla."

She bites her lower lip but listens right away, moving up to straddle my face. I grip her ass and spread her wide, her dripping cunt hovering over my tongue.

"Get back to work now. Suck my dick while I feast."

Layla pants, leaning forward and moving her hand down my shaft, chasing it with her mouth. Heat washes over me as she swallows my cock.

I lose it and thrust upward into her throat, and she gags around me.

"Just like that. Good fucking girl . . ."

She lifts up then moves her mouth back down before I can even get another word out. The tip of my cock hits the back of her throat, and I groan as I spread her legs wider. Her swollen pussy is dripping as I lay a tight little smack to her clit and she moans, sucking me deeper.

I don't deny myself any longer; my tongue flicks against her clit. Her back arches and I fucking love it. I give her another slap, then suck her clit into my mouth just to torture her.

"Christ, you have the prettiest fucking pussy," I tell her, sliding my finger through her as she keeps on sucking. She tries to clench her thighs together and I know I'm driving her crazy. I fucking love it. I give in then, devouring her.

"More," she moans, then swallows my cock again, but she's hesitating to put her weight fully on my face.

"I'll give you what you want, little dove, but first you have to *sit*." I grip her tight and pull her down forcefully until the weight of her is resting on my tongue as I slide the flat of it through her slit. "Stay right here." I lap her up again. *Fuck me*. She's the sweetest fucking thing I've ever tasted.

Layla moans as her drool leaks down my shaft and she turns wild, grinding her pussy down into my face. She sucks while I eat, and her nails dig into my thighs as my palms grip her hips and hold her pussy tight to my face, my tongue buried inside her.

The fucking sweetest. My cock slides out of her mouth and she cries out against me as she prepares to come. Her body shakes and I suction my lips around her clit and suck, hard. Her palm slaps my thigh and she rears up, pressing her pussy down into my face, riding my tongue—and my cock throbs, jealous.

"Holy fuck . . ." she cries out frantically.

I stop.

"I didn't tell you to stop sucking, Layla," I growl and she obeys, leaning back down to continue swallowing my aching cock. "I'm gonna . . . come!" she cries around me. I grip her tighter.

"We're gonna come *together*," I order, sucking her clit again. We continue like this, writhing together as I fuck her throat and she rides my face.

Within seconds, her legs shake as I push her over the edge, and my balls tighten.

"I'm gonna paint your throat with my come now, and you're gonna swallow every fucking drop," I say.

"Please . . ." she begs, and it does me in. Using the one firing brain cell I have left, I devour her pretty pussy as she pumps my cock with her hand once, twice, before sucking me hard into her mouth as I erupt down her throat, still sucking on her clit, groaning into her as she soaks my face. It's as passionate as it is downright fucking dirty.

Layla chokes and sputters around my cock for a few seconds as she struggles to swallow everything I've given her. Her lips make a popping sound as they slide off my dick and I lay a kiss on her clit as we catch our breath. Then she shudders, climbs off me and spins around, crawling right up into my arms, still soaking wet from the shower.

"I've never . . ." she sighs. "I've never felt anything like that." She looks up at me, the smile on her lips growing, and I love being the only man who gives her these experiences.

I swipe her half-dried hair from her face.

"Fuck, I've never wanted to wait," I tell her, hoping she understands. For the first time in my life, the want I feel for a woman hasn't disappeared after I've come. With Layla it's only grown, and I want to draw it out.

Her lips are swollen and pink, and just the look of her like this is making me want to bury myself in her and never come up for air. My dick starts to harden again with just the thought.

Layla reaches up and brushes her fingers across my cheek, then rubs her finger and thumb together, coated in my blood. The vision of her painted in my blood makes my dick twitch even more and I'm not even sorry about it.

"Well, that's good, because you're going to have to wait while you let me fix that. You're bleeding everywhere," she says with a smile.

I raise my eyebrow at her.

"What? You can tell me what to do but I can't tell you?" she asks. Standing up, she pulls her robe off the back of the door. "I have wound tape. We'll tape it. That's almost as good as stitches. So, *stay here.*" I wait while she disappears to the bathroom for a second and comes back with a first aid kit. Fuck if I know why, but I listen to her.

I'm sitting, still hard and ready for her, on the edge of the bed when she comes back.

She's quiet as she stands between my legs and dabs the blood from my face with a damp piece of gauze, but her lips turn up in a small grin. It grows bigger as she begins taping my gash, tilting my head so she can work.

"What's funny?" I ask as she tears open a butterfly bandage.

"Nothing. Just um . . . your prospect is still on my porch, probably sweating his ass off."

"*Fuck.*" I laugh with her, shocked at myself that I lost so much time and space, something I just don't do, but with her, it's like I don't give a fuck. I had totally forgotten Boyd was even here, and it has to be a hundred degrees out there in the late afternoon sun.

"A few more minutes won't kill him. He's a prospect, it's good for him to sweat."

Layla works carefully, telling me about the areas she's planning to work on with my back next as she gently squeezes my wound closed and tapes me up, and I listen. I also listen to her tell me what new kind of torture she's going to put me through later. Apparently, we're going to start doing yoga since I missed my massage.

I hear my phone start to ring from the bathroom counter but I ignore it. I just want a few more minutes like this before I have to shower and take her to the club. I've never wanted to listen to a woman ramble before, or have someone to talk to at the end of the day, but hell, right now I'm pretty convinced that's just because I hadn't found *her* to listen to yet.

CHAPTER THIRTY-TWO
Sean

FRANKIE

> I've called you three times. I have what you wanted.

> And you have to owe me something for this. This is something they would shit-can me for. I've been sitting at Lush for almost an hour. Kai said you guys were coming.

I sigh, opening Kai's text, the one telling me we're going to Lush. I send him a quick message before I answer Frankie.

> Calm your tits. I'll be there in thirty minutes.

Fucking cops. Having the deputy sheriff on our payroll is useful but he was calling and texting me incessantly while Layla was taping me up, though I'm glad to hear he's got the police sketch I've been waiting for. Seeing Layla's haunted face when she spoke about her mother forced me to move a little quicker in locating this piece of shit that killed her parents. The police haven't gotten anywhere, but they're gonna have to answer to me and my club. I won't rest until I have my hands on him. I see the look in Layla's eyes when she talks about her mother. It's the way I feel when I think about my father, like a small piece of me is gone. At least I had my club and my mother when I lost him. Layla had no one, and was learning all the secrets about her father that a girl should never have to know. From the sounds of it, her brother doesn't bother with her much. In fact, I wouldn't say this to her but he kind of sounds like a pompous prick.

"You can go back to the club, I'm heading to Lush," I tell Boyd. He's all red and sweaty standing in Layla's kitchen now. Over an hour on the porch with the direct sun beating down on him crisped him up. I give him a tap on his beet red arm just to fuck with him.

"Sounds good." He winces just as Layla comes down the hall in a simple black sundress.

"I called Amber, she took my shift. I'm going to take hers next—"

I don't even let her get the words out. I can't fucking help myself. I wrap my arms around her and kiss her while Boyd mutters *fucking hell* and heads back out to the porch.

"Christ, I want to bend you over right fucking here. That fucking *dress*." I smack her ass, maybe a little too hard, because it echoes and Layla swats me   worried that Boyd will hear, I'm sure—but I don't miss the way her breath hitched at first and now I'm fucking addicted to that sound. I'm addicted to her and my body is at my limit waiting to fully make her mine.

For the first time I can remember, I have a desire to blow off my responsibilities. To strip every bit of clothing from us both and just live inside of her for days. My phone buzzes in my pocket again, pulling me back to reality.

"Where are we going?" Layla asks as I text Kai back quickly and tell him to meet me on the outskirts of town so we can ride to Lakeside together. I know she'll be safe with me and I don't want to leave her behind. I also know there won't be any K6ers looking for us in a Disciples club out of town. I look down at her, already knowing the answer, but I ask anyway.

"Ever been to a strip club?"

Another text comes through from a paranoid Frankie during the ride between Layla's and Lush. The smell of smoke hangs in the air, mixed with cheap perfume, as Layla and I make our way into the old restored warehouse. It's plain black brick from the outside with a pink sign above the door. It's packed tonight, and a soft neon glow lights the large open room. A stage reaches from one end to the other, curving out into the space. There are stools around it, and tables litter the floor with comfortable leather chairs flanking them. Layla's eyes are wide as sultry music plays, and she takes it all in with open curiosity. Three girls dance at their respective places on the stage, all of them in various forms of undress.

I look down at Layla and wonder what exactly is going through her head, wishing I could climb inside for even a second, because if I didn't know any better, I'd think this place was almost turning her on.

There are two low-ranking Disciples members at the bar—guard dogs. One of them I actually know, so I tell him we're just here to give Layla an adventure. He chuckles as he looks her over appreciatively, and it takes everything in me not to punch his teeth in, but Kai steps in and puts his arm around me.

"Easy, Lover Boy. Another time." He pats my shoulder with

a huge grin. He's in his fucking element. "I'll find Trina and Ellie. We'll make it quick."

I grunt at him as he chuckles.

I haven't been in the club for more than two fucking seconds before Frankie's in front of me. I feel Layla stiffen the moment she sees our deputy sheriff. He looks at her for a moment before his face softens.

"Miss Monroe," he greets her. It hits me then *why* he knows Layla, and my stone-cold heart sinks in my chest for her. As deputy he was probably the one who had to come and tell her about her parents. I wonder if she's seen him since.

I grip her hand tighter, feeling her body relax a little. "Deputy Steadman." She offers him a curt smile as Kai squeezes Layla's shoulder with a smile. Always Mr. Right Place At The Right Time, I'll give him that.

"Come on, pretty girl, let's get us a drink and a place to sit."

Layla smiles, excitement in her eyes. Christ, she's gorgeous.

"Sure." She looks up at me.

"Go ahead. I'll come find you when I'm done." I kiss her lightly and then watch as she and Kai head to the bar. I know she's safe with him.

I look back at Frankie. I see the questions he won't dare ask: about why I'm looking for this information, and what I'm going to do with it.

"Don't ever fucking cut me off at the door like that again," I bite out the second Layla is out of earshot. I nod toward a dark corner and he follows me. "When I'm ready to talk to you, I'll find *you*," I reiterate.

"Sorry. Fuck." He rubs a hand across his jaw. "It makes me nervous to be here meeting you, man."

"Relax. This isn't even your jurisdiction. You got what I need?" I ask, straight to the point. Frankie reaches into his jacket pocket. He's off duty and in civilian clothes but I can see why he'd be nervous waiting around here. Even in civvies he can never know if he's gonna run into someone that he arrested from the next county over.

He pulls out a folded piece of paper and presses it into my palm. I don't look down at it yet. "Christ. Paper? What is this, 1999?"

"You know I can't leave a digital trail, Ax." He fills me in on what he found in the file.

"They think Layla's mother was an afterthought. Security cameras didn't work but the clerk who survived said it didn't seem like the gunman wanted to kill her . . ."

We talk for a few more minutes about everything else he thinks might be related to the case, but as another group of men pass by us to head to the restrooms, I can tell Frankie is antsy as fuck about being here.

I clap him on the shoulder.

"Okay, get the fuck outta here before you have an aneurysm."

He nods and scurries through the crowd faster than I can even get the words out. There's no one around me now, so I turn and pull out the sketch. I've never seen this man. He's maybe late forties, has a beard and black hair. He's got a wide jaw and deep-set eyes, looks solid. But the most standout feature is the tattoo of a joker playing card on the side of his neck. I memorize every feature on this prick's face, then I stuff the paper in my cut and head over to find Kai and Layla.

My eyes search the heavy crowd for my girl. There are probably a hundred people in here but my eyes land on Layla right away. She's sipping on a margarita, watching the dancer in front of her with fascination. Kai turns and gives me a double thumbs up with a grin. I shake my head and turn to the bar to grab a drink, watching her some more while I wait. There's a smile on her pretty face and her copper waves trail down the curve of her shoulders. She lifts the heavy curtain of her thick fiery hair off her back because it's hot as fuck in here, and as if she can feel my eyes on her, she turns to look at me over her shoulder. Her cheeks are flushed and she's got a glow about her under the pink neon lights.

All I want to do is hike that fucking dress up over those luscious hips and slam into her right in the middle of the bar—

"Hey Ax." I'm pulled from the vision of fucking Layla by a blonde I've seen around the clubhouse before.

"Trina." She offers her name, even though I didn't ask for it.

"Hey," I say, looking back over at Layla. She's watching me intently right now but it's obvious she's trying to pretend that she isn't.

"Um . . . I just wanted to let you know, that if you have some time, I have some time." Trina shrugs and looks up at me with a seductive smile on her face. That smile might have worked for me in another life. I know she has a reputation, and I might be the only one who hasn't "spent some time" with her.

I lean down so she can hear me a little better, just so I'm nice and clear.

"Did you see me come here with a woman?" I ask.

"Yeah." She eyes Layla up over my shoulder. "But you're not with her now, and I don't see a property cut or a ring. I've been thinking about you for a while. It could be hot?" she adds with a smile, reaching out to touch my arm. I remove her hand. "I thought maybe you were done with her—or you can bring her, that's cool too."

I wouldn't give this woman a second glance, but I don't even get the chance to tell her that myself because Layla is already stalking toward us with Kai scrambling to catch up. I have to admit, I find it highly amusing to see the look that she has in her eyes right now, one that I haven't seen before.

Jealousy.

CHAPTER THIRTY-THREE
Layla

The funny thing about pretending . . . if you pretend long enough, you forget why you were pretending in the first place.

I hate that he's right. But what I hate even more is that I immediately recognize the woman at the bar hitting on Sean, and I don't like it. It's the woman with the blonde bob I saw outside the clubhouse. The one who looked me up and down like I didn't belong there, and she's standing with Sean now, placing her hand on his arm and looking right at me, as if to taunt me. Now I know why she looked at me the way she did. She wants him for herself.

I've seen the way women look at him, but for some reason this one just got under my skin. The way she dismissed me *and* underestimated me makes me want to walk right up to where they're standing and kiss him. Lay claim to him right in front of her. It's unhealthy maybe, but unavoidable, and I'm already moving.

My back is damp with sweat after sitting in the crowd with Kai watching that woman bravely bare all, full of confidence, blowing kisses to the crowd. I admired her boldness and even respect it. I never expected to feel that way while visiting a strip club for the first time. I was having fun, but now I'm ready to show this woman that Sean Hunter is off limits.

I can't hear what they're saying to each other but she gives me that up-and-down look again as I approach, like I don't belong here with Sean. I swear she mouths the word *bitch* to me with an evil little glint in her eyes. It's apparent that if I'm with him, I'm going to need to thicken my skin a little, because some of the women who hang around the club just seem ruthless, mean and out for themselves. And this one is for sure.

I close the space between Sean and me, my eyes never leaving hers as I slide my hands around his waist, on a mission. I've never felt jealousy like this before and I don't like it. *What the hell is happening to me?*

"If you change your mind, Sean . . ." Her voice trails off.

"I won't." He doesn't even look at her, and I'll admit that his dismissal of her satisfies me a little.

"Trina!" Kai says on my heels, looking back at us as he locks arms with her. "I've been looking for you . . ."

"Finished working?" I ask Sean, nodding toward her.

"That's not work," he says, kissing me deeply. "She's a pain in the ass, always at the club. Most of those women just want to be someone's ol' lady. *Anyone's* ol' lady."

"And I'm the new girl who walked in out of nowhere, so they're all going to hate me?"

"Something like that," he says honestly, tightening his grip on me as sultry music plays through the club. The beat pulsates through me as the margarita I just downed warms my blood. "But none of those women matter. In case it isn't clear, I'm only looking at you, little dove."

His words wash over me and my chest tightens as Sean chuckles into my ear, letting his hands roam my hips.

"Trina has hooked up with nearly everyone in our club. She's not worth your time to worry about."

"Mmmm, I'm not worried, as long as she hasn't hooked up with *you*?" I ask, alcohol making me a little more vocal than I normally would be.

"Never, but I don't hate that my girl is jealous," he says low against my skin.

"I'm . . . not jealous," I manage to breathe out, but it sounds more like a moan because my hips just filled his palms as he squeezed them tight and his lips are trailing the length of my throat.

"I think you're a little liar. I think the thought of my hands on any other woman here is enough to make you crazy. And you know what?" He trails the pads of his fingers up my outer thigh to the hem of my dress, and oddly enough I don't even care if anyone sees him touch me. In fact, I think it makes his actions hotter as his lips come down over mine.

"What?" I ask as he pulls my bottom lip between his teeth.

"You being jealous is one step closer to you being mine." The depths of his vibrant green eyes shimmer with amusement. "Because I'm fucking crazy about you, Layla." The pad of his middle finger brushes over my nipple through my dress. "And I like that even though you won't admit it yet, you feel the same way for me."

His words, mixed with the idea of anyone, but especially Trina, watching us right now, are firing little cherry bombs through my blood. I pull back and look up at him, losing myself in his eyes and the way they fill with need as he looks down at me.

"I want you to fuck me, *here*. Right now," I whisper, pushing against his strong hard body, sliding my hands down to the top of his ass and gripping him tight against me. "*Please* . . . Sean," I whisper, begging him just the way he told me I would.

His response is a low growl in my ear, and before I know it, I'm moving with him down a dark hallway off the strip club floor.

CHAPTER THIRTY-FOUR
Layla

"*Fuck*, woman," Sean groans as he pushes me into the closest ladies' room in the club. There are black sconces on the wall giving out a soft light and music from the club is being pumped into the room. It doesn't look the way I'd imagined a strip club bathroom should look. Everything is a light marble, and a wide counter with two sinks sits at the far end. It's more like a high-end hotel in here, and impressively clean. Sean moves to lock the heavy wooden door behind us, but I shake my head and reach my hand out to stop him.

"*No.* Leave it unlocked," I say, looking up at him breathlessly.

He doesn't hesitate as he slides his hands down my thighs and lifts me, moving us toward the marble countertop. Then he sets me down and pulls the top of my black dress down, freeing my aching breasts.

His thumb and forefinger pinch my nipple in a tight roll and I squeeze my legs around his waist with a moan.

"You like the idea of being caught?" he asks, pinching me again, so hard that I whimper, before he bends down to flick his tongue over my nipple.

"Yes . . ." I admit. My God it feels good to say what I want without the fear of being judged.

"Mmmm . . ." he hums against my nipple. "I can't wait to fucking ruin this cage you've been living in." His whisper is so lust-filled it makes me feel empowered.

"Ruin it . . . ruin me. *Please*," I beg him as his lips come down on mine.

Sean slides me back so my head rests against the mirror, then he flips my dress up over my hips.

"My fucking filthy girl," he mutters as he sees I'm not wearing panties under my knee-length dress. "Heels up on the counter. Show me how soaked this tight little cunt is already," he demands as he backs up, watching me, and I've never felt so alive. The want I see reflecting back at me is almost too much to bear as Sean unbuckles his jeans and frees his solid cock.

I let my head fall back against the mirror and do what he says, letting my legs fall open, wide open, baring myself to him. His eyes grow wild, like he can't take it any more than I can. I watch as he spits into his palm and begins to stroke himself. The raw masculinity of his big inked hand handling his own cock is such a fucking turn-on, my mouth waters at the sight.

He pushes my legs open even wider and I lose what little inhibition I had left, giving him a show as I toy with my legs, closing them slightly, then opening them more. He sucks in a breath as he slides his first finger through my wetness and then brings it up, pushing it into my mouth. I hollow my cheeks around his finger and suck, eyeing him through my lashes as I flick my tongue against him like I would his cock. Something foreign and raw is waking in me. Something unstoppable. A dark need I've never understood. But with him, I'm able to be completely me.

"Let *me* spit on your cock Sean . . ." I tell him.

The sound he offers and the look he gives me tells me I could get anything I want from him right now, and it's so freeing to admit that I can't fucking wait.

He slides his thumb over the space just below the crown of his dick "Right here," he commands. I lean forward and spit as Sean's head falls back, and he strokes himself once, then twice, to coat himself in me.

He angles my face up to look at him. "Your eyes stay here while I fuck you," he commands, as he pulls me to him with one arm around my waist and lines up the head of his cock with my soaking pussy. "Later, I'll take my time with you, Layla. I'll fucking worship you the way you deserve, over and over . . ."

He slowly sinks that first inch inside of me and my eyes nearly roll back in my head. There's no friction, but he's so big that I stretch around him.

"But right now, I'm going to *fuck* you. I'm going to *use* you. I'm going to make you my own personal little cumslut, the way your eyes have fucking begged me to since the moment I first saw you."

"Yes . . ." I moan, pulling him closer. I'm frantic, aching, fucking desperate, like I'll never get enough. And knowing anyone could come in, knowing he's right here with me, it's everything.

"I'm not on the pill . . ." I whisper as an afterthought, because he's moving again, already starting to fill me, and I'm already lost to him. My head falls back as I clench around him.

"*Christ*," he breathes out, tipping his forehead to mine. "I know you're not, and I don't give a fuck." He's not gentle as he forces his way in, but I want it. He turns me on the counter just enough that my back is pressed against the wall.

"Deep breath," he orders as he pulls out slightly and then thrusts back in without any hesitation. We both groan as he buries himself deep and I grip his cut tight, wrapping my legs around him, already begging for more.

"This cunt . . . so fucking *tight*." Sean slides all the way out and slams back in again, sucking in a breath when he's filled me to the hilt. "So fucking greedy when it's treated right . . ."

One hand grips my ass as he finds his pace, and he makes good on his word—he isn't slow and he isn't gentle, he just fucks me in the most unhinged way, like he has no control. And watching the man who never loses control snap is such a beautiful thing.

"You're fucking *killing* me," he groans as his fingers grip the flesh of my hips while he struggles to hold it together, moving at a pace I can't keep up with, but I want it. I want to see marks tomorrow where his hands are.

"You love this, don't you? Laid bare, stuffed full of my cock, in a place anyone could walk in and see . . . so fucking naughty, Layla."

"Sean!" I cry out his name, unable to hold back.

"*Fuuuck*," he grunts deeply, taking his bottom lip between his teeth. At this pace, I feel like I might see stars or pass out before he's done. My back hits the wall, over and over. Fast and hard, Sean fucks me, hitting a place inside me every time that has my cunt tightening around his thick cock.

My eyes fly open at the sound of the door, but Sean doesn't stop or even seem to notice as a woman catches my eye over his shoulder.

Trina.

She stands in shock, her eyes wide, and her mouth falls slack as she takes in the scene before her. My heels hanging off my feet, legs wrapped around his waist, Sean holding me up. His jeans are just low enough to allow him to fuck into me viciously, as he groans lusty and deep with the way my pussy clenches around him. I don't take my eyes off hers as I whisper in his ear.

"Say my name, Sean," I coax, tightening my hold on him as he bounces me on his cock. Trina's hands fly to her mouth. I should be embarrassed. I've been taught sex is a private thing only for one man and one woman, and in another life I'd be appalled. But here with Sean? I lean into it.

"Layla," he growls as he fucks me. I throw one last smirk at Trina, before my eyes flutter closed as she scurries out of the bathroom to the sound of my moans. Her catching us sends me into a sort of tailspin. As Sean moves faster, he weaves one hand into my hair as he holds me with the other, tugging it hard. He takes my bottom lip between his teeth, and I whimper as my pussy clamps down around him and I rake my nails down his back under his shirt, hard enough to hurt him. He loves it. I know he wants more as he offers me pain in return, pulling my hair so hard I cry out.

My legs start to shake as an earth-shattering orgasm begins to take hold. I've never felt so high.

"Soak my cock now, Layla," Sean orders. "I want to feel this messy little cunt dripping all over me as you fall apart."

"Sean!" I cry out.

"That's fucking right. *Scream* my fucking name. Let everyone in this fucking place know who owns you," Sean says, slamming into me once more. I feel him growing even harder inside me.

"You, Sean," I tell him as I come undone. "You do."

"*Fuck,* Layla . . ." *Thrust.*

"My filthy . . ." *Thrust.*

"Fucking . . ." *Thrust.*

"Girl." Then Sean growls my name as he comes undone and his hand circles my throat, squeezing tight. Warmth spreads through my body as he spills into me. His brilliant green eyes focus on mine, then drift to where his hand is wrapped around my throat.

"All dressed up for me . . . *mine,*" he whispers.

A dull buzzing fills my head as I start to come down while his cock jerks. The whole thing took less than ten minutes but I've never been so spent.

The only sound is music and our breathing, and I know I'm completely ruined. I'll never want anyone the way I want him. All of him. I want hours and hours of him just like this, buried deep inside me.

Sean backs up and pulls out of me, sweeping his fingers up my inner thigh to push his come back into my pussy as he kisses me gently.

"All of me stays *here*. I want to still be leaking out of you later when I come back for more."

My pussy throbs, already tender from the way he just took me, but the idea of him again has me wanting more.

"You liked that she saw?" he assesses.

I narrow my eyes at him. "How did you know it was her?"

"Her fucking perfume. Chick wears way too much of it."

I start to laugh.

"You didn't answer my question," he notes, pushing back in with his still-hard dick. I whimper.

"Yes, I liked it," I whisper softly.

Sean chuckles. "That's my girl. There's nothing you can't admit to me. Never be ashamed to tell me what you want or need." He kisses my nose. "It'll be our secret."

CHAPTER THIRTY-FIVE
Sean

"Sean!" *Her big brown eyes flutter closed and her plush mouth pops open as she cries my name. The sound of pure peace as her tits bounce against me while I fuck into her perfect, tight, wet cunt.*

"I know him. He's from Lakeside, and I've seen him in Perrytown," Kai says, cutting into my memory of fucking Layla two hours ago. I can't stop thinking about her. My body is begging for her even more now that I've had her. We're back at the clubhouse after waiting for Kai to leave Lush. He came wandering out of a VIP room a half hour after Layla and I made it back to the floor, but he says it was worth it to get some good intel on Gator. And if I know him, probably to get his dick wet.

Jake and I sit across from him now at a desk as he cross-references the Baylor County police database on a second monitor.

"Yeah, that's what I thought. Their crew is involved with the casino there," I note. I've seen them in passing before.

"Part of the Wretched Souls MC." Kai's eyes move rapidly as he waits for the match in the database.

"Gotcha, fucker." He grins. "Alexander Ramos." Kai turns

the monitor to me and Jake to show us old mugshot photos from Lakeside, the town a few counties over.

"His tats are covered by the collar." Kai points to his neck.

"Looks like it," Jake adds from the other side of the desk.

"Now all we need to know is why the fuck a patched member of Wretched Souls is gunning down churchgoers in an Atlanta suburb."

I nod, looking from the grainy photo to the mugshot to the sketch. It's definitely him.

"You're right. It just doesn't make sense—their crew doesn't usually head up that way." I scrub my jaw, trying to put it together.

Kai shuts off the computer, stands and lights a smoke. He takes a long inhale. "We're close. We'll find him." He looks over at Jake then back to me. "We can get Mason in on the hunt. It'll give him something to focus on besides Nic."

I nod at him. "Good man. And speaking of Mase, what did you get tonight?" I switch gears.

"Besides your dick sucked," Jake chuckles, leaning back in his chair.

"Christ," I mutter. "Spare us."

"I don't kiss and tell." Kai grins on an exhale. "But the chick I talked to, she's worked at both Lush and Lavish, and she hasn't seen Gator. Not once in months, so that's a red flag in itself. She said he used to be there almost nightly."

"And I talked to Jesse." Jake mentions the leader of the Savannah K6ers. "We're good with them. Those guys we took out were stealing from their own crew. When I told him what we found in the house, he realized they were shorting them on the girls' percentages and what they were selling. He said we did him a favor. He fucking shook my hand and thanked me." Jake starts to laugh.

I stand. "So we're good to leave tonight."

"Yeah, there won't be any retaliation, but Jesse warned us to let him know next time we're in *his* territory." Jake smirks.

I laugh. Fucking rich. "Someone needs to remind him Bleaker *is* our territory. We have an arrangement. They don't deal within five blocks of the clinics."

"Another day brother," Jake pipes up. "Just let the dust settle on this one and we'll keep an eye out."

I nod and make my way out the door to search for Layla. She's sitting with my mom at a table watching the live band, and she flinches when I kiss her neck, then I feel her body relax.

"It's been a long-as-fuck day. All I want to do is get you somewhere and get you naked, *now*," I whisper in her ear, wrapping my arms around her.

She turns her face up to me, like she has a wicked little plan running through her mind. "Maybe. But it's only eleven, and I know your back must be tight, so you, Sergeant, are mine first."

CHAPTER THIRTY-SIX

Sean

"Be serious!" Layla looks over her shoulder at me and tests my will as she reaches up overhead.

Sun salutations. At fucking midnight. I just learned that term when we got back to her house from the club and she insisted that a yoga session with her to wind down was necessary. It'll help me sleep, she said. It'll help loosen the tight muscles in my back. Except she's standing in front of me in the smallest, tightest black shorts known to man, and it's actually having the opposite effect. Then add a tiny black bra top and her hair held back off her pretty face with a satin scarf and it's making my muscles more rigid by the second as I watch her move with grace through her routine. The living room is open and she has candles lit to create what she calls "ambience."

Surprisingly, as we move through the poses I'm able to pick up most of it with little trouble, and it does actually help loosen me up. Do I do it gracefully? Hell no. But fairly easily, considering she has me doing this in just my boxers—something about letting my energy flow. I'm skeptical of how my being almost naked helps, but at this point I'd probably do whatever she told me to if it meant watching her move like this in the candlelight.

Layla takes a deep breath as we wind down our practice, arms up over her head again. I follow her, taking in the dove on her shoulder, the curve of her spine, and the bottom of the vines peeking out from her top with *Jeremiah 29:11* scrawled underneath. Even Bible verses inked into her skin are fucking sexy.

She flows through her movements, rolling forward and touching her toes, rising up then dropping back down. The two dimples on either side of her spine become more pronounced when she's folded forward and I can't help but marvel at the fucking beauty and grace of her. The contrasting sides of her that I don't think anyone other than me has ever seen. I know now that she's outwardly sassy to protect the sweet vulnerability that lives inside, the side she's afraid to share with most people. And there's a dark side that lives in her, craving a little pain, craving a little dirty. Just watching her has me desperate for my reward for being such a dutiful student.

"Stop looking at my ass and focus." She glances back over her shoulder and it tempts me even further. I can't fucking believe how everything about this woman calls to me. I can barely stand being two feet away from her.

I offer her a grunt in response but follow her through the motions one more time, raising my arms up with my hands already flexing to touch her, but I promised to be dedicated to this plan and I'm a man of my word if nothing else.

As I watch her I can almost picture my name scrawled somewhere on her unmarked skin, and my cock swells even more.

The night is dark outside her living room window. Her house sits on a hill of sorts so the street isn't visible from here, only her yard and part of her neighbor's. The windows are open and the crickets rival the sound-bath loop Layla has playing through her TV.

"Last deep breath," she says calmly. "And close your eyes on this one," she adds, her voice barely above a whisper as she falls forward again, then takes one last swoop of her arms up toward the sky.

"Nah, I don't close my eyes," I mutter.

She looks over her shoulder again, then forward with a grin. "You do when you sleep."

"Of course, but I don't really sleep. Only with my gun under my pillow in my own house, which is locked up like Fort Knox."

"Suit yourself then, keep your eyes open," Layla says, looking at me through the space between her knee and her arm. Her smirk is smug, sassy. She drops her hands to her toes one more time and the need to tear through her yoga shorts overwhelms me.

I move behind her and grip her hips forcefully, pulling her into me. She yelps and then moans as I pull her to me even harder and my cock presses into her ass.

"I wasn't through my practice." She laughs as I plant kisses down the back of her sweaty neck.

"Alright." I tip her head back and kiss her. "Let's make us both happy then, hmm? What position would be best for you to be in while I feast on your dripping cunt?"

Layla doesn't miss a beat. She pushes away from me and drops down onto her hands and knees and looks at me over her shoulder. "That's easy. Cat pose," she says sweetly.

"Fucking little brat," I snap as I get down behind her, sliding a hand up her back then through her hair to untie the scarf she's wearing. I fix the folded fabric around her eyes and tighten it like a blindfold. Her breathing increases and my cock goes instantly rock hard.

"What are you doing?"

"Teaching you a lesson," I growl as I fist the seam of those fucking shorts that have taunted me for the last hour and tear them open from the center out.

"Sean!" she cries out. "I liked those!"

"Consequences, little dove."

I lay a punishing slap to her ass cheek and she fucking moans. I know everything is heightened for her right now with her eyes covered.

"Fucking Christ," I breathe out when I look down and see my handprint on her ass. I wind my hand in her long copper hair and force her upper half down onto the soft shag rug, then I hike her ass up high as she pants. Mine for the taking in the middle of her living room. My eyes roam over her. She's so eager to please me as I twist my first two fingers into the top of her thong. I pull it upwards, making it nice and taut over her clit, and she lets out a breathy moan. She's so swollen and needy that when I pinch her between her thighs over the soft cotton I can already feel how soaked she is. The way her body moves, the little sounds she makes, those fucking eyes. All of it is enough to break even the strongest man.

I pull tighter on her thong and she rocks her hips back as I use my free hand to reach forward and pull her bra down so her tits bounce free. She's a mess like this, spread bare before me, and I wouldn't have it any other fucking way. Her pink nipples pucker and beg for my tongue, my fingers. I can't touch her in enough places at once. She's fucking glorious, ass up before me with her sweet, soaking pussy ready to devour. I stand and make my way to her fireplace, taking one of the thick candles that burns there, which smells like vanilla. I look down at her and smirk, watching her grip the carpet in anticipation. Layla's breath increases with the uncertainty of what I'm doing, but quickly turns to the low whimpers of desire that I can't get enough of when she hears me retake my place behind her with the candle in hand, the hot wax pools at the top spilling slightly over the sides.

"You know, a side effect of an overactive brain means I study way too much, and in turn, I remember every detail of what I read," I tell her as I move her thong aside and slide my middle finger through her arousal, toying with her clit as I bite back a groan at the same time as I let one drop of wax land on the center of her spine. Layla flinches in surprise, her body tensing. As I let another drop fall, she understands what it is and relaxes.

"Sean . . ." She whimpers my name with the pain and pleasure combined, and I smirk as I let another drop fall below the last.

"Almost a hundred years ago, Bodhi Singh wrote about tantra. The aim of achieving liberation by embracing desires rather than suppressing them. The need to let ourselves be sexually free. Letting our souls find their optimum sexual counterpoint." I let another drop fall, pushing my finger into her just enough to counteract the burn of the wax on her back.

"It's said that, within the soul, humans have an absolute right to satisfy their sexual instinct in the way that feels physiologically proper." Another drop lands on her as I push my finger all the way into her tight pussy.

So fucking tight. I listen to her shallow breaths as she grips the carpet tighter with each drop of hot wax.

"That the joining of two souls is to treat all such acts as sacraments, ritual. Removing one's senses is a way to heighten that act to another level entirely."

Another drop, as I slide my finger out and sweep it up to pinch her clit. This time she cries out.

"Sean!"

I can't wait any longer, freeing my rock-solid cock as I drip more wax down her spine.

"I can't . . . take it . . ." she whimpers.

"Yes, you can," I tell her, coating the head of my dick in her arousal. "See, when I take your sight, you feel everything *more.* On a deeper level. And that connects us, little dove."

My eyes nearly roll back with just the feeling of sliding through her soaking lips, and I notch myself at her entrance.

"The lesson is to slow down. Not to eat as a brute, but to

savor." I grip her hip with one hand and let a little more wax roll above the cleft of her ass, just as I sheath myself inside her pussy with one fluid thrust.

The strangled moan that comes from Layla, mixed with the bliss of burying myself deep in her cunt, is the greatest type of euphoria.

"Ahhhh, *fuck*," I groan as her walls contract around me so tight I see static.

I set the candle down on the coffee table, giving in. I grip her hips tight and stay deep inside her for a beat, almost losing my own breath as she adjusts to my size.

"In order to enable true connection, true ascension, we must use every sense to further the one true objective of our existence." I'm fucking breathless as I slide out of her. "To fuck. Without shame." I keep my eyes trained on where we've become one as she moans softly, her arms flexing as she claws at the carpet.

Fucking beautiful.

"To fuck without a sense of sin or concealment." I thrust back into her deeply. And she whimpers. I wind my hand in her hair again and pull her up, her back to my front, and kiss her deeply while I slowly fuck her.

"It's tantric. To fuck, purely for the pleasure of it and not to be afraid of doing whatever you need to achieve your high," I whisper in her ear just before I nip tiny bites down the line of her jaw.

"Fuck me, Sean," she whispers in a moan, and I'm a fucking goner.

I set a rhythmic pace, moving deeper, edging us, getting us both almost there, time and time again.

Bringing us both to the precipice then slowing, knowing when I finally let us both come it's going to shatter any orgasm she's ever felt and take hold of us both in a way neither of us has ever experienced. Because I've never fucked a woman before with any sort of feeling. I've never wanted to know the deepest parts of a woman's soul the way I want to know Layla.

"Sean . . . please, *please* let me come," she begs sometime later as her legs shake and her hips rock back into me.

"No, little dove, not yet. You're going to remember what it feels like to be properly fucked. My perfect little cock whore. My own special little toy," I groan as I feel my balls tighten and my release lick at my spine again. It must be the third or fourth time I've been ready to come since I began. I pull out of her, needing a fucking break myself.

I lie back on the rug, turning her and guiding her down to straddle me. She's still blindfolded, but inch by inch she sinks down on my cock, her hair falling over her shoulders.

"You're too big like this . . ." she whimpers.

"No I'm not, you can take it."

She sinks down a little more and shudders.

"Don't tease me, little dove, slide that messy little cunt down on my cock or I'll do it for you. Every inch."

Her nails make little crescents in my chest as she slinks down inch by fucking mind-blowing inch until I'm fully rooted in her. I still, just enough to bring us both back down, then pull the blindfold from her eyes. She focuses, her eyes desperate for me, and we're both covered in a veil of sweat with the hot and heavy air around us.

"You don't come until I tell you . . ." I warn her, desperate to come myself.

Layla is boneless above me, rocking her hips, her hands pressed to my chest, whispering her begging words as I reach between us and pinch her clit. She's wound so tightly, and every muscle is engaged as she tries to hold it together.

"Now you're ready, little dove, when you get to *this* point. When I don't even have to move to make you come."

"I can't anymore, Sean . . . I have to."

Fuck, she's dripping down the sides of my dick and I'm one shift of her hips away from unloading in her.

"Come for me then, Layla." I grip her hips and look up at her, thrusting my hips just enough to give her what she needs.

"Yes . . ." she cries. "Sean!"

"Christ, I love the way you look at me when you come, like you know I belong to you . . ." I tell her as she cries out and her pussy strangles my cock. "Atta girl . . . give us what we both want." Another thrust, another cry. "Ride me like my good girl. Let *my* cunt take every fucking drop I have to offer you."

"Holy fuck, Sean!" she cries, her full and perfect tits bouncing. She chants my name like a prayer, mixed with some form of *please, please, please* as she soaks my dick and pulls my own release from me with a force I've never felt before. This time, I have no choice—I come with her as I sit up and wrap my arms around her, thrusting deep and fast.

"Fucking Christ, *Layla. FUCK.*" A growl rips through me as I grip her so tight my knuckles whiten. I come so fucking hard, barely even moving within her. I have no idea how much time passes like this, but when I open my eyes she's looking down at me.

"Oh my God, that was . . . just . . ." she stammers, the pads of her fingers tracing my face, under my eyes, then over my cheeks. I lower us down onto the rug in the candlelight, flipping her off me, and hover over her, looking down at her beautiful breathless face. I nip at her ear.

"Life-changing . . ." I finish for her. "And that had *nothing* to do with God."

"Well, that feeling should be a religion," she mutters with a satisfied sigh. "A religion where the only members are us . . ."

I kiss her copper waves. "Now you're getting it all figured out." I chuckle, lying down beside her, sated. She crawls into my arms and my chest twists with the intense feelings of her snuggling in, but I don't think, I just pull her closer and stroke her shoulder. Layla looks up, her eyes growing serious as she watches me.

"Why don't you sleep well?" she asks, reaching up and covering my jaw with her warm hand. Looking at me with the concern of someone who's known me for years, and I'm reminded how difficult it is to make sense of this connection between us. It's almost otherworldly. As if I knew her in another life, and maybe I did. I was only drifting through time until the moment her eyes met mine, and then I became grounded. By *her*.

"Too many demons live here to sleep." I point to my head.

Layla's brows knot in concentration. "From your club life or another?"

"Both," I answer instantly. "From the life I've lived, overseas and here. It's not that I just remember what happened, I remember the sounds they made when I shot them, the look in their eyes. I fucking remember the smells, the weather . . . everything."

I expect her to push deeper, to ask me how I feel, or tell me I can get help for it. I can't get help. I've tried that. My brain is too detailed to forget. But instead Layla pulls my face to hers to kiss me, then slides out from under my arm, standing in her torn clothes as they half hang from her body.

"I'm going to shower. Some barbarian just ripped my clothes to shreds. Join me if you want to," she says, giving me the grace to keep my demons to myself. She peels her bra off on the way to the shower and tosses it to the floor. One simple action of not prying or trying to fix me and she just solidified what I already knew: Layla Monroe is it for me. She bleeds light everywhere she goes. Even into the places of me that have always been pitch black.

I stand and chase her sassy little ass down the hall, scooping her up and dropping her on her bed as she laughs. She isn't getting to that shower just yet.

CHAPTER THIRTY-SEVEN
Sean

There is really no way to describe what goes through your mind when you think you're about to die.

My life doesn't flash before my eyes. I don't see any "light." There's no time for any of that.

The blast consumes the right side of the truck, causing all of the doors to blow open. It must compromise the buckles on the left-side seatbelts, because both Wolfe and I are ejected onto the dusty barren road, I think I hit my head and then I slide. For a full seven seconds, I slide. When I'm able to open my eyes, I can see Wolfe through the clouds of dust maybe fifty feet away.

A crippling groan leaves one of us, or both of us, as I raise my head trying to see our Humvee through the haze. A small part of my brain understands that my side is torn to shit from road rash, but I can't feel it yet. Wolfe is calling something. His words echo, I can't make them out, but I see him already up and running to the truck. I force myself to try to stand.

Yup, my back is fucked.

Pain radiates down my leg and makes it feel weak as I stand. I probably shouldn't run, but it's either that or risk being shot.

There's so much adrenaline pumping through my blood that I use it and just go, patting myself down as I run to make sure I still have all my limbs. My Staff Sergeant, Keenan, is alive and seemingly okay. Blood leaks from his left arm and his forehead has a nasty gash from the glass. I can hear him on the radio as I frantically search for Buck. It's been seconds, maybe a minute, but it feels like an eternity before I hear him moaning.

Fucking Christ. His body is partly pinned under our Humvee, face down in the dirt, but I can see the bottom half of his leg and his toes are pointing toward the sky. My vision tunnels as the opening strings to that fucking Clapton song start all over again; it's on repeat. I try to comprehend how Keenan's makeshift sound system is even still working as I skid into the dust beside Buck's broken body. My shirt is sticking to my arm, soaked in blood. I ignore the pain that starts to shoot through me. I can't feel it fully yet.

I always sit right. But I chose left so I didn't have to sit behind Keenan's beefy body like a sardine and smell his rank chew on the drive. It should be me pinned under this thing with my hips rotated one hundred and eighty degrees, not Buck.

"Chhh-cchhheeseburger," Buck says, his face half in the dirt, as I lie face down, covering him with my body. There is hardly any part of him still intact. My guts churn and pain shoots through me like multiple daggers are being thrust into my back all at once.

"Cheeseburger, bud?" I say, my voice shaking with shock, but I understand him. "That's your first choice for dinner?" I whisper, talking to Buck like he isn't gonna die right here in my arms.

But he is. There's no question. He's ripped wide open and I've never actually seen a living human body this fucked up before, and after almost three full tours out here, that's saying a lot.

"Aaaand f-fries," he stutters.

"Cheeseburger and fries it is. Just gotta get you out of here first, you hang tight. Help is on the way."

"Three minutes out!" Wolfe echoes in a grunt as he assesses his own injuries.

The sound of a chopper can already be heard in the distance. I flip over onto my back and bite into my lip so hard it bleeds as my teeth chatter and the adrenaline from moments ago starts to leave my body. My arm is ripped open for sure, it's definitely broken, and I'm skinned alive with road rash.

One of the tires spins slowly above us on our upside-down vehicle. I let my head fall back to the earth, my hand still gripping Buck's shoulder, whispering to him to hang on as I look toward the clear blue sky. I might fall in and out of consciousness for a short time, I'm not sure. Ringing and the muffled sounds of the music fill my ears as I focus on a lone dove that has just landed on the truck; its wings settle and the lyrics of the song play on. The dove is calm, looking around from the top of the truck as if our world wasn't just blown to all hell. Nature versus carnage. The shade of the dove's feathers is almost the same shade as the doors of our now mutilated truck. I don't know how long I watch the bird for, and I wonder why it doesn't leave. It can simply fly away at the sight of danger. It should fly away. It should get the fuck out of this desert, but it doesn't. The dove stays, looking down on me, and I use it to keep my focus as long as I can. The chopper gets closer. Buck groans beside me, the garbled sound of certain death.

"You fuckin' stay with me, Buck," I mutter.

He groans again, and I feel my stomach lurch, knowing these are his last seconds. He'll die out here, and for what? They won't know he had a wife. A daughter he's never met. That he loves the Detroit Lions and Bud Light. They won't know that when all of us are tired he tells us the stupidest fuckin' jokes, just to keep our spirits up, until someone starts throwing shit at him to get him to stop.

Numbness spreads through my right leg and I do my best to stay awake as the song continues, and the guardian dove keeps a watchful eye.

"Stay . . . please stay," I whisper to it, fighting to hold on. Peace spreads through me just as I realize that I have no idea what my internal injuries are. I could die any time now, but I'll hold my focus for as long as I can, talking to Buck or no one and focusing on the dove as long as I can. It's not until I feel the gust from the chopper that the dove finally takes flight. I close my eyes and let the darkness swallow me as the lyrics echo around us . . .

"Sean." I blink and see her eyes just as the dove flies overhead. She's reaching for me but I can't sit up. The pain is too much.

"Sean." I feel a hand on my arm and adrenaline rushes through me as I rear up, ready to kill whoever is touching me.

"Sean!"

My eyes snap open, and hers come into view, only she's under me now, and I'm pressing my forearm against her throat. It takes me a second to realize this is here and now. I'm not in the desert. We're naked in her bed. I let her go right before I cut off her airway completely and I bend down to kiss her. My whole body trembles. I don't even know what I'm saying besides, "I'm sorry, I'm so fucking sorry," as she struggles to get her breath back.

CHAPTER THIRTY-EIGHT
Sean

"You were . . . calling my name," she rasps. Her eyes are wide with fear and she's panting. "I just tried to wake you and then you were on top of me."

She takes a deep breath as her body starts to steady. I'm shaking like I do in my dream. I'm right back in the desert; I can feel the shock taking over my body. Layla backs up on the bed, clutching her throat. I give her space, though my hands are desperate to touch her.

"If that happens again, don't try to wake me up, just get out of bed," I bite out.

Fuck. This is why I sleep alone.

"W-where'd you go just then? Was that a nightmare?" she stutters.

"Layla. You'll get out of the bed," I reiterate. "It's non-negotiable. I never want to hurt you, and when I dream like that . . . sometimes . . . I just don't have control—"

"Yes, I promise," she agrees quickly, tears glistening in her eyes in the dim room, her knees clutched to her chest.

I reach out to touch her, and she flinches. I pull my hand away.

"I'm sorry, it just scared the hell out of me," she offers. "Touch me."

I do, hesitantly grazing my knuckles over her leg before sitting up on the edge of the bed and running a hand over my head. It's been a long time since I've dreamed in that kind of detail about those moments.

"There were demons in your eyes when you opened them." Her voice is shaky and I know I owe her something, because I'm sure that scared the shit out of her. I stand and move toward the window, staring out at her sprawling backyard.

"There's more to it . . . the way I felt when I first saw you. There's a reason I know you're the one for me, and it's because of that day, the flashback I just had."

"What happened?"

"When I was on my last tour, I was part of a simple run. Move embassy staff from one city to another. It was supposed to be routine. My Staff Sergeant was with us, but my job was to protect the men in the Humvee with me. Wolfe was there, and two others." I turn and face her. "I told you we drove over an explosive device en route. It blew our Humvee to shit. Wolfe and I were on the left side, our doors blew out and we were tossed. That's how I fucked up my back and broke my arm. The glass is how I got my scars."

She nods and sits up a little more, wrapped up in the white sheets, and in the moonlight her beauty stuns me.

"Wolfe was in the best shape, but Buck, my bunkmate, he was . . . let's just say there wasn't much left of him. I lay there with him thinking he was going to die, not knowing if I was going to die too."

"But you were calling out my name . . . I don't understand," she whispers as I come closer, crawling into bed with her. I lean back on the headboard and pull her close, my breathing settling and my body finally relaxing as I stroke her shoulder and down her arm.

"My Staff Sergeant drove me fucking crazy." I smirk in the dark. "He only listened to Eric Clapton, and when we detonated, the music never stopped. It played on a loop, the same fucking song over and over until the chopper came, but it gave me something to focus on and I needed that. I figured if there was something logical in all that carnage maybe I was still alive."

"That makes sense," she whispers, kissing me on my chest.

"But I was fucking tired. I just wanted to close my eyes and let the darkness take me. That's when a dove landed on top of the Humvee. It watched me, just sitting there oblivious to all the destruction around it. That bird and that song on repeat are the most vivid parts of that memory. They're what kept me awake, kept me talking to Buck. They're what kept him alive until the chopper came for us. The thing is, the song that kept playing . . . it was 'Layla.'"

CHAPTER THIRTY-NINE
Layla

My stomach drops with his words and I find it hard to breathe. Is it possible? Of all the songs in the world, the one playing in his worst moments bears *my* name?

"It sounds crazy, I know, because I never believed in fate, Layla. It scientifically never made sense. I couldn't see it, couldn't feel it. I never believed in 'meant to be,' or destiny. I thought I made my *own* fate. But the night I met you, I had a gut feeling so strong that you were meant to be mine, and then when you turned around and I saw the dove on your shoulder, it was like . . . a reunion. Then when I heard your name, it was like my past had collided with my future."

He runs his fingers over the spot where my tattoo sits, as if he's memorized its precise location on my body. My eyes fill with tears as I listen to his truth.

Is this truly what I've read about in books? *Written in the stars*? *Love at first sight*? And why can't that exist? Why have I been fighting this? Why have I been afraid? I've seen the couples who have been together all their lives, who say they knew the moment they met that they were destined for each other. Why is the world so quick to assume something like that can't be true? And why *can't* it have happened to me?

"Everything in me slowed in those moments in the desert . . . the dove, the lyrics, they all felt like my end, but they weren't. They were a change in the direction of my compass, a new north, and everything I've done since has led me to you." He kisses my forehead and my chest twinges. "And now you know why."

I have no words to offer him. From nearly being strangled when he woke up to the intense words he's speaking now, it feels almost like a physical manifestation of what I'll always have with him. One extreme to the next, but nothing unintentional. No boundaries or secrets, just us and the truth we're meant to live. I reach up and kiss him; it's all I have to offer after being told a story like that.

Sean pulls me into his arms and kisses me for so long that it feels like a promise, solidifying what's next. There's no fighting this any longer. I have no idea what the future with him holds, but I'm in too deep now not to find out.

"Mmmm," he groans into my lips as the sky outside the windows begins to lighten. "I think I owe you a real apology for scaring you like that . . ."

I smile into his lips, my core already heating with anticipation. "You definitely do."

One strong arm flips me over onto my back so quickly that I yelp as he settles between my legs. He looks out the window at the morning sky.

"I'm going to take you somewhere today, but I think there's just enough time for you to come on my tongue before I cook us breakfast . . ."

I think I must have drifted back to sleep for at least an hour, but now I'm leaning against the kitchen doorway watching Sean, who's cooking blueberry pancakes for us. The morning sun is shining in and he's wearing his usual pair of jeans and black t-shirt.

I admire the beauty of him. He doesn't look up but I'm sure he knows I'm here. My eyes trace the hard lines of his face, the dog tags at his neck that are always there, the way his arm flexes as he grips the handle of the pan, and the way he moves, always so calculated and intentional. It might be the perfect view to wake up to. I realize he must have left to get a change of clothes and I wonder about his home. How he lives in his own space. I imagine it's tidy, organized and minimal.

He finishes cooking and shuts off the burner, covering the plate of stacked pancakes. The moment his eyes lock onto mine, I feel *it*. It's the rush I imagine you'd feel taking your first step onto a tightrope, or in the first second after you jump from a plane.

It's the rush of free falling.

There's nothing particularly special about this scene before me, but I swear I see the future in this *one* moment. I see him cooking for me like this, years from now, our children coming in and out of the room at all different ages, with Sean stealing kisses from me in the corner while our kids tell us how gross it is. I see him older, still wearing his cut as he heads out the door. Salt in the pepper of his beard. I see it all. I want it all, and I can't find one scrap of logic in that after only days of knowing him, but maybe he's right. Maybe our souls are tied.

I make my way over to where he's standing and reach up to kiss him before I grab a coffee.

He unravels the tie holding my robe closed and slides his warm hands over my waist, bending down to kiss me deeper, and I instantly break out in goosebumps. His face is almost pained when he pulls his lips from mine, like he just can't kiss me enough. Right now, I feel the same way.

I think of the phone call I overheard on the first morning he cooked me breakfast and his confession yesterday about taking a man's life, and I know I want to learn more about this man that I'm dreaming of forever with.

"Tell me more about what you do," I say, as his thumbs graze my waist.

"I work for the government." He smirks as he backs away to wipe the counter. My eyes drift to his wide shoulders, which lead to those thick arms that feel so good wrapped around me . . .

Shit, you're hopeless, Layla.

I force my eyes back to his face.

"And for the club, what do you do? I want to know more."

He side-eyes me cautiously, unsure. "These aren't secrets I share with just anybody."

"I'm ready," I promise him.

He takes a moment before answering, setting down the towel he was using before turning to face me, watching me, judging my ability to handle who he is. I wait as he pulls a knife from its sheath on his belt, holding it in his hand. "The people who know these details about me, the ones I trust . . . we're bonded by blood."

My breathing increases as I watch the blade glint in the morning sun.

"We've taken an oath," he adds, pulling me close with his free hand.

I look down to the knife then back up to his eyes. *He's actually fucking serious?*

"A-are you asking if you can cut me?" I swallow nervously as Sean brings his fingers up to slide under one side of my robe, pushing it off one shoulder, then the other, so it falls to my feet on the floor. He turns his knife so it's sideways, running it across my chest. The cool dull side of the blade instantly causes my nipples to harden as he trails it down my arm.

"No. I'm not asking you, little dove." He slides the knife back up. "If my secrets are what you want, then you're asking *me* to cut you."

The knife passes under my collarbone. I don't look down, I just feel it as it moves between my breasts, my breath a shallow pant as he trails it over my ribs to my belly, and I shudder as he pauses there.

"I protect my president from threats to him or the club. Sometimes slowly, sometimes quickly."

The knife rests on my stomach, just on the inside of my hip, and I suck in a breath when he suddenly flips it over without warning, the sharp tip against me so fast that I never even have time to think about stopping him. I don't move. I barely breathe. I just look up at him in horror as my fucked-up body starts to heat in anticipation of what he might do.

"Shall I go on?" His voice is low, and I realize he could push that knife into my flesh any time he chooses. I realize that, in his mind, the trust I'm putting in him to cut me without actually hurting me is the same trust he has in me not to share his sins. But it's the man he is that I want, and without thinking I simply nod.

"Please," I whisper, and I see his eyes heat.

My heart pounds in my ears and I feel almost dizzy as Sean presses the knife lightly into my skin. I barely feel it until he's lifting it from my stomach. It's when he's done that I look down and realize just how sharp the knife is, and I feel the slight sting as I begin to bleed from a small shallow slice. My eyes focus as I realize that the cut isn't just a cut. It's a tiny S. He's fucking carved his initial into me. He looks at the blood dripping down from my stomach to my hip then back up to my eyes, and a hunger is there that I can't explain but I understand.

It's the same hunger I feel for him as I bleed. Letting go

of my body, he places the knife in my shaky hand. The tiniest amount of blood runs along the edge. My blood. I watch as he pulls his shirt off from behind his neck; it lands on the floor and he unbuckles his jeans, quickly losing them and his boxers too, so we stand naked together in the warm morning sun in the middle of my kitchen.

Sean doesn't speak, he just moves closer, putting his hand over mine, gripping the knife to turn it again. The dull side is now pressed against his skin.

"Now you choose where to mark me," he commands, dragging the flat side down his chest, leaving a hint of my blood behind. My pussy throbs with this ritual, what I'm saying by allowing this, what I'm committing to as he lets go, his arms falling at his side and the trust lingering in his eyes.

I could kill him right here and he knows it, yet he watches me with a heated want as I give in to the oath. I find the place on his belly equivalent to mine and flip the knife over, then look up into his eyes. He reaches out and grabs my arm to stop me.

"If you cut me too deep here, we're going to have a problem. So lightly, little dove. This knife has taken fingers in a single slice."

I nod, trying to catch my breath as he kisses me. As our lips mesh together, I drag the knife down as lightly as I can then pull it back. He breaks our kiss and looks down. "*Fuck*," he mutters. My eyes grow wide as I follow his. I didn't even feel like I was cutting him, but his mark is deeper than mine; it may need stitches and he's already bleeding more than me. It runs down his center and onto his thigh.

He grabs the knife from me and tosses it down on the table before pressing his body to mine in a searing kiss. I feel the blood from him and the blood from me, sliding over our skin. Even Sean is breathless as he speaks. "Now, little dove, ask me whatever you want to know."

CHAPTER FORTY
Layla

"When someone wrongs you, do you torture them?" I ask, as he brings his lips down to my neck and kisses me there before speaking under the base of my ear, his hands sliding over me.

"If someone steals from us, I take their hands." His voice is gruff and makes me break out in goosebumps.

I don't know what it says about my morals, but God help me, I whimper with the idea of him being capable of such a violent task.

"If someone shares information about our club, or if someone is a rat, I take their tongue." I imagine the darkness in his eyes in those moments, the man he'd have to become and the certainty with which he'd strike.

I feel my wetness gathering. For all the reasons it shouldn't turn me on, it does, and Sean knows it. His hands slide over my hips, and he coats his cock in my blood and my eyes roll back.

"I will hunt down and beat any man who threatens us." His lips press to mine as his thick middle finger slides through my center, bringing my wetness and our blood up to my clit.

"T-then what?" I ask breathlessly.

"Then, if need be, I would repeatedly bring them to the point of death, until they talk. When they finally do and I no longer have a use for them, when I've gotten what I need, I watch the life drain from their eyes in a way that satisfies me." His finger slides into me, pumping slowly, in and out. It's methodical and intentional, curving into me, coaxing that tight coil of heat to grow as his thumb slides over my clit. My eyes flutter closed and I wonder just how fucked up I am, because I've never been this turned on. The sight of our blood together, becoming one, fuels me as I seek more.

"What do you mean, *in a way that satisfies you*?" I push him to tell me more.

Sean adds another finger, working faster as his lips trail up my neck, to my earlobe, sucking it into his mouth before he bites down then speaks low.

"It means that when I remember, when I look back on that kill and how I carried it out, I know there were no loose ends left untied."

"No loose ends?" I moan. "*Fuck*," I bite out, gripping his shoulders as my legs begin to shake. Sean holds me steady with his free arm around my waist as he pumps in and out of me roughly.

"It will be clean. It will be decisive, and it will be swift."

"That's . . . fucking savage," I mutter.

"That's the man I am," he whispers.

"But the cross . . . on your finger." I can barely speak. *I'm so fucking close.* "You must believe in something . . . a higher power, a judgment of some kind?"

"This cross is simply a reminder that all the sins of the men I kill are absorbed by me when they die. I bear this cross like my father before me. It's part of my truth." He kisses my lips as I rock my hips into him. "*A man who injures his countryman—as he has done, so it shall be done to him.*"

231

Listening to Sean talk about the shameless violence he's capable of while quoting the Old Testament as he fucks me with his bloody fingers is a contrast I would never have expected to drive me over the edge, but it does—almost instantly.

"An eye for an eye, little dove," he adds. "Watching them die, knowing they won't hurt me or anyone I care about ever again, brings me satisfaction."

I moan loudly as his lips come down on mine, kissing me deeply. My pussy clenches around his fingers as my orgasm begins to crest. I *want* the madness, the beast in him. I want all of him and I'm helpless to stop it.

"I'll take care of you, Layla, above anyone else, because the only place I've ever found peace is with you."

"Sean!" I cry out as I ready to come all over his fingers with his confession. The strength of this man who would protect the people he cares about without hesitation. It's so natural, so instinctive, it *makes sense*. Without warning, he lifts me up, carrying me to the kitchen table. He swipes my placemats onto the floor before depositing me there, lining his now bloody cock up with my aching core. He's so hard and leaking precome, and his eyes tell me he's about to wreck me.

"Your blood is now mine," he growls, feeding me the first inch. "And mine is now yours." He lifts his fingers, still covered in me and our blood, and pushes them into my mouth. I suck them, tasting us and copper, inching myself closer to him, desperately trying to take more of his cock, *needing him* as my pussy clenches around him. What kind of woman *wants* to hear that the man her body begs for is a ruthless killer? What kind of a woman wants him to fuck her like this as their blood coats his cock?

Me.

I am that woman. The way he lives his life goes against everything I've always been taught, but it doesn't matter. Sean

Hunter is the most honest man I've ever met, and he wants me for exactly who I am, untamed needs and all.

"You're a good girl on the outside, but inside you want nothing more than to be fucked by the immoral savage."

I look up at him as he pushes into me more. His blood drips onto my thigh and I moan, tightening my legs around him. Welcoming him.

"Fuck me . . . please," I beg. "I want every brutal piece of you. I want it all . . ." I don't even get the words fully out before Sean is pulling back out and thrusting in to the hilt, deep inside of me. I cry out as my head falls back, then I close my eyes and give in completely.

Everything in my body is heightened, every cell, every nerve. I feel Sean's movements like we're one. The warmth of his breath, the blood on my skin, the bite of his teeth on my neck as he fucks me, the pleasure and pain of him stretching me, claiming me. Making me his.

"*Fuck*, the sight of your bloody cunt . . . sucking my cock in so deep . . ." Sean growls as he watches himself fuck me slowly. "Clenching me so tight, look at the dark side of *you*, Layla June." He drives into me again and again, and all the while our blood leaks and blends together, smearing across my stomach and his.

Somehow, the sight makes my pussy throb even more. He's right, I do have a dark side.

He grunts unintelligible words, pushing back into me again as he watches where we become one. "*Christ*, you're fucking destroying me, Layla."

He doesn't even let me fully adjust. Sean is on a mission to mark me, claiming me for his own pleasure, and it's only heightened by the brutality of this moment between us. His name leaves my lips in a moan as his hand, coated in our blood, angles my face down. He slams into me, pulls out all the way to his tip, then drives back into me again, hitting a place deep inside me that makes me feel faint. I cry out, but just when I think I can't take him any deeper, my core begins to tighten, and my body begs for more of the animalistic way he fucks me.

I'm begging him, "Harder . . . harder . . . please . . . " as I wrap my arms around his strong shoulders. I move with him, my nipples grazing his chest and hardening further. My entire body feels ready to explode as I back up just enough to look down to where we connect.

"You want to watch me fuck you? See how this tight little cunt milks my cock? Begging for my come?"

"Yes!" I cry out. "Deeper Sean, more . . ." My words trail off, watching us move together.

There are no words as the pain blends into pleasure the same way our blood becomes one, until there's no line between the two.

"That's it. Beg me Layla," he growls, showing me that he craves my submission as much as I crave the dark in him. He's lost in this moment as much as I am. His hand tightens around my throat and his eyes are crazed as he sees me like this, covered in our blood.

There's nothing I can do but whimper as Sean drives into me relentlessly. I've given up on trying to even breathe properly, but the limited oxygen is heightening everything and my body begs him to keep going.

"Seeing you like this, bloody and helpless," he murmurs.

"You're marked by me now . . ." He thrusts.

"The things you know . . ." *Thrust.*

"They belong between us, just like our blood." *Thrust.*

"Sean, please," I moan as my orgasm takes hold of every fiber of my being.

"Yes, scream my name. Remember this moment."

"Sean . . . !" I cry out. I have nothing left as my pussy tightens and I come hard, all over his cock. His growl is deep and unforgiving as he murmurs my name into my lips. My body tenses and I grip his shoulders so tight I think I could cut him, but it's the pain he craves right now. It's what he wants.

"Do you understand what this is?" His eyes glimmer with intensity. "Do you understand this man that I am? Who owns you? Who fucks you now?" He brings his face down to mine, his hand still circling my throat. "Make no mistake, we can be one, but I will slit your fucking throat if you betray me."

I have no idea how it's possible but I feel the heat center between my thighs, exploding again as he begins to wrench another orgasm from me. He kisses me as he groans, squeezing my throat tighter so I can't breathe at all, as if he realizes it will make me come harder. Dots line my vision, and as I start to come I feel him grow harder inside me. Then he loosens his grip, and I come undone, clenching his cock as he releases the deepest growl, biting into my bottom lip so hard the taste of copper fills my mouth.

"*My* blood, *my* body now." Sean grips my hips as he circles his own, his actions growing rough as his cock jerks and pulses inside me. "Fuck!" he bites out through clenched teeth.

I just let him claim me, because there's no turning back now. No matter how wrong it *should* feel, it doesn't. It feels right.

Everything about this savage man is my home.

CHAPTER FORTY-ONE

Layla

The air between us has shifted when I come down the hall after getting dressed to see Sean opening a duffel bag at my front door. First, we ate semi-warm pancakes, both of us still covered in blood like the true savages we are, then we had to clean ourselves up in the shower, where he took me again until the hot water ran out. I'm sure the gash on Sean's stomach needs a stitch or two, which he promised to punish me for later. He also said it wasn't my fault and that now he needs to teach me how to handle a knife properly.

The kitchen is clean and you'd never know what went on in here not long ago. I watch with curiosity as he pulls a soft, plain black leather jacket out of the bag and makes his way over to me. I stare up at him as he slides it onto each of my shoulders.

Sean scrubs his face with the palm of his hand. "*Fuuuck*, you look good in that. The way your hair looks over that leather? Christ, woman, you're stunning," he murmurs into my neck, wrapping his arms around me. "Soon, it'll have my name on it, so everyone will know you belong to me, but I wanted you to have it for this ride. If you're gonna be on the back of my bike, you need your own leather."

Sean slides his hands under the jacket and his thumbs graze my nipples through my shirt. They instantly harden. I have no idea how, but I'm already on fire for him again with one simple touch.

"We need to leave *now*," he says gruffly. "We have a long ride ahead of us. One that doesn't allow for me to fuck you again for at least an hour." His eyes roam over me hungrily. "And if I have to look at how fucking hot you are like this for one more second, the choice will be made for me."

My stomach flutters in anticipation as I grab my bag and toss on my shoes with a laugh, trying to behave as un-sexily as possible. I have no idea where he's taking me today, but I'll admit I *want* to know. The more I find out about Sean, the more I realize the true complexity of him. His layers run deep. And with every new layer revealed, I fall a little more.

The sun is hot on my leather-clad back as we ride down the open highway into Savannah. The flat terrain of the Georgia country-side is broken up by rows of billboards and advertisements as we close in on the city. I lean my head on Sean's strong back and breathe him in. He smells so damn good.

As we make our way through Savannah, stately homes turn to modern buildings then back to homes again. Spanish moss clings to the trees that form canopies over the streets, and day lilies perfume the air with their sweet scent. Summer is in full bloom here. Tourists and locals alike line the streets, shopping and lunching. It's when we're almost through to the other side of the city that we turn off onto a side road and drive for a few min-utes, before the trees open up and a large compound of redbrick buildings fills my sightline. It looks like a hospital but there's no emergency entrance that I can see, and as we pass the gates I note the large sign with directions to the different outbuildings.

John R. Mackie VA Hospital and Rehabilitation Center.

I don't know what to think as we pull up and Sean parks his bike in a spot within a row of reserved ones. His is labeled just for him: *Sergeant Sean Hunter.*

He has his own parking spot?

"What is this place?" I ask as I pull my helmet off and take in my surroundings. The main building we're in front of has floor-to-ceiling glass doors, and just outside the entrance is a courtyard of sorts with a large gazebo structure. Medical staff are pushing patients in wheelchairs around on a trail. Two men are playing chess at a table. On the other side of the glass doors are tables, one full of what looks to be a family—a woman patient in hospital clothing, a man, and two children running around chasing bubbles the woman is blowing. Sean hangs our helmets off his grips and pulls his black bandana down from his face.

"This is my job, the brick-and-mortar part, for Veterans Affairs."

My jaw falls slack as I look around. "What do you do here?"

He grins. "I keep the government liaison for these programs on his fucking toes. I've been here since the plans were drawn six years ago, and I'm the single-largest private donor. On paper I oversee the treatment of every Vet that comes through the door. I do my best to make sure they aren't left behind."

I blow out a breath. "Holy shit" is all I can offer.

Sean runs his hand down my arm and laces his fingers through mine. "Come on, we're late."

For what?

I let Sean lead the way as we enter through the glass doors, the older woman at the front desk offering him a large smile as he enters.

"Sergeant," she greets him. "Beautiful day out there."

"Connie," Sean answers. "This is Layla, she's going to be with me today for my visit. Can we get her a pass?"

"Of course," she answers, looking me over in a friendly way.

"And is there a cafeteria delivery for me?" he asks.

Connie gets me a badge, and passes Sean a brown paper bag. I listen curiously as she tells him about some of the patients as he inquires about their progress. She tells him about a new therapy program happening in the construction shop.

"How big *is* this place?" I ask as Sean hangs the badge around my neck and pulls his own out of his pocket. I eye the photo on it, and note his freshly shaven face and Marine uniform. Goddamn. I'll be saving that image for a rainy day.

"Massive." He chuckles. Obvious pride fills his tone. "There's the main hospital where we are now. This has been here for the last sixty years but it was modernized when Veterans Affairs took over. In the last few years we've added a long-term residence, and five other buildings that house outpatient and inpatient programs for Vets. Physical and mental therapy, job training, addiction services and hobbies to keep their interest while they're recovering. My job is to make sure these men and women are supported from the moment they return home. Some people can handle it, some people can't."

"Why? Because they've seen more than others?"

We stop in front of a set of double glass doors and Sean swipes a key fob over a console on the wall to open them. The sign above says: *Long Term Care Wings A & B.*

"We all live with our ghosts and demons, Layla. There's no measure of what affects one man to the next. Only how he chooses to pay his penance for the mistakes he's made. I've made mine. Being here, doing this work, is the only way I know how to make up for it."

On the other side of the doors, the hustle and bustle of the hospital is all but gone. Soft music plays through the hallways and the lighting is natural and warm. The walls are painted a pale sage color and there's a huge glass skylight, like a dome. It feels almost like we're outside. There are little shops, their fronts the same red brick as the exterior of the building. There's a café that we walk through, and as we go, various people wave or say hi and a couple salute Sean. He stops to speak to a few and I'm introduced before we move on. This part of the complex almost feels like a resort. There are patients everywhere. Some are being pushed around by staff, some sit in the café with friends or family. The smell of freshly baked goods is in the air.

"What are we doing here, Sean?" I ask as I look around in awe.

He moves closer and pulls me in, looking around with me. "When you told me your name, it was like an invisible cord tethered us together. I want you to know what *drives* me to live my life the way I do. Why I sacrifice my safety with everything affiliated with the club. Why I justify everything my club does." He looks around. "This place is it." He scans his fob over another door and pushes inside. I follow him into the room. It's almost like a little apartment. The walls are the same sage as the hallways outside. In the center is a hospital bed, and the entire east wall is windows that look out over trees and the plant-filled courtyard. There's a small table and a sofa and a little kitchenette. In a wheelchair facing the window is a man; he's paralyzed from the neck down—or so I assume because a brace holds his head in place.

Sean moves to the window and greets the man with a warm smile on his face. The man uses his first finger to turn the wheelchair to face him.

"Fuck, you get uglier every time I see you," Sean says. "Fries, nice and fresh, from Connie." He bends down and covers the man's head with his hand, kissing the top of it. The man's first two fingers work speedily to type on a tablet. He doesn't even look down to see what letters he's hitting as they fly. He looks at me and gives a friendly smile while Sean reads.

"Like fuck, she's mine," Sean says to him with a chuckle before he makes his way around the back of the wheelchair and turns it fully to face me. The man is handsome. Around the same age as Sean with deep blue eyes and he wears dog tags around his neck too.

"Layla, I'd like you to meet my friend, Private First Class Christopher Buckman. Buck."

For the last hour I've watched in awe while Sean sits with Buck and they talk, Sean using his words and Buck typing out his answers. I've learned Buck's C5 vertebra was shattered in the accident and that he's had a lot of surgeries. Twelve. I learned he had a stroke that has impeded his speech but that he can eat, drink and he has the use of three fingers on his right hand, which allows him to communicate by typing on his small tablet. They've brought me into the conversation a little, with Buck asking me what Sean did to convince me to hang around such "an ugly chump."

This side of Sean has me rethinking everything I've been told since my childhood. It has me rethinking my own morals and values as I watch him help Buck eat his fries. I think of all the times my parents and members of our church condemned the members of the Hounds of Hell. Judging them without knowing any of them, their lives, the stories that make up their existence or the driving reasons they do the things they do. *Sometimes you have to do a little bad to do a lot of good.*

I remember Sean's words as I look around. This place *is* good.

It's incredible. And so is the way Sean gives his heart and makes this place his passion. Giving back to the veterans that weren't as lucky as him. It has me seeing the real him as he laughs and jokes with Buck. And something tells me there are very few people in this world who have ever seen this side of Sean Hunter.

"I wonder if adding more massage would help you," I offer as Sean and Buck talk about the possibility of helping Buck's circulation and blood flow to his legs.

"That's something we've been wanting to get more of on staff here. I like where your head is at," Sean says, looking from me to Buck.

I shrug. "I'm happy to help, if you want to set it up." I smile at Buck and then look back at Sean. The look he's wearing is one of pure adoration. I wait patiently while they chat for a little while longer, and then as Buck starts to look sleepy, Sean stands and heads toward a bookcase. He grabs a book off the shelf and walks back over. He looks down at Buck's tablet.

"He says it was nice to meet you," Sean tells me. "He wants to talk to you."

I stand and make my way over to him. I put my hand over his. "It was an honor to meet you, Buck."

Buck grins and types out, "Keep this fucker in line and come back and visit anytime."

I laugh. "I'll do my best. He isn't the easiest to keep in line though." I lean in. "Kinda stubborn."

Buck smiles then looks up at Sean. "Ain't that the fuckin' truth," he types. "But he's a good man. My brother." Our eyes lock in understanding and I nod. Buck is telling me to see more in Sean. See the other side—and the funny thing is, I already do.

Sean makes his way around the back of the chair and turns Buck toward the window again. Then he takes a seat beside him and cracks open the book. Rosalia de Castro, *Selected Poems*. It's old, but it's an English translation. I take my place on the sofa behind them and listen to Sean read the beautiful words with tears streaming down my face. He reads to Buck from the weathered old book until Buck's eyes fall closed and then Sean stands, offering him another kiss on the top of his head, and says quietly, "See you next week, bud."

There's something so familiar and simple in their exchange. I can tell Sean doesn't do this out of guilt or remorse, although I'm sure he feels some. I'm sure he does it because underneath that tough exterior that has seen the things of my nightmares, Sean has a heart. *An amazing heart.* He told me he would have me surely falling for him in two weeks, but as I sit here and watch him cover Buck with a fleece blanket, I realize I already have.

CHAPTER FORTY-TWO
Sean

Every time I come here and see Buck, I'm hit with the guilt of knowing that I couldn't save him from this. Every fucking time. If I'd sat on the other side of the Humvee I would *be* Buck. But I don't show that weakness or guilt to him. Instead, I come to him with a smile on my face and life's simple pleasures: the cheeseburger and fries I promised him he would get out there in the desert. Every single week.

"My heart breaks for him. He's so young," Layla says as we walk back to the main building.

I stop and she follows suit. "That's the one thing you're not allowed to do, little dove," I tell her, taking her hand and looking into her eyes. "I realize his injuries are hard to stomach, but to pity him is the worst way you can treat an injured soldier. He knew what he was signing up for when he enlisted. In his mind it was his honor, he told me himself. He doesn't feel sorry for himself, so we don't either, understand?"

Layla swallows and offers me a soft smile. Her full, pink lips turn up just enough to exaggerate her pretty cheekbones. "I understand," she agrees.

I hold her hand tighter and we continue to walk.

"Does he have people to support him besides you?" she asks.

I nod. "Yeah, his wife Sophie. They were high school sweethearts. She comes to see him every other day. She lives here in Savannah and they have an eight-year-old daughter."

Layla breathes out a sigh. "I'm really happy about that, but why doesn't he live at home with them?"

"Sophie works as a schoolteacher. She brings their daughter to visit a lot, and Vets can do out days, so they make day trips, or sometimes weekend trips between the long-term care home and their family home. He spends every holiday with them, but Buck won't live with her full-time. He's adamant. His only wish was for his care not to consume their life. He didn't want Sophie to have to quit her job and spend every waking second offering him round-the-clock care, which he needs. He wants their love to stay alive. He said he didn't fight so hard to live so that he could end up a burden. Instead, he wants the time spent with his family to be a joy. And it is."

"And he has you. It's amazing that you spend so much time here with him."

We make it back to my bike and I clip Layla's helmet on for her, checking the strap the way I do every time. "It's not amazing, little dove. I give him my time because he's my brother." I notice the admiration in her eyes as I bend down and kiss her on the tip of her nose then climb onto my bike and pop the kickstand.

It's late afternoon now, and I still want to do one thing with her before I take her home and fuck her ten ways to Sunday. I wait for Layla to climb on behind me but she doesn't, and I turn and glance over my shoulder to see her just looking at me.

"Come on, woman, we're burning daylight. I have to stop at the club quick before we go for dinner. My mother wants you to come by so you can give her your opinion on a cake for Flip's party."

"Well, we don't keep Shelly waiting."

"Fuck no," I respond.

Layla just shakes her head at me as she climbs on and wraps her arms around my waist. The closest thing I've ever felt to love fills me when she leans her head on my back as I tug her closer and she whispers, "You're a good man, Sean Hunter. A beautiful soul."

Of all the things I've ever been called, a good man isn't one of them. But for Layla, I want to be the best version of myself that I can.

"Have you lost your fucking mind?" Shorty asks me. He's our club's resident tattoo artist and right now he's looking at me like I'm insane.

Layla is with my mother and Maria making food to feed the members that are here tonight, and I'd still like to talk to Kai before I leave, so I know I don't have long.

"Nope, and I don't pay you to ask questions. I pay you to work." I drop cash in the middle of the table. "And I want it *exact.*" I tap the piece of paper in front of him. He looks down at it then back up at me. Shaking his head, he smiles at me, his eyes crinkling in the corners. He picks up the piece of stencil paper and places it where I asked, in the exact place Layla ran her fingers the first night I met her. Just over my cheekbone, under my eye. He holds up a mirror so I can see where he's about to start to ink. I nod.

"Yup."

Shorty chuckles. "Alright, man. You're the boss."

The hum of his gun fires up, and as he raises his hand I don't feel an ounce of hesitation—in fact, I've never been more sure of anything, ever. I can't wait to see the look on my little dove's face.

CHAPTER FORTY-THREE
Layla

"*What* did you do?" I gasp, my hands flying to my mouth, because Sean has only been out of my sight for thirty minutes when he comes back into the main room at the clubhouse while Maria and I are chopping veggies. Shelly just left to go get napkins from the storage shed out back.

"Gave you your own place." Sean pulls me in close and kisses me way too inappropriately for all the people around us. I push him back and he grimaces with the way I stopped him from kissing me, but I'm in shock—because under his left eye, in *my own* slanted, cursive handwriting, is *my name* in fresh, new ink. As clear as day.

Layla

"Is that? . . . Did you? . . . How did you?" I stutter, not understanding what I'm seeing.

"You like it, little dove?" he asks, leaning in, his voice doing the lower-octave thing that makes my core come alive. "My initial is in you forever now, so I thought it was only fitting if your name was on me."

"How did you get my signature?" I'm pretty sure my mouth is hanging open, but Sean appears to be loving every second of my reaction.

He reaches into his pocket and pulls out a slip of paper. I take it from him. It's the receipt I gave him at the bar the night I met him. He kept it? And got it tattooed? On *his face*?

"He's probably had that planned out since the moment you gave him that," Maria says, then turns to me. "And there's no changing his mind when he has it set on something," she adds.

I turn and look back at him. "Apparently not," I say, but in truth, as crazy as it may seem, with his rugged features, and the look of my girly handwriting under his eye, the way he shamelessly inks my claim on him is . . . fuck, it's hot as hell. I reach up, not wanting to touch it but wanting a closer look. I grasp his jaw and turn his head slightly, examining.

I blow out a breath and shake my head. "You have a big problem."

"What?" His brows knot. "It's an exact replica. I made sure."

"It may be exact, but what are you gonna tell the next woman you haul into a cooler?" I joke.

Sean growls and picks me up with his hands under my ass, squeezing tight. He kisses me on the lips then whispers gruffly in my ear, "I promise you this, Layla, there is *no* next woman after you. In fact, you better fucking understand that."

"Is that so?" I ask, the butterflies in my stomach fluttering about as I let his lips trail down my throat.

"Fuck yes. Now let's get the fuck out of here."

"Ax, got some info for you . . . !" Kai calls out from behind us.

Sean shakes his head.

"Ax!" Kai says again.

Sean just kisses me and ignores Kai. "Fuck it, I'll just talk to you later!" he calls with a chuckle in between kissing me.

"Where are we going?" I ask him, smiling into his lips.

"My house."

CHAPTER FORTY-FOUR
Layla

As we cruise through Harmony, the summer night air is thick and humid. I cling to Sean and watch the lights of the town go by, and I realize that I have no idea what to expect from the home of Sean Hunter. He's never talked about where he lives and won't give me any sort of hint. The mystery that surrounds him makes me want to learn every last thing about him.

I'm surprised when we continue almost to the outskirts of town and we turn down Hillcrest Avenue, the main road in a century-old neighborhood lined with trees. They form a perfectly curved canopy over the road, and the houses sit far back on manicured lawns with BMWs and Audis in the driveways. We move further into the community, taking a few turns onto streets that are just as exquisite. I grew up with kids from this area. My best friend, Brinley, still owns her late parents' home in this neighborhood. This isn't the neighborhood where I'd expect an outlaw to live, but maybe that's the point. We make one last turn onto Bishop Court and take it all the way to the end. There, on the curve of the street sits a lovely 1920s Craftsman home. It's unassuming dark brown brick. The large property is well manicured and the driveway is wide and concrete, leading to a two-car garage behind the house. It has a window overtop with a light on, like an apartment or at the very least a room up there. We park in front of this garage, which is the same dark brick as the house, and when I get off the bike and look around I'm once again confused about this man and his Jekyll and Hyde lifestyle. The bad-boy biker who helps his fellow Vets and lives in an upper-class family neighborhood.

"Not what you expected?" Sean asks, unclipping my helmet and hanging it from his handlebars.

"Honestly? Not at all."

"What did you expect?"

"Either . . . all white walls and stainless-steel furniture, or a manly cabin somewhere in the middle of nowhere." Sean tugs on the lapels of my leather jacket and pulls me close. "I didn't expect an upscale home in the middle of one of the nicest neighborhoods in Harmony, but I've resolved myself to the fact that, when it comes to you, I'll always be a little nervous because I have no idea what to expect, Sean Hunter."

"Good. I like you a little nervous, little dove," he says bending down to grip my face between his broad palms. His delicious cedar and leather scent washes over me as he kisses me, my insides pooling with fire as his tongue sweeps into my mouth and meets my own.

He pulls back just short of my knees giving out and looks deep into my eyes.

"I'm nervous because this . . ." I motion between us. "This intense sort of feeling, a man who claims you as his own and tattoos your name on his face within days of meeting you? It just doesn't happen in real life."

Sean takes hold of my hand and places it under his cut over the thin cotton of his black t-shirt, where I feel his heart beating fast under my fingers.

"What is real life?" he asks. "*This* is real."

There are no sounds aside from insects buzzing in the night. Sean slides my hand down to feel his cock through his jeans. It's hard and ready for me. "*This* is real," he whispers. "Nothing else matters, Layla. You just have to open the door to that cage and fly out."

"I want to," I say honestly. "But the people I loved left me alone with their ghosts and lies. What if . . . you're just like them?" I add meekly.

"I'm just like *me*. I'll never lie to you about who I am. I'll never hurt you and I will skin any motherfucker alive who does you wrong. *That* is who I am. I don't give a fuck about anything else—what is normal or accepted. Those things are illusions. *Those things* aren't real."

He kisses me again until I'm breathless and desperate for him. Then he chuckles and runs a thumb over my swollen bottom lip.

"Let's go inside before I tear your clothes to shreds in my driveway," he says gruffly. Sliding his hand down my arm, he laces his fingers through mine. I recognize it as a gesture he does often and find comfort in the familiarity of it as we walk.

"Is that an apartment?" I ask looking over my shoulder at the garage as he leads me to a door at the side of the house.

"Yeah, my mom lives up there," he says as he unlocks the door.

Of course she does. "That's sweet you gave your mom her own space."

Sean looks back at me as he walks into the house. "*Sweet* has nothing to do with it. If she's here, I can keep her safe."

Oh.

Sean flicks on a light as we enter the kitchen. Of course his house is pristine. It smells clean and like Sean. There are walnut beams lining the ceiling in the kitchen. It's vaulted and there's a skylight overhead. The cabinets are walnut on top and white on the bottom and the counters look like polished white concrete. Everything is modern but keeps with the traditional style of the house. The island has to be eight feet long, and on the other side of it is a dining room with a big harvest table and bench seating. It's apparent the space was opened up at some point. The stools at the island are iron and leather, and the counters are clean and bare, save for a fancy-looking blender and a coffee maker. Should I be surprised that there aren't any pictures on the stainless-steel refrigerator, or even a magnet?

I notice the rest of the house is absolutely spotless as he takes me around, showing me the living room with overstuffed leather furniture. The only thing on the walls is a large mirror behind the sofa. The floors are polished hardwood, and there's a long narrow table on the other wall near the front foyer, but nothing is on it. It would be the perfect place to display photos.

He shows me his bedroom—light gray walls and a massive king-size bed with a wooden headboard. It's rustic and masculine just like the rest of the house. His bathroom is white tile and there's a clawfoot tub in the center that looks too big to be original yet still somehow fits with the style of the house. A state-of-the-art home office that I imagine was once another bedroom is behind double glass doors.

"That's where I work, for both the club and my job," he offers simply. I nod and look around.

"Do you have anything personal?"

Sean shrugs. "The past is the past. But I'm not a complete heathen. I have a box of things that mean something to me."

"I think maybe I'd like to see that." I smile up at him and he nods.

"I'd like to see you spread out on my bed naked." He begins to unbutton my jacket. "Now."

"Uh-uh, Sergeant. First you need your massage. I'm not

neglecting my job. You hired me for a reason, and we said massages every other day. We're already behind."

"I don't have a massage table," he says. "And my back is fine."

"I don't need it. Just take your clothes off and stretch out on your bed for me," I say as sternly as I can. "*Now.*"

"Fuck," he growls into my lips. "I don't know why, but that commanding shit is totally working for me."

"Good." I reach up and peck his lips. He gives me a look that says he doesn't hate me bossing him around. I go with it just to test him. "Then do as you're told."

Fifteen agonizing minutes later, Sean is struggling to get through his massage, doing his best to touch me and distract me every chance he gets. As I lean over him and move my hands in slow, deliberate strokes on his oil-soaked back to work out the knots he has around the area of his slipped disc, he's busy sliding his hands up the backs of my jean-clad thighs.

I laugh and back away as he squeezes the fleshy part of my upper thigh tight, and he even bites my thigh in his best effort to entice me. I tilt his chin up and he gives me the mischievous smirk I'm starting to find impossible to resist.

"You're touching me. It's only fair I can touch you," he says mischievously.

"*You* promised dedication. You can make it five more minutes."

Sean pulls me closer, his upper arms flexing deliciously as he does, and buries his face between my legs over my jeans, groaning, "I told you, I'm weak. I don't think I can."

"I'll tell you what," I say, backing up again. I'm learning

his love language is physical touch and connection, so I think I can use it to my advantage to get through this massage. "Every minute you make it, I'll remove a piece of clothing. I only need five uninterrupted minutes, and then if you play your cards right, you'll have me naked by the time I'm through," I offer with a grin.

"Deal," he says without hesitation. "Although I don't know why I didn't think about having you naked the entire time. From now on, I'll let you give me as many massages as you want if you aren't wearing any clothes."

"We'll never get through it." I shake my head with a smile.

Sean folds his arms under his chin and I pull my phone out of my back pocket and set a five-minute timer. I crouch down and kiss him on the lips, realizing I *love* to make Sean weak for me. I love feeling in control of a man who doesn't give up his power easily.

"Now be a good boy, and I'll give you a prize."

"Fucking Christ, woman. I'm not going to last one *second* with you talking to me like that," Sean rasps into my lips. I straighten up and he grabs at me. I place my first finger on the end of his nose.

"*Stay*," I hum with a laugh, to which he snarls at me then barks like a dog, and even that is somehow hot. I laugh, pushing him as he groans and drops his face down.

"Let's get these five minutes over with," he grunts.

I stand and press start on the timer, leaving the phone on the bed so he can watch it, and then I begin to finish his massage, uninterrupted. At four minutes remaining I lift my shirt off over my head and toss it to the floor. At three, just to fuck with him, my socks, but Sean doesn't argue; I think he likes the anticipation of what's to come just as much as I do. At two I don't have a choice—he unbuttons my jeans and yanks them down before I have a chance to stop him. I kick them aside and stand before him in just my red lacy bra and thong.

"Red lace?" he deadpans. "Are you trying to fucking kill me?" He immediately moves to bury his face between my thighs.

"Uh-uh," I remind him, sternly. My pussy throbs with my own words, my dominating stance with him turning my insides to fire before he's even touched me.

The last minute begins, and I remove my bra, widening my legs just to torture him. He groans as he keeps his eyes trained on the timer. I don't think he even blinks as I finish the last few seconds. The moment the alarm sounds Sean moves to his knees, his hardened cock bobbing as he grabs me by my waist and tosses me down onto the bed. My breasts bounce as my back hits his soft comforter and he tears my panties from my body, dropping the scraps aside and staring down at me hungrily. I wait, my breath shallow. Eager and desperate.

I take in the sight of him, his hard body flexed and the veins in his arms bulging as he strokes his thick solid cock.

My eyes lock with his as every dirty, depraved thought he brings out in me comes rushing to my lips.

"Time for my massage now, *Boss*?" I beg way too sweetly, just to fuck with him.

A deep growl erupts from Sean's chest as he flips me over, squeezing my ass so hard I whimper.

"No, little dove. Time for your punishment."

CHAPTER FORTY-FIVE
Sean

There isn't a single thing I love more than to see Layla become the woman she always was inside. To see her breaking free of whatever held her back, because fucking Christ when she called me a good boy, I almost blew a load all over my bed. I want that from her—one side a dominant queen, the other a submissive little slut.

I'll never get enough, but the way she taunted and tortured me has turned me from a man into a beast really fucking quickly.

I hike her ass up, ready to consume, and she props herself up so she's on all fours. I chuckle darkly, wrapping my hand in her long fiery hair roughly and pulling tight. She hisses in response but rocks her hips back as I use the hand in her hair to push her upper body down into my bed.

"You don't get to decide how to move right now," I say darkly, releasing her hair. It splays out around her. So fucking pretty. "You wanted to torture me? Taunt me? Degrade me?"

She whimpers as I grip her ass tight.

"You're *my* little toy now, so you'll do exactly as you're fucking told." I knee her legs even further apart and take in the sight of her dripping pussy. She rocks back again, so fucking eager at my rough treatment of her, and I can't wait to fucking make her suffer more before I fuck her.

I use my thumb to spread her arousal through her center and up over her tight, pink asshole. She shudders, but she's relaxed enough for me to play, and the need I have to claim every hole this woman possesses is overwhelming.

I grab the bottle of oil she was using and squeeze it gently over her ass. It drips down between her cheeks as I add more pressure, losing the tip of my thumb to her. She moans into the bed and her pussy glistens more.

"Does my little toy like her massage?" I ask as I line my cock up with her pussy, sliding it through her lips, tormenting her.

"Sean . . ." she moans as I pull my thumb out then push it in deeper. I use my free hand to stroke my cock, so ready to fuck.

"Yes, my filthy little slut?"

She moans at my degrading words and it strikes a chord in me. "More . . ." she mutters, trying to rock against me. I don't let her. Her punishment is staying fucking still and waiting until I'm ready to ruin this tight little pussy. On *my* time.

"More?" I ask, just to fuck with her. "Nah, use your words. Tell me exactly what you want, Layla."

"I need you, please, fill me . . . *please, please*," she chants, and I almost give in.

Almost.

"You want to be stuffed full? You want to come with my thick cock crammed in your clenching cunt as I fill your tight little ass too?" I slide my cock against her pussy again and she's fucking soaked now, dripping down her inner thighs.

"Yes!" she moans as I slip my thumb in and out of her ass with ease. I spit right above it and my cock throbs, begging to take its place. She pushes back to take me a little deeper.

"Please use me, Sean . . . I'm sorry. I'll be such a . . . good little toy . . . just *fuck me* . . ." she cries.

Holy fuck.

I lose it, thrusting my cock into her pussy so deeply, she practically strangles me. This fucking woman. Every time I try to break her, she fucking breaks me instead.

I grip her hip with my free hand and fuck her so hard and deep, she's crying out into the bed. She's too much, too fucking tight at this angle, and her ass clenching my thumb, rocking back to take more, has me desperate to empty my balls into her womb.

"Such a deviant little brat. So desperate and needy, trying to make me come." I fuck her harder, punishing her as I fight my own need. "Is this how you want to be fucked hard, Layla? To be used?"

"Yes!" she whimpers as I don't let up. I slam into her with another deep growl and slide my thumb deep into her ass. Every part of her is slippery and ready for me.

"So full . . ." she moans as I pause, holding all the power as she quivers around me.

"You can take it, now fuck *me*," I tell her, remaining still.

She begins moving, rocking back on my cock. What a fucking sight.

"Thank me. Thank me for letting you fuck me." My voice is a growl as I pull my thumb from her ass and help her, using her body to fuck. I grip her tight with both hands and slide her forward, then back, taking my time. She's fucking perfect as her ass bounces back on my cock and I'm seconds from unloading in her. She writhes beneath me, just as consumed as I am, and the exhilarating notion of putting a child in her—a child of *mine*—suddenly washes over me.

"Thank you, Sean," she hums, so submissively, so sweetly, that fucking *Christ*, I'm coming, I have no choice.

Her pussy grips my dick so tight, I unload in her the second she comes, calling out my name as her body turns rigid first, then boneless beneath my hands.

"*Layla, my good fucking girl . . .*" I mutter, squeezing her hips tight while my cock jerks inside of her, unleashing hot ropes of come. Her fingers flex and release on the sheet as she comes down.

My head is buzzing as our breathing slows. I'm completely out of my element. I've never been out of control in my life, but since the day I met her all the control has been hers. And I know, without a doubt, I never want it back.

As I fall to the bed and she crawls up into my arms, I kiss her, never wanting to let her go. Seeing the future with her, knowing this woman will be my wife. For the first time in my life, it almost feels like everything is perfect.

CHAPTER FORTY-SIX
Layla

CHANTEL

Black leather, bitches.

It's a photo of her in a black leather dress.

AMBER

Cute, but that dress is gonna be hard to take off for the biker you decide to take home after a night of dancing.

CHANTEL

Shit.

I snort out a laugh, almost choking on my water.

"We really need to spend some time going through these and get a better filing system. You have to be organized, Lay." I glance up from my phone at my brother Dell, and the stack of papers strewn across the kitchen table. I still have five hundred words to write for my practical theory essay, before working the lunch shift at The Palm Club and then rushing back to get ready to meet Chantel and Amber tonight before the party.

My day was organized until Dell showed up two hours early for cutting the grass in search of last year's equity loan papers for the house. Which is why I'm sitting here with him now, rummaging through paperwork.

"Can't you just look them up online? I really have a lot of work to do."

"I could, but you know I like to have original copies. I can pop by after dinner if you have time to look after work," he says with a shrug, stacking his papers up in a nice, neat pile.

Dell is the epitome of neat and clean-cut. Tall, well dressed, with brown hair and a friendly smile. Not a stitch of ink on him. I don't think he's ever even drunk a beer. He's a good guy. Too good. I worry one day he'll just snap and follow in my dad's footsteps—that he'll end up sneaking around, and hiding things from his wife.

I clear my throat. "I, uh, actually have a date tonight."

Dell's brow furrows. "It's not with the motorcycle guy, is it? Those men are dangerous, Layla."

"His name is Sean and you don't even know him." I stand and wander to the sink, not wanting to get into this with him.

"I don't need to know him," Dell answers right away. "Mrs. Fielding said he was wearing an H.O.H. cut."

"So that makes him a bad person?" I ask, filling a glass with water. I'll admit, having my glasses beside the sink is a lot handier than the cupboard they were in before Sean moved them.

"If he's a criminal, yes." Dell stands and straightens his pants. I take a long drink and turn to face him.

"At least he isn't afraid to admit who he is," I spit out. I never noticed how damn ridiculous my family and the people I grew up with were until now. "Dad hid his sins but went to church, so that makes what he did okay?" I ask, placing a hand on my hip.

"Shit, not this again. They're gone, Lay. Can't we just let their memories rest?"

I scoff, "You can, apparently, but I'll never forget."

"So this is a rebellion then? This biker?" He spits the word out like it's poison. "Dad had some faults so you're going to date a *criminal*?"

"*Had some faults?* He was a bad man, Dell. He *abused* her! And this has nothing to do with Mom and Dad!" I yell, leaving the kitchen. I head to the living room and take my seat on the sofa where my laptop is. "You can go."

"Come on, something must be going on, Lay. The fact that you're seeing someone like this, are you okay? I'm just worried about you."

I look up at him and smile softly, shaking my head. "I like him, Dell, a lot. More than anyone else. And I'm fine. I'm better than fine. Besides, doesn't your church teach you not to judge someone when you haven't walked in their shoes?"

"It used to be your church too," Dell says, folding his arms over his chest as his eyes are drawn out the front window. He shakes his head and swallows. "Speak of the devil," he mutters, swiping a hand through his hair nervously.

I turn and follow his eyes, and the moment I do I can hear Sean's Harley. He's following what looks like my mom's Lincoln, only it doesn't have any rust on it and it's actually running.

I wait for the white Navigator to turn into another driveway, but it doesn't. As it gets closer and then pulls into my driveway, I realize it's Boyd driving. How the hell? Sean took it from the garage and I didn't notice? When?

"Is that *Mom's* car?" Dell exclaims as the prospect and Sean park side by side behind Dell's pickup truck.

"I guess so," I murmur as Sean walks up to the front door, and Boyd goes to stand at the end of the driveway. Sean moves in easy strides, looking back at Dell's truck as if he already knows it's Dell's. Then I realize he probably does.

I beat him to the door and swing it wide open. Sean stands on my porch, looking over my shoulder.

"How did you? . . . When did you?" I blurt out.

"Your brother is here?"

I place my hand on his chest. "Yes," I answer quickly, my touch bringing his eyes back to mine. "How did you take my mom's car?"

"You have a lock on the garage that's as effective as the one on your house was," Sean deadpans. "I towed it to the mechanic a few days ago. Your alternator and battery were shot. Your brakes needed changing too, but it should run just fine for you now. Oh, and the body's been repainted."

I look at my mom's SUV, shiny and new-looking, my eyes stinging with the sweet—and of course, boundary-pushing—gesture.

"I can't pay you back," I whisper. "At least not right now."

Sean smiles wide and reaches for my hand, dropping the keys into it and folding my fingers over. "That's good, I wouldn't take your money anyway. Big Mike owed me a favor. And this is a gift for you. My girl doesn't take the bus." Sean leans in and kisses my lips. Dell clears his throat and swings the door open wider, standing behind me with an arrogant attitude.

Sean locks eyes with Dell and the muscles in his jaw flex, knowing all I've told him about Dell dismissing my feelings and the truth about our parents.

"Sean, this is my brother Dell. Dell, this is Sean," I say, looking between them pointedly. "Can both of you just be nice?"

CHAPTER FORTY-SEVEN
Layla

Sean's jaw softens at my command and he nods. "Sean Hunter," he says gruffly, moving toward Dell and extending a hand. Dell takes it and then his eyes grow wide when he sees the tattoo under Sean's eye. He swallows hard and looks between Sean and me, but he doesn't dare say a word. He pulls his hand back as his eyes move to Sean's neck.

"Military man?" Dell asks, swallowing. I can tell he's nervous, the same way I was when I met Sean.

"Marine," Sean answers.

Dell's eyebrows shoot up, relaxing a little. "Were you overseas?"

"Three times," Sean answers. "You a soldier?" he asks. I stifle a laugh. Dell wouldn't make it through boot camp.

"No—I, uh, I'm an architect," Dell answers. It's apparent he's skittish and even that pisses me off. He has no reason to be afraid of Sean. "So you're, uh, dating my sister then?" Dell asks, trying to sound brave and unaffected by Sean's size and stature.

Sean smirks. "You could say that," he answers, looking between me and Dell. "What brings you by, Dell?" Sean's voice is commanding; right now, he's the man of the house.

"Just came to check in on my sister," Dell answers.

"Your sister is just fine," Sean retorts. *Fucking hell*.

"Dell actually just came to get some paperwork of our parents', which I just remembered might be in the office." I look at Dell. "And then he's leaving."

I glance between them. The testosterone is way too thick in here. Dell folds his arms over his chest, which thoroughly amuses Sean. Dell is fit but I don't think he's ever thrown a punch in his life. Sean would pummel him into the ground with a flick of his thumb and forefinger.

"I'm not leaving, I'm going to cut the grass," Dell retorts.

Sean chuckles and I roll my eyes, losing my patience.

"Both of you, sit! I'm going to grab your paperwork." *Fucking* men. "I'm twenty-four years old. I *don't* need the two of you acting like barbarians, especially when I'm in the damn room. Dell," I turn to face him, "I'm old enough to date whoever I want. I don't need you giving Sean the wannabe-Dad staredown." I turn to Sean. "And you don't need to speak for me like you *own* me."

Both the men take a seat on the living room sofas across from each other and I nod, satisfied they listened before turning to head down the hall for Dell's paperwork. When I'm halfway down the hall I hear Dell speak to Sean.

"Well, she's damn touchy today."

"She doesn't like being told what to do." I hear Sean chuckle. *Now they're friends?*

I rummage through my dad's office desk and grab the papers Dell needs and take a breath. I knew the two of them would run into each other eventually. With me being around Sean almost every minute that I'm not at work or school it was inevitable, but for some reason my two worlds colliding makes this *real*. Sean stormed into my life and hit me like a hurricane. The connection between us feels both impossible and undeniable. The invisible thread between us isn't made from thread at all. It's more like corded steel, unwavering just like Sean—and even though it's been so little time, I'm willing to admit that there's something special here. Dell is just going to have to accept it.

I make my way back to find the two of them sitting exactly where I left them. Dell stands, as does Sean, and I make my way over to Dell, pushing the papers into his chest.

"So what, you're going to cut the grass now?" I ask Dell.

Sean laughs. "You're cute when you're pissed off." He pulls his sunglasses out of his pocket. "I'm leaving anyway, so hang out with your brother. I have some work to catch up on."

He kisses me gently then looks at Dell, his eyes serious.

"Since you're wondering about how long-term this is—to be clear, I'm not going anywhere." Sean pats Dell on the shoulder. "So you're just gonna have to get used to me."

He puts his sunglasses on and gives us both his megawatt smile.

"Be good this afternoon." Sean looks down at me. "Do you want to drive, or for me to take you?"

"I'll drive," I tell him, excited to have that freedom back. "And Chantel and Amber want to pick me up tonight for Flip's party."

Sean gives me a wary look. "It'll be fine," I tell him "I'll see you tonight."

Sean nods reluctantly and walks through the door. When the rumble of his Harley fills the driveway, Dell looks at me.

"He has your name tattooed? On his *face!?*" he whisper-yells.

"Yes," I answer honestly. "And I don't need you telling me what's right or wrong, Dell." I let my expression soften as I fold my arms over my chest. "Do you enjoy feeling this caged up all the time?"

"What do you mean?"

"I mean you don't have to be who *they* want you to be." I

search his eyes. "You can be a good person and do it on your own terms." I move closer and place my hand on his arm. "Do you love Mandy?" I ask. I've seen the way he looks at her and it isn't the look of a man in love.

"Mandy is very sweet. She comes from a great family. It makes sense."

"But do you *love* her?" I repeat. Dell hesitates.

"What, are you an expert after however many days you've known Tattoo Face?" he bites out.

"The funny thing is, Dell, I don't think I'm an expert but I'm starting to feel like maybe I understand. You only have one life. Don't waste it for one second if what you're doing isn't your passion. That's all I'm saying," I offer.

Dell looks out the window to where Sean was parked just moments ago.

"It was nice of him to fix up Mom's Lincoln for you," he allows.

I smile and nod. "Yeah, it was. Just trust me on this. Not everything is black and white, okay? Give him a chance."

Dell starts to laugh. "I don't think I have a choice, because I'm pretty sure he could easily kick my ass."

"True." I push his shoulder with a laugh. "He might seem rough around the edges, but I've never felt more cared for," I say seriously.

Dell blows out a breath. "Okay. I really respect that he was a Marine. It's an amazing thing to serve our country. I guess I can't fully judge a book by its cover." He looks at me expectantly.

"He also graduated from Duke, with honors," I say just to see the shock on Dell's face. It doesn't disappoint. Duke is a better school than he went to. "And he still works for the government. He's a good man. He cares deeply about those men and women he fought with. It's his passion. The club isn't all he is."

"No shit?" Dell asks, his voice rising at the end in surprise.

I pat him on the shoulder. "Told ya, there's always a gray area. Don't be *them*." I mean my parents, the church. "Be open-minded and think about what I said. You deserve to be happy on your terms, Delly Bear."

I poke fun by using his nickname from when we were kids and then straighten up, pointing to the door. "Now get lost, I have schoolwork to do." I say jokingly, as Dell surprises me and pulls me in for a hug.

"I trust you, Lay. I just worry. Ever since Mom and Dad . . . you're all I have left. Just promise me you'll be safe," he says, pulling back from the hug.

"I will," I tell him. Hoping that, even with the danger that lurks in Sean's world, I'll be able to keep that promise.

CHAPTER FORTY-EIGHT
Sean

"So, is no one gonna fuckin' say it?" Kai asks, leaning against the table in the chapel.

"I've just been waiting for business to conclude so I could say it," Mason chirps.

"Fuck you all." I say with a chuckle, knowing exactly what they're talking about, and that even though they're joking, none of them will challenge me on my decision.

"Your face, bro? This is fuckin' extreme speed dating," Jake laughs.

"Whether I've known her a week, a day, or one fucking minute, time is irrelevant. Layla isn't going anywhere. She's mine. So, *extreme*? Not a chance."

I glance at Wolfe. He's stroking his beard and analyzing me.

"You heard the man. Layla is one of us now," he says, snapping the gavel down. Everyone rises as our meeting ends, and a few of the guys pat my head and shake my hand. They all know. It's an unwritten rule. If I lay claim to Layla as my ol' lady, every single one of these men will protect her and respect her as their own.

"Ax," Wolfe says, using his two fingers to signal me over. He's still sitting at the head of the table, leaning back in his chair. The other guys filter out and I take a seat next to him. He leans in.

"Does she know what this means?" he asks.

I nod. "Mostly," I answer honestly.

"She needs to understand completely," Wolfe says, with no room for argument. "That package you're waiting for, it has to do with her?"

I nod.

"Then don't fuck around. Show her what it means to be one of us. If a woman is going to be in the fold, if we're going to trust her, she needs to understand the truth. Let her decide what she does and doesn't want to know going forward, but she needs to be aware of what it means to be with you. To be with us. There's no other way."

I know this already, of course, but I was hoping to ease her into it. I'm not an unfeeling beast. I don't want her to be a part of the dark things we have to do. But I know Wolfe is right. I have no choice. She needs to know the lengths we go to for the club and for our family.

"Will do," I answer.

Wolfe smiles, which is highly fucking unusual. "Then I'm happy for you. A fuckin' one-woman man. Never thought I'd see the day."

I smile back. "Neither did I, but this woman will be the mother of my children," I say firmly. Because I know it, with everything in me. "You know she has a couple of friends coming tonight," I add offhandedly, just in case he's looking for something new. Wolfe has been known to run through every sweetbutt in this place.

Wolfe chuckles deeply and takes the final swig of his bourbon. "Don't try to fuckin' drag me into your domestic bullshit."

"Never say never." I shrug. "That's what I used to say."

"Never," he adds as we stand to leave the room.

I don't even clear the doors of the chapel before Kai pulls me aside to where he's talking to Jake.

"Steadman came through. That package you wanted? We located it," Kai says.

Jake nods. "Where does Layla live? How long before you pick her up? I could use some help on a run and Donny wants to talk about Gator. You want to ride with me?"

"She lives on Pine Lawn. She's coming with her friends at seven, so yeah, I've got you."

"Good." Jake grins, patting me on the shoulder.

"The prospect and Mason are in Lakeside. They'll bring the package," Kai adds. "Can't believe we found him so easily. Fucking cops are useless."

"You could always trade your patch in for a badge," I offer.

"Wouldn't get near as much pussy with a badge," Kai jokes. "You guys need me to come with?"

"Nah man, we're good," Jake tells him.

Kai lights a smoke and I nod to him. "Thanks for the help with this, man." Then I grab my phone and make a quick call to Steadman's burner.

"You came through for me," I say when he picks up.

He breathes a sigh into the phone. "Yeah. Whatever you're gonna do with him, Ax, just keep it neat. I don't want . . . anything left in this jurisdiction that I have to deal with tomorrow." *Anything*—meaning a body.

"Don't worry. We're just gonna have a little chat," I assure him.

"That's exactly what I'm afraid of, Ax."

Chapter Forty-Nine
Layla

God, it feels good to drive my own car again. Even though it was way over the top as a gesture, my heart warms all the same with the idea of Sean having only known me for a couple days before getting my car towed to his mechanic and getting it fixed for me. Sean may not even realize it, but he hasn't just given me back my freedom from taking the bus. He's given me back a piece of my mother. I settle with the reality that this is just what he does, and protesting these big acts of service won't stop them. I can try to pretend I'm in control of this situation, but I'm just not. At this point, when it comes to me and Sean, I'm just along for the ride—and damn it feels good to just give in.

After my conversation with Dell this morning, I've realized there's no one else on earth I care to impress or explain myself to. This is my life, and if anyone wants to judge me for jumping in too fast with the biker who has the biggest heart of any man I've ever known, so be it.

I turn the volume up and sing along with Dolly Parton as I drive home from The Palm with the windows down and the warm summer breeze blowing in. Even the inside of my car has never been so clean. It smells like vanilla.

It was the typical Saturday afternoon crowd during my shift today. Shoppers, tourists and couples getting out for a day date. Amber and Chantel were texting back and forth nonstop in our group chat about what each of them is wearing tonight.

The odd thing was that I missed the steady presence of Sean at the bar, though I know he has club business to tend to today. I think of the past week and try to come to terms with Sean and me, and everything that's happened as I pull into my driveway, dreaming about a hot shower and imagining the look in his eyes when he sees me after being apart all day.

It hits me then that I'm starting to crave that look. The one that tells me I'm the only woman on earth for him—and I already know I don't want to let it go.

My house is quiet as I walk in and eat quickly, then shower, taking my time to blowdry and style my hair. My phone rests on my bathroom counter playing Eric Church while I carefully apply my makeup and then select a lacy black thong and bra, and another set of the exact same style but in red. I know both of them will drive Sean half mad when he sees them. I snap a photo of them on my bed and send him the picture, asking him which one he prefers.

Even my house doesn't seem lonely anymore as I lay out my clothes while I wait for his answer, knowing that very soon he'll be with me, replacing the ghosts with new life and joy.

> **YOUR BOSS**
>
> Always red.
>
> Christ, now I'm half hard while I'm working.

I smile down at my phone as I put on the red set and snap another photo blowing him a kiss, and hit send. My light jean shorts will be comfortable and cool for tonight in the warm club-house when it's packed with people, and I toss on a black tank that fits me perfectly and makes my tits look great.

YOUR BOSS

> Tell the girls not to bother, I'm coming to get you.

It's a photo of his face in a scowl outside the clubhouse.

I laugh as I realize what he means: he's coming here to have me first and he isn't waiting for me to arrive at the club with Chantel and Amber.

I set my phone down on my dresser and fluff my hair in the mirror, then expertly apply my lipstick. I'm mid-press of my lips when I hear the familiar creak of the back door. I freeze, knowing Sean can't be here yet, and knowing Dell is out with Mandy tonight. I wait, looking around my room, not knowing what to do. Didn't I lock the door behind me when I came in? I can't remember.

Then I hear footsteps. My heart rate skyrockets as I realize I have nothing here in my bedroom to protect myself with and no way out. So I do the only thing I can think of and dial Sean's number, put it on speaker and slide it under the pillow on the bed. I turn as the footsteps get closer, and make to dart behind my heavy bedroom door as my heart pounds in my chest. I decide to slam the door against anyone who tries to come through it, but I'm not fast enough. Before I can even get behind it, I'm faced with a man standing in the doorway.

He's tall, thick. His hair is black; his eyes are piercing and dark. My eyes flit to the tattoo on his neck of a joker card. He's a real person, but he's also the sketch I've had memorized for almost two years and I'd know this face anywhere.

275

CHAPTER FIFTY
Sean

Layla is going to be the death of me with photos of her fucking underwear laid out on the bed. I'm gonna take her every fucking way I can tonight. Jake and I have just finished giving Kai the info we found out about Gator today, which was basically nothing. Jake's lead ended up being a dead end, and the safehouse we thought we might track Gator down to did have Disciples members in it, but none of them were him. We couldn't even risk busting in and questioning the ones who were there, because we didn't want them to know we were even watching them.

"This is a long game," Kai says, noting the address and adding it to the list in his phone as the majority of us sit around the table in the chapel.

"We'll put that place on rotation and we'll just keep watching," Wolfe adds from the head of the table. "That's all we've got for today. I want everyone to have fun tonight and cut loose a little." He turns and looks at me. "When are you getting that delivery?"

I look at Kai for direction.

"Mason's heading to the Barracuda to get him now." Kai

mentions an escort house in Lakeside—one we know the Wretched Souls hang out in, and where we know for a fact Alexander Ramos will be tonight. Jake might be a shithead but he's got good connections with other MCs and street gangs, and he's rarely wrong. After having the deputy sheriff and Kai on it all week, we've found Ramos and now Layla will get her closure.

Jake leans back in his chair. "Flip is already shitfaced and we get to lay a beatdown? This night is looking up." He smiles wide. The table chuckles.

"We aren't giving Frankie a body to worry about tomorrow," I tell them. "He got me the first bit of intel as a personal favor, not a club one."

"What about body parts?" Kai grins.

I shrug. "We'll see."

"Your girl on her way?" Jake asks, taking a swig of his drink.

"Coming with two of her friends, yeah."

"Fuck, is one of them the blonde from the bar?" Kai asks like an eager fucking dog.

"I think so."

He pulls a smoke out of his pack. "Fuck yes, it's a good day, boys."

"Alright, let's go have a drink with Flip." Wolfe snaps the gavel down and we all stand as another photo comes in from Layla. This time she's fucking wearing the red lingerie I picked out, and my dick instantly twitches. Her perfect tits spilling over the top, mixed with her shiny copper waves and pretty pink lips, are enough to make me change my plan entirely. I push through the clubhouse door, my mind already made up. I snap a photo of my best grimace and send it, telling her to call her girls off. I'm gonna need to fuck her before the night even gets started.

I haven't even made it to my bike when my phone rings. I pick it up, only waiting a split second to speak as I tuck it between my ear and my shoulder, but I freeze when I hear a muffled scream and a man's voice.

"I had to get to you before they got to me . . ." I hear him say.

She cries out my name once and then I'm muting the call so whoever is there can't hear me but I can hear them, and I'm on the back of my bike before my brain even has time to think.

Ramos. He's gotten to her first, and I wrack my brain trying to figure out how and why. My mind races and my hands flex as I ride, and by the time I reach her street I'm ready to fucking gut him for thinking he can just show up and threaten her without his certain death following.

CHAPTER FIFTY-ONE
Layla

We stand in suspended silence for a beat before I make a move, trying to get behind the door and doing my best to slam it shut, but this man is faster, pushing his hand out to stop me. I swing frantically, and some of my punches connect and he grunts, but then he grabs me by my shoulders and begins to pull me down the hall to the living room.

"Layla!" he says. The fact he knows my name shocks me, and I look up at him in horror. How does he know my name? "We need to talk, you and me." He smells of cologne and I can't place it but I've smelled it before. I claw at him with my nails and I kick, trying anything I can to get free, and all the while he begs me to stop as he holds me. I grab for a picture on the wall of my mom and me when I was small, and hit him with it over the head as I cry out. The glass shatters, falling to the floor, and he yelps. "Fucking Christ!"

I make a run for it but I don't get far before he's cornered me in the living room, his hands holding my shoulders tight. He's strong, so I can't escape. My house is growing darker with the setting sun and I know my property is big enough that no one will hear me scream.

"You need to fucking listen to me! I knew this was the only way I could get to you without *him*." He pins me against the wall, and he takes a moment to look me over, slowly. My mind races with all the reasons he'd want to get me alone. "Fuck, you have her eyes," he says as he searches my face, and I can't make sense of why he's here. "It's like . . . seeing her fucking ghost."

I hate what I see when I look at him. It's not rage. He's looking at me like he *knows* me.

"I'm *not* listening to you! Let me fucking go!" I cry out, closing my eyes as I struggle, waiting for a fist or an assault that doesn't come.

Instead, he loosens his hold. I try to run and he slams me back against the wall, speaking clearly. "I don't have to hurt you if you just fucking cooperate! You're looking for answers and I'm gonna fucking give them to you . . . but you can't fucking run!"

"I don't want anything from you!" I bite out, trying to raise my leg to knee him. Then a shadow catches my eye and I suck in a deep breath of relief when I see Sean over this sick fuck's shoulder. I didn't even hear him come into the house but he's here, pulling back my attacker's head in a blur.

The look in Sean's eyes is terrifying, like a monster has been set loose from its chains. It's as if he doesn't even see me while his fist connects and a sickening crack fills the air. I know by the sound that my attacker's nose must be broken and then Sean's arm is wrapped around the man's thick neck and he's dragging him toward the back door. He didn't even get a chance to fight Sean at all.

Sean pushes through the back door and I follow quickly, trying to stop him from killing this man out in the open, but when we reach the yard Sean pulls him behind a thick row of cedars, away from any eyes or visibility.

Sean doesn't hesitate, tossing him to the grass behind a bush as the man mumbles around a mouthful of blood.

"Motherfuck—" I hear him mutter as Sean hits him again.

"Alex fucking Ramos," Sean growls at him. "I was fucking coming for you. But here you are, offering yourself up to me." He hits him again before the man can even speak, and the sound of his jaw cracking seems to fuel Sean. I watch Sean hit him over and over. I should stop him but I don't. I don't know how long Sean beats him for, but I know that, as long as I live, I'll never forget the sound of Sean's fist connecting with his face. Ramos goes limp and stops trying to fight and I know if I don't say something Sean will kill him. I want to stop him. Not because I don't want this man to die but because I have some questions for him first.

"Sean." My voice is steady and calm from behind him. Sean stops, as if he's come out of a trance, as he looks down on Ramos, letting go of his bloodsoaked t-shirt collar, and turns to face me. "That's enough," I order softly. Sean looks up at me and stands, moving toward me with a look on his face that I can't quite place. Just before he reaches me he drops to his knees, hitting the earth with a heavy thud as he wraps his arms around my waist, burying his face in my stomach.

"I'm so sorry, baby, did he hurt you?" There's a guttural sound that leaves him as he chokes out, "I'll fucking kill him," over and over until he's quiet. I have no idea how long we hold each other for. His arms grip my waist, clutching my shirt then moving under it as I kiss the top of his head before he looks up at me from his knees. I run my hand over his head and bend down to kiss his lips.

"I'm okay," I whisper as his eyes come back to me from somewhere else entirely. As if he's reliving something I can't understand.

Sean rises and moves on silent feet to the side of my house to turn on the hose. He washes his busted and bloody hands and then rips a piece of fabric from the bottom of his t-shirt. He runs it under the water carefully and comes back to me, wiping away the tears I didn't even know were streaming down my face, and what I assume is Ramos's blood from Sean's first punch. He takes his time, making sure every speck of me is clean, washing the places he once painted me with in his own blood.

"Why did he come here?" I ask, shivering as Sean tosses the fabric down and runs his hands over my bare shoulders. It's not cold out but I think I'm in shock and his warm hands comfort me.

"His name is Alex Ramos. He's a patched member of the Wretched Souls. I don't know how he's connected to your dad yet, or why he did what he did. Kai and I just found him a few days ago. I'm gonna figure out how he found you though." He brushes my now messy hair from my forehead and kisses me before bringing me to his chest, cradling me in his arms. I'm swallowed completely by his size and I'm able to take my first deep breath since he arrived.

"That's better," he whispers, breathing me in.

"He says he has answers . . . could he?"

"I'm gonna figure that out."

"What do we do now?" I ask into his chest.

"I do what I do, and you decide how deep into my world you wanna be."

I look up at him, not quite understanding.

"He was right. I was hunting him. I wasn't planning to kill him, but now . . ." He flexes his bleeding hand. "You know exactly who I am . . ." His thumb comes up to stroke my cheek softly.

"Yes." I place my hand on his jaw, needing to feel him.

"But knowing that reality and *seeing* it are two totally different things, understand?"

I look over at Ramos.

"Of course."

Sean ducks his head to bring my eyes to his. "Don't look at

him. He's lying there like that because he took from you, and I will never tolerate that. No one will ever harm a single hair on your head, or anyone you love, ever again."

I think about this man dying at Sean's hands because he threatened me, and I can't think of a better fate for him. He took my mother, and I'll forever be without her because of him.

I look up at Sean. A moment of clarity in the midst of the storm. He's my center. I barely know him, yet I know unequivocally that he's all I want and all I'll ever need.

"I don't have many of those . . . people that I love," I mutter softly. "But . . . do you think he does?" I don't even know why I ask.

"Don't do that." He tilts my chin up. "Look at me. He isn't worth an ounce of regret. He made his choices in life, the wrong ones. This is his fate."

The funny thing is, I would kill him myself right now if I knew there would be no consequences. Maybe there's something wrong with me, but I don't feel guilty as I look down at Ramos bleeding on my grass.

I remove Sean's steady hands from my face and straighten up. I won't let Ramos take one more thing from me or one more moment of my life. After tonight I will never think of him again.

I push past Sean and move to stand over my attacker's unconscious body. I breathe evenly. Flashes of my mother run through my head: her holding me when I was scared, humming softly as she sat with me when I was sick, laughing as we ran through the sprinkler in our yard. Her face beaming with pride when I sang in church. Her cheeky smile when she said something she thought was naughty. How she loved butterscotch ripple ice cream and would hide it in the freezer so Dell and I wouldn't eat it. Her eyes, whenever she looked at me. Filled with love.

"I'm stronger than you think, Sean," I offer before dropping to my knees. Fire rises in my belly and a rage that I can't explain brings my hand up. I cry out as I hit Ramos in the chest. The feeling exhilarates me.

"An eye for an eye." I choke back a sob as I pick up a heavy rock from the garden and raise my arm to hit him again, but Sean is faster. I don't even know how he got down beside me so quickly, but he grips my hand tight and pulls me back, pushing my hair out of my face as he shakes his head.

"No, little dove. Not yet. I will fucking gut him if you want me to, *after* I get the answers you need and you have some time to think clearly. Taking a life will change you, but I understand why you'd want it." He kisses me. "What happens to him is your call because he took from *you*. My only intention was to bring you peace, and in doing that I was the one to put you in danger." He bends down and kisses me again, his eyes full of regret as he focuses on me.

"Don't look at me like that. It's not your fault. However he found me doesn't matter. It's all part of our truth, remember? I don't care what you have to do to him. I want to know *why* he killed my parents."

"Then you will," Sean says firmly. The sound of Harleys in the distance has him looking over my head. "That's Kai and Jake. Did you tell the girls not to pick you up?"

I shake my head quickly. "I didn't have time."

Sean nods. "Call them now and tell them to meet you at the club in an hour. I'm not letting you out of my sight until I know there's no longer a threat." He kisses me softly on the lips. "Or maybe ever."

I kiss him back. "I can live with that right now." My heart is still pounding but the moment I saw Sean in my kitchen, I knew I was safe.

CHAPTER FIFTY-TWO
Layla

"This place is like a baddie's dream," Chantel says to me and Amber as they come through the clubhouse doors and look around at the party that's raging. I'm still shaken from Alex Ramos being in my house, and I know Sean has him in the back of the building now with Kai. I also have no idea what he's doing to him back there, but I know he'll come and get me when he has the answers I'm looking for. Why he killed my parents. It's all I've wanted to know for the last two years. The clubhouse is packed with well-wishers for Flip's fiftieth. Shelly is running around making sure everyone has drinks, and that the food will be ready on time. There's a pig-roasting company out back with a full pig on a spit. The local catering service providing all the fixings is a friend of the club. The back wall is lined with salads, fruit and veggies, there will be roasted potatoes, and the cake was made by a local bakery and Shelly had it made with a replica of his bike for the top. The entire air is festive, happy and familial. No one would ever guess there's a murderer most likely being tortured in the back.

"I've got dibs on the one who looks like he should be in the yacht club magazine," Chantel says, looking at Kai, who just walked into the large room from the back hallway.

I laugh. "That's Kai."

She smiles at me. "Well, Kai is welcome to make a home between my thighs."

Amber tips her head back and laughs. "Go get him, tiger."

Remi hands Chantel and Amber their drinks as Kai comes up to us, as if he can sense Chantel's intrigue, eyeing her up the way she's eyeing him up.

"You wanna come sit with me, gorgeous?" he asks, nodding to the table a few feet from us where a couple of members sit with women I've seen around here over the last week. One of them is Trina. She's clearly moved on to someone else in the club after walking in on me and Sean.

Chantel nods and looks back at me. "Don't wait up, Mom," she whispers with a wink.

Amber takes a seat with them, eyeing up the available men.

We sit at the table and I listen to Kai and Chantel flirt for what seems like way too long. Sean has been gone for quite a while, and the entire time I have an uneasy feeling in the pit of my stomach. A gnawing. The feeling like something is coming that I don't want to hear. Because of that I don't drink. I dance, and I smile because Chantel and Amber are having the time of their lives and the clubhouse is alive. There's a live band playing outside and people are out on the dance floor. The music filters into the clubhouse itself, so even though there are a couple hundred people here it doesn't really feel packed. I check my phone and note that it's been well over an hour since we got here.

I get through another half hour with a very drunk Chantel and Amber. The way Chantel is eye-fucking Kai across the room, I'm pretty sure she'll be going home with him, or at the very least, going somewhere with him. I make my way over to the bar and try to push from my mind the look in Sean's eyes as he attacked Ramos. The savage glare that made him seem a million miles away. That, coupled with the fact that I haven't seen Wolfe or the other big one, Mason, since Sean left leads me to believe that things might not be going completely as planned, wherever they are.

"Staring at the door won't make him come back any faster, darlin'," Remi says to me over the music from behind the bar. I smile softly at her for reading my mind.

"You need a drink." She grins. I blow out a deep breath.

"You're right. Can I get a double Hellbender?" I ask her. She nods and pulls a glass out, pouring the amber liquid into it with a smile. "Take it from me, hun. I've seen a lot here. Have fun, relax, and he'll be back when he's done doing whatever it is they do."

I take the drink from Remi and tip my head back, swallowing the entire double shot in one go. Before I'm even done with it, Remi has gone to make a drink for someone else. I turn and lean against the bar and watch the room. People are happy. They're dancing, eating, drinking and laughing. But I can't focus. I need to know what the man who took my mother from me is saying, what his reasons are, if any.

I've just convinced myself to go and look for Sean, knowing I might see anything, when I see him push through the door to that mysterious back hallway.

He's still wearing his cut, but my heart drops into my stomach. I'm frozen in place as he closes the space between us with his confident easy stride, and I realize that his shirt is covered in blood. No one else even looks up as he comes toward me. As if a man covered in blood from beating another man is a normal, everyday occurrence.

I look down at his bloodsoaked shirt then back up to his face as he knocks on the bar. Remi makes her way over and pours him a shot that matches mine from moments ago without him even asking. I try to find his eyes, to find that softness he's looked at me with before, but I don't. These eyes belong to someone else. They're hard, emotionless, and they're utterly terrifying.

He takes his drink and swallows it down, placing the glass on the bar, then nods toward the door he came from.

"Come with me, now." It isn't a question, it's an order. I don't hesitate—I make my way through the crowd to the back of the room, and when we reach the door, he pushes it open. Once it closes behind us it's much quieter. "Last door on the left at the end of the hall," he says firmly.

I move slowly. There are various doors down this hall and the lights are low.

Sean wouldn't hurt me, I know that much. I know he would try to protect me from anything that could hurt me, even Ramos's words. But in my gut I feel there's something he isn't telling me. I don't just feel it, I *know* it.

"Here," he says, lightly grabbing my arm and stopping outside a heavy wooden door. There is no sound from inside the room.

"What aren't you telling me?" I ask with a shaking voice.

"I just want to prepare you." He gives my shoulders a light squeeze.

"So prepare me then. I can handle it, Sean," I say, my eyes flitting to the door, then back to his.

"I never want you to be hurt." When I don't speak, he continues. "This"—he nods toward whatever is beyond the door—"is nowhere near the story you think it is, little dove."

"What does that mean?" I ask.

"It means I'm offering you an easy out," he says firmly. "But make no mistake, the choice is yours, because I promised you I'd always be honest with you and I don't doubt for a second how strong you are." He grazes my arms with his thumbs as he speaks. "You can either live with the memories you have or you can come in here and find out for yourself. If you do, you'll learn the truth."

My throat thickens with his words. I imagine what he had to do to get the truth from Ramos and I shudder.

"It will give you closure, and it will answer your questions. But it will also change your view, permanently. You can choose to face it with me, or you can choose to say no."

I watch as he flexes his fist.

"We fucked him up good, but it had to be done. He kept saying he wanted to talk to you first, and you need to understand that I would never let that happen without knowing what he was coming to you with. It took some extra convincing to get him to tell us first. It's not just his secrets. It's his club's business too." He reaches up and swipes his calloused thumb against my cheek.

Sean kisses me softly on the lips. "Take as long as you need to decide if you want to enter." I weigh the decision as we stand outside the room, as if I'm on the edge of a knife and I can no longer balance. I have to go one way or the other. I try to gather the words to make him understand how I feel after such a short amount of time with him. It's unheard of and unconventional but it just . . . is.

"That's the thing, Sean. You say you never had a choice when you saw me? Well, neither did I." There's nothing more to say. I lace my fingers through his with one hand and grip the handle to the door with the other, turning the knob and pushing into the room. My eyes land on Wolfe standing in the center of the space. The very battered body of the man in front of Wolfe is bleeding. The man I now know for sure shot my parents. A strange feeling of strength and power washes over me as I watch him bleed all over the tarp at Wolfe's feet.

CHAPTER FIFTY-THREE
Layla

"You got this?" Wolfe asks Sean as we enter the room and he closes the door behind us. Where the hall is dark, this space is brightly lit. It's a utility room of sorts—solid concrete, floor to ceiling, with a utility sink in the corner, a table and a few chairs. On the table are various knives, tools, a soaking wet cloth and jugs of water. Some of the jugs are empty, some full, and leaning against the table is a baseball bat. I'm frozen in place. After seeing him at my house and now in this brighter light, I'm unable to believe how accurate the police sketch was with all of the smaller details, even down to the shape of his eyes and the joker card that's tattooed on the left side of his neck. How the police never found him while knowing such details is beyond me. The thought that maybe they didn't want to find him, that someone was on his club's payroll, runs through my mind.

Sean nods and Wolfe looks at me; his gaze feels hot, like he could kill me if he stared too much longer.

"Welcome to the family," he says, bending down to kiss me on the cheek.

Alexander Ramos sits before us, beaten to a pulp. His left

eye is almost bulging out of its socket, his cheek is clearly broken and so are some of his fingers. It's an odd moment, as I take in the scene before me while Sean's club president is welcoming me to the family. But somehow it's settling and comforting. After losing my mom, this is the first time I've felt like I belonged to someone or something—maybe even more so because I know Sean and his club are my family no matter who I choose to be. No judgments, no stipulations. They just want me for me.

Wolfe moves toward the door and leaves Sean and me alone with Ramos. I stare down at him. So many nights I imagined him as a monster. Tonight, I saw the monster as he stood over me. I thought he was someone from my nightmares—the man who stole my mother and her freedom. But now, he looks scared, weak. I take in his bloodstained jeans, and his cut lying on the floor. *Wretched Souls.*

The silence in the room is deafening.

"Are we in a hurry?" I ask. Sean turns to look at me. It must have sounded like an odd question.

"We're here until you tell me you want to leave," he answers.

I can feel him watching me, deciding if I'm going to snap. The odd thing is, I've never felt calmer.

"This was a bad idea," Sean says, facing me and bringing his eyes to mine. "I'll tell you whatever you want to know. I don't like you being in here with—"

"Sean," I tell him, placing my hand on his chest. "I'm okay." Sean looks at Ramos then back to me.

"Tell her what you told me," Sean says to him, sounding defeated. The fire I've felt burning under my skin ever since my mother died intensifies. I *feel* the life he stole from her and me. My innocence. The love I had for my mother, the love she had for me. He took it all. And all I can think to ask is, "Why?"

The word leaving my lips is so quiet it's almost a whisper.

My eyes brim with tears. His eyes start to roll back as he hovers in and out of consciousness.

I gain some confidence when he doesn't answer. "Why did you kill my parents?" I ask louder, moving closer. "Why *her*?"

His eyes snap open at the mention of my mother. "That's what I was trying to tell you." His voice is garbled. "She wasn't supposed to be there." He starts to cry. "Fuck . . . you look so much like her."

Sean doesn't hesitate, hitting him in the gut, hard. He starts to choke on blood and drool as Sean grips his face. "Don't you fucking say that to her. You don't have the fucking *right*." Sean's voice booms in the concrete room.

"What . . . what do you mean?" I ask, not understanding.

Sean lets go of him and pulls me close. "The reason they died. It wasn't because of your dad, little dove. It was your mom."

The room reels and I stumble backward. Sean comes with me and I grip his arms with both my hands. "What do you mean?" Tears fill my eyes as I look from Sean to Ramos. Her killer's eyes beg for mercy.

"Tell her," Sean says to him, keeping his eyes on me.

"She was leaving him . . . you know that, she told you. I fucking loved her so much." Ramos's words are almost a whisper and I think I'm having an out-of-body experience as they sink in. How the fuck does this man know about my mother and father?

I look back at Sean and his eyes are soft—pained as it all comes together. My stomach lurches when I realize what he's saying to me. *They were having an affair?*

"No," I tell him, shaking my head, tears spilling over my cheeks. "No, she wouldn't cheat on my dad."

"Your dad hit her. Did you know that?" Ramos asks, blood dripping from his lips. "She hated him. I made her happy . . . we were happy." Tears streak his cheeks and I look down at him, seeing what she would have seen. A man from a world that was nothing like my father's, a man who wouldn't judge her. Who would maybe give her what Sean gives me. A man who was there for her. A man who wanted her for *her*.

"We met at Gamblers Anonymous. She was there for *him*. And your dad, fuck, he was gambling and cheating on her for years. She was so unhappy."

I gulp back another round of sobs because I know all of that is true. Sean must see me sway because he puts a chair behind me and helps me into it while Alex continues talking.

"We started meeting for coffee. We had something between us, I can't explain it. We couldn't stop it."

I grip the bottom of the chair so tight my knuckles start to numb. "If you loved her so much then why the fuck would you *kill* her!?" I bite out through clenched teeth as I lunge for him. Strong arms wrap around me.

"Easy, pretty girl," Kai says, coming through the door, smoking a cigarette as Sean grabs me and holds me back.

"If you want to hear it, don't kill him before he can tell you," Sean whispers. I barely feel him deposit me back into the chair.

"Fuck . . ." Ramos mumbles. "I went to take care of your dad that night, so he couldn't hurt her anymore. The bruises . . . you didn't see them. He'd never hit her face." Tears stream down my cheeks as Sean holds me while I cry, on his knees beside me.

I know he's right. I *did* see them. She always had an excuse. For one insane instant my heart goes out to Ramos, knowing he was there for her in some way at least.

"She wasn't supposed to be there, she said she was leaving. I just thought . . . if he was gone, really gone, she would be free." His words hit me like a ton of bricks being slammed into my chest. *Free.*

"After I shot him she went crazy. She was hitting me and crying."

"So you fucking shot her?!" I yell as Sean's hold on me tightens.

"Say the word and I'll end him."

"No . . ." I cry. "I need to understand."

Ramos raises his head. "I fucking loved your mother. I loved her with my whole heart. I've lived with this for two years, but I had no choice. She tried to call the police. When I . . ." he sobs. "When I pointed the gun at her, she lunged at me, it just went off."

"You just left her there while she bled out on the floor?" I ask, not understanding how you can love someone and just leave them to die like that.

"I had no choice . . . I couldn't implicate the club. I called 911."

"You left her and you *chose* the club." My voice breaks and I close my eyes, fresh tears spilling over my cheeks. "You *always* have a choice."

"I loved her, we were happy. I've had that gun in my mouth so many times," Ramos pleads, and the worst part is that I know he's telling the truth.

A fiery sort of white-hot haze takes over my body. My cheeks heat and I feel like I can't swallow. Like my mouth is full of sand. I think I'm shaking. I don't know where I'm going but I'm moving. "But you didn't pull the trigger, because you're a fucking coward!" I say, and then someone starts yelling, and all I see is white.

You took her from me.

You should have shot yourself.

I wasn't alone.

She was just like me.

You stole her . . .

My arms ache as I fight my way through my screams. I fight so I can breathe again, and all the while I think I'm hitting something hard as I cry. It doesn't feel stable or unforgiving, it's spongey. It's going to break but I want to keep hitting.

Something strong grabs hold of me as I feel my breath

burning in my lungs. I'm unable to move now. I blink my eyes once, maybe twice, and try to focus. Sean is holding me, gripping my wrists tightly, and he pulls something from my hands—the baseball bat?

"No, Layla. You're too good to finish this, baby," he says, and then I'm being kissed. "She loved him, she *was* brave, little dove. Just like you." He kisses my forehead as he whispers in my ear. I think of her face in those last weeks, the glow she had, how ready she was to start over. She *did* seem happy.

"But he took her!" I sob, then I look down and see Ramos even more bloodsoaked now. His breathing is shallow and he's unconscious and there's blood all over my shaky hands.

Everything becomes painfully clear. I lost myself to the rage building inside me. I could've just killed him.

"Y-you stopped me," I whisper, looking up at Sean. He's still holding me in his arms.

"I've got you, baby," he whispers as sobs rack my body. I give in, and I just cry harder.

"I'm so sorry it's not the words you wanted to hear, but it's the truth and now you know it," he says. Kai unties Ramos and he slumps to the floor then Kai drags him into the corner. I look up at Sean as he gently swipes my hair off my forehead. I'm covered in sweat and another man's blood.

"Maybe it was wrong to seek him out so you could learn this. Maybe I shouldn't have subjected you to this, and that's something I'll live with for a long time. But I couldn't keep it from you. I wanted to give you the choice."

"No, you weren't wrong. I wanted to know. It's been haunting me for two years. I'm so sorry you had to do this to him for me."

Sean strokes my hair as he speaks. "This is what it means to be mine, Layla. You're always in control. What you say goes. This is the iron-fisted chokehold you have me in. I'm at your service. Whatever you want is yours."

My body trembles as Sean holds me and strokes my face, letting me know he'll always hold me. "I'd line up twenty more of these fuckers without a second thought and pick them off one by one with my bare hands if it meant I could give you peace," he says. He bends down and kisses my lips, my cheeks, my throat. His voice is a rasp against my ear. "I'm no longer just my club's soldier, little dove. Above all, I'm *yours*."

CHAPTER FIFTY-FOUR

Sean

I don't know how long I just hold Layla on the floor. But I do until her sobs stop and she's not shaking anymore. She looks back at Ramos in the corner. Kai is oblivious to the carnage in this room—the fucking guy lives for this shit. He's probably champing at the bit to shoot him. He sits in the corner smoking and scrolling on his phone. I won't tell her what she doesn't need to know, so I keep to myself that one of the things Ramos uttered to me, between us waterboarding him, was that he found Layla because someone left a note on his bike with her address, telling him that I was coming for him. My head races knowing they've been watching us—and her. Either that or someone from our circle gave intel to them, which seems impossible. The only thing I'm sure of is that I'm going to make it my life's mission to tear apart with my bare fucking hands anyone who was behind Ramos getting to her. But first I'm going to look after her until she recovers from this.

"What will happen to him?" she whispers after a time.

"Whatever you want," I tell her, stroking her tearstained face.

She looks back at him then up to me. "I don't want him to

hurt anyone again." She shrugs. "But she wouldn't want me to take his life. I know it." I watch her red-rimmed eyes as she decides his fate. "I want him to live and be reminded of her every day. I want him to regret his choice to kill her every single day until he dies. Can you do *that*?" she asks.

I nod and kiss her face. Layla has had enough trauma for one day, and I can make sure he'll never shoot another gun or ride ever again. It goes against everything in me not to make sure he's put into the ground, but if that's not what she wants I'll give her that. She doesn't need this man on her conscience. My girl is too good to sentence a man to death.

I kiss her and stand, helping her up in the process. Then I make my way to Kai, telling him quietly enough that she won't hear what my plan is as she rips a piece of paper towel from over the sink and blows her nose.

Kai stops and squeezes Layla's arm as she rejoins us. "We've got you now," he says as she nods to him. "We'll make sure he never hurts anyone else."

"Will he come back or send his club to hurt you?" Worry lines her pretty face as she asks us.

"No, little dove. They wouldn't dare."

"They could try." Kai grins. "It'd be the last thing they'd ever do."

Layla nods, but as Kai moves back to the table, her eyes harden. "Sean. I want you to know, your club life and this stay with me. No matter what it is you have to do." She reaches between us and takes my hand, tracing the ink there, flipping my wrist over to trace the compass. "I will never breathe a word of it, but I have some conditions if I'm gonna be your . . ." Her face crumples up. "Ol' lady."

I chuckle, kissing her forehead. "And they are?"

She takes a deep breath and steadies herself, reaching her hand up to my face. "Thank you for finding me the truth. But

298

the details of this, what happened with my mother and him . . ." She looks around, her eyes landing on Ramos. "Those memories stay here too. If I want to talk about it I will, but I never want to focus on why she died, only the positive."

"The positive?" I ask, always trying to get a step ahead of the way her beautiful mind works.

"She lived, she loved, and even though he took her from me, he gave her happiness in those last months. That's what I want to remember, and I'll take her secret affair to my grave. I expect you to as well."

I nod. "Of course."

"As far as your club life . . . this sort of thing." She waves a hand toward the blood on the floor. "Unless I specifically ask, I want only *you* when you're with me. The things you have to do to be this man?" Her eyes focus on Ramos's battered body. "You leave *those things* here, with the club, understand?"

Her words are full of command. A woman changed, a woman coming into her own.

Fuck, she's breathtaking.

"I understand," I say.

She looks at Kai as he comes back through the door, Mason behind him. She turns to him. "Thank you for caring about my parents. You've never even met them."

Kai hits her with the grin that's earned him his fuckboy reputation. "You're with us now, pretty girl. Your boy here will have to get you your own official cut with his name on it."

Fucking right I will. The thought of that makes my cock start to swell even in the midst of the devastation and carnage.

"And hey," Kai adds as she looks at him questioningly. "Remind me not to get on your bad side when you're holding a bat." He chuckles, mocking a swing and clucking his tongue. "Fucking beast mode."

Layla laughs, already looking less in shock after that ordeal.

Kai moves closer and shakes my hand. "I've got this. You guys get out of here."

"Not a fucking chance in hell," I retort.

Kai grins at me. "Always gotta ruin my fun."

I shake my head. It's not about ruining his fun; it's my need to make sure this is done right.

Layla looks up at me for direction. "Go to my room, it's right at the end of the hall." I pull my keys out of my pocket and hand them to her, holding the one to my space here at the club. There isn't much in there—just a bed, a dresser and a small bathroom. "You can get cleaned up, then head out and find a prospect. They'll all be sober. Tell them I said to take your friends home," I tell Layla.

"Nah, that I'm on top of," Kai calls out from the other side of the room.

I smirk. "So fuckin' helpful tonight."

Kai sharpens his knife as he grins. "That's me, Mister Helpful. Tell your friend I'll see her soon, Layla." He winks at her.

"What will you do to him?" she asks, curious.

"What you commanded. I promise he'll live, and by the time you've asked someone to take Chantel and Amber home, I'll be out there with you."

She looks up at me, trusting but still curious.

"Need to know, little dove."

She nods and kisses my lips, so soft and so sweet, and I fight the urge to kiss her deeper. "Thank you, Sean," she hums, reaching up to place her hand on my cheek. Tonight, her world came crashing down around her for the second time—and if I can help it, it'll be the last. But even though she didn't take a life today, her compass is forever altered too.

I kiss her head, not saying anything as I open the door to let her out. The second I close it and turn to Kai he's holding the ten-inch tanto knife with an even bigger grin on his face than before.

"Take this fucker's hands?" he asks.

"You read my mind." I nod. "Then get Mason, and dump him outside St Vincent." I mention a hospital the next town over.

Kai holds the knife out to me but then pulls it back as I reach for it. "You take one and I take one."

I chuckle. *Fucking Kai.*

I swipe the knife from his hand. Ramos is so out of it this won't be as satisfying as I'd like it to be, but I speak anyway as I slide him downward on his tarp so he's lying flat on the ground.

"You put your hands on my girl, so I should be slitting you from your guts to your mouth."

He makes a garbled sound. Layla really did a fucking number on him already with the bat. I pull his hand away from his body, laying it flat beside him. He's so weak he doesn't even fight it as I admire the blade. This fucker is sharp. I calculate the weight of it, as I've never used this knife before so I have to judge how hard I'll have to strike. Kai might take his time, humming himself a song as he saws through the small bones of Ramos's wrist, but I'm eager to get back to Layla so I'll do this as quickly and cleanly as possible.

"Every day after this, every fucking morning when you wake up and you can't hold your own cock to piss, I want you to remember my face and remember the woman who allowed you to live." I line up my strike. "And if I ever see your face around here again, it will be your head that I take next." I lean down so I know he can hear me. "I'll hollow it out and hang it on my fucking wall."

I raise the blade and tighten my grip before I bring it down, taking Ramos's hand clean off. The monster in me rears its head, breathing deeply. Satisfied even without the kill, knowing above all else I've made *her* happy.

CHAPTER FIFTY-FIVE
Layla

"Let me just look at you," Sean says as he wraps a towel around me. He stands behind me in the bathroom mirror, brushing my wet hair to the side and kissing my shoulder. We're back at my place and clean, after stopping at his house for clothes and some of his things. I don't want to stay at my parents' house alone, but there is already no trace of Ramos left. Sean had Boyd come over to clean and saw to that.

I've thought a lot about what I've learned over the last two hours. I think about my mother and how I am more like her than I realized—she was strong, she almost made it. Maybe she would've been happy after she left my father, if she'd had the chance. Ramos is a lunatic, but I know by the look in his eyes he'll live forever with the regret of killing her, and I heard Sean tell Kai to take his hands. I remember Sean's words: if someone steals from us, we take their hands. It does seem fitting.

Sean's fingers trace my skin softly. "So fucking beautiful," he murmurs as his lips find their way to my neck, my earlobe, softly biting. I whimper under his touch.

"Truth?" he asks, probably assuming what happened tonight is weighing on me.

"Truth . . . when I saw him there . . . beaten, weak . . ." My eyes sting as I picture the way Ramos looked at me when he said, *"I fucking loved her."* I look into Sean's eyes in the mirror as he strokes my skin softly. "I was . . . glad. It was like understanding my mother's secrets and the life she hid from me for the first time, and saying goodbye to a ghost that's haunted me for almost two years. I understand, I think, how you compartmentalize this."

The muscles in Sean's jaw flex. "You have to compartmentalize. You have to believe every single thing that happens is part of our path."

"She made her choices, and it was her path to intertwine with his—to die when she did."

"Exactly," he says. "And *our* paths were always meant to intertwine," he adds, kissing my shoulder.

"I thought you didn't believe in fate?"

He looks down at me, so very much mine in this moment. "I didn't before, but now the idea of something unexplainable, unquantifiable yet I can feel it with everything in me . . . your mother and father dying so you ended up working at the club, the storm that meant I found you there . . ."

"Not everything has to be explainable, Sean," I offer with a raised eyebrow. He turns me toward him and looks down at me, his green eyes light.

"I know that I see my path, but I don't know where it leads. Not knowing where I'm going is what inspires me to travel it."

"Philosophy from the outlaw biker," I comment, letting a soft smile take over my face. "A Sean Hunter original?" I ask.

"Rosalía de Castro." He smirks. "Call it fate, call it choice, but I know my path and every bump in this fucked-up road I've been on has led me to you, to this moment." He continues the line of kisses down my arm. "And since you're on this path with me now, we'll ride it together." I think about the blood and ruin in that room. I think about what Kai will do to Ramos.

Sean tilts my chin up to him, as if he sees my thoughts.

"And one thing you need to understand is there's no right or wrong way to feel after fighting pain and coming out the other side of it." He kisses my shoulder. "Just like there's no right or wrong way to feel after retribution. Everything you think you know about your emotions is because someone told you how you should feel."

"I just feel . . . grateful it's over." I breathe out a sigh as his knuckles slide down my arm. "I feel strong. I feel like *she* was strong," I admit in a whisper.

Sean uses his thumb and forefinger to unhook the soft towel from between my breasts. It falls to the floor and the cool air makes my nipples harden. Tiny embers of heat ignite as I stand bare before him. He uses his hand to grasp my throat gently and lift my chin.

"This is the face of a strong woman," he says softly, tracing his finger over the places he marked me with his blood, like it's burned into his memory. My skin sparks as he turns my face to his and pulls me into a deep kiss filled with new passion, connection and emotion. I moan into his lips as he pulls back and turns my face toward the mirror again.

"Her world fell apart yet here she stands, on her own two feet. She's bold." He trails a hand between the valley of my breasts, my skin pebbling in its wake.

"She's wild." He pinches my nipple and presses his lips to my neck, a tiny smirk taking over his expression when he feels a quick flutter of my pulse there.

"She is so fucking beautiful." He murmurs softly.

I stare at the woman he sees. Her eyes glassy and lust-filled, her stance is confident beneath his worshipping gaze. I see the change in myself in the short time I've known him. I've lived through loss for a second time and come out the other side. I'm the woman my mother never fully became. I want to be her, always.

"She was made for this life. She was made for me. She is *mine*," Sean adds as his hand slips down, over the curve of my hip. "And we are infinite." His naked body presses into mine and I feel more myself than I ever have. I'm proud of this woman before me. This woman who wants to belong to Sean Hunter in every way possible.

He grabs a brush from my drawer and carefully pulls it through my hair, taking his time to care for me after a life-changing night, and I marvel as I watch him, not understanding how this came to be, but I'm going to let our truth guide me the same way it guided him.

He came into my life as a storm, and even though he's already taken my heart captive, the woman behind the bars is free with the wings he gave her. I should feel trauma after what I've seen and what I know, but I don't. I just want to be his. A fresh new start, no cages, no boundaries, just me and him.

When my hair is brushed through, Sean pushes it around my shoulders, then he reaches down and grabs some gauze and tape from the drawer, covering his initial on my stomach. His still bleeds, uncovered from the shower, but I already know as long as I'm alive, he'll look after me first—it's just the way he is. Which tells me, one day, it won't just be me first, it will be our children too.

"I have a feeling I'm gonna be sore tomorrow." I look up at him over my shoulder.

"Your body is coming down," he notes. I nod. After fighting Ramos, the trauma and the tension in my body is already starting to come out. My muscles ache in a wave of fatigue after the adrenaline rush.

"Now we have to get you cleaned up." I eye his cut in the mirror. "And I still say you need a stitch."

"I'll be fine." He wraps both his arms around me, kissing my shoulder. "Mmmm . . . Just stay, Layla," he chants into my hair. "Just for a minute."

"Don't try to distract me with that sexy, manly voice. It's time to clean you up. And then it's time for yoga."

He groans deeply.

"Uh-uh," I scold, patting his face. "Just because *we're infinite* doesn't mean I'm giving up on healing your back."

He chuckles and reaches around to turn my face up to his, kissing my lips. "I'm all for healing my back. And more *naked* massages are definitely in order, but fuck, I have to tell you . . . I paid your tuition the day after I met you. You were already mine, Layla, I just had to convince you."

I laugh. Of course he did. I kiss him, tears filling my eyes. "I shouldn't be surprised but I am." I kiss his jaw, closing my eyes. "Thank you, Sean, for finding me," I whisper, and I know even though it seems impossible, I love this man already.

"Do you know what they say about love at first sight?" he asks as my eyes focus on him, as if he's reading my mind. One tear spills onto my cheek as I smile at him.

"No, but I'm sure you do."

"It's an unbreakable promise that happens in an instant. That's what this is. What we are. I fell irreversibly in love with you the moment you pushed me up against that cooler wall." He chuckles, kissing my neck, and I laugh with him. Then his face grows serious. "I knew then that you were my match in every single way, Layla."

"Is that so?" I ask.

"It is." He drops his lips to mine. "And I have another promise. As sure as I stand here breathing"—he strokes my cheek—"I promise, by this time next year you *will* be my wife."

Chapter Fifty-Six
Layla

*Two Months Later (because Sean and
Layla don't move slowly)*

"There you go, little dove, just relax, open up for me."

We haven't had sex in two days, which is the longest we've gone in the two months since we met, but Sean says being patient will give us the best reward.

I breathe as Sean pushes the largest-size plug into my ass, and sigh as it settles inside me.

"*Fuck*, I'm rock fucking hard right now." He grins, shaking his head as he looks down at my ass. The final stretch to being ready for him.

"How do you think I feel?" I bite out, slightly annoyed. I'm so full, and I go to move but he stops me, smacking my ass—and even that makes my pussy throb.

"Just burning this image into the memory bank." He points to his temple with a wide grin and I laugh at him as I turn and pick up my cotton panties, sliding them up over my hips.

"Where are we going?" I ask, because he's been very evasive all day.

"We just have one stop and then I need to see Wolfe before we come back here." He kisses me then hands me the leather jacket he gave me, only now it has a *Property of Ax* patch on the back with the Hounds of Hell insignia, and on the front *Sean* is embroidered over my heart.

"It'll take us a couple hours, and by the time we're done you'll be good and ready to take my thick cock in this tight little ass."

I pull my dress up and push my arms through the straps. "Don't remind me how thick it is, or I might change my mind." I smirk at him over my shoulder.

"You have no fuckin' choice at this point," he says, low, dropping his lips to my neck.

I kiss him on his cheek, where my name is inked forever. God, he's gorgeous. His trademark black t-shirt is tight on his strong upper arms, and his thick neck pulses as he watches me in the mirror. Every single day I think he gets even more beautiful, and not just because of how he looks, which is incredible, but because of who he *is*.

As my semester comes to an end, I've started going to his weekly visits with Buck, and Sean had me brought on staff so I could start more massage therapy on his legs to encourage better circulation. When I'm there, I see how much Sean cares for him. How much he cares for all the Veterans in the center. I've learned that the club helps fund local recovery clinics because of Sean and Wolfe's love for their military brothers and sisters. So many of them end up on drugs or lost when they return home, but if Sean and Wolfe can help even one of them with what they do, they will. Even if the way they help fund the programs is on the wrong side of the law. And if I can help while I start my career, I will too.

Sean is renting a space for me come fall where I can set up

my own massage therapy clinic. I've continued working with him twice a week and we've seen a vast improvement in his pain and lower back strength as a result. My plan in my new space is to offer my services to injured Vets who might not be able to afford extra care. Coupled with their therapy, it will help with their anxiety and PTSD. Sean is inspiring me in a way I never thought possible when I first met him.

I remember his words every time I go to the center or think about our future: *Sometimes you have to do a little bad to do a lot of good.*

I believe that with my whole heart.

"What *is* this?" I breathe out. "Where are we?" I add as I take in my surroundings. We've just pulled up to a historic inn on the bluffs on Tybee Island. Lighthouse Landing. It's elegant and quaint, but the real beauty is in the scenery. Beyond the rustic white building is the ocean, as far as the eye can see, and a dock that stretches out into the water. And it does in fact have a lighthouse on it. The waves lap around it and the sun is just beginning to set.

I think I hear music playing as we get off Sean's bike, leaving it parked right in the circular drive. There's a parking lot out back that I can just see the outline of, but Sean insisted we park here. It sounds like there are violins, or an acoustic guitar maybe, as we walk to a wide, flat grassy area and more of the water comes into view. I pause when I realize there are people lined up along the bluff in the distance. They all wear uniforms of some kind, but I can't tell what for. There are at least a dozen of them facing us and they're all standing behind large cages.

Cages full of . . . doves.

I look up at him in shock and confusion, not knowing what the hell is going on. Just when we get a little closer and I think I couldn't be any more confused, he drops to his knees in front of me, his back to the cages as he faces me.

"This is the place we're going to get married very soon," he says gruffly. "I've been breathing for approximately one hundred thousand, four hundred and eighty-eight minutes since the moment I laid eyes on you, but it would only take *one* second of living without you for my lungs to take their last breath. I say we're infinite, because there is no quantifying you and I. If I lived a thousand lifetimes and loved you in every one of them, it still wouldn't be enough. This isn't just love. It's *unending* love."

My hands fly to my mouth as Sean pulls out a box and holds it up to me. It's all so fast, but am I surprised? No. Am I hesitant? Not a chance. I know this man is everything I'll ever want, forever.

"And I'm hoping it takes you less than that one second to say yes." He opens the box and my eyes are met with the most beautiful diamond I've ever seen. "Will you marry me, little dove?"

My eyes trail upward, because with just a slight nod of his head, every cage has opened and doves are ascending into the sky, feeling freedom under their wings. The same freedom I feel under mine when I'm with Sean. And as of this moment, the only cage I'll ever live in for the rest of my life is his arms. A cage I'll welcome.

"Yes, I'll marry you!" I cry out as he stands and kisses me.

"Fuck, I love you, Layla," he growls into my lips as he slips the ring on my finger. Of course it's a perfect fit.

"And I love you, Sean Hunter."

"Can we come out now?" I hear Shelly's voice from around the corner and I gasp.

"They wanted to celebrate with us." Sean smiles, then kisses me again and then pulls me around the back of the inn, and I'm greeted by over a hundred people and their cheers when Sean shouts, "She said yes!"

Twinkle lights and greenery decorate the scene, and flameless candles and lanterns light the space. There are round white iron tables and a full spread of food and drinks, and a man with an acoustic guitar is playing softly as we're surrounded by family and friends. I glance to the other side of the space and lock eyes with Dell. He looks nervous as hell but he's here, and it touches me. So many people are hugging us at once it's hard to tell which way is up or down.

I hug Dell tight once he makes his way over, and he congratulates me.

"I'm glad you're happy, Lay."

Having him here is gesture enough to tell me he may be opening his mind—even if it's just a small corner of it—to the fact that life isn't so black and white after all. He even laughs when Sean picks him up in a bear hug, lifting him right up off the ground and calling him "brother" before offering him a shot of bourbon. It gives me hope that I might have some semblance of my brother back.

"My sweet and sour girl. I knew you were the one," Shelly says, gripping both sides of my face. She has tears streaming down her cheeks as I see Sean hug Robby J behind her.

"And I've always wanted a daughter," she adds. "Now I have one."

I swipe a tear away. "I love him so much, Shel."

"I know you do, baby. And he loves you," she tells me as she beams. "I hold a lot of pride for that boy, but I hold guilt too."

She reaches down and squeezes my hand.

"The first time Sean ever took a life, it was for me." She looks up at me and I see the regret there. It's lived in her every day, I'm sure. "It was inevitable, but he was young, and it was to protect me. He never looked back after that, and that says everything you need to know about him. He'll never fail you. He'll never let you down. As long as you love him for the man he is, he'll love you more than anything in this world."

"I always will," I say, hugging her again. I know it from the tips of my toes to the top of my head as Sean looks over at me hugging his mom, as if he feels me watching him. His knowing eyes gleam as he mouths, *I love you.*

My gladiator, my protector. I love him alright, and this was beyond the proposal of my dreams, but I'm still going to give him a piece of my mind for proposing to me in front of everyone we know with a heart-tipped plug buried in my ass.

"We're celebrating, little dove." Sean pushes into our room at Lighthouse Landing three hours later. The entire club is staying overnight.

"Don't be angry. I'm still gonna fuck you, but it will be a lot more fun if you aren't angry."

I let him kiss me. I'm anything but angry after three hours of this plug in my ass and him looking at me all night—the night he proposed, gorgeous and rugged by the candlelight with all our family and friends. All of that combined was torture.

"I'm not angry, Sean. I'm bothered, I'm ready to combust and I'm dying for you." I back up and pull my dress straps off my shoulders, cocking a hip as I look up at him through my lashes.

"In fact, if you don't take me right here, right now, I might take back my yes."

Sean scoops me up so fast I don't even have time to think. I yelp as he tosses me right over his shoulder and smacks me on the ass. The plug pulses inside me and I moan as he places me down on the bed, yanking what's left of my dress off my body and burying his face in my soaking pussy.

"Christ, so fucking wet for me and I haven't even touched you yet."

"You haven't," I mutter as he licks a trail through my slit and groans against me.

His hand goes to the plug and he pushes it in a little more. I moan. I feel like an animal begging for his touch, and he's a fucker because he knows it and he's loving every single second.

CHAPTER FIFTY-SEVEN
Sean

"This is coconut oil." I smirk as I say the words Layla said to me when she gave me my first massage while I shake up a little bottle of the clear oil. "Any allergies?" I chuckle down at Layla on all fours in the middle of the bed in the executive suite. I don't even notice the look of the room itself with Layla before me, eager and ready for me.

"Fuck," she mutters as the oil hits her ass and slides down over the plug that's still inside her. Fuck, what a sight. I don't wait as I rub her arousal all over her slit and use both hands to spread her ass even wider, admiring how pretty she looks like this as I sheath my cock in her—deep, desperate, because not fucking her for two days just about killed me.

"Holy fuck!" she cries out as she's filled by both me and the plug. I stay rooted in her, my cock pulsing as I toy with her, pulling the plug out slightly then pushing it back in.

"Sean . . ." She's already wrung out, desperate and boneless beneath my hands.

"Layla . . ." I mimic, fucking her slowly, just slow enough to keep me from coming as her tight cunt vises me.

"Please . . . let me come."

I continue to toy with the plug, pushing it in as I fuck her, pulling it out as I withdraw, and every time I push it in she rocks back into me. She's so fucking ready.

"You'll come, little dove, don't worry." I bend down and kiss her shoulder as I pull the plug from her ass and toss it on the bed. Then I spread her wide and stare down at her perfect ass, ready to take me, slippery and soon to be mine. "And I can't wait to feel it while I'm claiming this ass." I grip her hips tight as I pull out of her cunt, and she whimpers with the loss as I line myself up. I'm coated in her and she's coated in the oil.

"You're so much bigger," she murmurs, half in a moan.

"You're going to love the feeling of me taking this tight virgin ass, Layla June. My filthy fucking girl wants to be filled in every hole she has," I coax her. I stroke her pussy with my fingers, sliding up to pinch her clit as I slowly sink my cock the first inch into her ass. She pants in shallow breaths as I toy with her clit, relaxing her, opening her up for me. "That's it . . . good and ready."

"Yes . . . good and ready . . ." she murmurs as I sink in another inch. *Un-fucking-real.*

"Yes . . . my filthy girl, you've started to crave it, haven't you? You want this ass filled while I fill your cunt too?"

"Yes . . . *pleasssse,*" she moans as she rocks back.

I sink in further and my eyes roll back. Slowly but surely her ass takes my length as I fuck my first two fingers into her pussy.

"Soon you'll be my filthy wife and I'm so fucking proud of you. You're such a good girl letting me train your ass like this. You should see how well you're taking me now. How well you're swallowing my cock."

Layla starts to move, pushing back against my fingers, and she takes me deeper. She's relaxed, she's open, she's begging and she's mine.

Her back arches and she cries out when I reach my full

depth, and I take a second to breathe myself because goddamn she feels incredible. I let my hand roam her spine, her hips, never stopping my fingers working over her clit as she does the work for us, fucking *me*. And I wonder if she'll ever stop surprising me.

"Fucking Christ," I breathe as I pull all the way out and then push back in, her ass taking every inch of me.

There isn't a part of her that isn't mine now and I'll never let her go. I've loved her since the moment I laid eyes on her. I kiss her gently as her orgasm crashes into her, and she cries out my name as she writhes, gripping the sheets, her whole body quivering around my cock. I'm so far gone that mine prepares to chase hers just as quickly in return.

"This ass . . . so . . . fucking . . . mine," I emphasize each word with a punishing thrust. "Just like you, Layla, just like you."

Layla June Monroe was born to be my wife. And no amount of science or logic could convince me otherwise.

Do I believe in fate now?

Fucking right I do.

EPILOGUE
Sean

Nineteen Years Later

"Are you guys *fucking* kidding me?"

I turn and cuff our seventeen-year-old son, Rhys, in the back of the head for cussing like that.

"Eh, your sister doesn't need to hear it," I tell him gruffly as Calli, our fifteen-year-old daughter, pushes through the side door with a huge smile on her face and her dark hair flying out behind her as she chases her brother.

"Sorry, Cal," he calls, looking back at her. "But holy shit!" he exclaims as he takes off down the driveway. He's wearing a suit but that doesn't slow him down. Layla tucks herself into the crook of my arm with a stunning smile as we watch our son open the door to his completely overhauled and redone 1993 Dodge Ram. His dream truck I've been working on for months. It's a beast with flat gray paint and black rims done by his uncles, Kai and Wolfe.

"That's it, I no longer have control over where he goes and when," Layla says softly, emotion lining her face. "He was just five years old yesterday, sitting in the lawn chair while you worked on your bike in the garage."

Her copper hair blows in the breeze, and with the way she looks in her black dress, ready for Rhys's graduation, it's a wonder I don't sneak her into the bathroom and hike the skirt up over her ass before we leave. I think about how much we still have to do before we go today and promise myself to fit the time in. I still can't fucking get enough of her after almost twenty years.

I bend down and kiss her head. "Gotta let him grow up, little dove. At least he'll be driving something safe when he's at Duke in the fall." It was our proudest moment when he got accepted to my alma mater, cursed and blessed with a brain like his dad—only he's going to put it to better use than I ever did and become a doctor.

"Never seen her look so happy for her brother before . . . about anything," I comment about our daughter, who's currently sitting in the passenger side checking out Rhys's new ride.

Layla starts to laugh her all-knowing mama laugh and looks up at me with the beautiful brown eyes I've loved for a lifetime. She never ages; in her early forties, her face is still unlined and her skin is bright. She still has the long thick waves I love, only they're a darker copper now, and I have no idea how it works but her fucking body only gets better with age, I swear to Christ.

She pats me on the chest as I breathe in her sweet citrus scent. "She isn't happy for him Sean, she's happy for *her*," she whispers with a giggle. "She graduates in two years, and she knows this means there'll probably be a gift like this for her in the driveway."

I scoff. "Only if she changes her dream car from a VW Bug to something that will actually protect her."

It's no secret that Calli is my baby. At fifteen she's bound to make me take at least one boy's life before her eighteenth birthday for looking at her the wrong way. She's a beautiful soul inside and out just like her mother, and is Layla's spitting image only with my dark brown hair and green eyes.

"Well, she'll be riding in Micah's truck to Rhys's grad, so you know she'll be safe in that," Layla comments, mentioning her best friend's son who is a year older than Calli as she kisses me on the cheek and then backs away.

"Like fuck. That's how you're gonna try to tell me she's driving with him?"

I know Micah is a good kid, but no one is good enough for my baby—and how much I like the kid and his parents means nothing. I'll still break his hands if he touches her, and his dad would understand.

"Gotta let her grow up, *babe*." Layla smirks, turning back around to scoop our four-year-old baby boy Max from the yard and taking him to see his brother's new truck.

I stand in the sun of a perfectly clear May morning watching my family, knowing how fast the last twenty years have gone and knowing it all wouldn't have been possible without every step of the journey it took me to get to her. Layla has only grown more amazing every single day that I've known her, and there hasn't been one second where I've doubted my gut instinct from the first day I met her. The way she balances worlds to keep everyone and everything running in our family is nothing short of incredible. I've watched her raise two kids almost to adulthood and then get the surprise of being pregnant with Max in her late thirties. And she embraced that with me the same way she's embraced my club, my job and hers. She runs her own wellness clinic in town and has for ten years, employing a naturopathic doctor, two other massage therapists and an osteopath. I fall more in love with her every time I look at her, and I did make good on my promise. We were married in *less* than a year.

Rhys turns up his custom sound system which is playing The Black Keys and Max dances in the yard. I chuckle as I fold my arms over my chest and head toward them to join the driveway party. Over the years, I've come to love the way my brain doesn't forget a single thing, because the more years that pass with Layla and our kids by my side, the more memories fill my head, pushing out the ones that came before her.

It leaves me with nothing but peace, and changes my truth from one I want to forget to one I strive to remember every single day.

Layla

"He's coming around that corner too fast," Sean says, coming up behind me on our porch. Inside, our house is packed already and we've only been back from Rhys's graduation for thirty minutes. Our house isn't small, but with over sixty people inside and out it feels a little claustrophobic. That's why I stepped out onto the wide covered porch with a glass of wine, and of course Sean followed me. He's been following me every moment since the day I met him, and although life hasn't always been easy or perfect, we're still here, still in love, and I know we always will be.

"He's fine." I set my wine down on the rail and reach up to pat Sean on his neck as his strong arms wrap around my waist. We watch as Micah makes his way down the street at a completely acceptable speed with Calli in the front seat.

"Hmmph," Sean grunts as he bends down to kiss my neck. "It was a good day, little dove."

"It was," I say, swallowing down the tears that are brimming. Our family has always been so close, and with Rhys going away to school in August I wonder how I'll survive the loss of him in our home. He's so much like Sean, and at seventeen he's almost as tall and getting bigger by the day. But unlike Sean he's only known joy and love his whole life. He knows who his dad is and has already got his learner's permit to ride, but he has other aspirations that don't include a life in the club. Namely, right now, whatever girl is following him around that week. I blame his uncle Kai's influence for that.

"He'll be home every six weeks and it's only until spring," Sean says, knowing exactly what I'm thinking.

He strokes my hip as Calli and Micah get out of his dad's truck, and she smiles at him. She's way too beautiful for her own good, and I watch him melt for her as she tells him she'll be inside in a second and then swerves to the side of the porch to speak to us where no one can hear.

"Could you two *not* make out on the front porch when I bring my friends here?" she whispers at us before rolling her eyes and rushing after Micah.

I look up at Sean and we both laugh. I kiss him once, then twice. The same familiar fire for him I've felt for almost twenty years creeps up my center. At just over fifty he has more salt in his beard than pepper but he's fitter than most twenty-five-year-olds. He's in better shape now than he's ever been, after years of massage, acupressure and osteopathic healing for his slipped disc. Not to mention he's continued his intense training sessions almost daily. He still works with the Vet hospital and even helped Buck move back home with his wife ten years ago, after life-changing surgery gave him more use of his upper body and back.

With mostly the same crew after all these years and Wolfe still president, the Hounds of Hell has settled into a phase of peace, forming a truce with the clubs they once had conflicts with. Sean has definitely calmed down some since our early days. He's still got the same fire inside him, but he's really settled into our family and into being a dad. I know there are still things he has to do in the name of the club, but I've always lived on a need-to-know basis with those things and it's worked well to balance the club life and our family life.

"Okay, my love." I reach up and kiss him. "I'm going to get Rhys's cake." I nod toward the staircase below the porch that leads to our cold cellar. "Check on Max?" I ask. "He's with your mom."

Sean groans and leans in, kissing me just a little longer. "Later . . . you're mine," he rasps.

"Deal," I tell him.

"Fuck, I love you," Sean smacks my ass then squeezes it tight.

"I love you too, baby," I whisper back, kissing him then turning on my heel to head down the steps while he goes inside. Since meeting him, there hasn't been a day gone by that I haven't felt loved and safe. Sean Hunter healed a hole in my heart after my mother's death. He gave me stability and a family of my own, and I'm grateful for him every single day I get to wake up beside him.

I stop to grab Rhys's grad cap out of my car that I'm definitely making him wear while we eat cake, even though he'll hate it. As I walk, I think about our life and how it's passing by in the blink of an eye. The king of my family isn't a knight in shining armor with sweet words and a squeaky-clean appearance. My king is the vice president of the Hounds of Hell motorcycle club. An outlaw. Always clad in black and leather. He's messy, depraved and loves me with every fiber of his being, and I wouldn't want it any other way. This life I live is only possible because Sean knew we were meant to be the moment he laid eyes on me. Even when I wasn't sure, Sean never wavered and he knew enough for the both of us.

We're as permanent as my name inked under his eye and the dove on my shoulder that now has his name scrawled below. We're unstoppable. Unshakable. Infinite. It's something I haven't doubted since that first week with him.

The crickets are loud and plentiful as I crack the door to the cellar. I step over the threshold and flick the light on, crossing the clean dry space to where our extra fridge and chest freezer are. I'm thinking about where the birthday candles are when I open the door to the fridge, but the moment I do, the light in the space flicks off. I flinch and my breath hitches when I feel strong arms wrap around me. The moonlight shines in the small window under the porch.

I spin around in his arms and look up into the green eyes I've never been able to resist.

"So, you want to help me with the cake then?" I ask, one eyebrow raised.

Sean slowly shakes his head as his hands slide down my waist. I take my bottom lip between my teeth, understanding what he wants as I breathe evenly, starting to back up slowly.

"Hmmmm." I look up to the ceiling thoughtfully. "Are you trying to fuck me in our cellar while our guests wait upstairs?"

"Fucking right I am, little dove," he growls at the precise moment I turn on my heel to sprint the few feet to the door, knowing just what he wants. For me to put up a fight.

I've just grabbed the handle when Sean reaches over and stops me, pulling my hips back so my ass slams into his rock-hard cock. He groans as his hand slides over my hip to cup my pussy from behind.

"No, Layla. *Stay*."

I moan as I let him do exactly what he wants with me. Sean Hunter never has to worry, because I'm never going anywhere.

Acknowledgments

I had the most incredible time telling Sean and Layla's story! To my amazing husband for being the backbone of our family. For countless moments on our porch talking plot points with me and outlines – as well as, at least once a book, coming up with a few banger one-liners. Thank you for taking a back seat to every MMC I write and for just being you.

To Jess Muscio and the entire team at Evermore and Deb Werksman and the entire team at Sourcebooks Casablanca for believing in my writing and this series. Your encouragement, guidance and kindness are always unmatched.

With multiple people in multiple countries working on my stories, it's hard to list everyone in a small space, but I figure this is the best way to try. To my unwavering teams of dev and copy editors in North America and the UK, my *incredible* Alpha and Beta readers without whom these books would not be their best, my content creators, artists, a truly awesome TikTok manager, my amazing street team and my ARC readers and all readers alike.

And lastly, a little shoutout to my own little dove, for always checking on me when I go MIA in the writing cave. Thank you. I may not do it better than anyone else, but I pour my whole heart and soul into these stories, and every time one of you comments, likes, shares, edits or mentions me, it is noticed and loved.